VAULT

DAMIAN A. WASSEL
PUBLISHER

ADRIAN F. WASSEL
EDITOR-IN-CHIEF

NATHAN C. GOODEN
ART DIRECTOR

TIM DANIEL
EVP BRANDING/DESIGN

REBECCA TAYLOR
MANAGING EDITOR

DAVID DISSANAYAKE
DIRECTOR OF PR/RETAILER RELATIONS

IAN BALDESSARI
OPERATIONS MANAGER

DAMIAN A. WASSEL, SR.
PRINCIPAL

WRITER
JUSTIN RICHARDS

ARTIST
VAL HALVORSON

COLORIST
REBECCA NALTY

LETTERER
TAYLOR ESPOSITO

STORY BY JUSTIN RICHARDS & SABS COOPER

VAULT COMICS PRESENTS

FINGER GUNS

A SHOT IN THE DARK

ONE

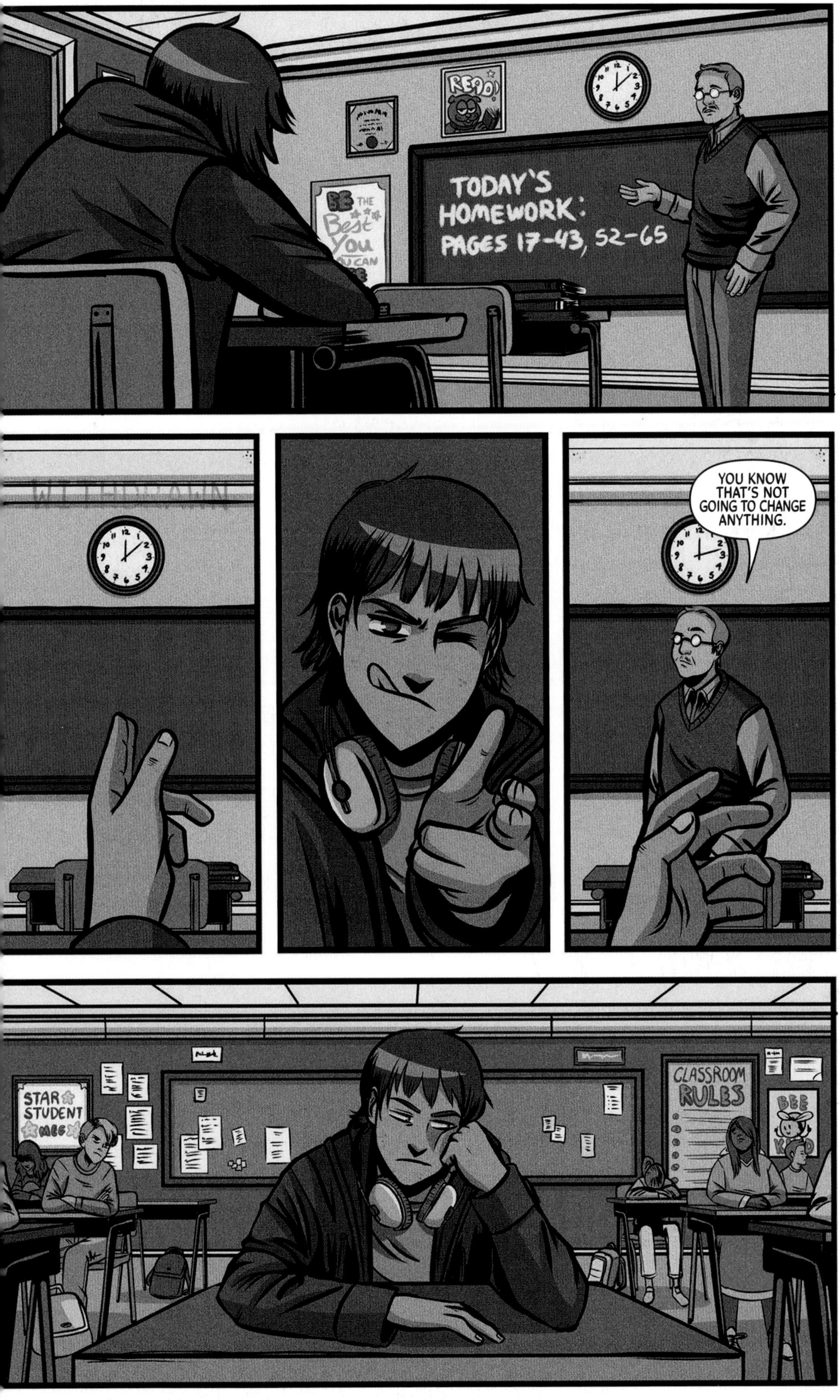
READ!
TODAY'S HOMEWORK: PAGES 17-43, 52-65
YOU KNOW THAT'S NOT GOING TO CHANGE ANYTHING.
STAR STUDENT
CLASSROOM RULES

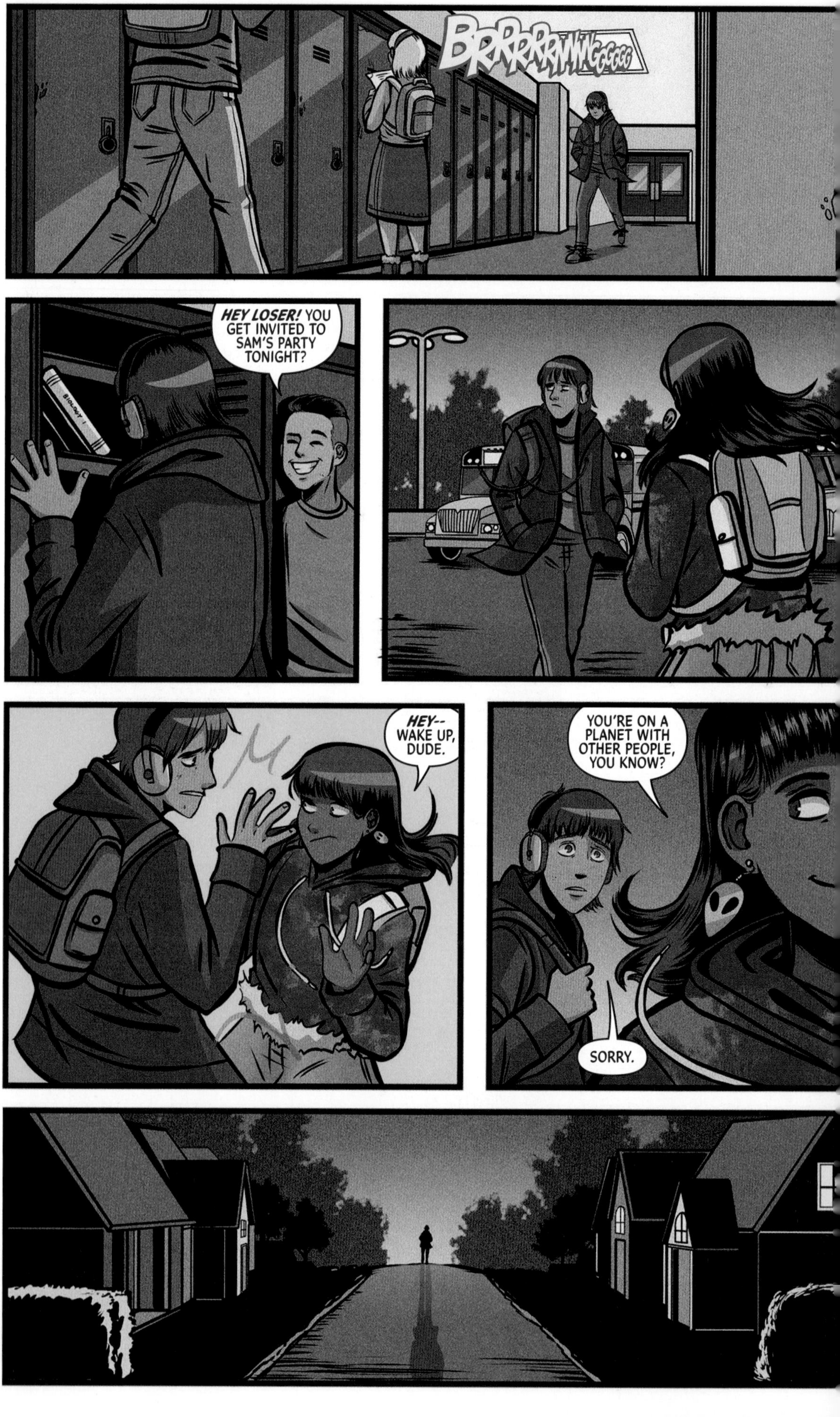
BRRRRRIIINNNGGGGG
HEY LOSER! YOU GET INVITED TO SAM'S PARTY TONIGHT?
BIOLOGY I
HEY-- WAKE UP, DUDE.
YOU'RE ON A PLANET WITH OTHER PEOPLE, YOU KNOW?
SORRY.

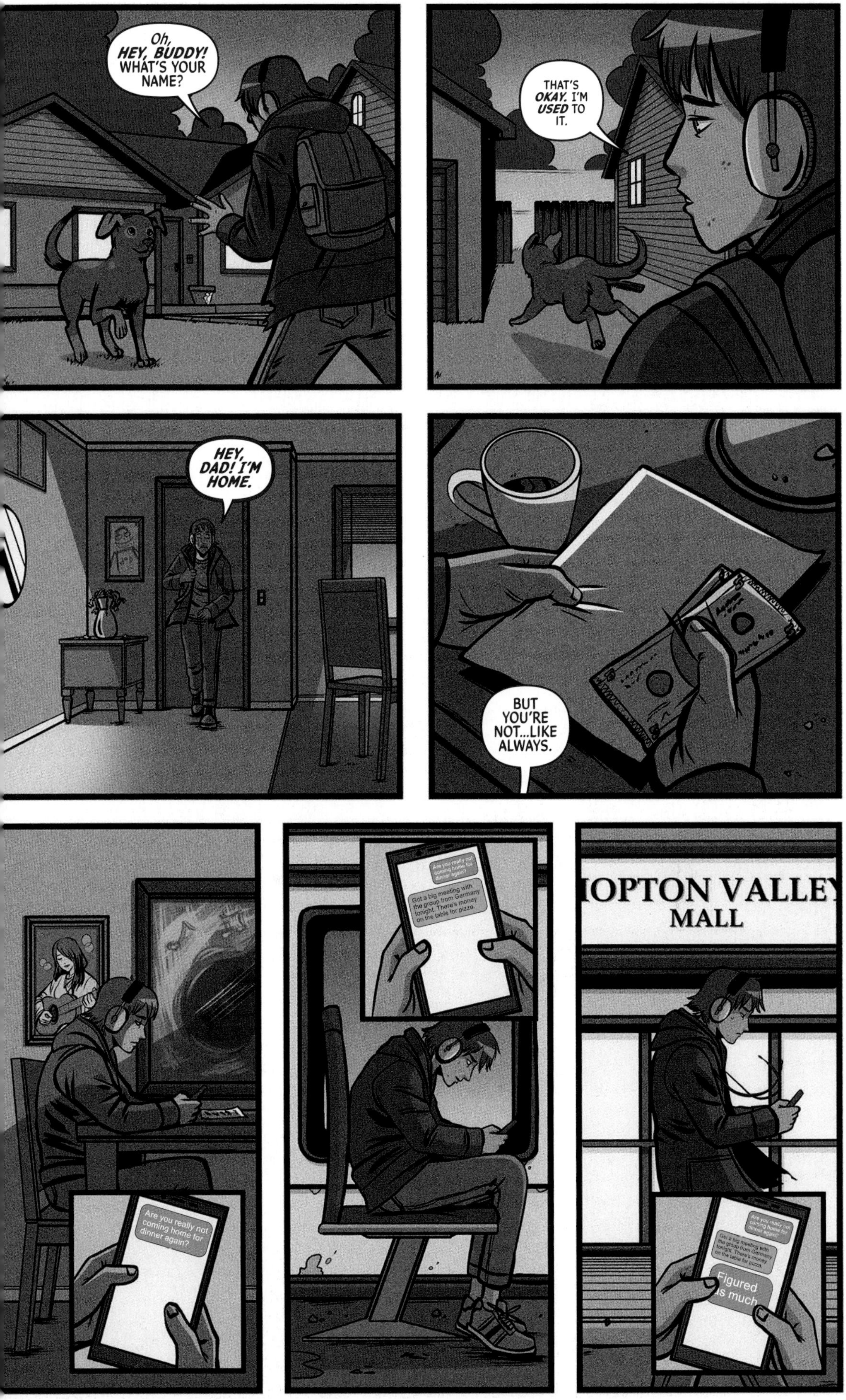

Oh, HEY, BUDDY! WHAT'S YOUR NAME?
THAT'S OKAY. I'M USED TO IT.
HEY, DAD! I'M HOME.
BUT YOU'RE NOT...LIKE ALWAYS.
Are you really not coming home for dinner again?
Are you really not coming home for dinner again?
Got a big meeting with the group from Germany tonight. There's money on the table for pizza.
OPTON VALLE
MALL
Are you really not coming home for dinner again?
Got a big meeting with the group from Germany tonight. There's money on the table for pizza.
Figured
s much

BUT I WANTED THE *GREEN* RANGER!

IT'S THE SAME THING, JUST A DIFFERENT COLOR.

ANOTHER DAD WHO DOESN'T GET IT.

KRAK

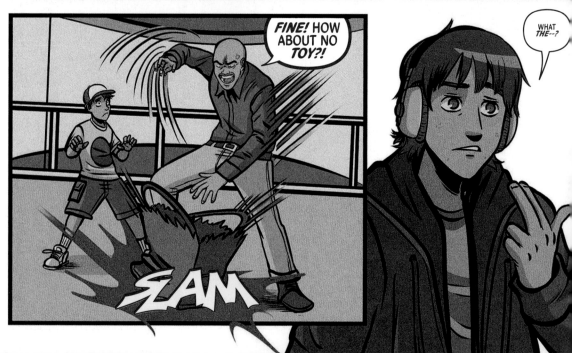

FINE! HOW ABOUT NO *TOY?!*

WHAT *THE--?*

SLAM

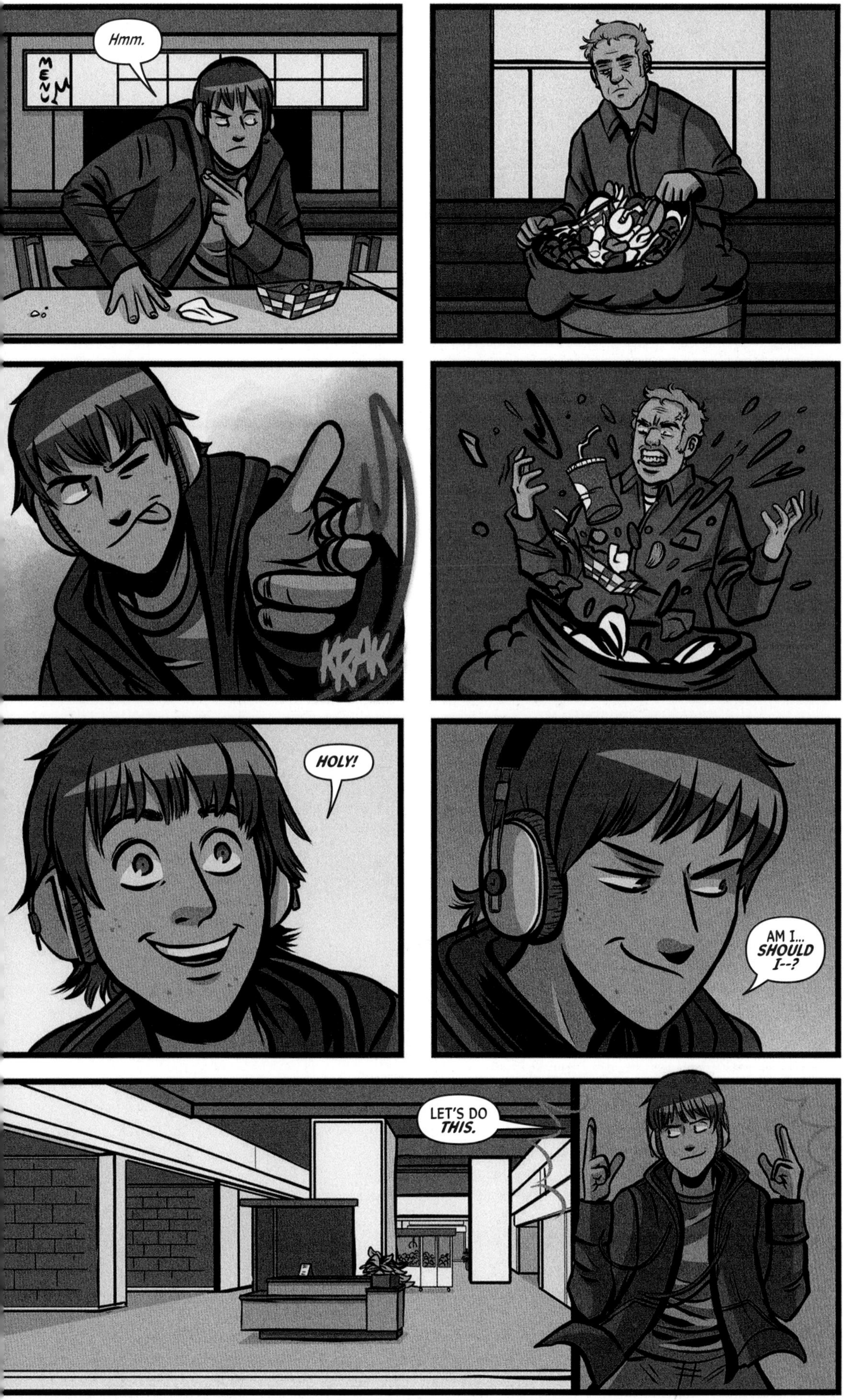
Hmm.
MENU
KRAK
HOLY!
AM I... SHOULD I--?
LET'S DO THIS.

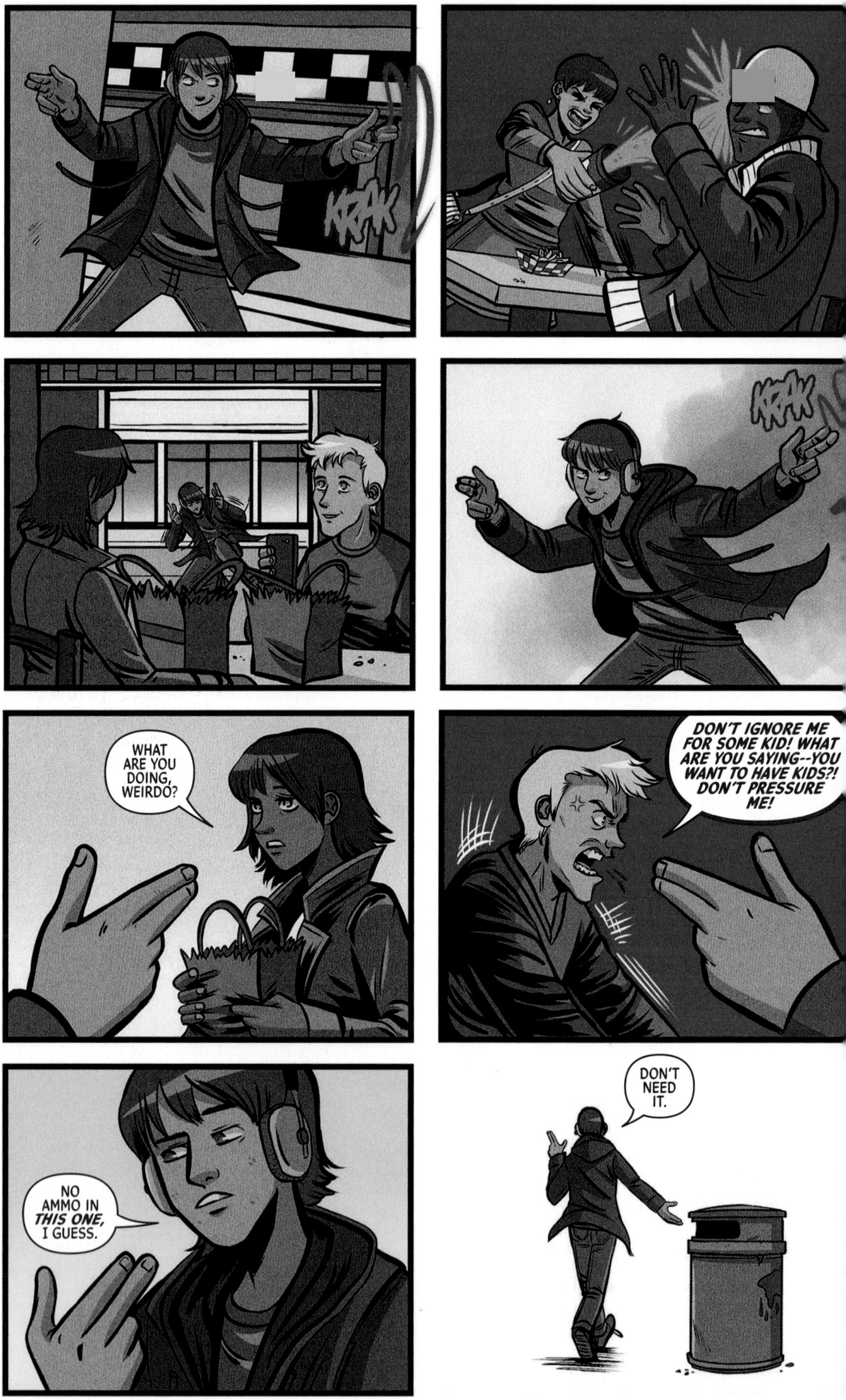
KRAK
KRAK
WHAT ARE YOU DOING, WEIRDO?
DON'T IGNORE ME FOR SOME KID! WHAT ARE YOU SAYING--YOU WANT TO HAVE KIDS?! DON'T PRESSURE ME!
NO AMMO IN *THIS ONE,* I GUESS.
DON'T NEED IT.

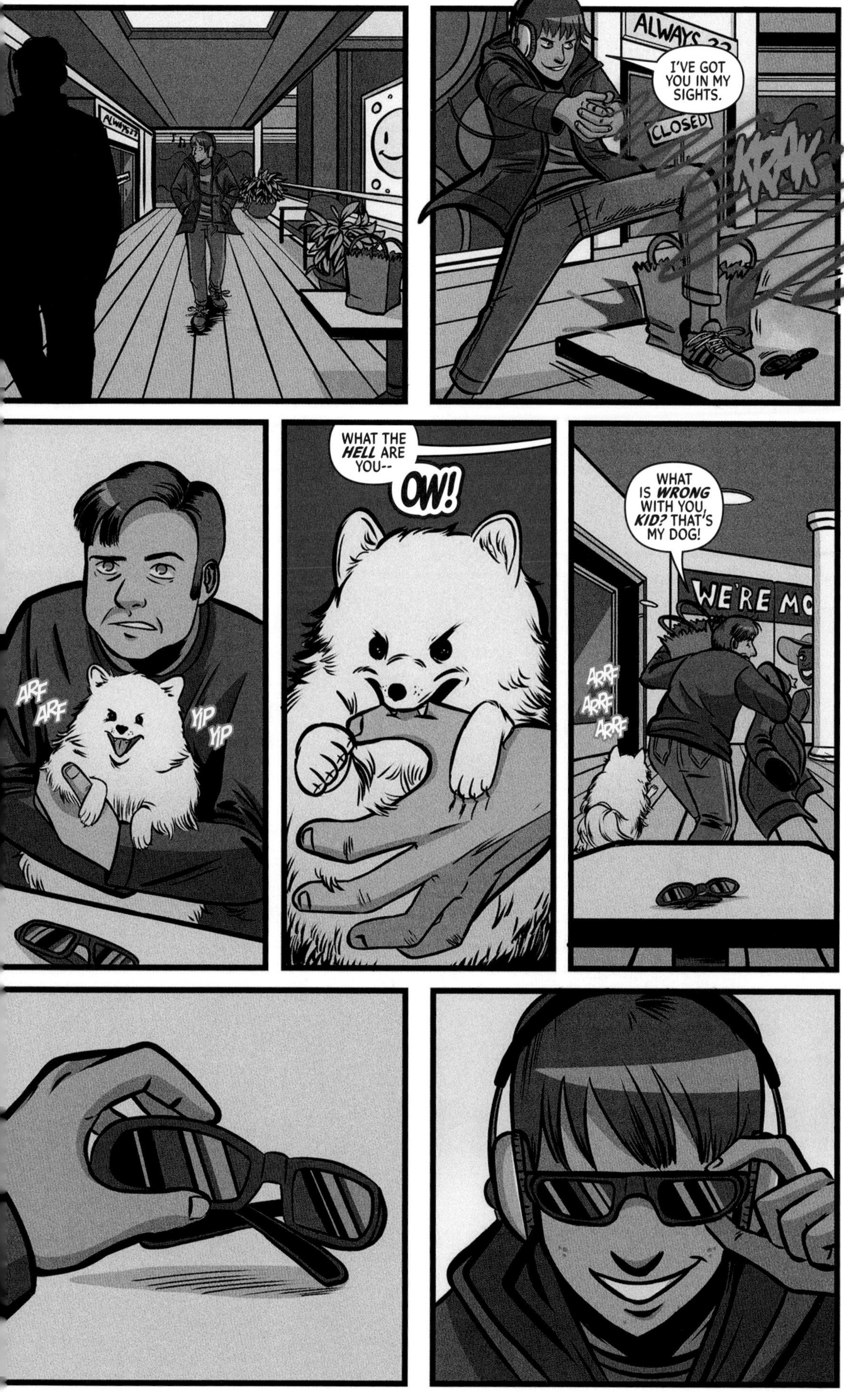
ALWAYS 22
I'VE GOT YOU IN MY SIGHTS.
CLOSED
KRAK
ARF ARF
YIP YIP
WHAT THE HELL ARE YOU--
OW!
WHAT IS WRONG WITH YOU, KID? THAT'S MY DOG!
WE'RE MO
ARRF ARRF ARRF

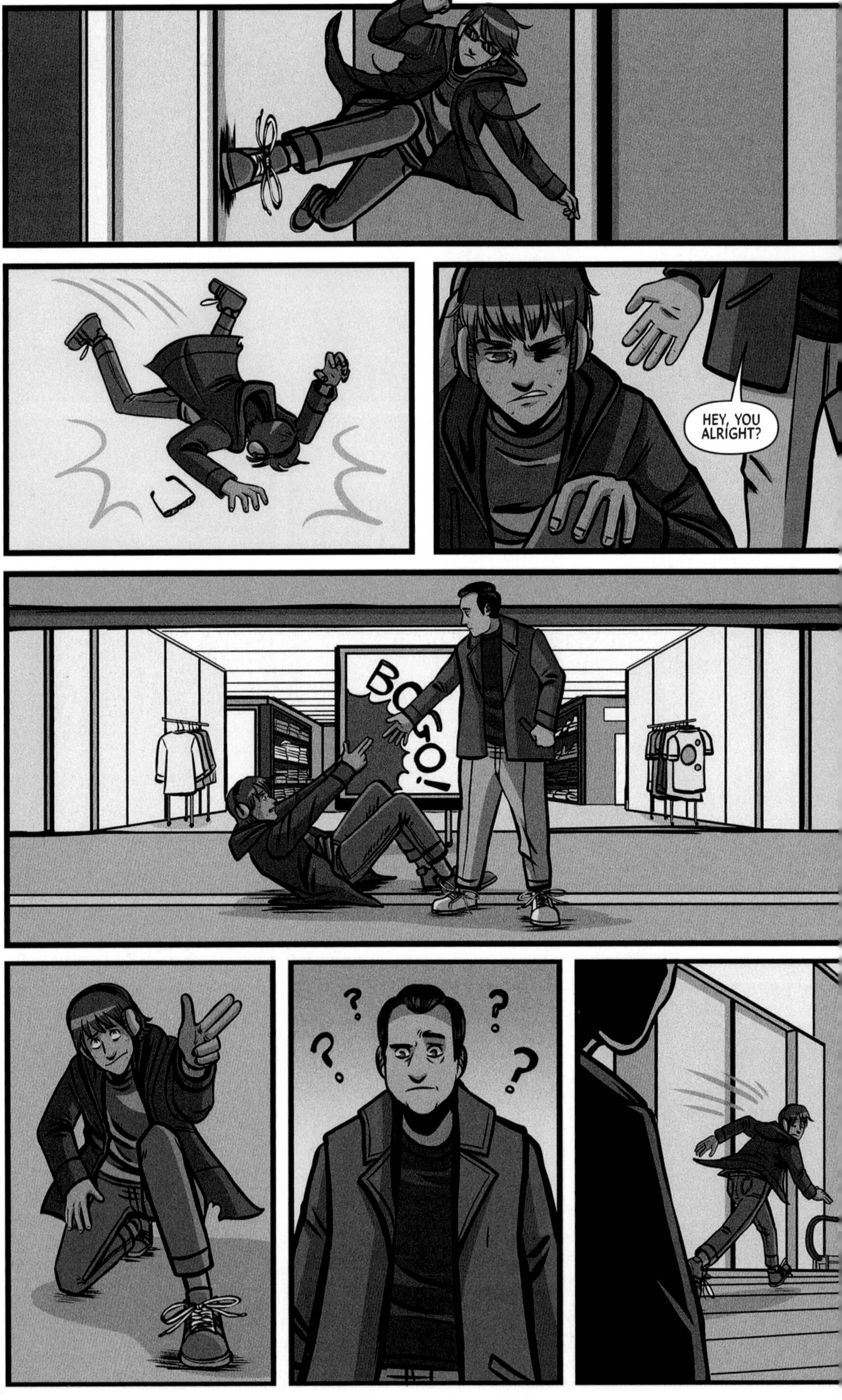
HEY, YOU ALRIGHT?
BOGO!
?
?
?
?

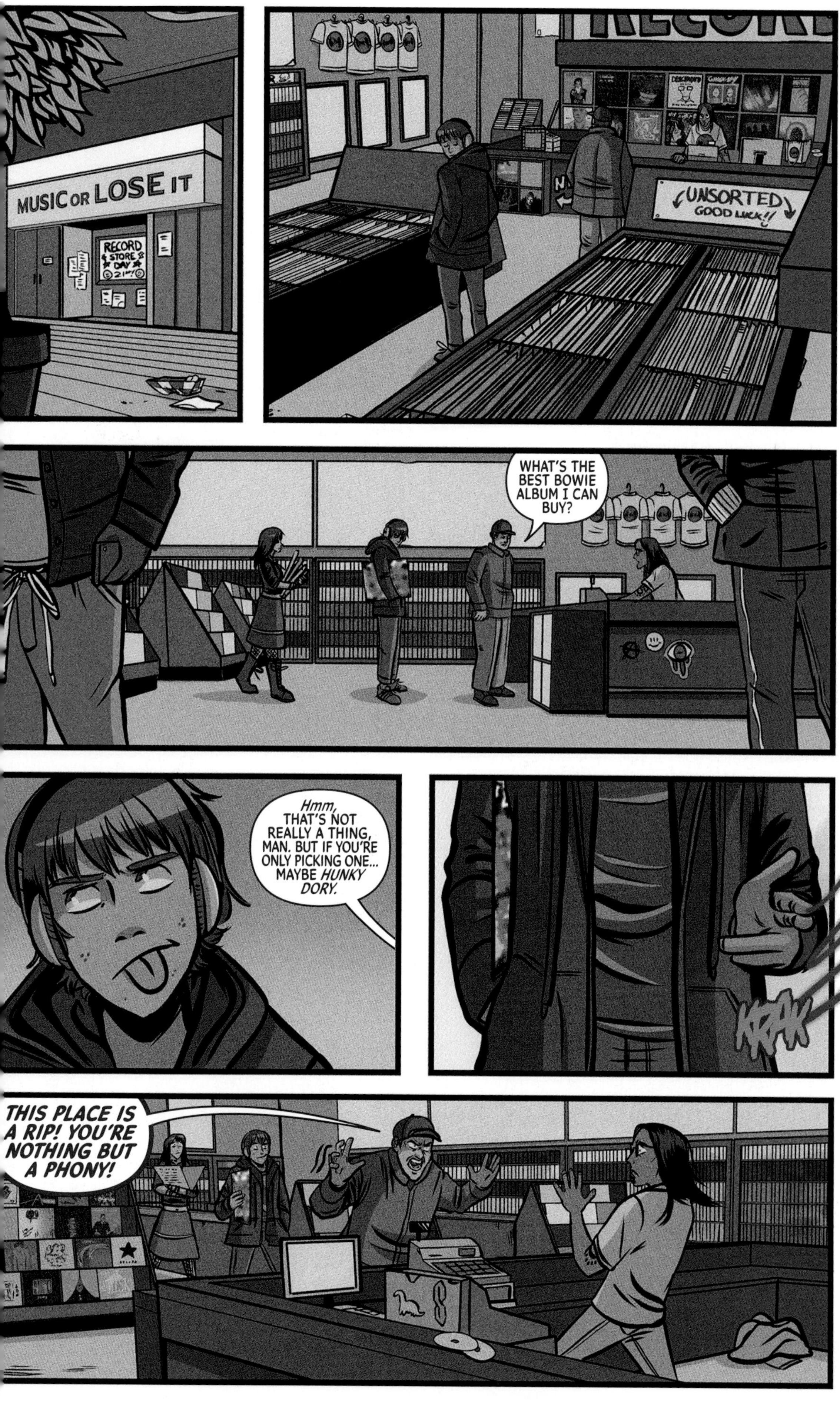
MUSIC OR LOSE IT
RECORD STORE DAY
UNSORTED GOOD LUCK!!
WHAT'S THE BEST BOWIE ALBUM I CAN BUY?
Hmm, THAT'S NOT REALLY A THING, MAN. BUT IF YOU'RE ONLY PICKING ONE... MAYBE HUNKY DORY.
KRAK
THIS PLACE IS A RIP! YOU'RE NOTHING BUT A PHONY!

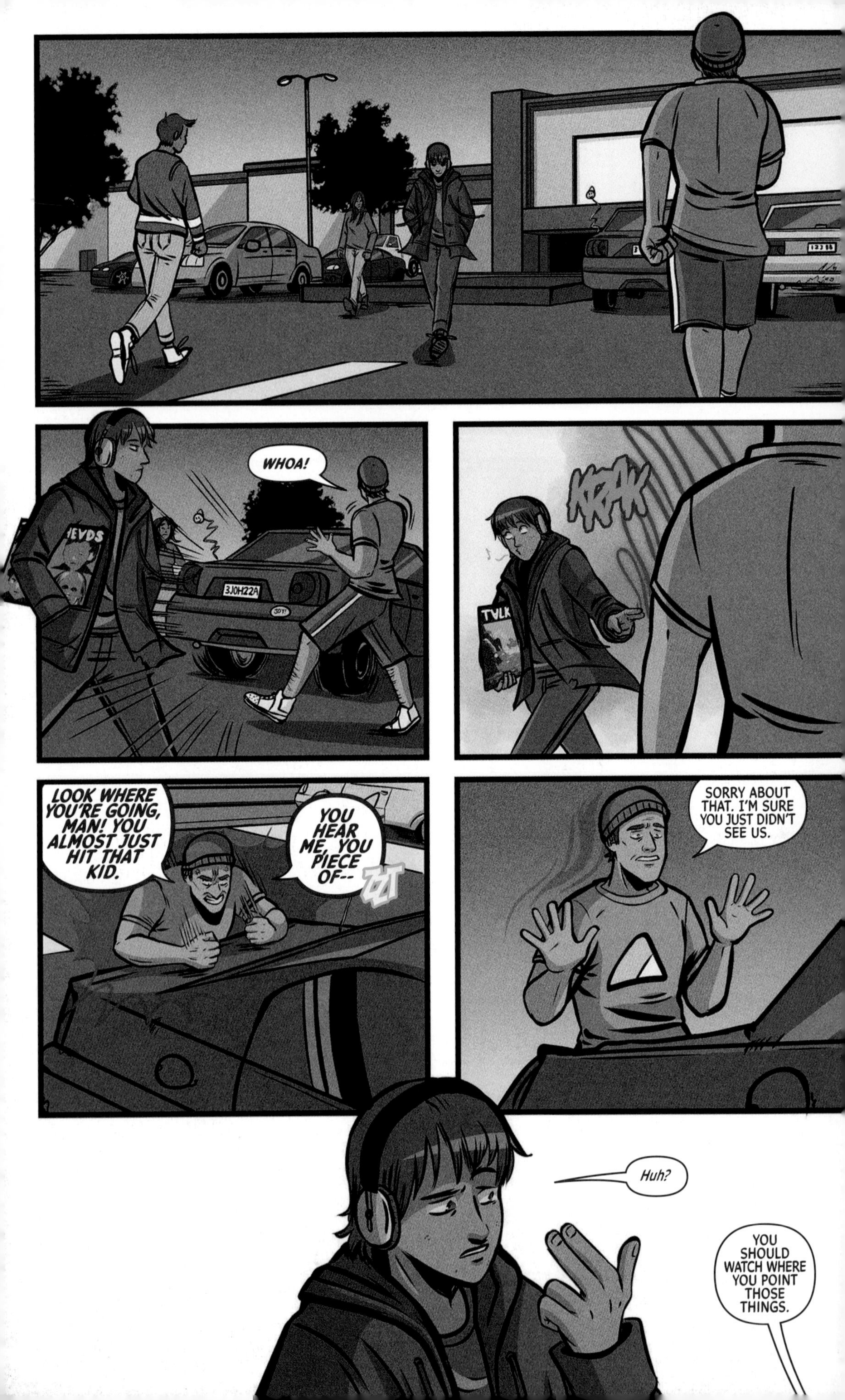
WHOA!
KRAK
LOOK WHERE YOU'RE GOING, MAN! YOU ALMOST JUST HIT THAT KID.
YOU HEAR ME, YOU PIECE OF--
ZZT
SORRY ABOUT THAT. I'M SURE YOU JUST DIDN'T SEE US.
Huh?
YOU SHOULD WATCH WHERE YOU POINT THOSE THINGS.

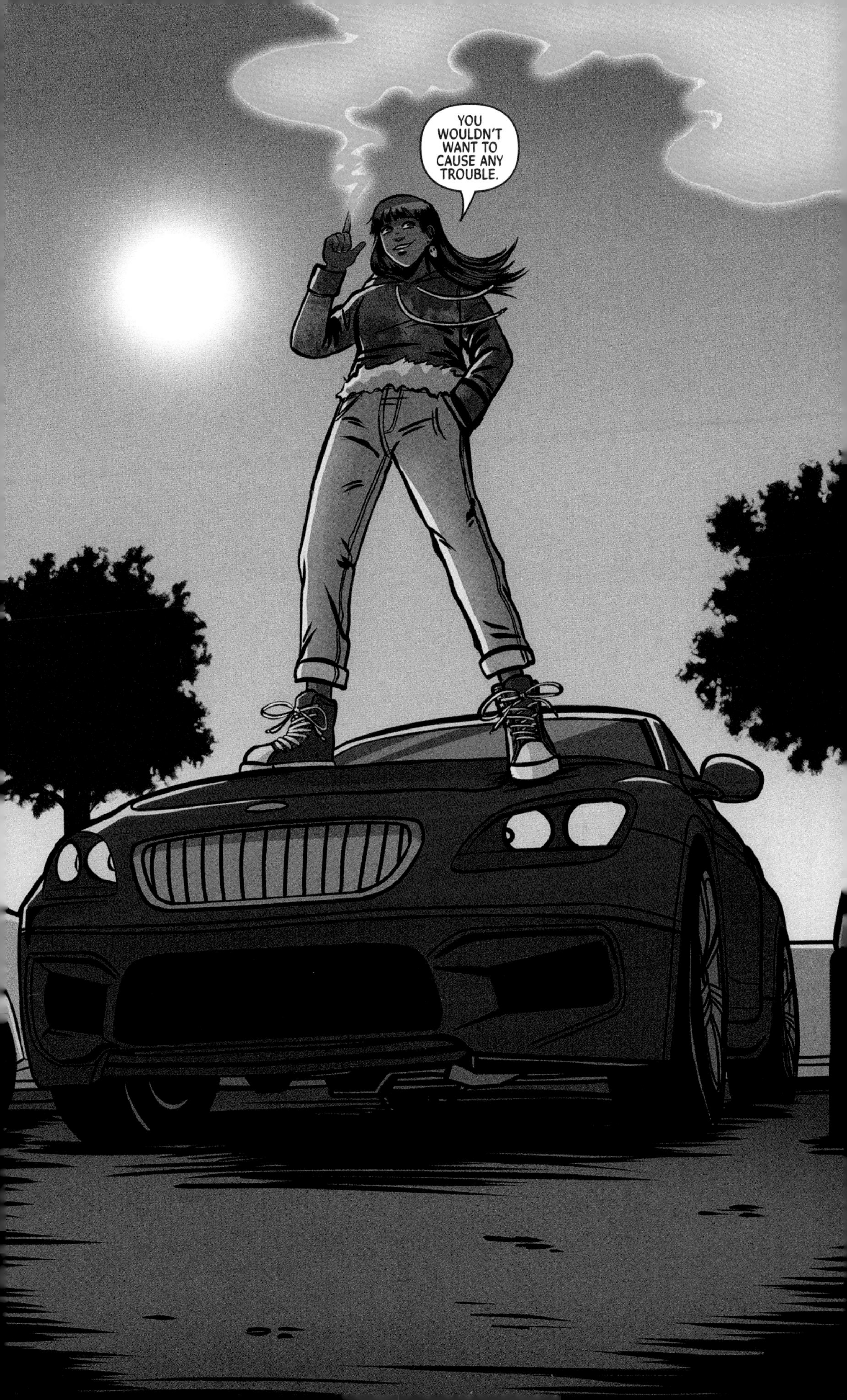
YOU WOULDN'T WANT TO CAUSE ANY TROUBLE.

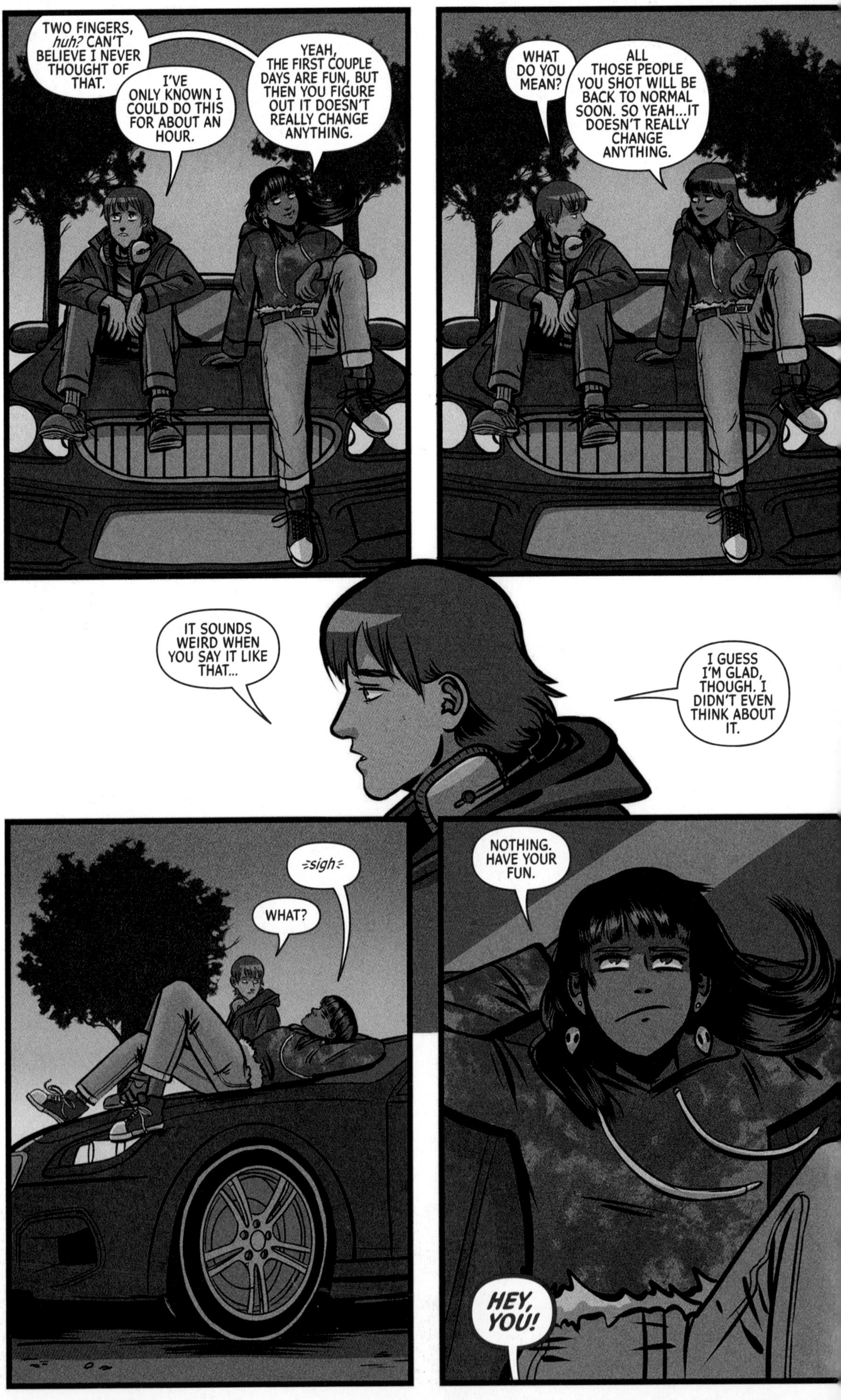
TWO FINGERS, *huh?* CAN'T BELIEVE I NEVER THOUGHT OF THAT.
I'VE ONLY KNOWN I COULD DO THIS FOR ABOUT AN HOUR.
YEAH, THE FIRST COUPLE DAYS ARE FUN, BUT THEN YOU FIGURE OUT IT DOESN'T REALLY CHANGE ANYTHING.
WHAT DO YOU MEAN?
ALL THOSE PEOPLE YOU SHOT WILL BE BACK TO NORMAL SOON. SO YEAH...IT DOESN'T REALLY CHANGE ANYTHING.
IT SOUNDS WEIRD WHEN YOU SAY IT LIKE THAT...
I GUESS I'M GLAD, THOUGH. I DIDN'T EVEN THINK ABOUT IT.
sigh
WHAT?
NOTHING. HAVE YOUR FUN.
HEY, YOU!

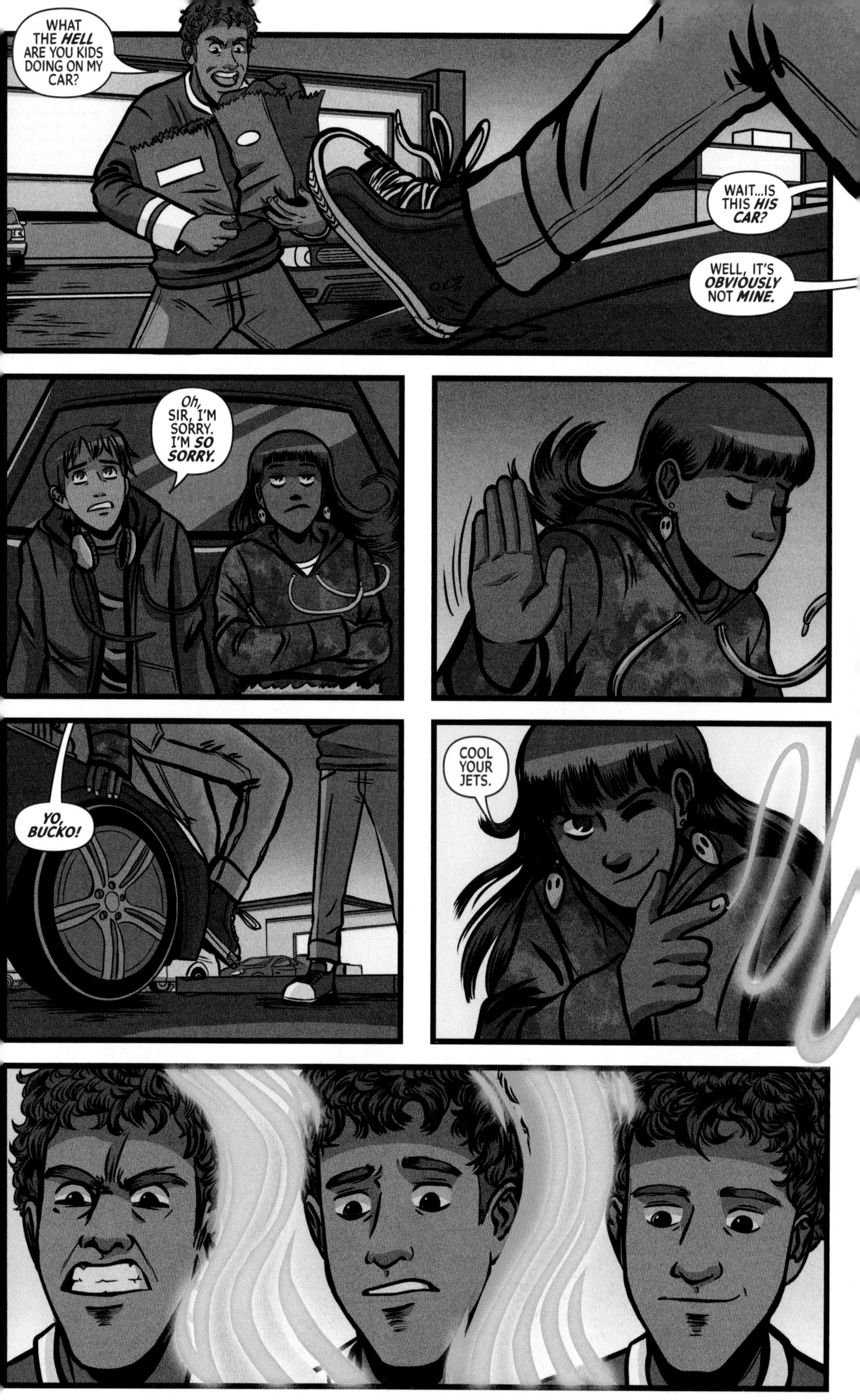
WHAT THE *HELL* ARE YOU KIDS DOING ON MY CAR?
WAIT...IS THIS *HIS CAR?*
WELL, IT'S *OBVIOUSLY* NOT *MINE.*
Oh, SIR, I'M SORRY. I'M *SO SORRY.*
YO, BUCKO!
COOL YOUR JETS.

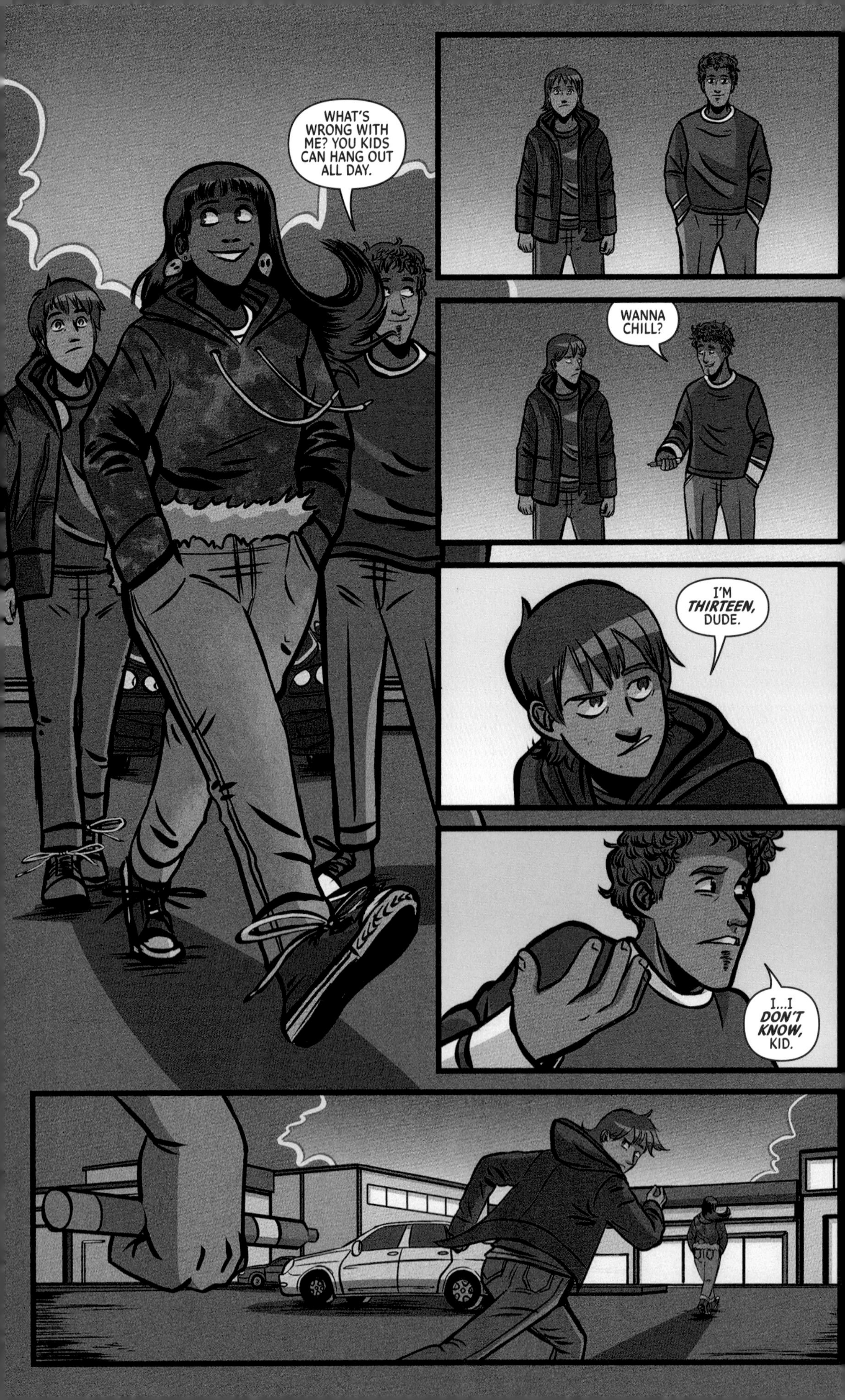
WHAT'S WRONG WITH ME? YOU KIDS CAN HANG OUT ALL DAY.
WANNA CHILL?
I'M *THIRTEEN,* DUDE.
I...I *DON'T KNOW,* KID.

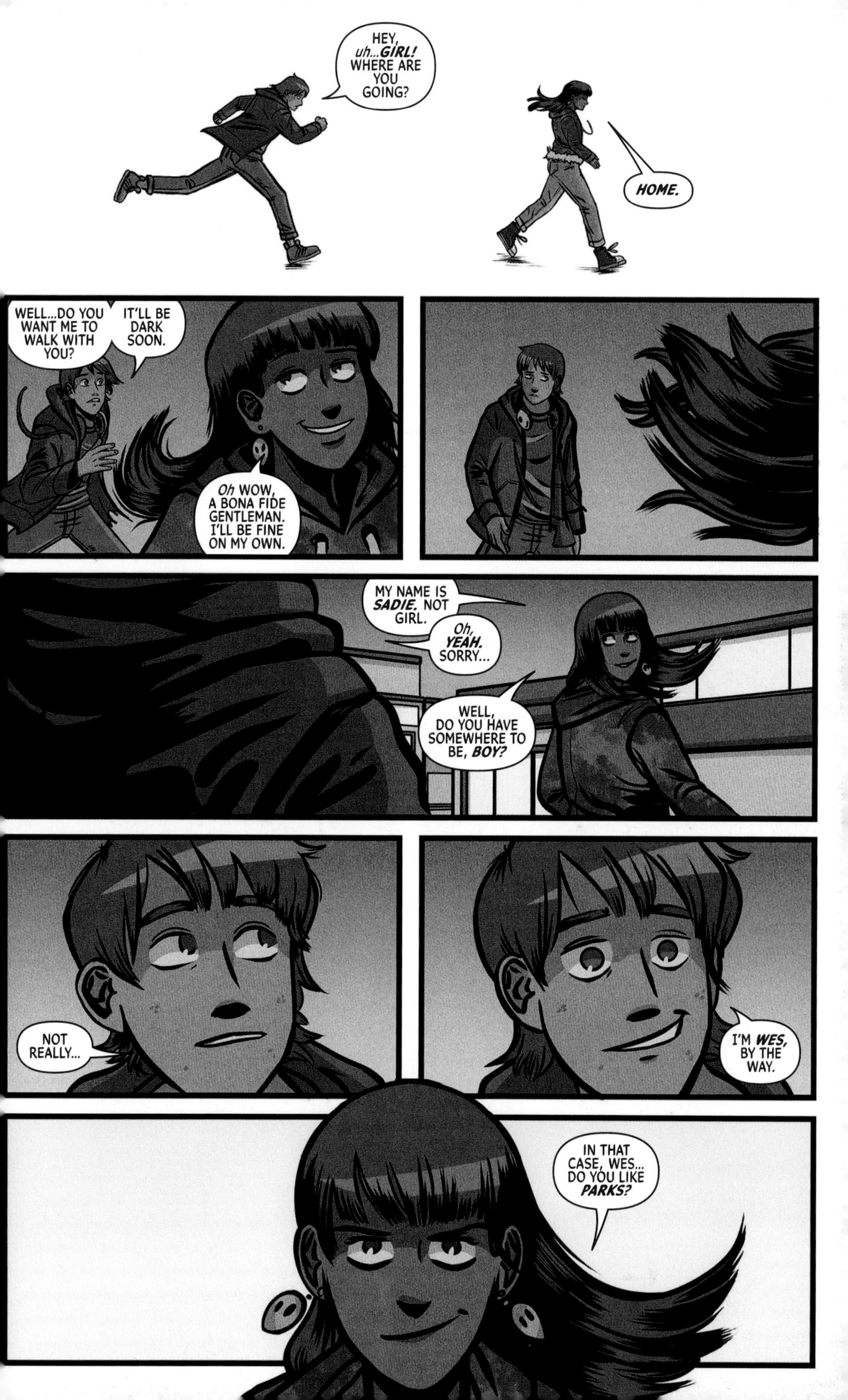
HEY, *uh*...**GIRL!** WHERE ARE YOU GOING?
HOME.
WELL...DO YOU WANT ME TO WALK WITH YOU?
IT'LL BE DARK SOON.
Oh WOW, A BONA FIDE GENTLEMAN. I'LL BE FINE ON MY OWN.
MY NAME IS **SADIE.** NOT GIRL.
Oh, **YEAH.** SORRY...
WELL, DO YOU HAVE SOMEWHERE TO BE, **BOY?**
NOT REALLY...
I'M **WES,** BY THE WAY.
IN THAT CASE, WES... DO YOU LIKE **PARKS?**

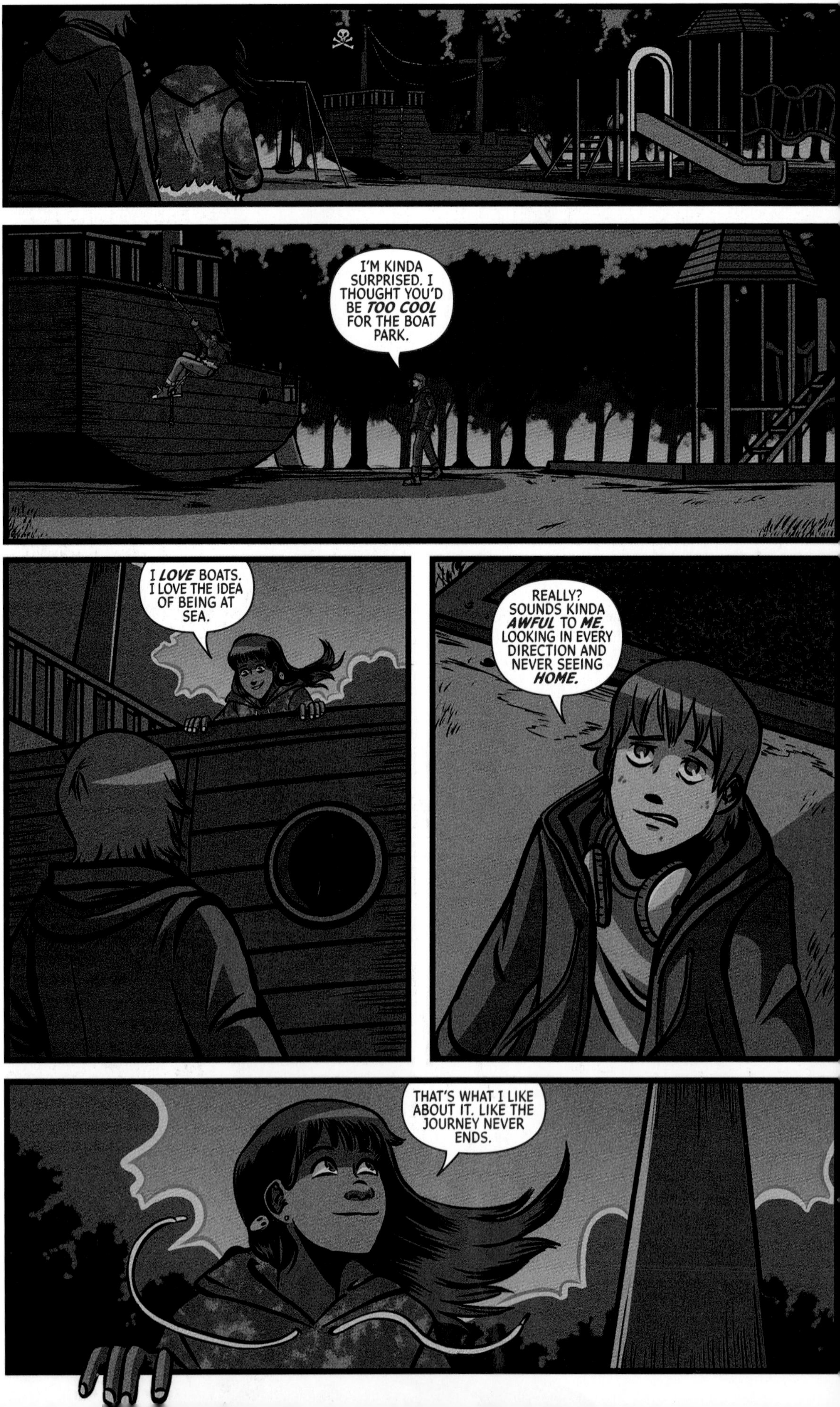
I'M KINDA SURPRISED. I THOUGHT YOU'D BE *TOO COOL* FOR THE BOAT PARK.
I *LOVE* BOATS. I LOVE THE IDEA OF BEING AT SEA.
REALLY? SOUNDS KINDA *AWFUL* TO *ME.* LOOKING IN EVERY DIRECTION AND NEVER SEEING *HOME.*
THAT'S WHAT I LIKE ABOUT IT. LIKE THE JOURNEY NEVER ENDS.

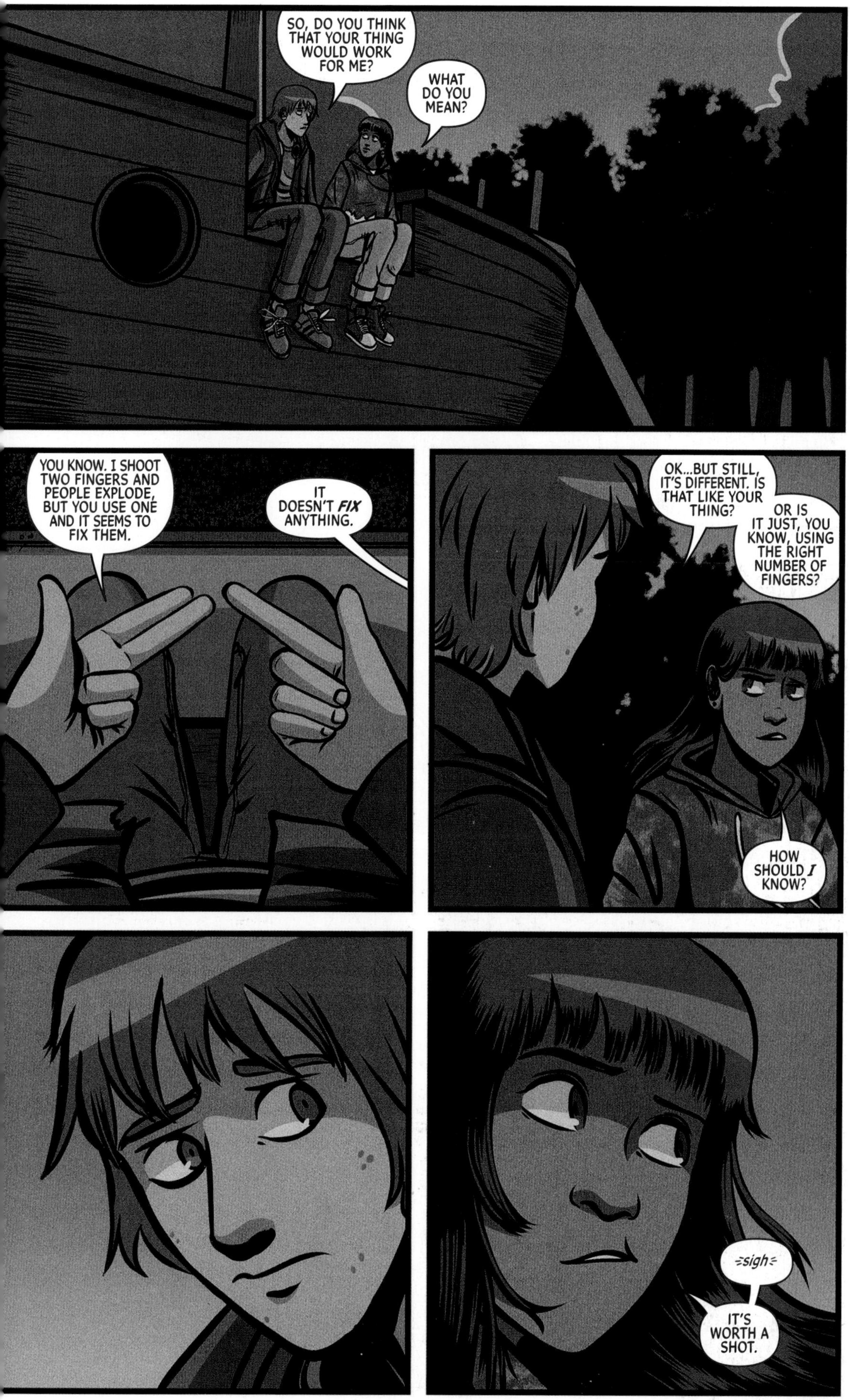
SO, DO YOU THINK THAT YOUR THING WOULD WORK FOR ME?
WHAT DO YOU MEAN?
YOU KNOW. I SHOOT TWO FINGERS AND PEOPLE EXPLODE, BUT YOU USE ONE AND IT SEEMS TO FIX THEM.
IT DOESN'T *FIX* ANYTHING.
OK...BUT STILL, IT'S DIFFERENT. IS THAT LIKE YOUR THING?
OR IS IT JUST, YOU KNOW, USING THE RIGHT NUMBER OF FINGERS?
HOW SHOULD *I* KNOW?
sigh
IT'S WORTH A SHOT.

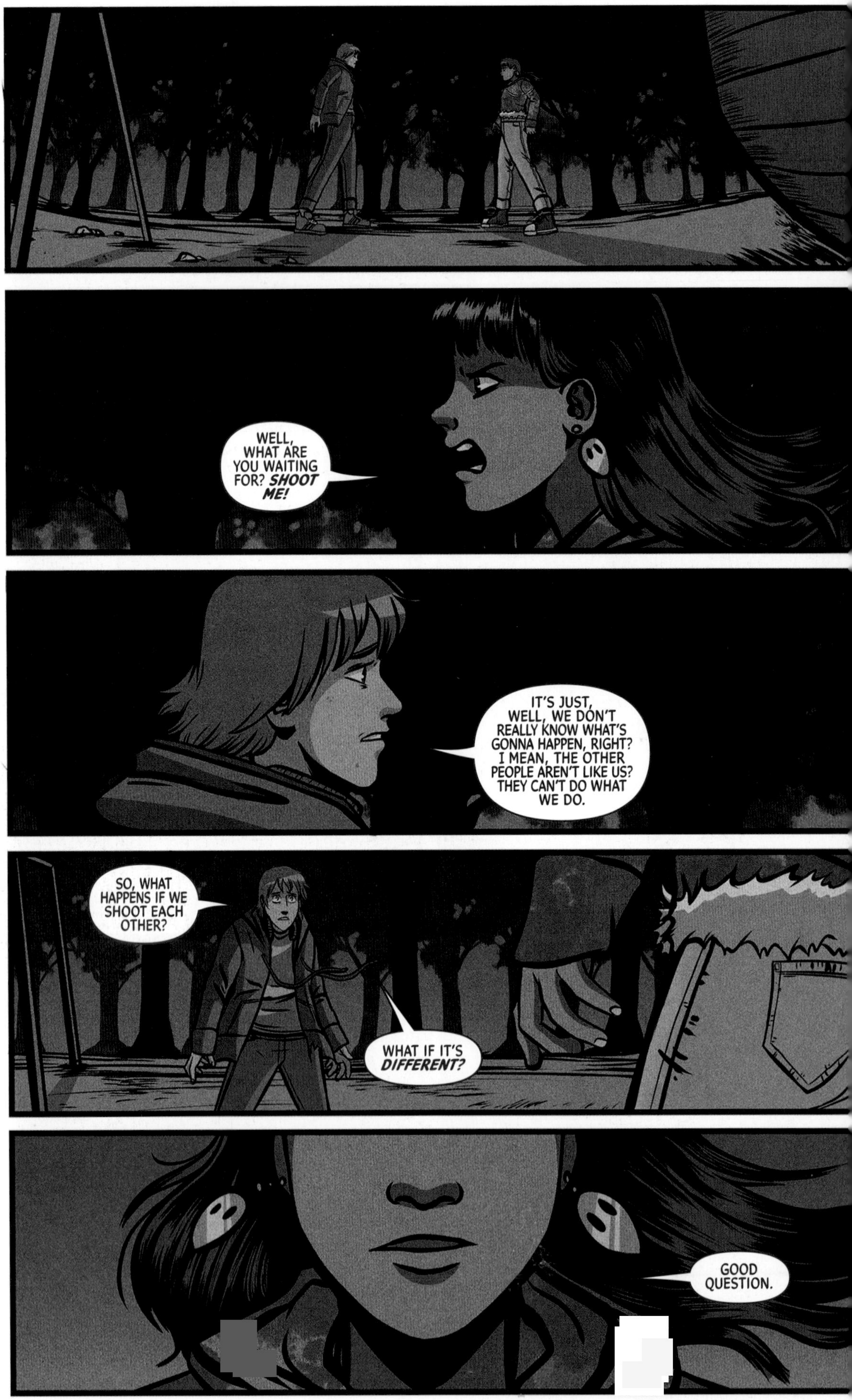
WELL, WHAT ARE YOU WAITING FOR? *SHOOT ME!*
IT'S JUST, WELL, WE DON'T REALLY KNOW WHAT'S GONNA HAPPEN, RIGHT? I MEAN, THE OTHER PEOPLE AREN'T LIKE US? THEY CAN'T DO WHAT WE DO.
SO, WHAT HAPPENS IF WE SHOOT EACH OTHER?
WHAT IF IT'S *DIFFERENT?*
GOOD QUESTION.

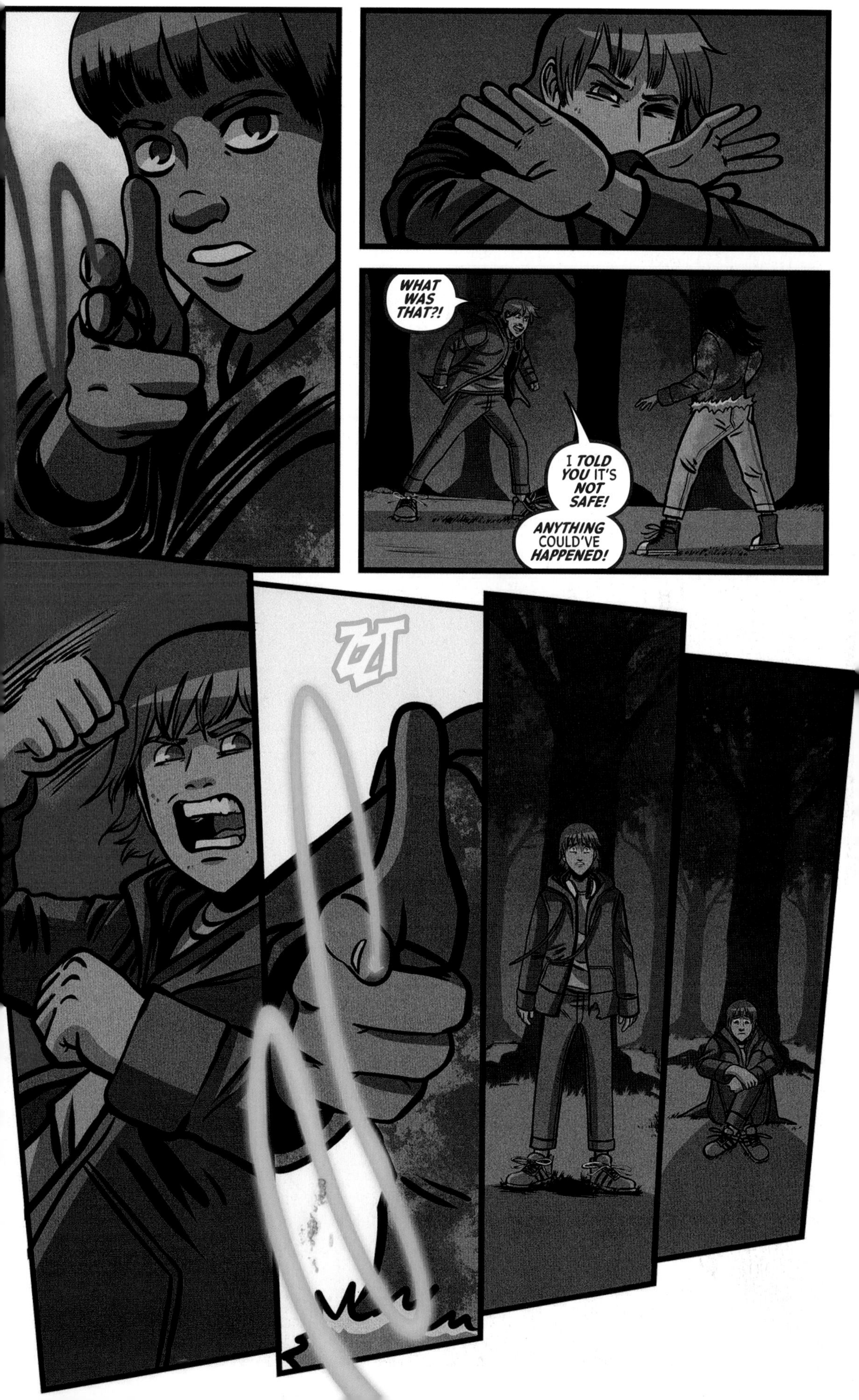
WHAT WAS THAT?!
I TOLD YOU IT'S NOT SAFE!
ANYTHING COULD'VE HAPPENED!
ZAT

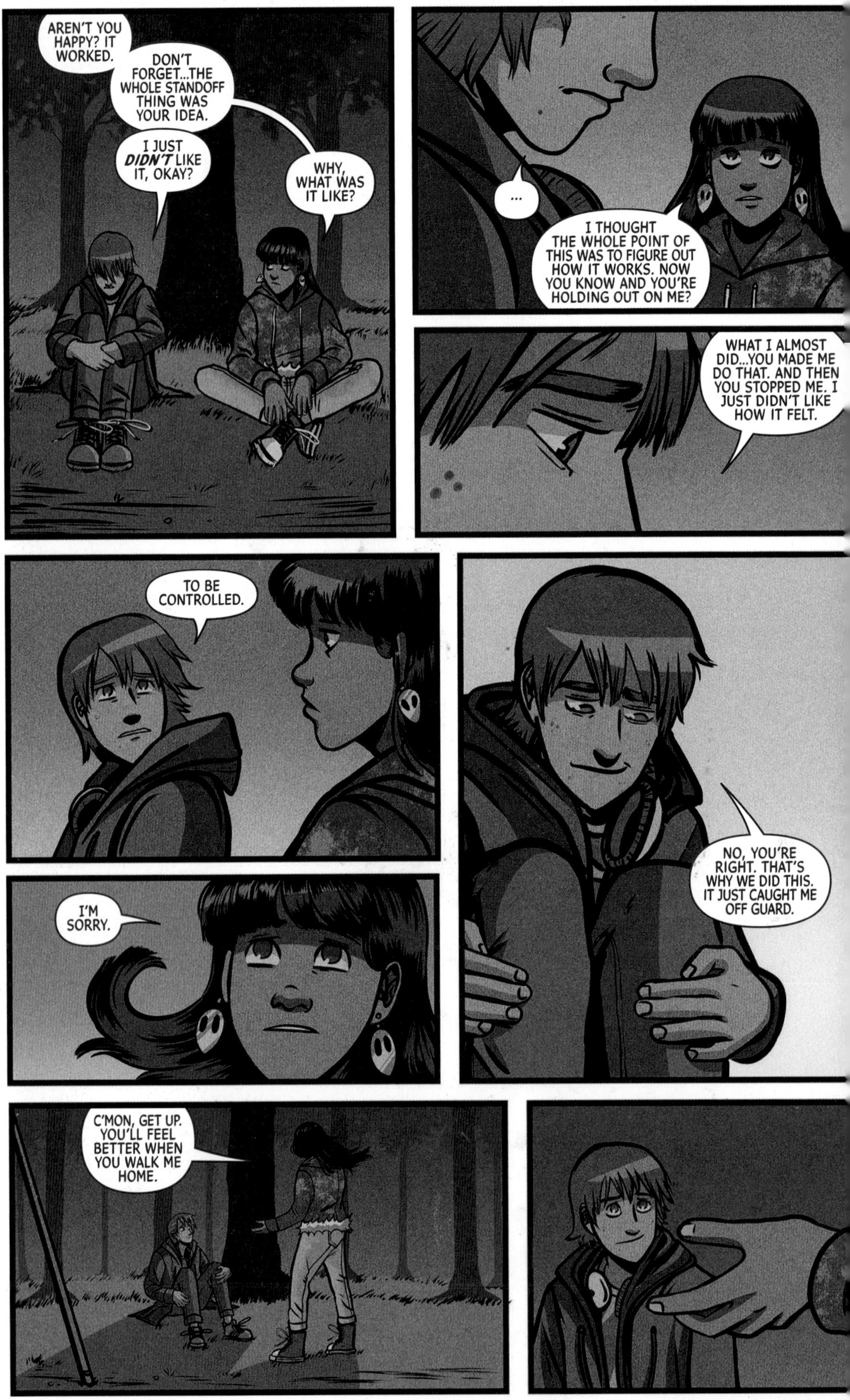
AREN'T YOU HAPPY? IT WORKED.
DON'T FORGET...THE WHOLE STANDOFF THING WAS YOUR IDEA.
I JUST *DIDN'T* LIKE IT, OKAY?
WHY, WHAT WAS IT LIKE?
...
I THOUGHT THE WHOLE POINT OF THIS WAS TO FIGURE OUT HOW IT WORKS. NOW YOU KNOW AND YOU'RE HOLDING OUT ON ME?
WHAT I ALMOST DID...YOU MADE ME DO THAT. AND THEN YOU STOPPED ME. I JUST DIDN'T LIKE HOW IT FELT.
TO BE CONTROLLED.
I'M SORRY.
NO, YOU'RE RIGHT. THAT'S WHY WE DID THIS. IT JUST CAUGHT ME OFF GUARD.
C'MON, GET UP. YOU'LL FEEL BETTER WHEN YOU WALK ME HOME.

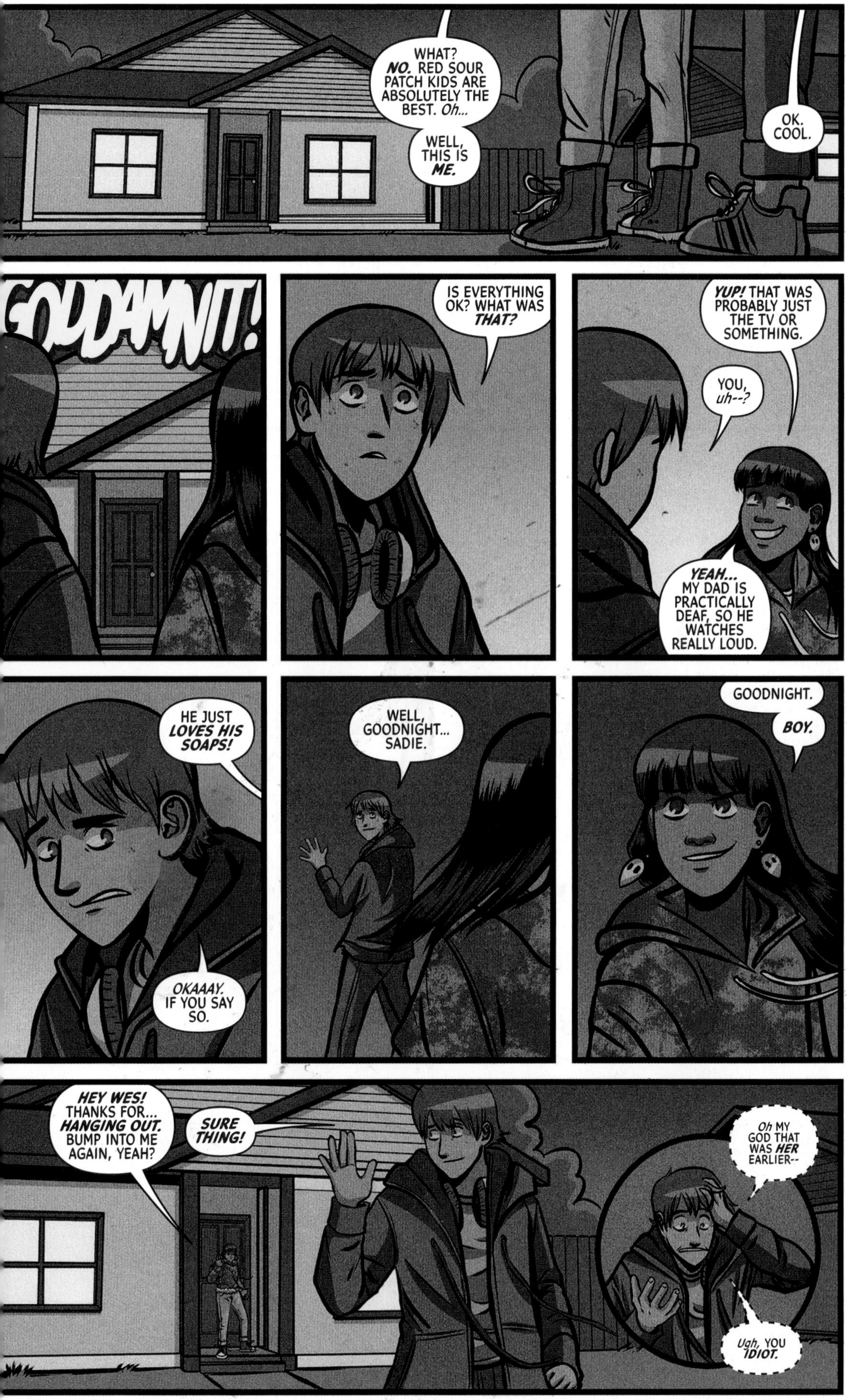
WHAT? *NO.* RED SOUR PATCH KIDS ARE ABSOLUTELY THE BEST. *Oh...*
WELL, THIS IS *ME.*
OK. COOL.
GODDAMNIT!
IS EVERYTHING OK? WHAT WAS *THAT?*
YUP! THAT WAS PROBABLY JUST THE TV OR SOMETHING.
YOU, *uh--?*
YEAH... MY DAD IS PRACTICALLY DEAF, SO HE WATCHES REALLY LOUD.
HE JUST *LOVES HIS SOAPS!*
OKAAAY. IF YOU SAY SO.
WELL, GOODNIGHT... SADIE.
GOODNIGHT.
BOY.
HEY WES! THANKS FOR... *HANGING OUT.* BUMP INTO ME AGAIN, YEAH?
SURE THING!
Oh MY GOD THAT WAS *HER* EARLIER--
Ugh, YOU *IDIOT.*

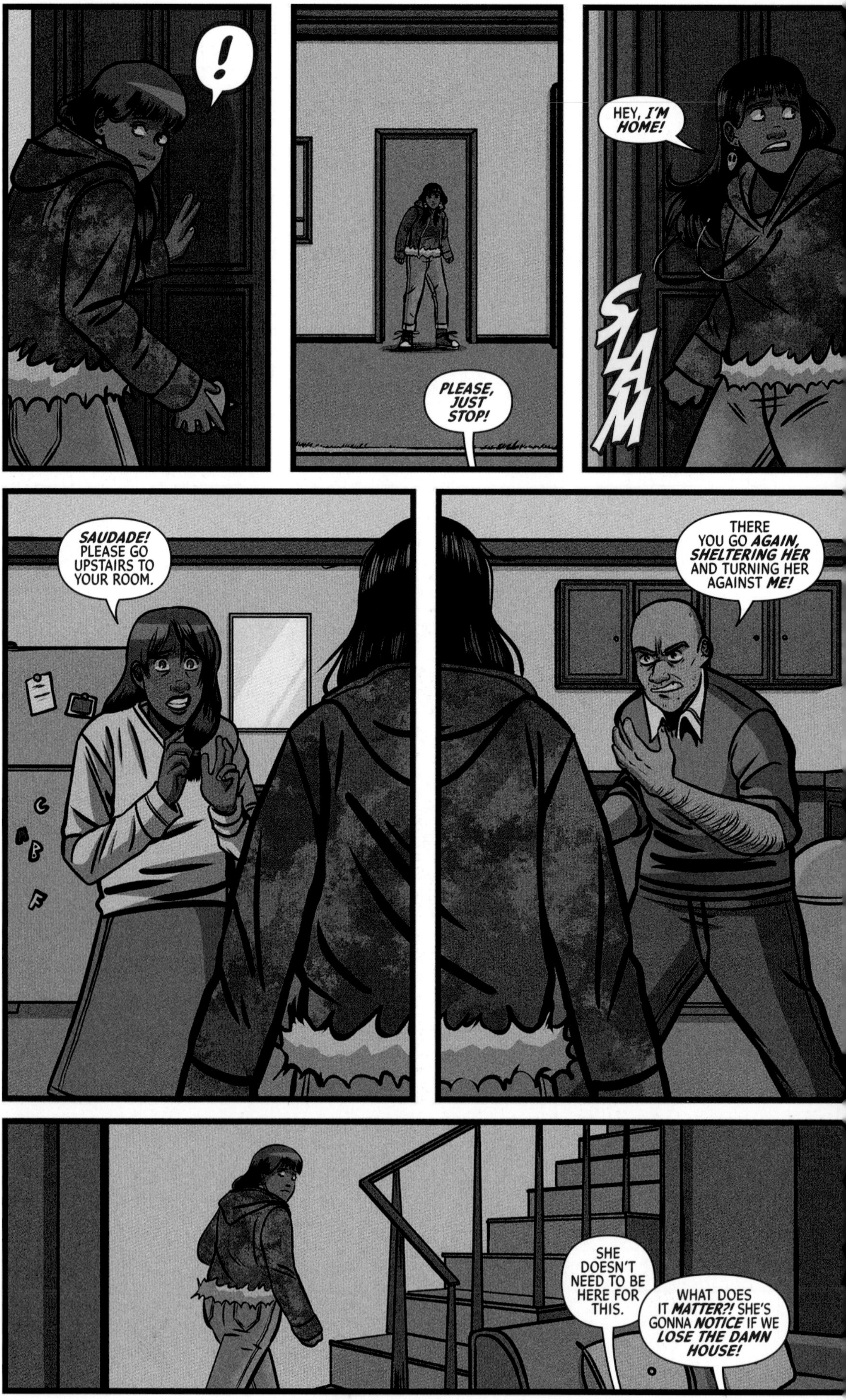
!
PLEASE, JUST STOP!
HEY, I'M HOME!
SLAM
SAUDADE! PLEASE GO UPSTAIRS TO YOUR ROOM.
THERE YOU GO AGAIN, SHELTERING HER AND TURNING HER AGAINST ME!
SHE DOESN'T NEED TO BE HERE FOR THIS.
WHAT DOES IT MATTER?! SHE'S GONNA NOTICE IF WE LOSE THE DAMN HOUSE!

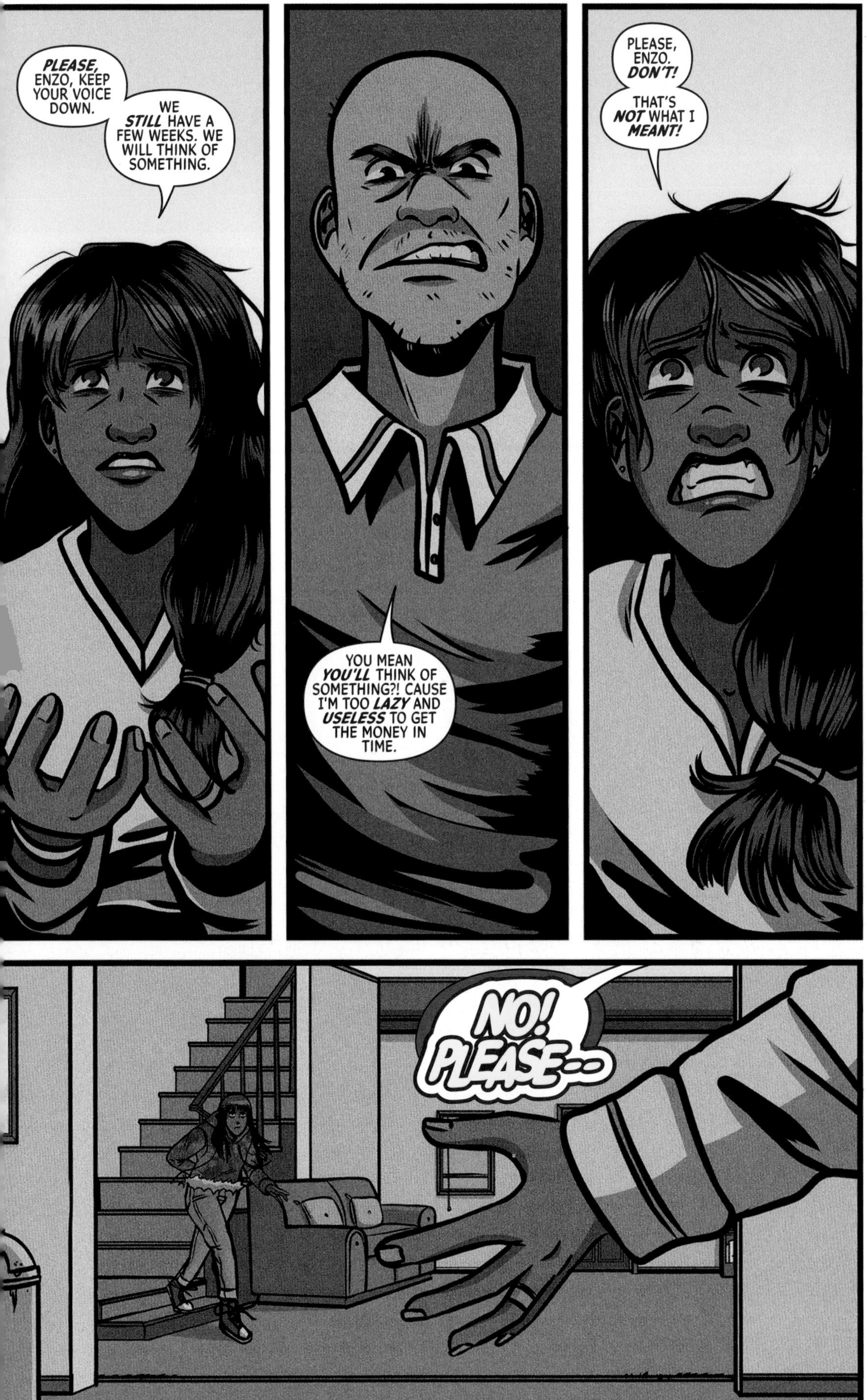
PLEASE, ENZO, KEEP YOUR VOICE DOWN.
WE STILL HAVE A FEW WEEKS. WE WILL THINK OF SOMETHING.
YOU MEAN YOU'LL THINK OF SOMETHING?! CAUSE I'M TOO LAZY AND USELESS TO GET THE MONEY IN TIME.
PLEASE, ENZO. DON'T!
THAT'S NOT WHAT I MEANT!
NO! PLEASE--

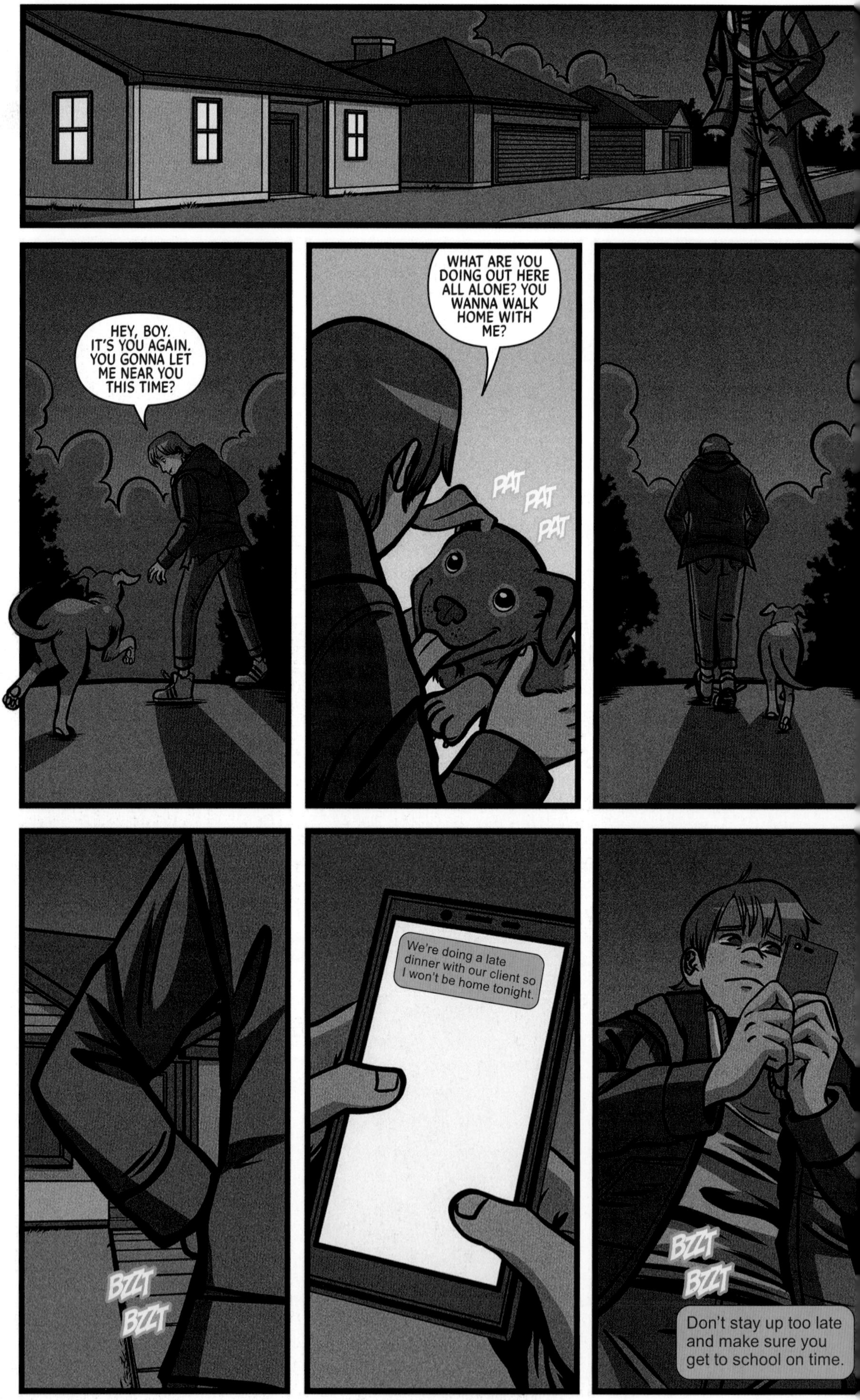
HEY, BOY. IT'S YOU AGAIN. YOU GONNA LET ME NEAR YOU THIS TIME?
WHAT ARE YOU DOING OUT HERE ALL ALONE? YOU WANNA WALK HOME WITH ME?
PAT PAT PAT
BZZT BZZT
We're doing a late dinner with our client so I won't be home tonight.
BZZT BZZT
Don't stay up too late and make sure you get to school on time.

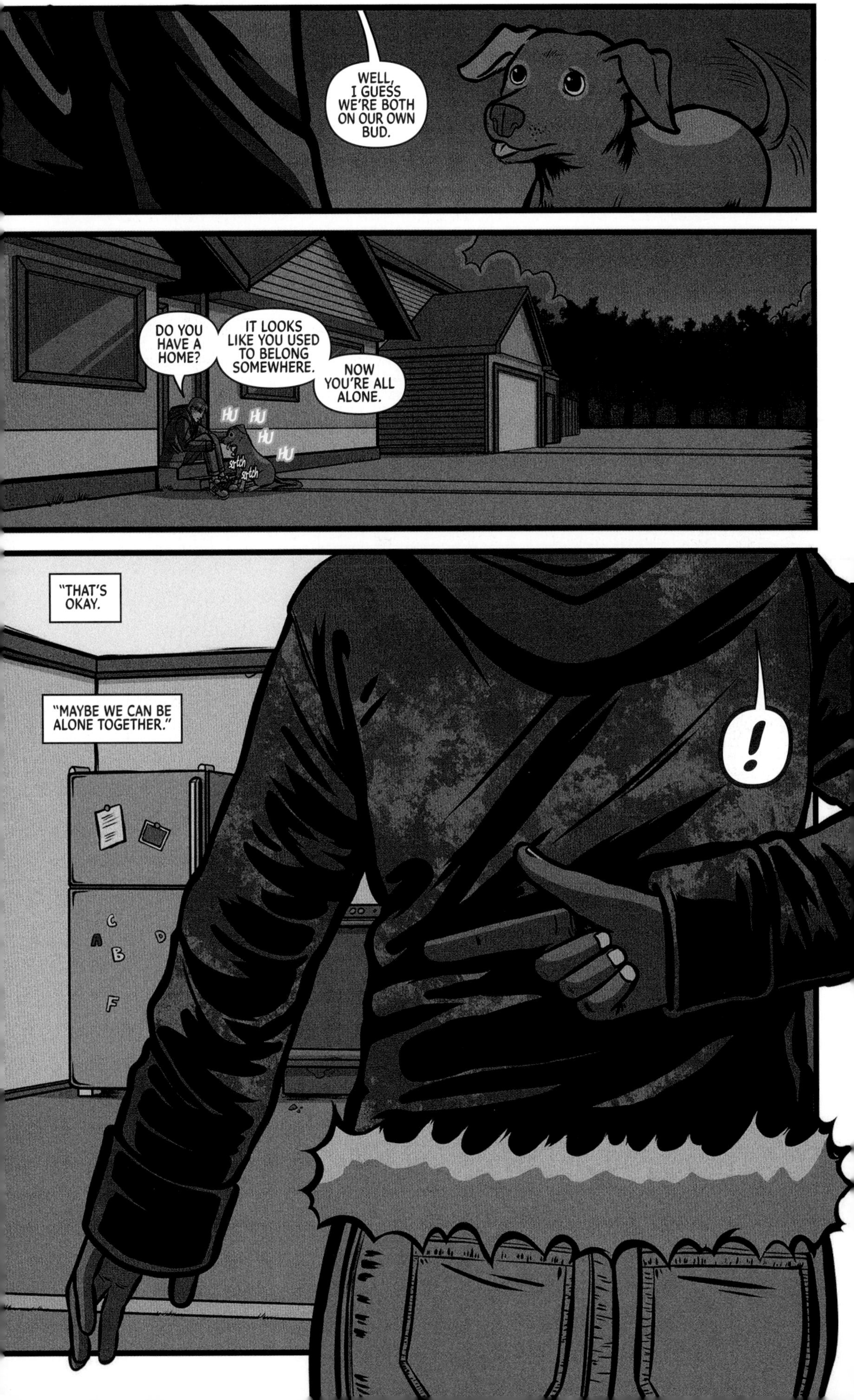
WELL, I GUESS WE'RE BOTH ON OUR OWN BUD.
DO YOU HAVE A HOME?
IT LOOKS LIKE YOU USED TO BELONG SOMEWHERE.
NOW YOU'RE ALL ALONE.
HU HU HU HU
"THAT'S OKAY.
"MAYBE WE CAN BE ALONE TOGETHER."
!

TWO

UNDER THE GUN

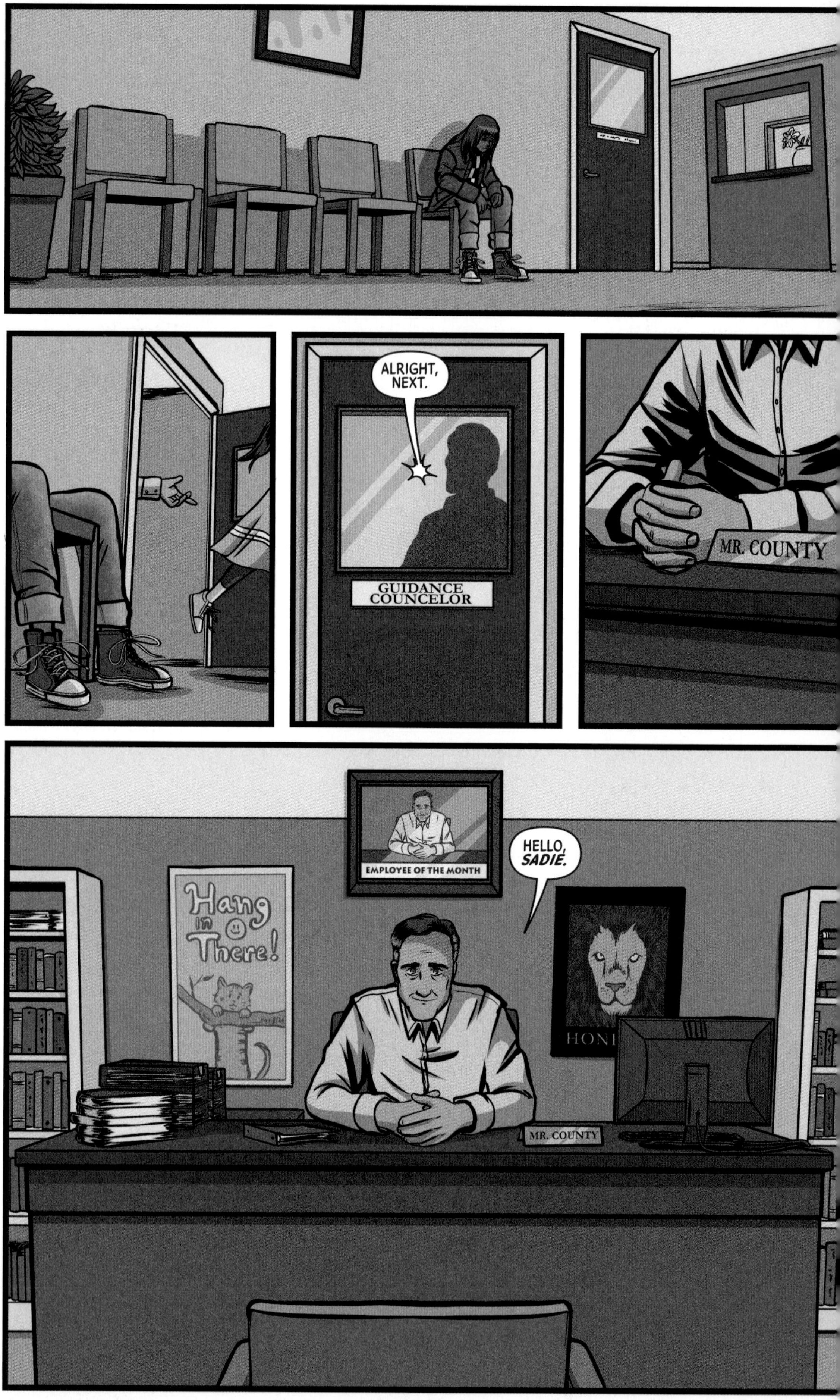

ALRIGHT, NEXT.
GUIDANCE COUNCELOR
MR. COUNTY
EMPLOYEE OF THE MONTH
HELLO, *SADIE.*
Hang in There!
HONI
MR. COUNTY

IT'S GOOD TO SEE YOU AGAIN. I WASN'T SURE IF WE'D BE CHATTING TODAY.

I'VE HAD A LOT ON MY MIND.

SAUDADE... WHAT ARE YOU DOING? GO BACK TO YOUR ROOM.

YOU LOOK AT *ME*. I'M NOT DONE *TALKING TO YOU!*

ENZO, PLEASE, I'M JUST TALKING TO OUR DAUGHTER.

NO! YOU ARE TALKING TO *ME!*

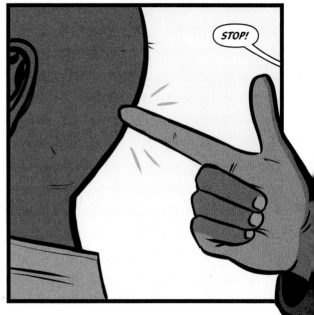

STOP!

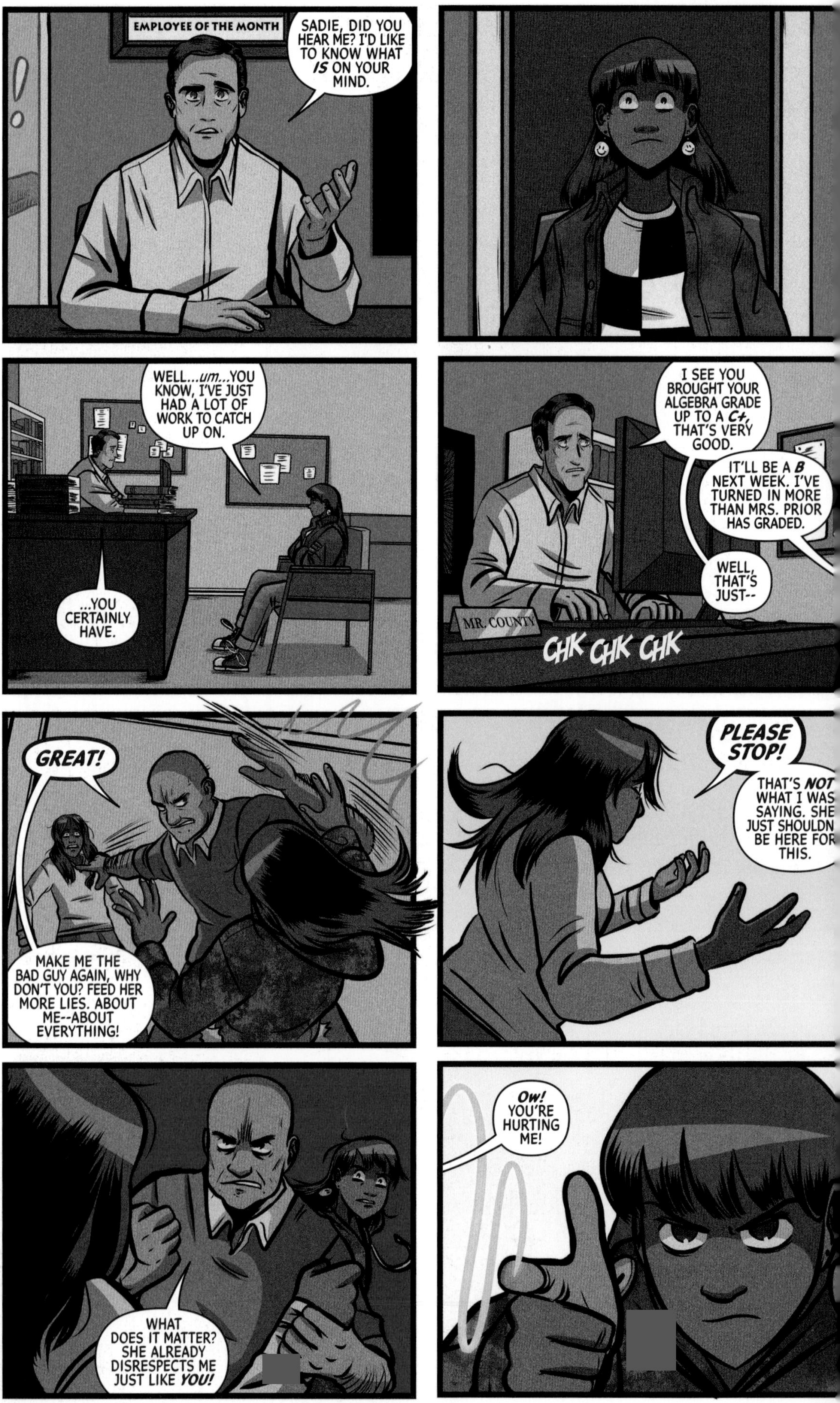
EMPLOYEE OF THE MONTH
SADIE, DID YOU HEAR ME? I'D LIKE TO KNOW WHAT *IS* ON YOUR MIND.
WELL...*um*...YOU KNOW, I'VE JUST HAD A LOT OF WORK TO CATCH UP ON.
...YOU CERTAINLY HAVE.
I SEE YOU BROUGHT YOUR ALGEBRA GRADE UP TO A *C+*, THAT'S VERY GOOD.
IT'LL BE A *B* NEXT WEEK. I'VE TURNED IN MORE THAN MRS. PRIOR HAS GRADED.
WELL, THAT'S JUST--
MR. COUNTY
CHK CHK CHK
GREAT!
MAKE ME THE BAD GUY AGAIN, WHY DON'T YOU? FEED HER MORE LIES. ABOUT ME--ABOUT EVERYTHING!
PLEASE STOP!
THAT'S *NOT* WHAT I WAS SAYING. SHE JUST SHOULDN BE HERE FOR THIS.
WHAT DOES IT MATTER? SHE ALREADY DISRESPECTS ME JUST LIKE *YOU!*
OW! YOU'RE HURTING ME!

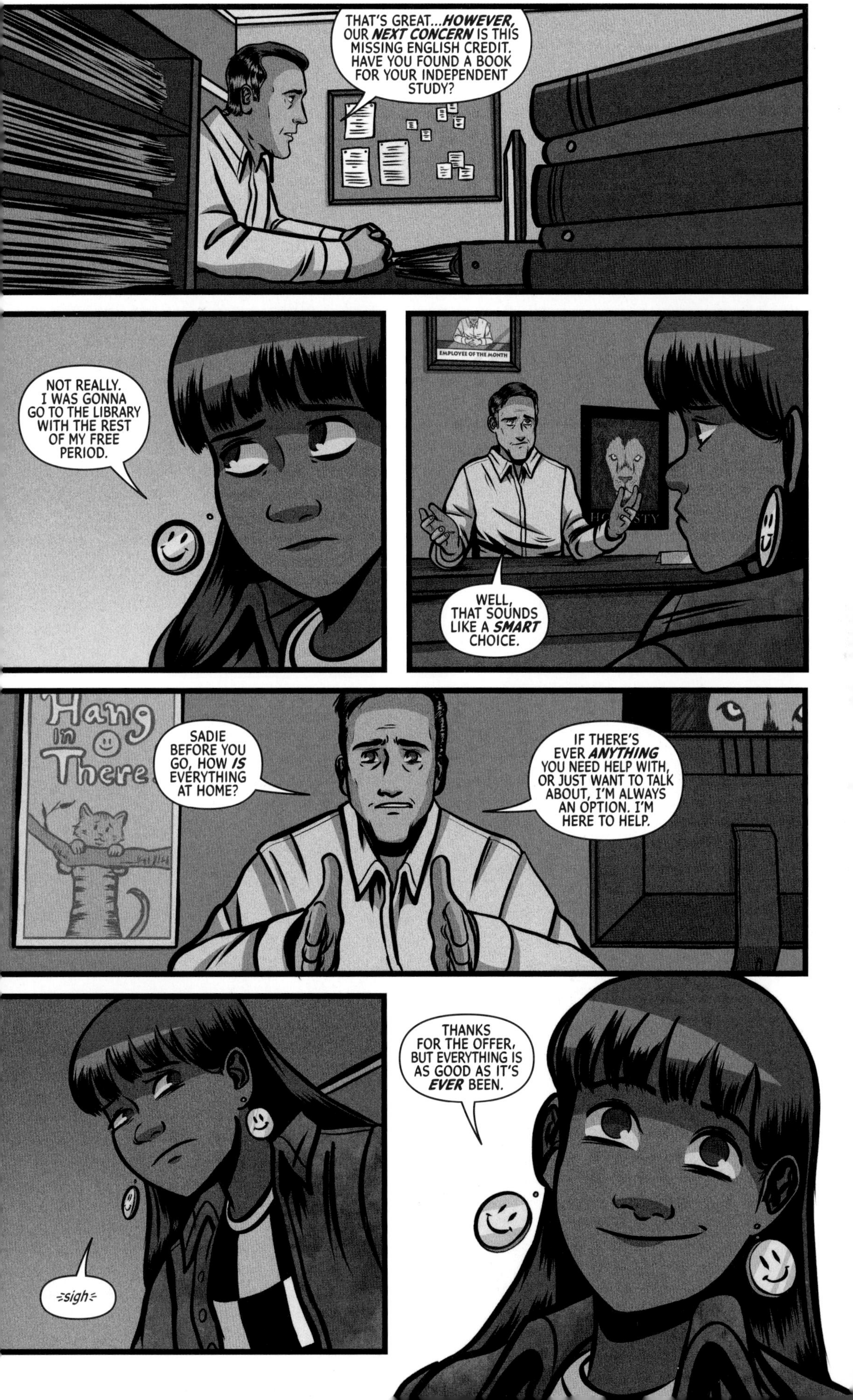
THAT'S GREAT...*HOWEVER*, OUR *NEXT CONCERN* IS THIS MISSING ENGLISH CREDIT. HAVE YOU FOUND A BOOK FOR YOUR INDEPENDENT STUDY?
NOT REALLY. I WAS GONNA GO TO THE LIBRARY WITH THE REST OF MY FREE PERIOD.
EMPLOYEE OF THE MONTH
WELL, THAT SOUNDS LIKE A *SMART* CHOICE.
Hang in There.
SADIE BEFORE YOU GO, HOW *IS* EVERYTHING AT HOME?
IF THERE'S EVER *ANYTHING* YOU NEED HELP WITH, OR JUST WANT TO TALK ABOUT, I'M ALWAYS AN OPTION. I'M HERE TO HELP.
sigh
THANKS FOR THE OFFER, BUT EVERYTHING IS AS GOOD AS IT'S *EVER* BEEN.

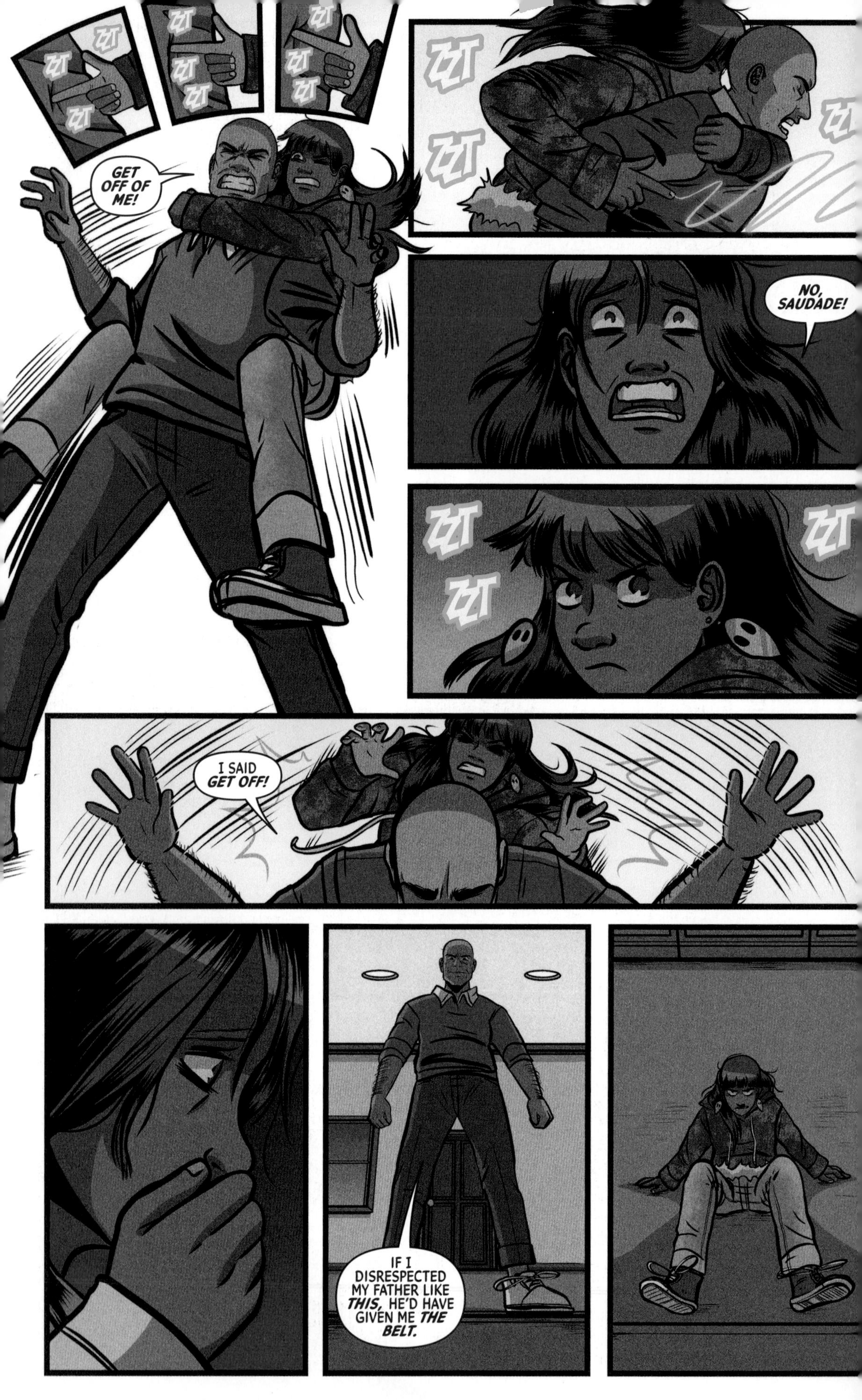
ZZT
ZZT
ZZT
ZZT
ZZT
ZZT
ZZT
ZZT
ZZT
ZZT
GET OFF OF ME!
ZZT
ZZT
ZZT
NO, SAUDADE!
ZZT
ZZT
ZZT
I SAID GET OFF!
IF I DISRESPECTED MY FATHER LIKE THIS, HE'D HAVE GIVEN ME THE BELT.

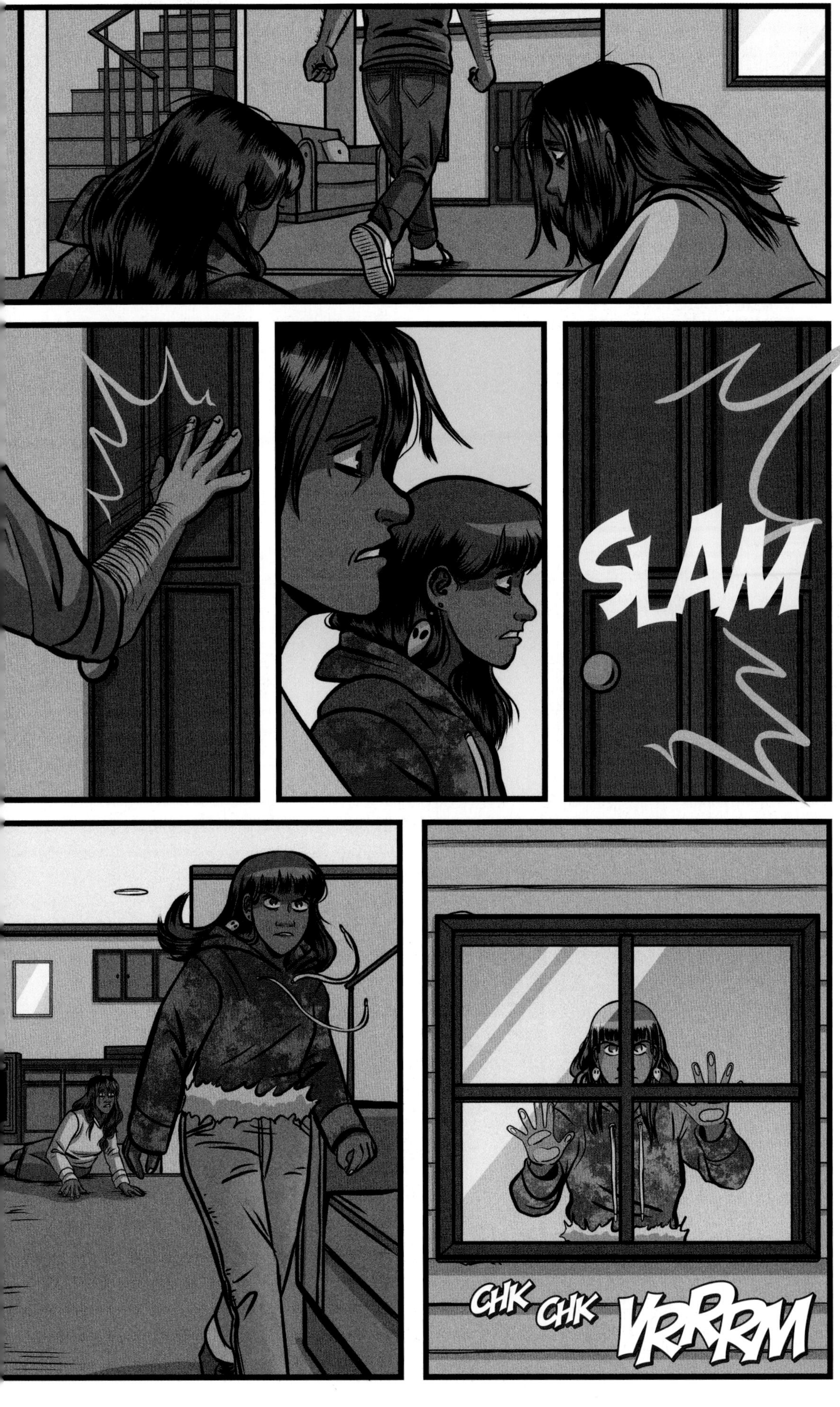
SLAM
CHK CHK
VRRRM

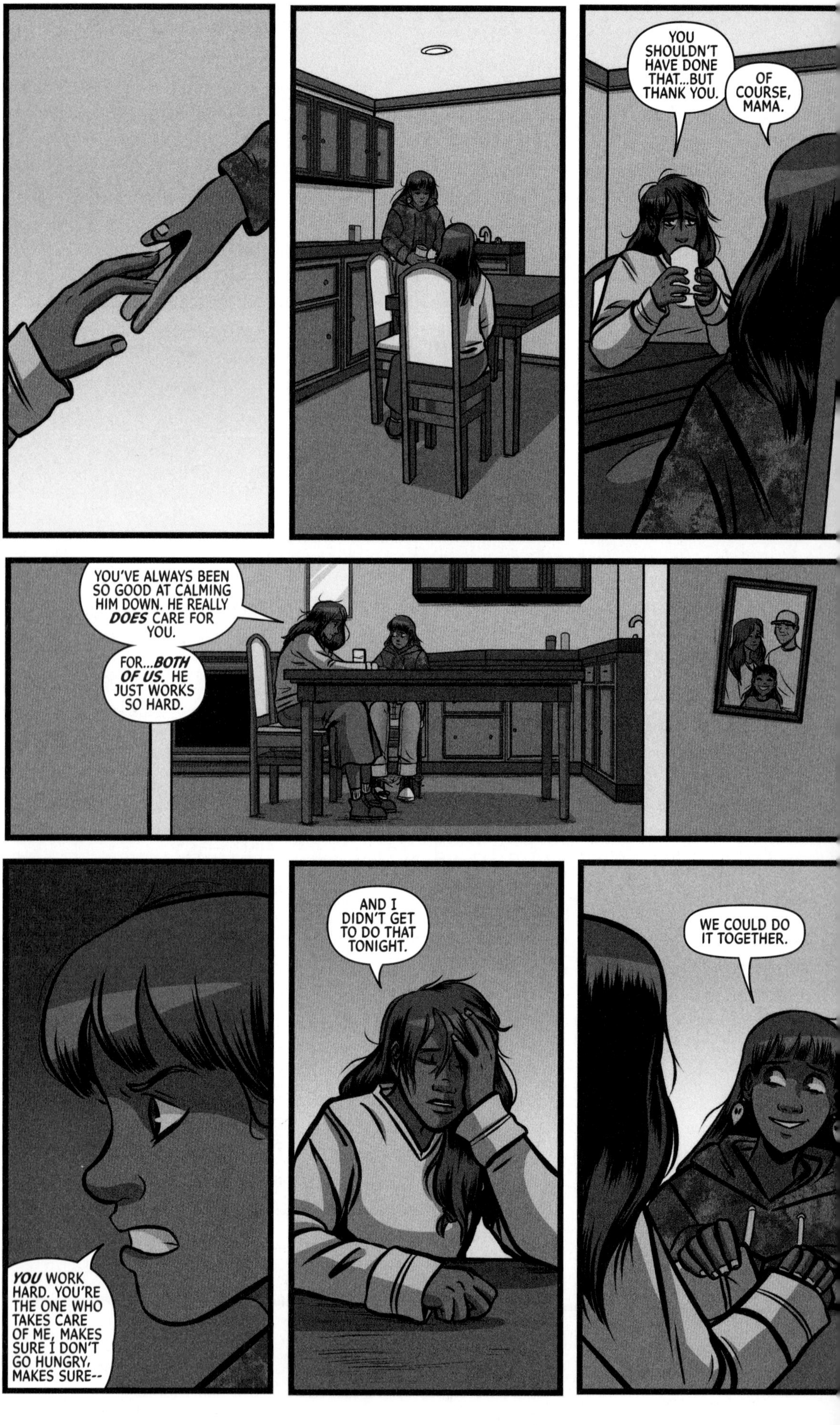
YOU SHOULDN'T HAVE DONE THAT...BUT THANK YOU.
OF COURSE, MAMA.
YOU'VE ALWAYS BEEN SO GOOD AT CALMING HIM DOWN. HE REALLY DOES CARE FOR YOU.
FOR...BOTH OF US. HE JUST WORKS SO HARD.
YOU WORK HARD. YOU'RE THE ONE WHO TAKES CARE OF ME, MAKES SURE I DON'T GO HUNGRY, MAKES SURE--
AND I DIDN'T GET TO DO THAT TONIGHT.
WE COULD DO IT TOGETHER.

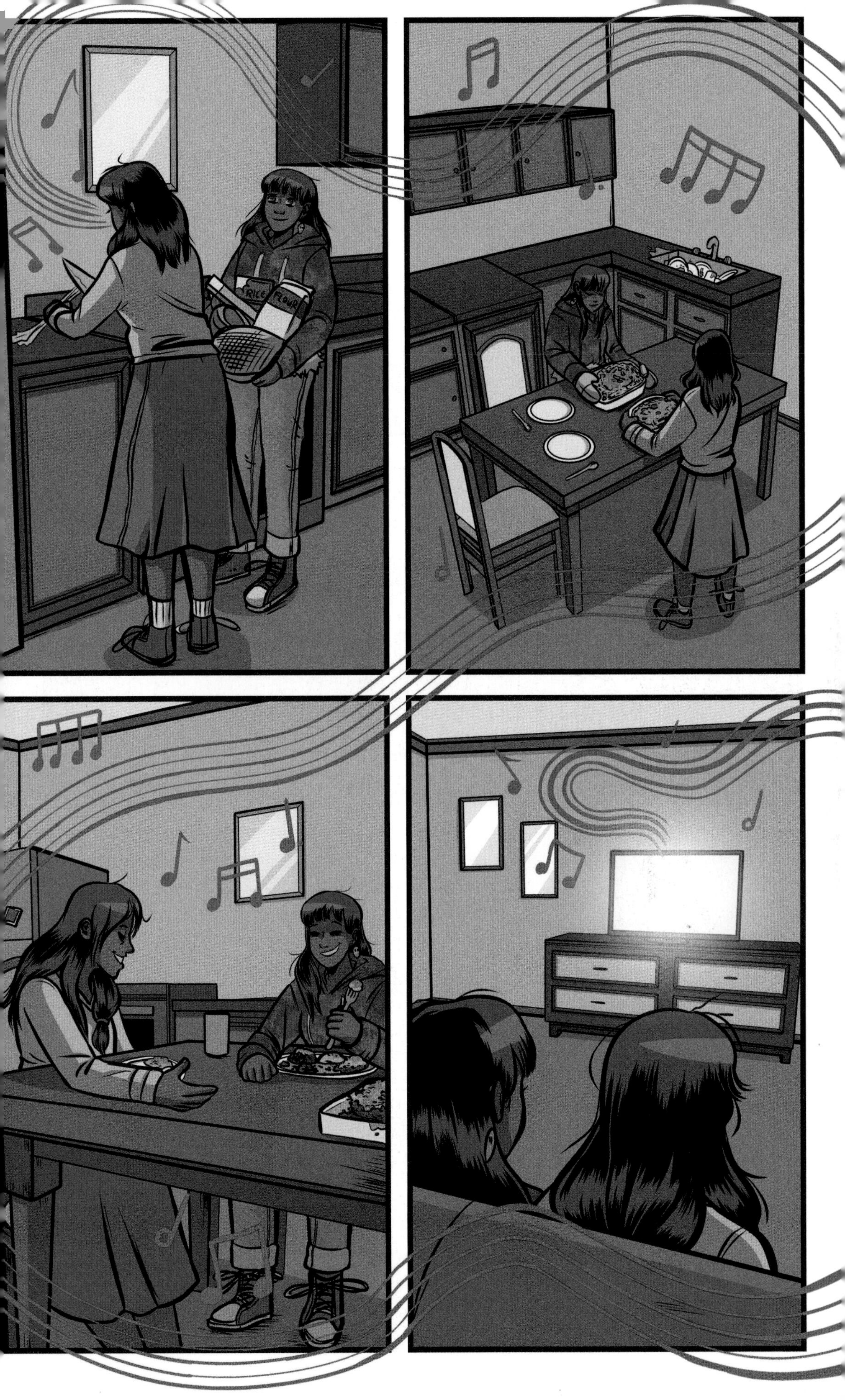
RICE
FLOUR

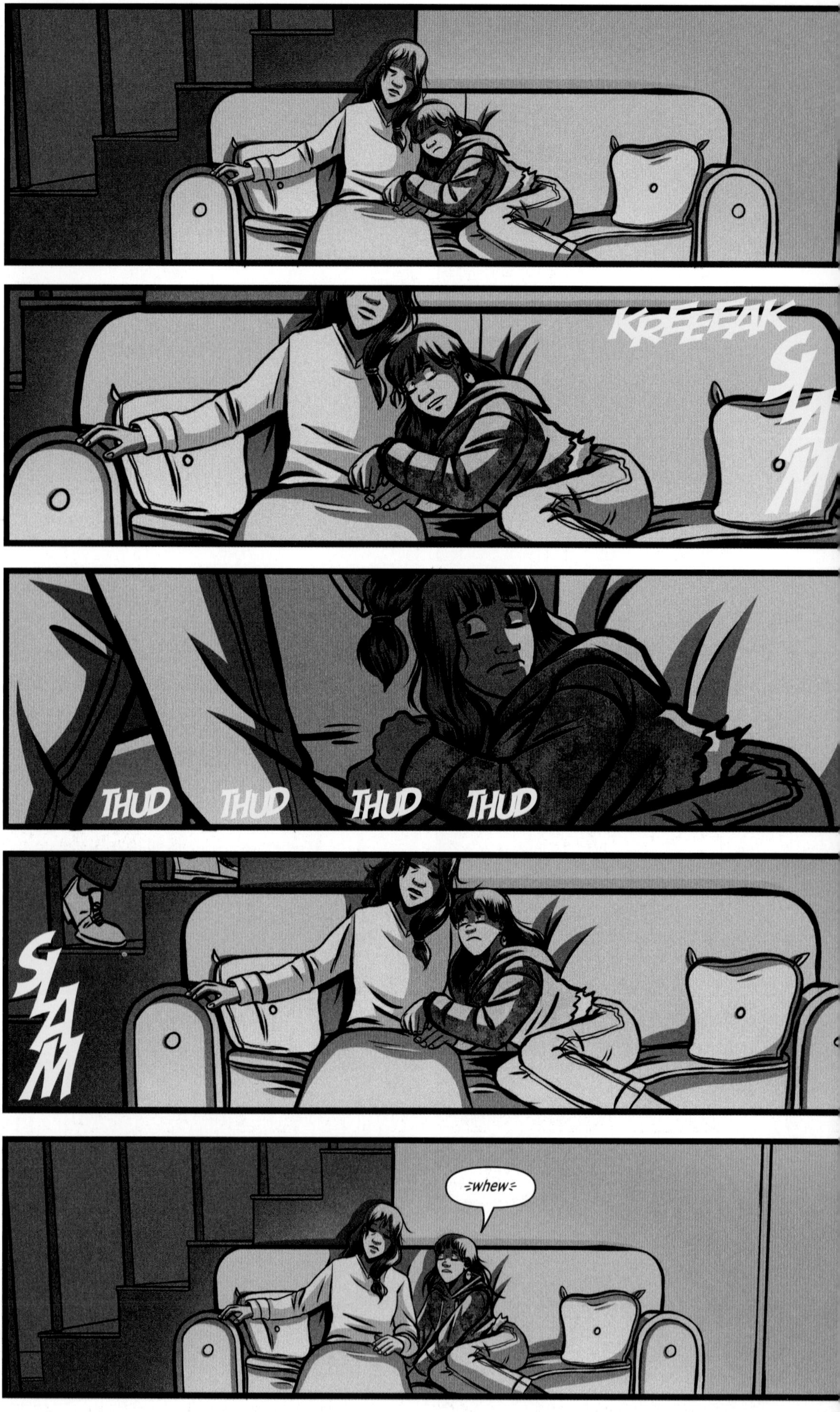
KREEEAK
SLAM
THUD THUD THUD THUD
SLAM
whew

SEARCH
FINGER GUNS
ALL
Finger Guns — Wiki
Finger Guns —
...REALLY?
THANKS, URBAN DICTIONARY.
Ssshh!
WASTE OF AMMO.
PRINT
GOODBYE, MRS. OVERCASH!
Oh, IT'S ALWAYS NICE TO SEE YOU, SADIE!
HOW ARE YOU STILL INTERRUPTING EVERYONE?

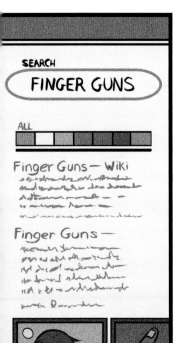

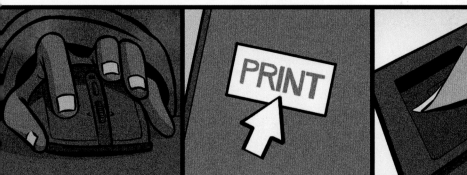

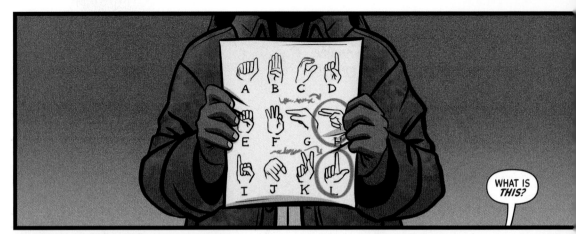

WHAT IS *THIS?*

IT'S THE SIGN LANGUAGE ALPHABET, BUT I THOUGHT MAYBE IT COULD BE CONNECTED TO WHAT WE CAN DO.

IS THERE SOMETHING I'M *NOT SEEING* HERE?

WORTH A SHOT, I GUESS--

HEY, SADIE!

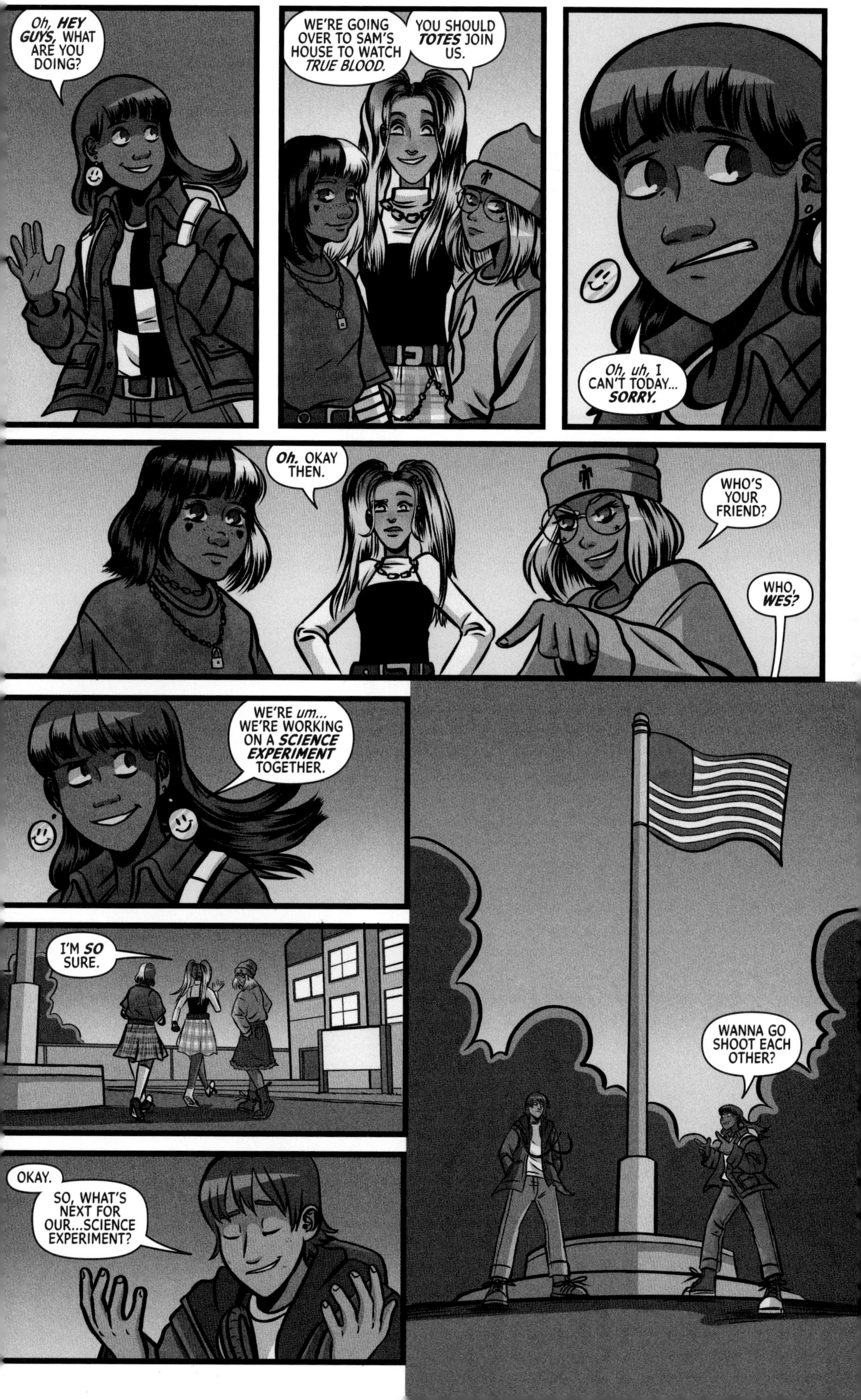
Oh, HEY GUYS, WHAT ARE YOU DOING?
WE'RE GOING OVER TO SAM'S HOUSE TO WATCH TRUE BLOOD.
YOU SHOULD TOTES JOIN US.
Oh, uh, I CAN'T TODAY... SORRY.
Oh. OKAY THEN.
WHO'S YOUR FRIEND?
WHO, WES?
WE'RE um... WE'RE WORKING ON A SCIENCE EXPERIMENT TOGETHER.
I'M SO SURE.
OKAY.
SO, WHAT'S NEXT FOR OUR...SCIENCE EXPERIMENT?
WANNA GO SHOOT EACH OTHER?

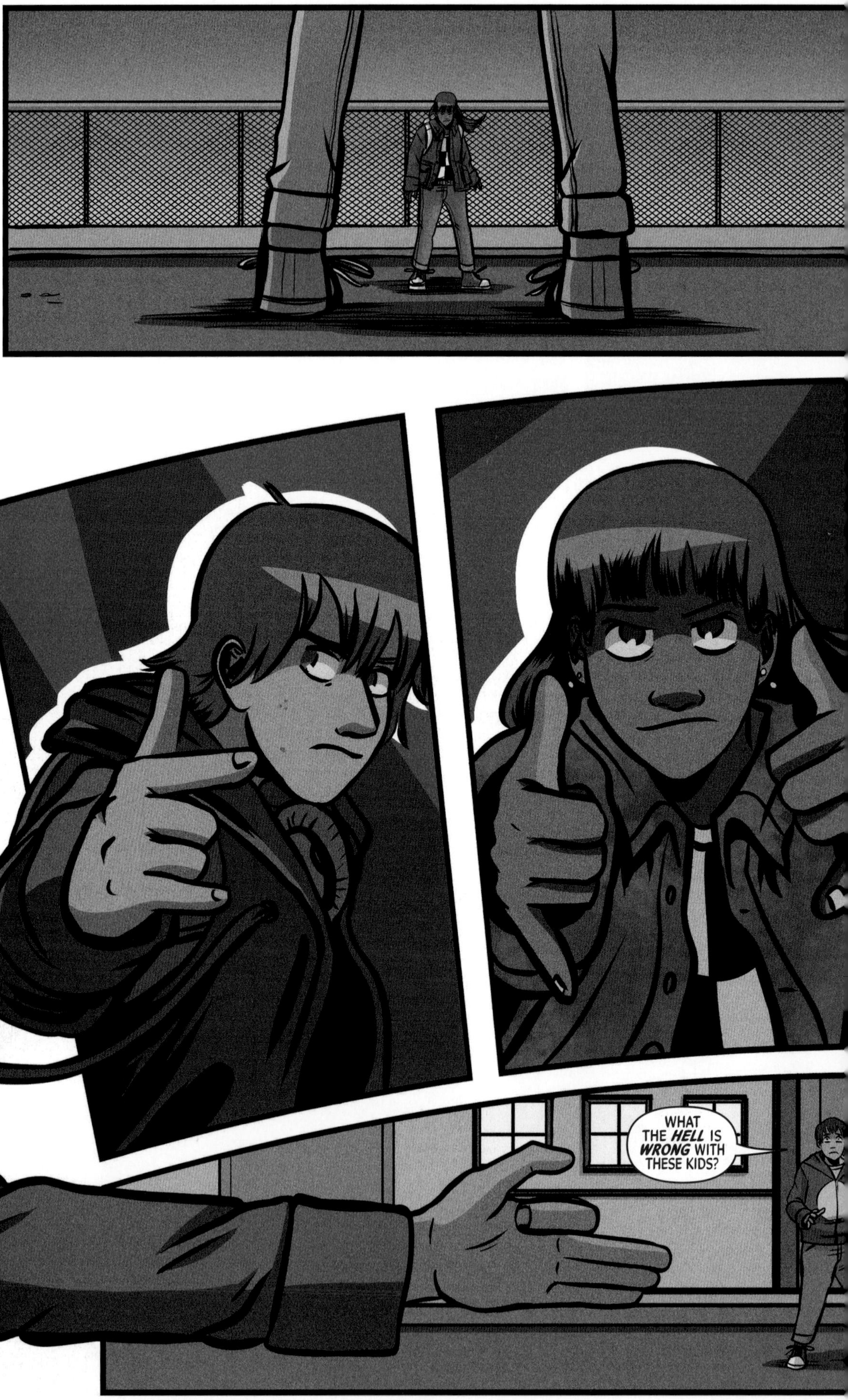
WHAT THE HELL IS WRONG WITH THESE KIDS?

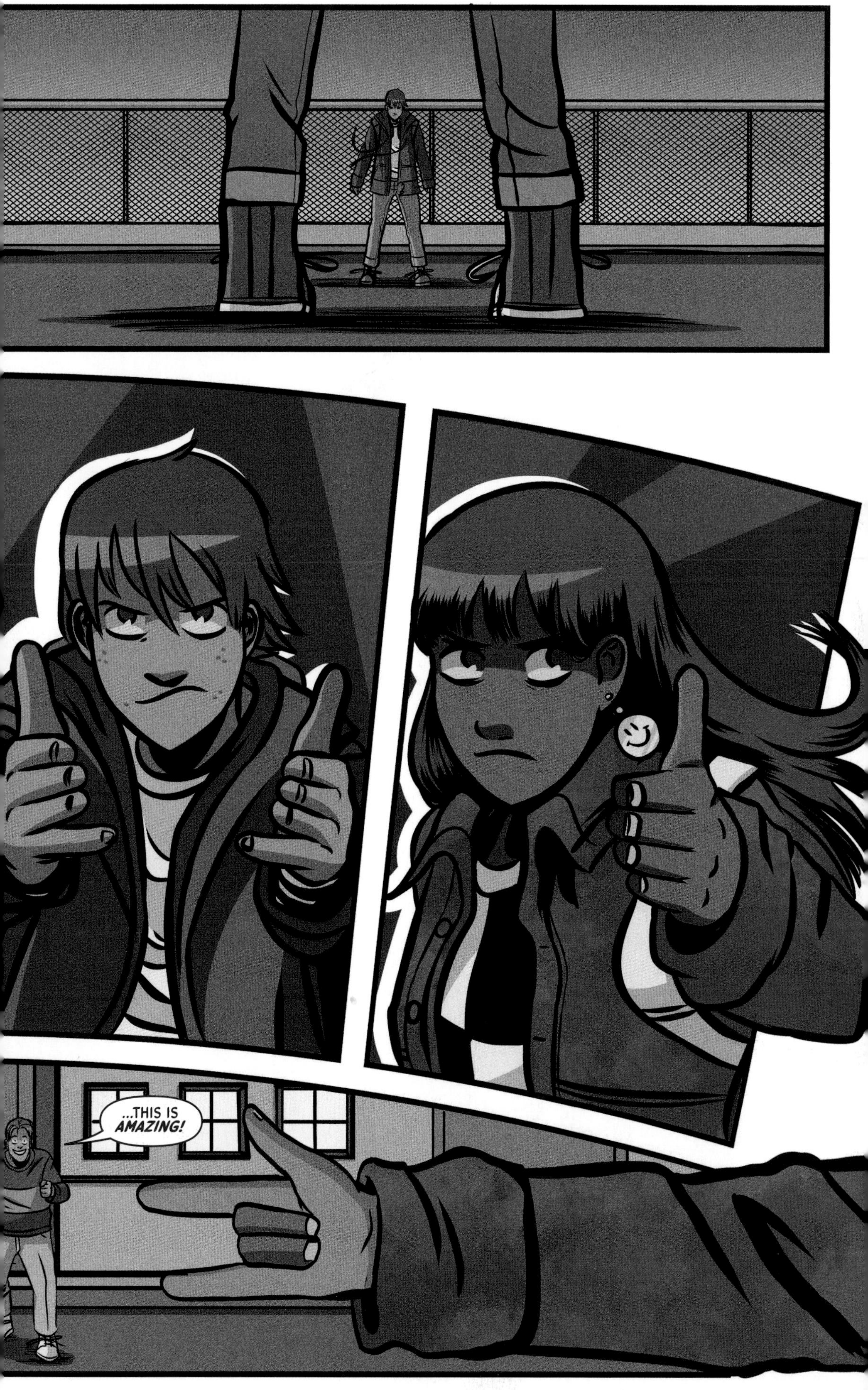
...THIS IS AMAZING!

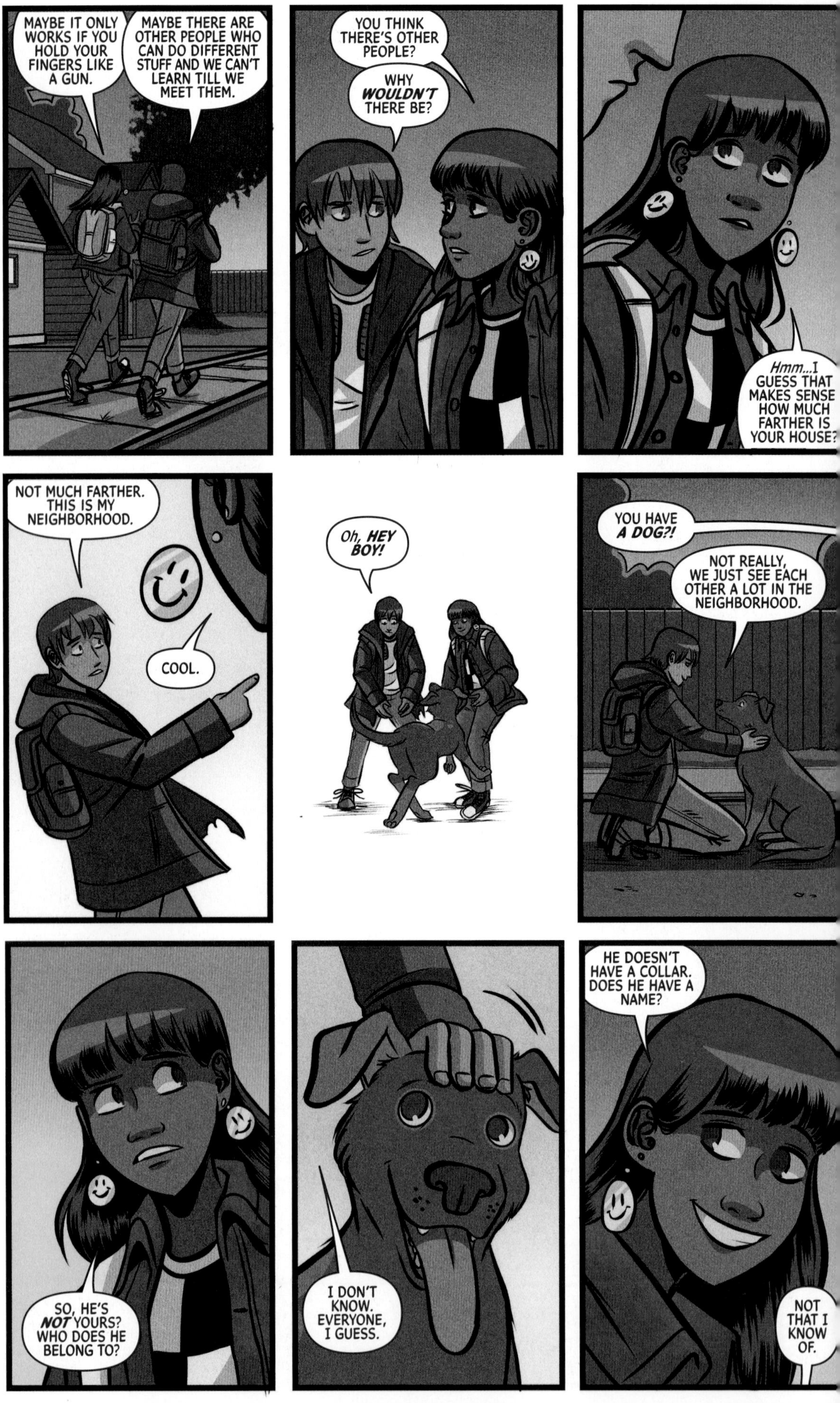
MAYBE IT ONLY WORKS IF YOU HOLD YOUR FINGERS LIKE A GUN.
MAYBE THERE ARE OTHER PEOPLE WHO CAN DO DIFFERENT STUFF AND WE CAN'T LEARN TILL WE MEET THEM.
YOU THINK THERE'S OTHER PEOPLE?
WHY *WOULDN'T* THERE BE?
*Hmm...*I GUESS THAT MAKES SENSE HOW MUCH FARTHER IS YOUR HOUSE?
NOT MUCH FARTHER. THIS IS MY NEIGHBORHOOD.
COOL.
Oh, *HEY BOY!*
YOU HAVE *A DOG?!*
NOT REALLY, WE JUST SEE EACH OTHER A LOT IN THE NEIGHBORHOOD.
SO, HE'S *NOT* YOURS? WHO DOES HE BELONG TO?
I DON'T KNOW. EVERYONE, I GUESS.
HE DOESN'T HAVE A COLLAR. DOES HE HAVE A NAME?
NOT THAT I KNOW OF.

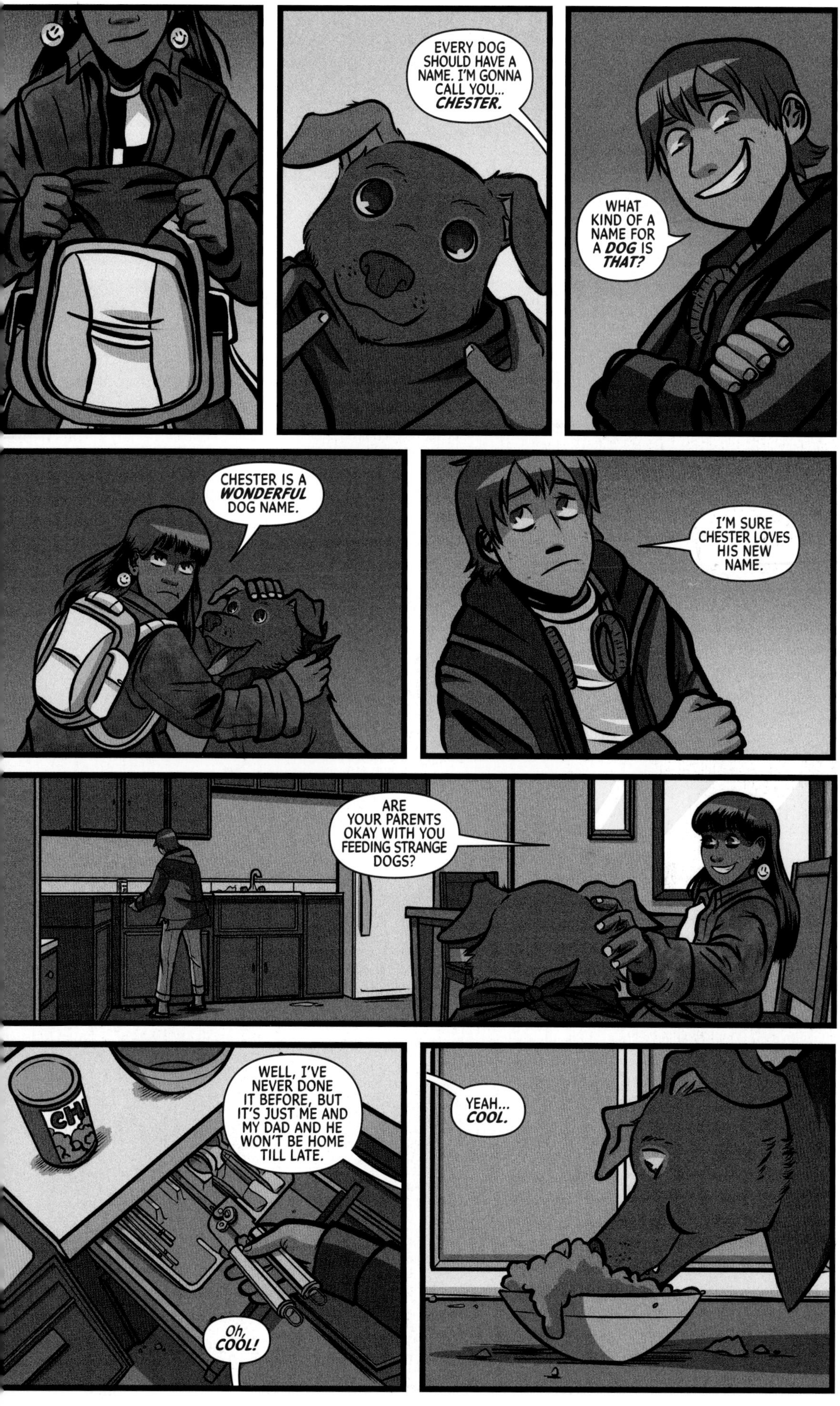

EVERY DOG SHOULD HAVE A NAME. I'M GONNA CALL YOU... ***CHESTER.***
WHAT KIND OF A NAME FOR A ***DOG*** IS ***THAT?***
CHESTER IS A ***WONDERFUL*** DOG NAME.
I'M SURE CHESTER LOVES HIS NEW NAME.
ARE YOUR PARENTS OKAY WITH YOU FEEDING STRANGE DOGS?
WELL, I'VE NEVER DONE IT BEFORE, BUT IT'S JUST ME AND MY DAD AND HE WON'T BE HOME TILL LATE.
Oh, ***COOL!***
YEAH... ***COOL.***

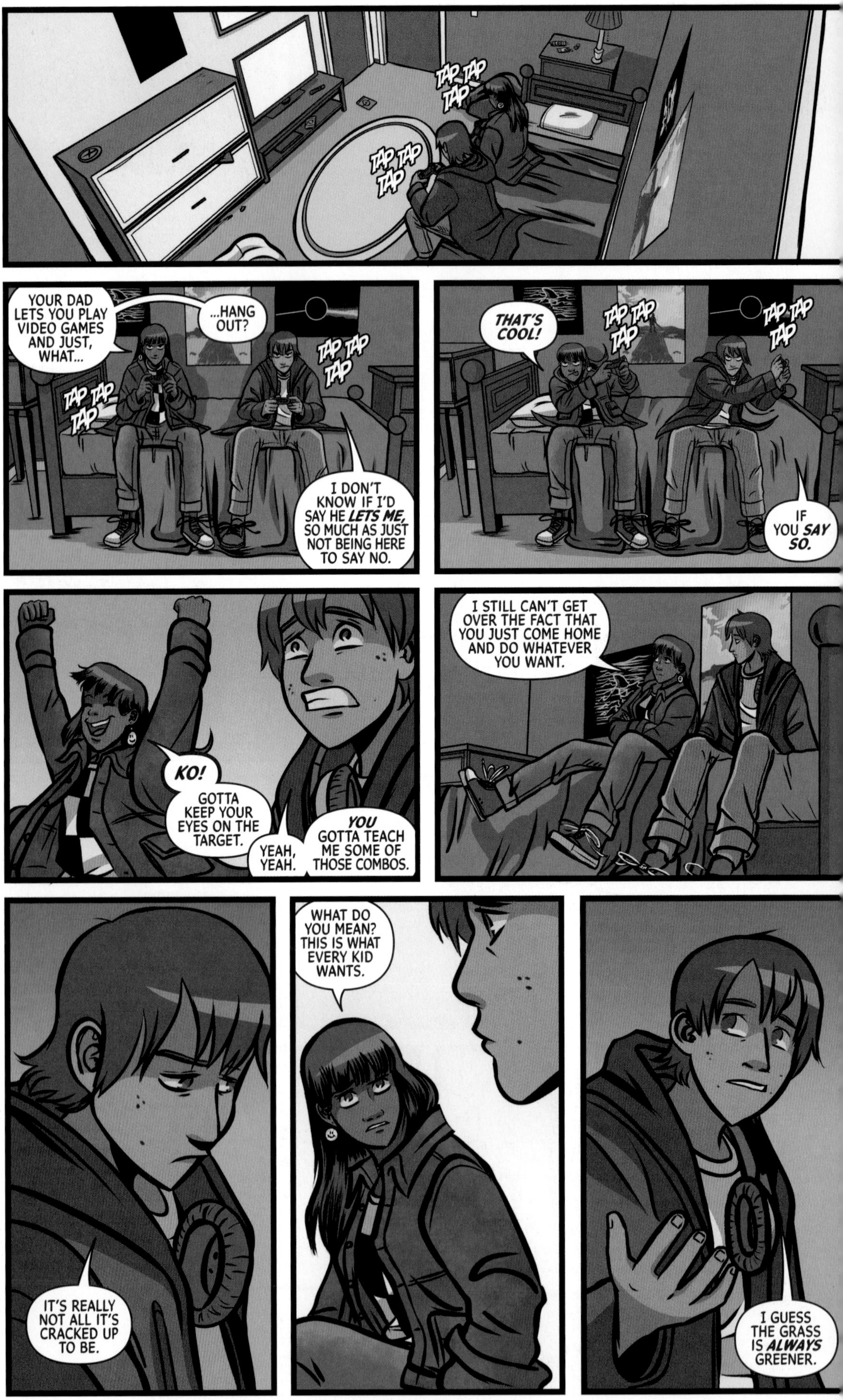
TAP TAP TAP
TAP TAP TAP
YOUR DAD LETS YOU PLAY VIDEO GAMES AND JUST, WHAT...
...HANG OUT?
TAP TAP TAP
TAP TAP TAP
I DON'T KNOW IF I'D SAY HE *LETS ME,* SO MUCH AS JUST NOT BEING HERE TO SAY NO.
THAT'S COOL!
TAP TAP TAP
TAP TAP TAP
IF YOU *SAY SO.*
KO!
GOTTA KEEP YOUR EYES ON THE TARGET.
YEAH, YEAH.
YOU GOTTA TEACH ME SOME OF THOSE COMBOS.
I STILL CAN'T GET OVER THE FACT THAT YOU JUST COME HOME AND DO WHATEVER YOU WANT.
IT'S REALLY NOT ALL IT'S CRACKED UP TO BE.
WHAT DO YOU MEAN? THIS IS WHAT EVERY KID WANTS.
I GUESS THE GRASS IS *ALWAYS* GREENER.

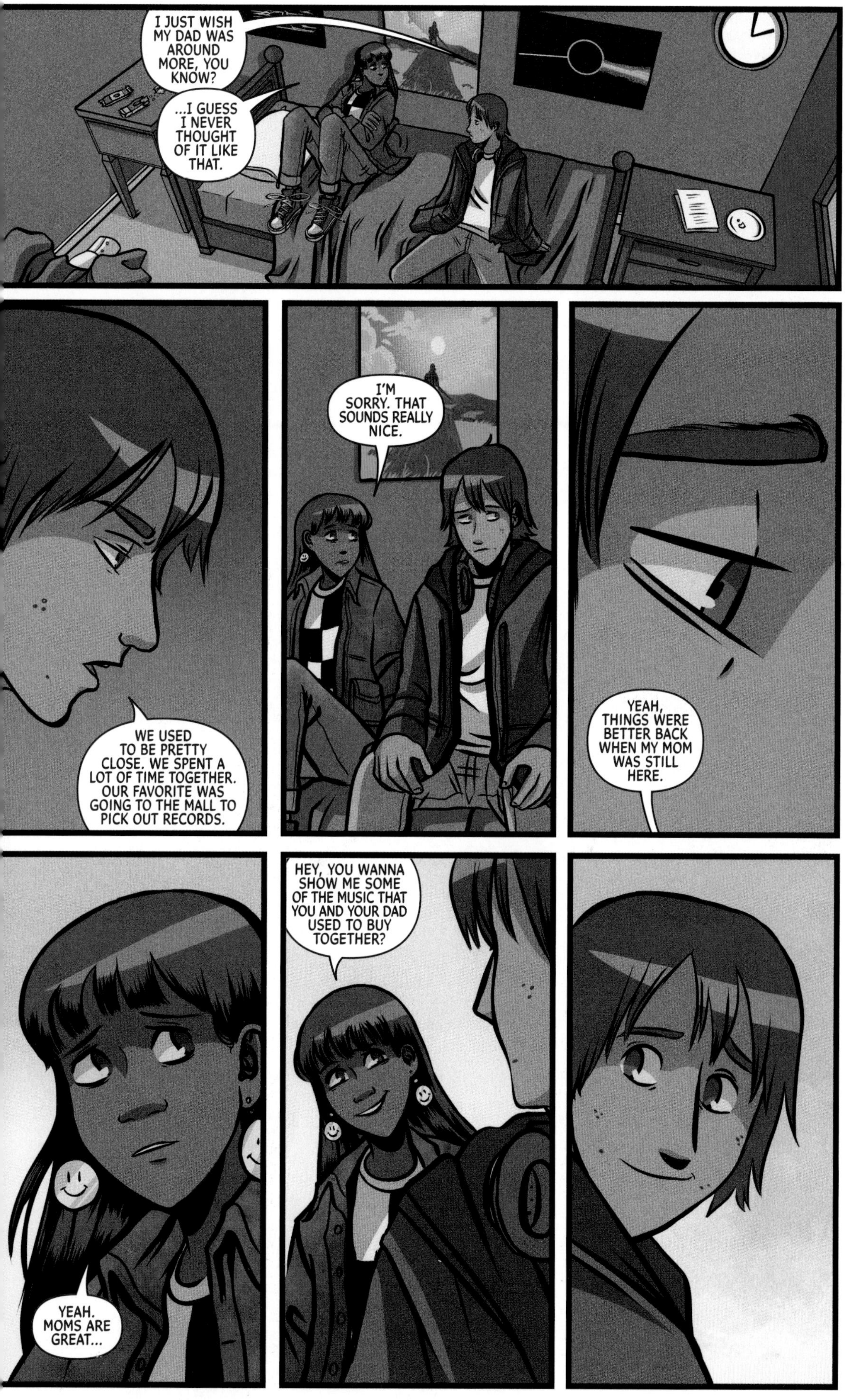
I JUST WISH MY DAD WAS AROUND MORE, YOU KNOW?
...I GUESS I NEVER THOUGHT OF IT LIKE THAT.
WE USED TO BE PRETTY CLOSE. WE SPENT A LOT OF TIME TOGETHER. OUR FAVORITE WAS GOING TO THE MALL TO PICK OUT RECORDS.
I'M SORRY. THAT SOUNDS REALLY NICE.
YEAH, THINGS WERE BETTER BACK WHEN MY MOM WAS STILL HERE.
YEAH. MOMS ARE GREAT...
HEY, YOU WANNA SHOW ME SOME OF THE MUSIC THAT YOU AND YOUR DAD USED TO BUY TOGETHER?

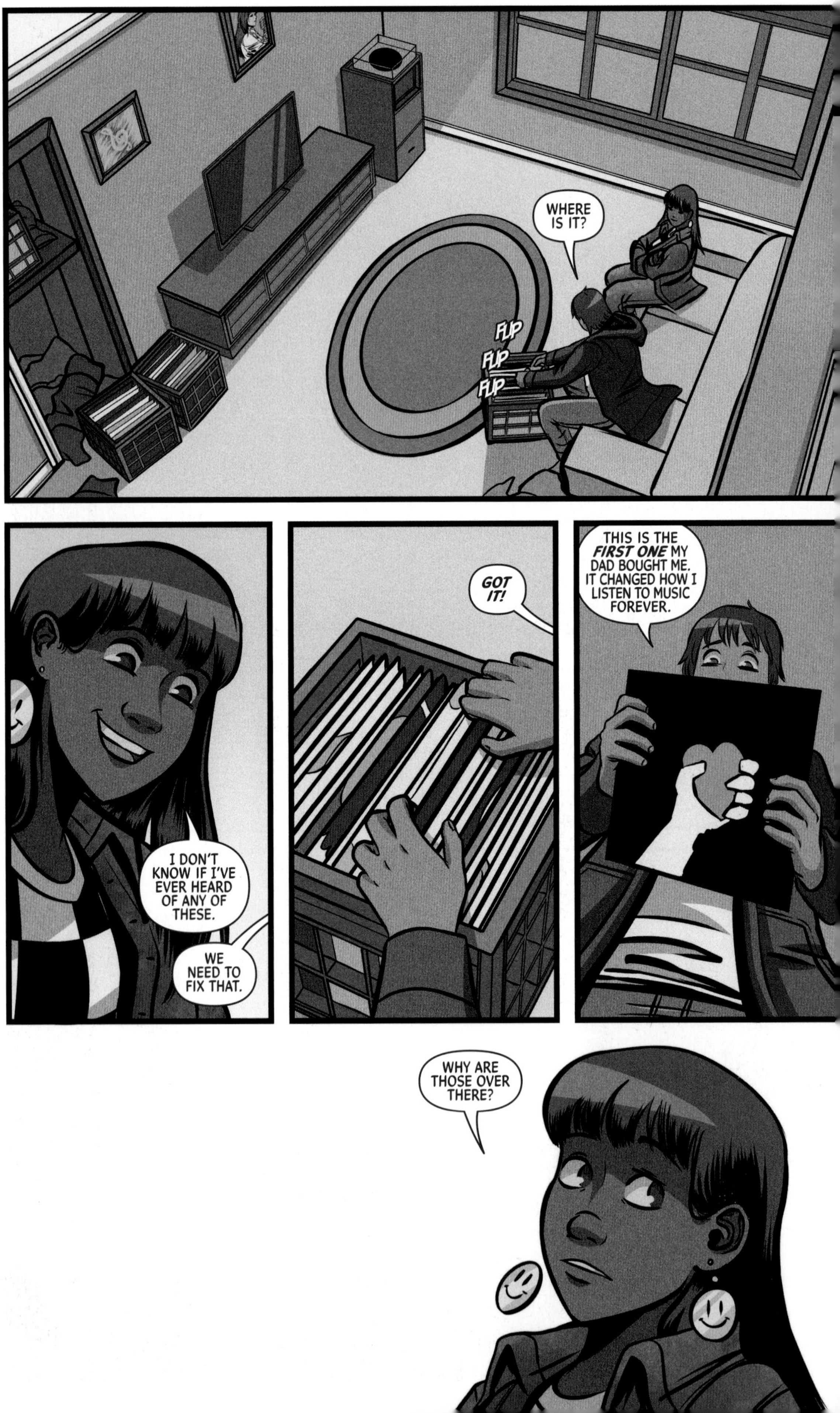
WHERE IS IT?
FLIP FLIP FLIP
I DON'T KNOW IF I'VE EVER HEARD OF ANY OF THESE.
WE NEED TO FIX THAT.
GOT IT!
THIS IS THE *FIRST ONE* MY DAD BOUGHT ME. IT CHANGED HOW I LISTEN TO MUSIC FOREVER.
WHY ARE THOSE OVER THERE?

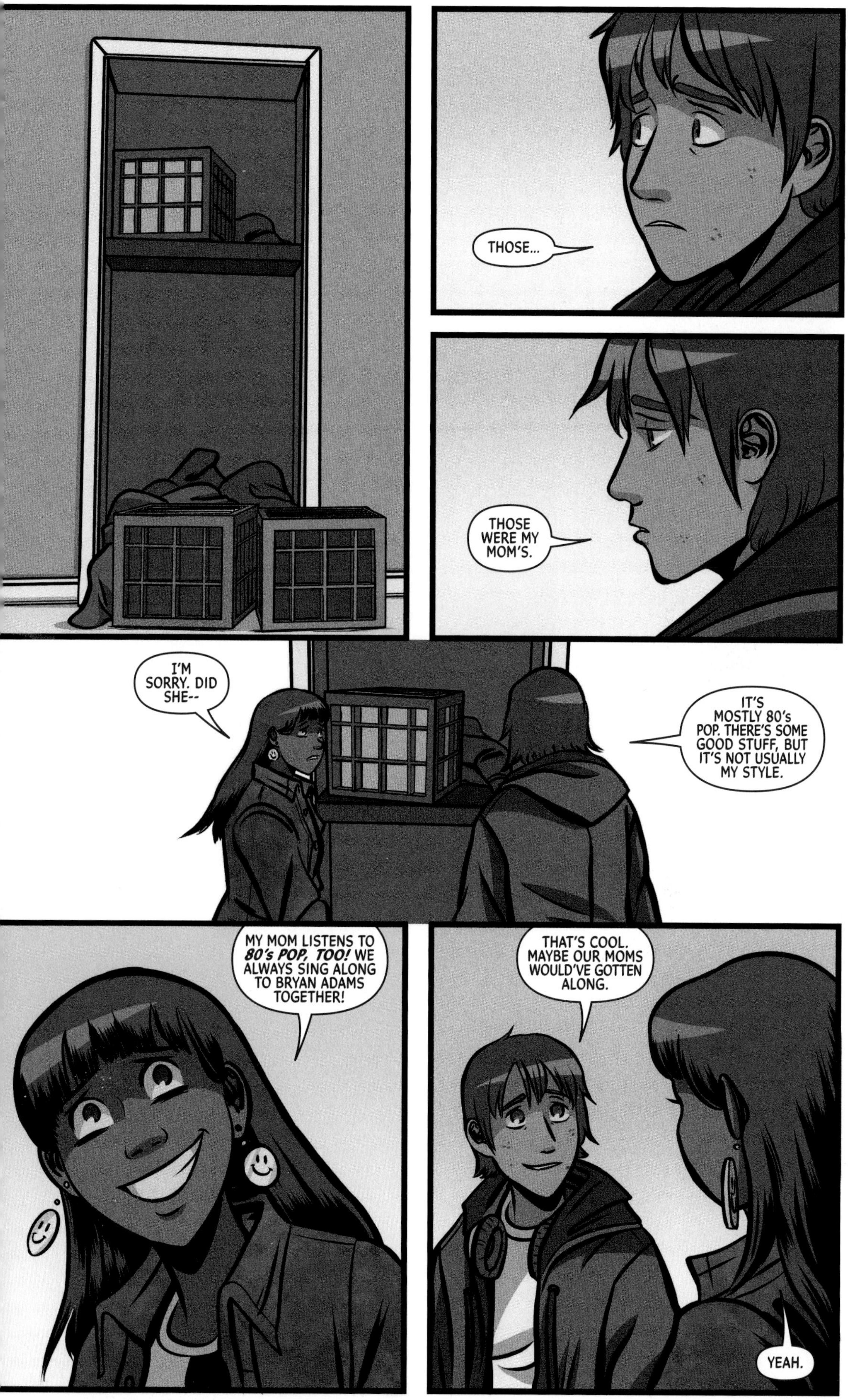
THOSE...
THOSE WERE MY MOM'S.
I'M SORRY. DID SHE--
IT'S MOSTLY 80's POP. THERE'S SOME GOOD STUFF, BUT IT'S NOT USUALLY MY STYLE.
MY MOM LISTENS TO *80's POP, TOO!* WE ALWAYS SING ALONG TO BRYAN ADAMS TOGETHER!
THAT'S COOL. MAYBE OUR MOMS WOULD'VE GOTTEN ALONG.
YEAH.

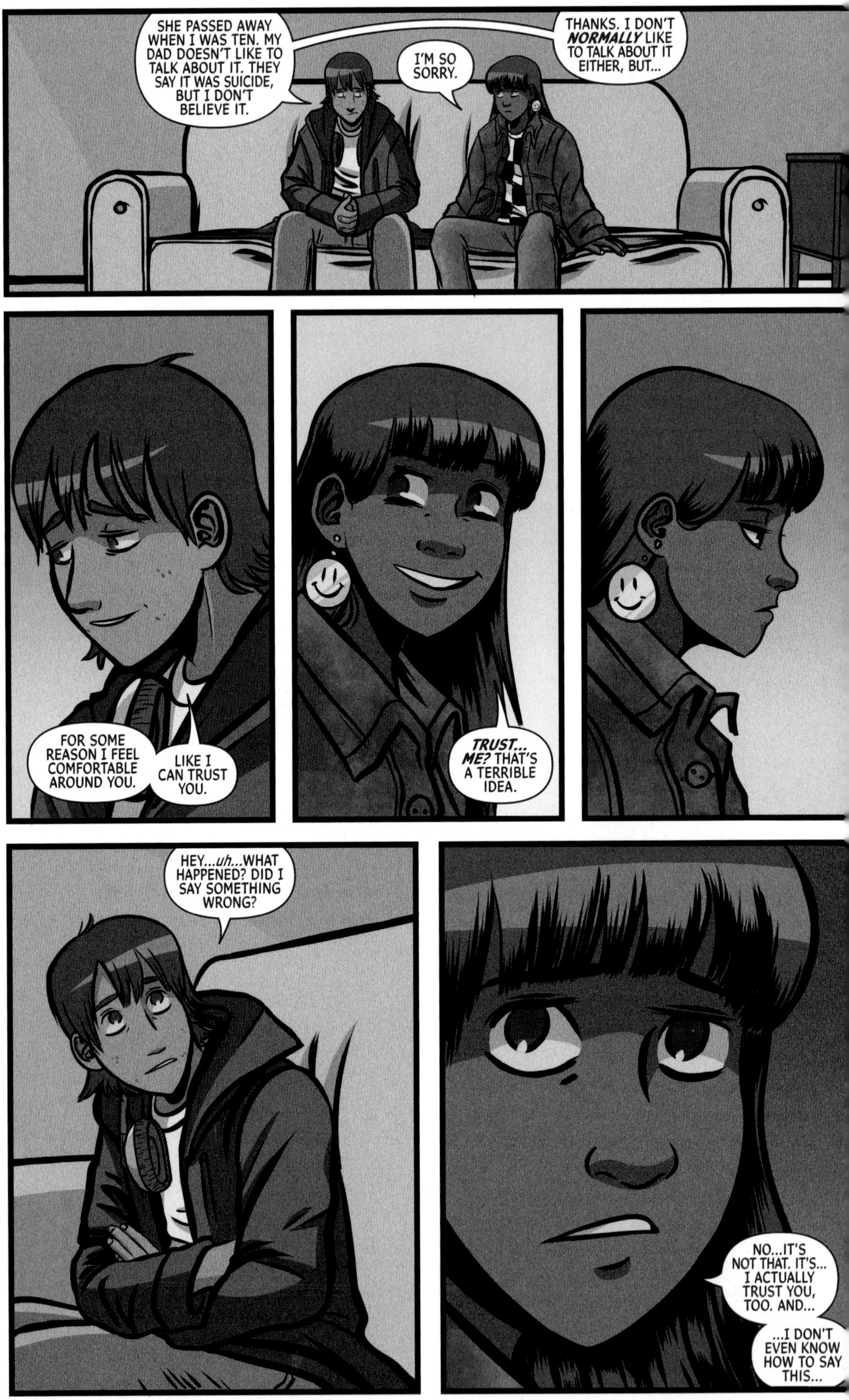

SHE PASSED AWAY WHEN I WAS TEN. MY DAD DOESN'T LIKE TO TALK ABOUT IT. THEY SAY IT WAS SUICIDE, BUT I DON'T BELIEVE IT.
I'M SO SORRY.
THANKS. I DON'T NORMALLY LIKE TO TALK ABOUT IT EITHER, BUT...
FOR SOME REASON I FEEL COMFORTABLE AROUND YOU.
LIKE I CAN TRUST YOU.
TRUST... ME? THAT'S A TERRIBLE IDEA.
HEY...uh...WHAT HAPPENED? DID I SAY SOMETHING WRONG?
NO...IT'S NOT THAT. IT'S... I ACTUALLY TRUST YOU, TOO. AND...
...I DON'T EVEN KNOW HOW TO SAY THIS...

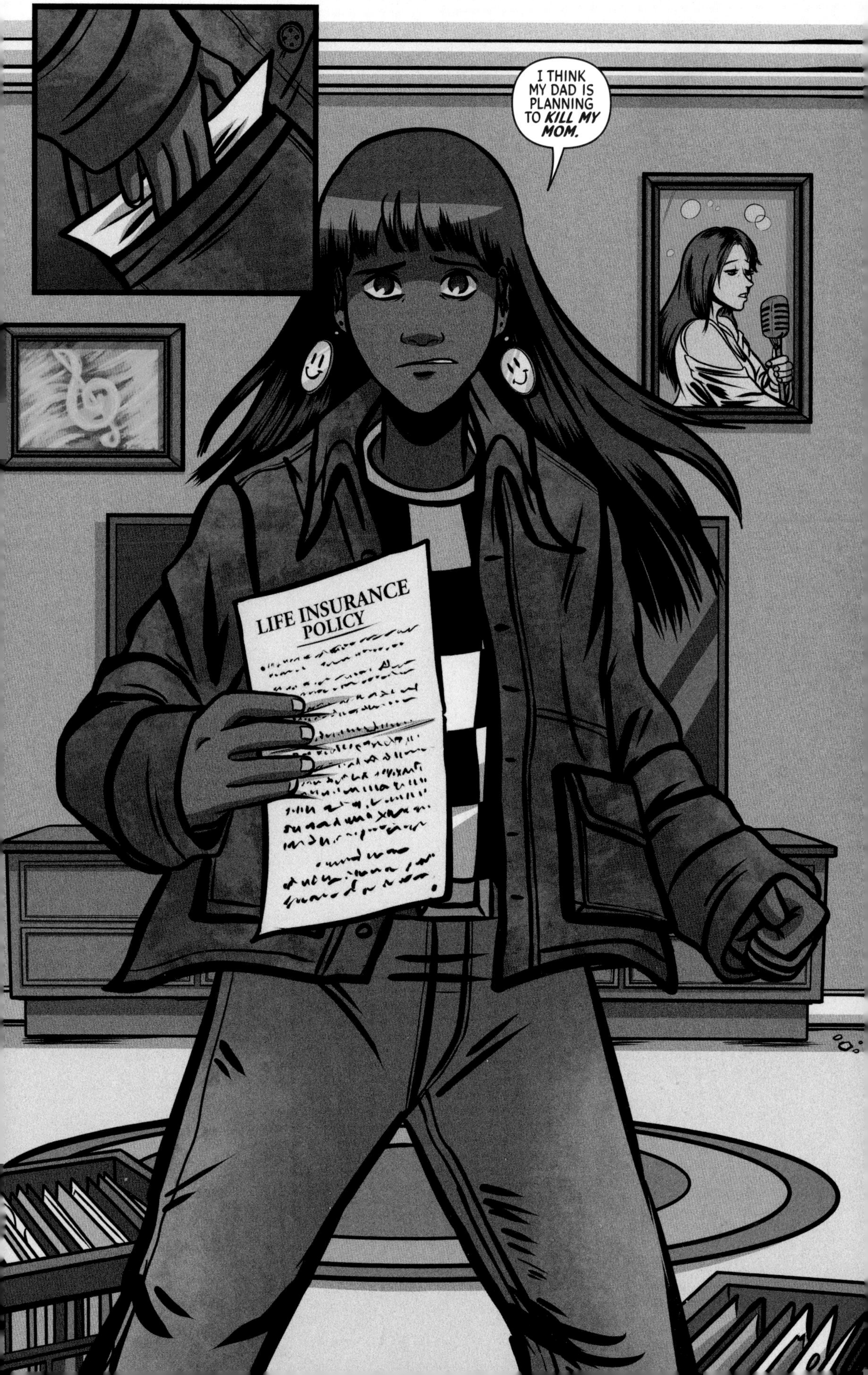

I THINK MY DAD IS PLANNING TO KILL MY MOM.
LIFE INSURANCE POLICY

FRIENDLY FIRE

THREE

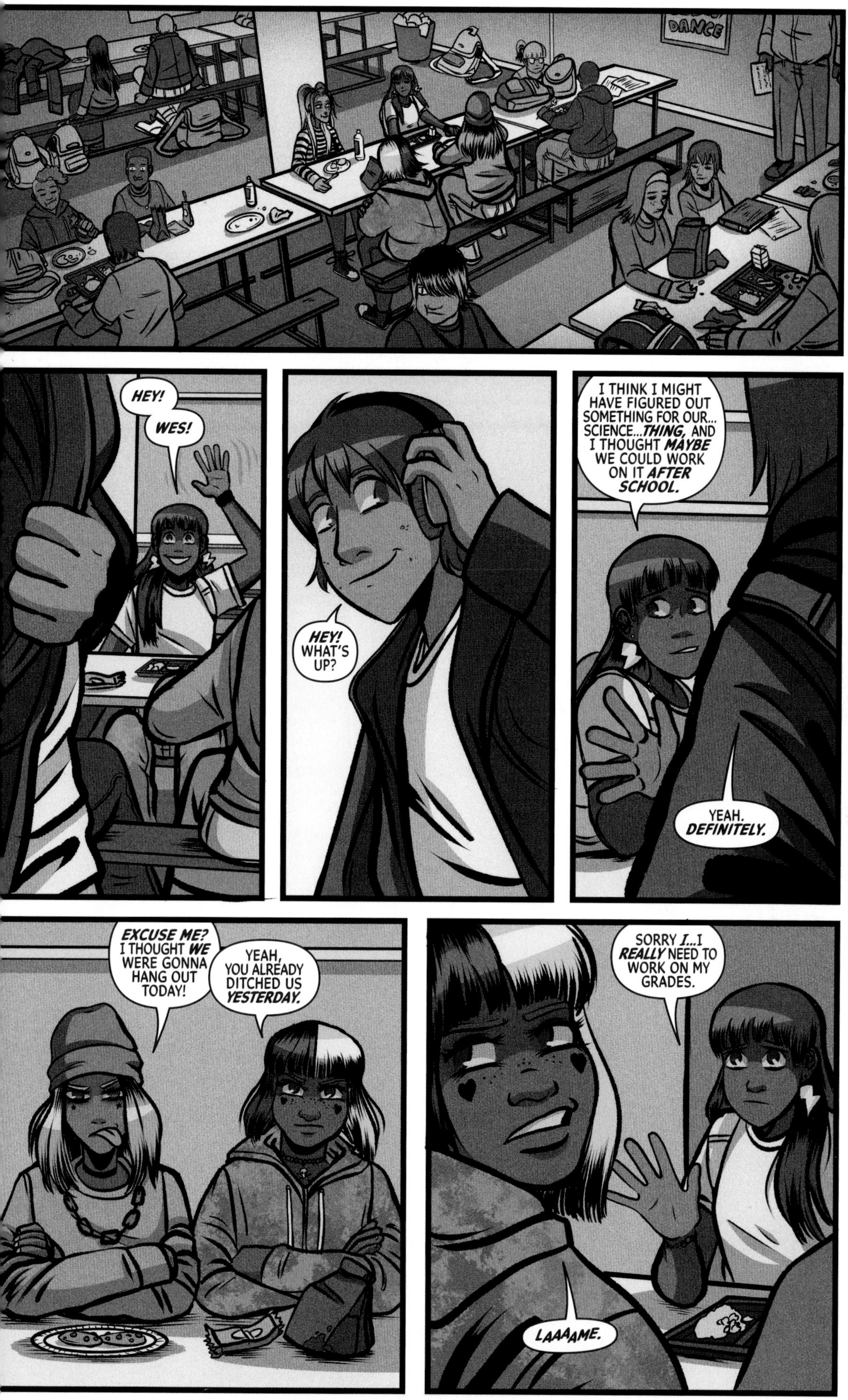

DANCE
HEY!
WES!
HEY! WHAT'S UP?
I THINK I MIGHT HAVE FIGURED OUT SOMETHING FOR OUR... SCIENCE...THING, AND I THOUGHT MAYBE WE COULD WORK ON IT AFTER SCHOOL.
YEAH. DEFINITELY.
EXCUSE ME? I THOUGHT WE WERE GONNA HANG OUT TODAY!
YEAH, YOU ALREADY DITCHED US YESTERDAY.
SORRY I...I REALLY NEED TO WORK ON MY GRADES.
LAAAAME.

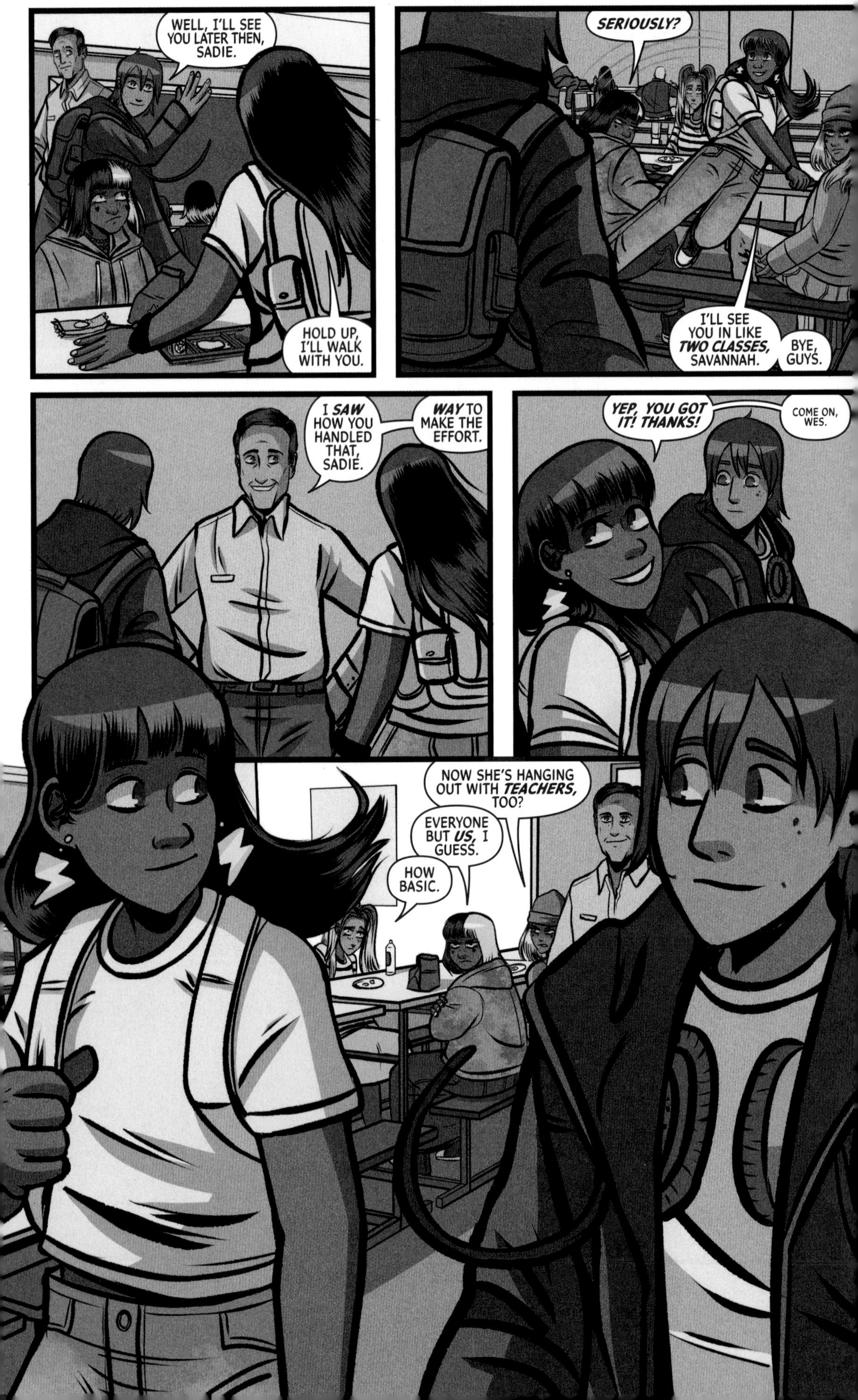
WELL, I'LL SEE YOU LATER THEN, SADIE.
HOLD UP, I'LL WALK WITH YOU.
SERIOUSLY?
I'LL SEE YOU IN LIKE *TWO CLASSES,* SAVANNAH.
BYE, GUYS.
I *SAW* HOW YOU HANDLED THAT, SADIE.
WAY TO MAKE THE EFFORT.
YEP, YOU GOT IT! THANKS!
COME ON, WES.
NOW SHE'S HANGING OUT WITH *TEACHERS,* TOO?
EVERYONE BUT *US,* I GUESS.
HOW BASIC.

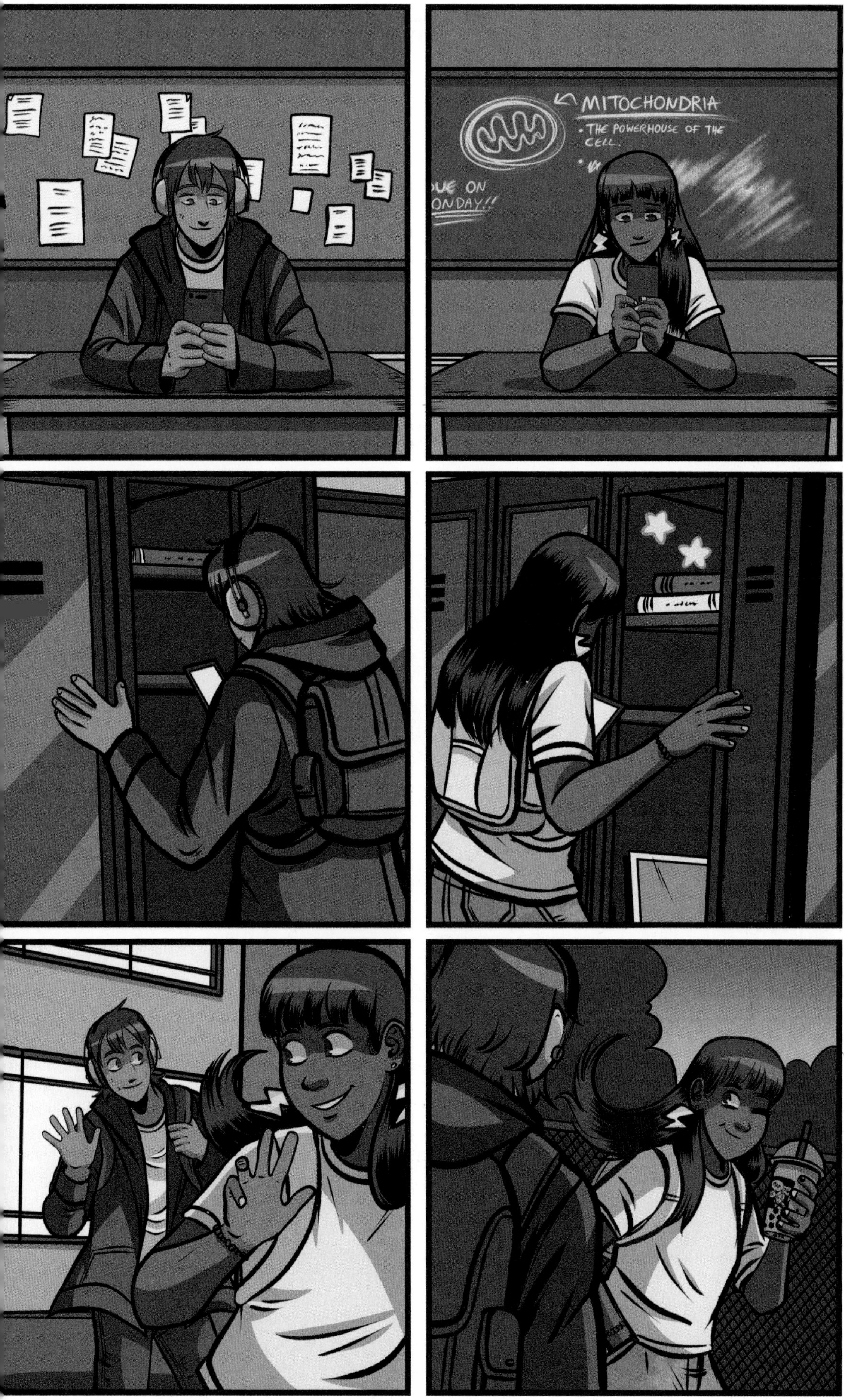
MITOCHONDRIA
• THE POWERHOUSE OF THE CELL.
DUE ON
ONDAY!!

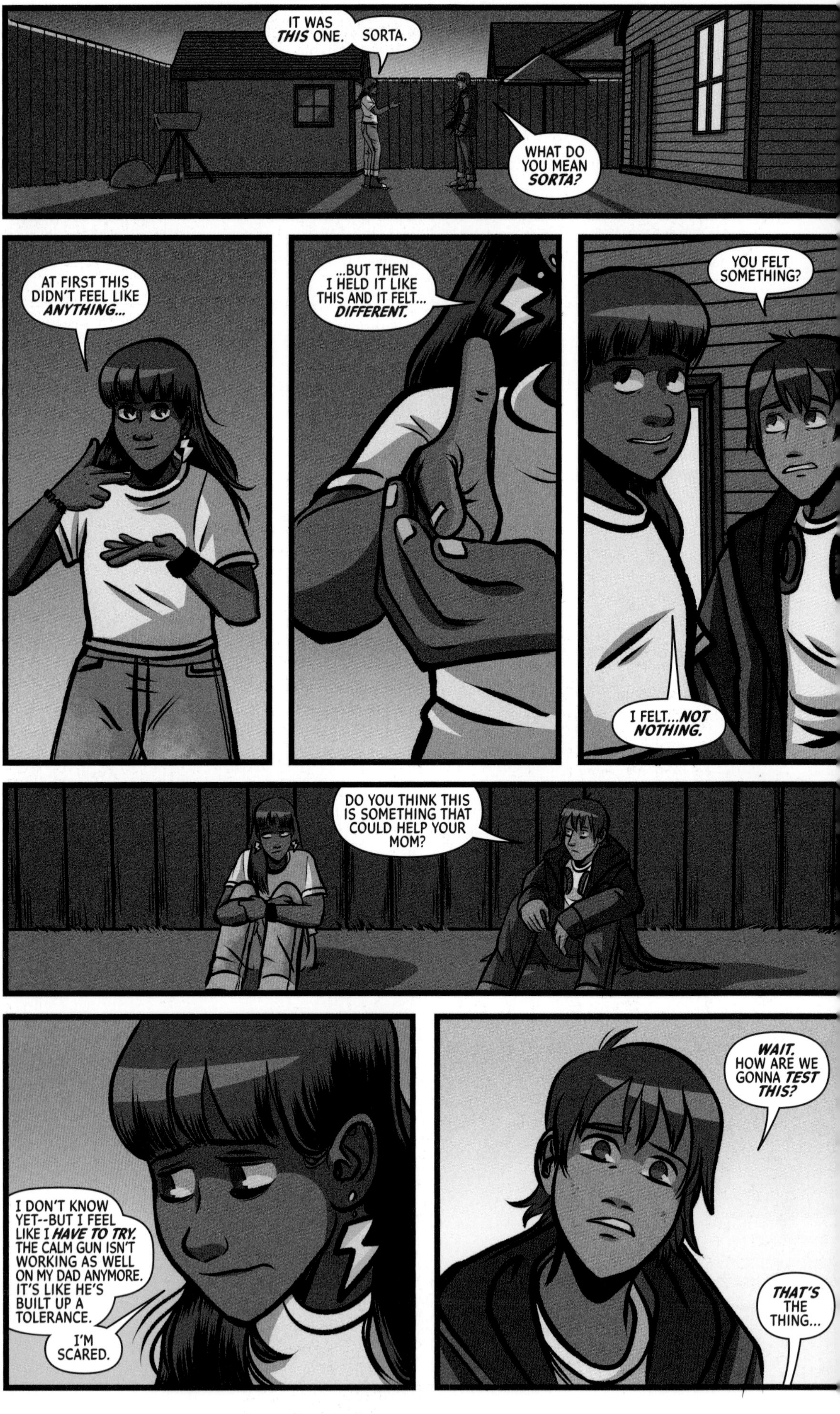
IT WAS *THIS* ONE.
SORTA.
WHAT DO YOU MEAN *SORTA?*
AT FIRST THIS DIDN'T FEEL LIKE *ANYTHING...*
...BUT THEN I HELD IT LIKE THIS AND IT FELT... *DIFFERENT.*
YOU FELT SOMETHING?
I FELT...*NOT NOTHING.*
DO YOU THINK THIS IS SOMETHING THAT COULD HELP YOUR MOM?
I DON'T KNOW YET--BUT I FEEL LIKE I *HAVE TO TRY.* THE CALM GUN ISN'T WORKING AS WELL ON MY DAD ANYMORE. IT'S LIKE HE'S BUILT UP A TOLERANCE.
I'M SCARED.
WAIT. HOW ARE WE GONNA *TEST THIS?*
THAT'S THE THING...

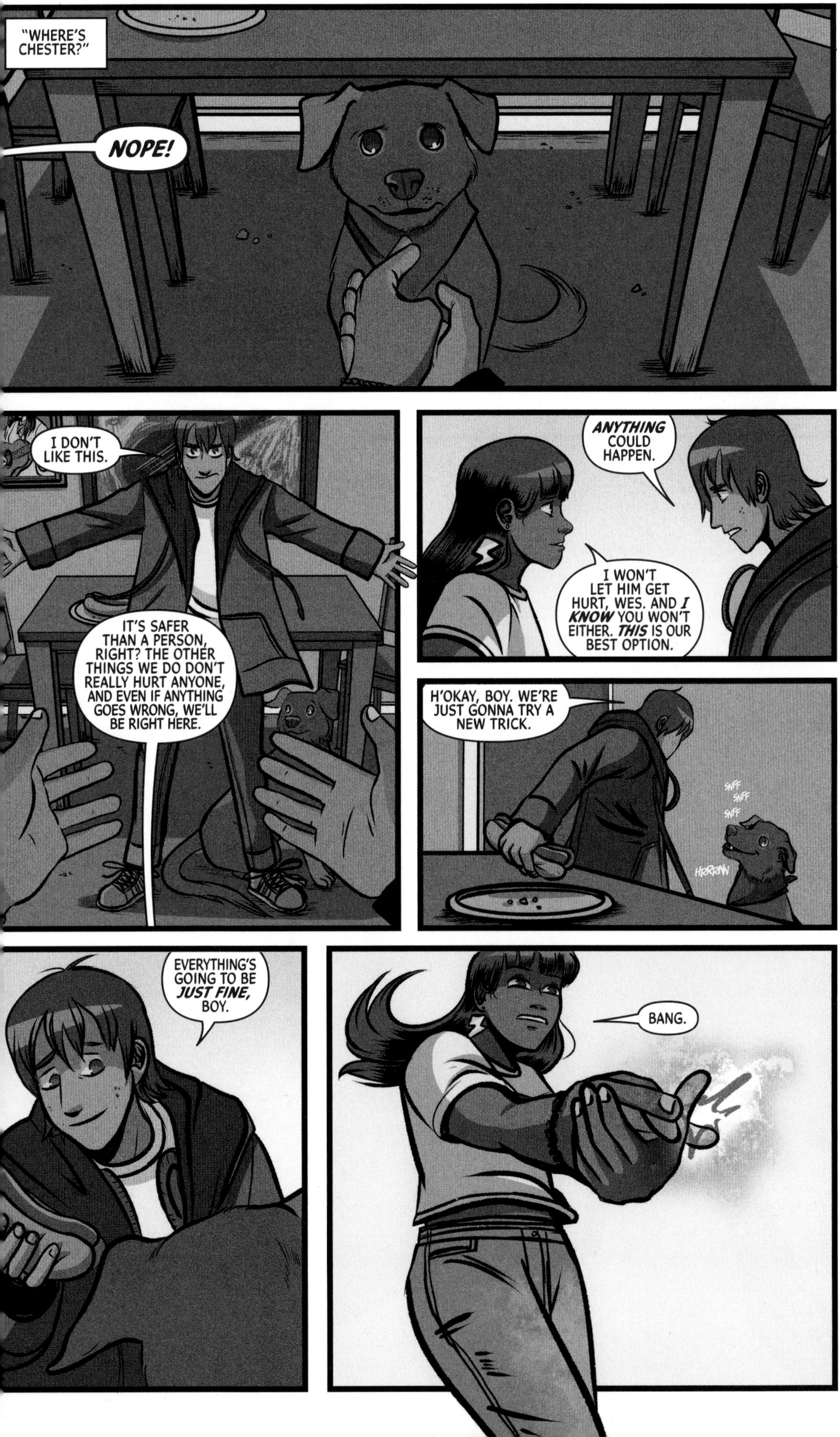
"WHERE'S CHESTER?"
NOPE!
I DON'T LIKE THIS.
IT'S SAFER THAN A PERSON, RIGHT? THE OTHER THINGS WE DO DON'T REALLY HURT ANYONE, AND EVEN IF ANYTHING GOES WRONG, WE'LL BE RIGHT HERE.
ANYTHING COULD HAPPEN.
I WON'T LET HIM GET HURT, WES. AND I KNOW YOU WON'T EITHER. THIS IS OUR BEST OPTION.
H'OKAY, BOY. WE'RE JUST GONNA TRY A NEW TRICK.
SNFF SNFF SNFF
HRRRNN
EVERYTHING'S GOING TO BE JUST FINE, BOY.
BANG.

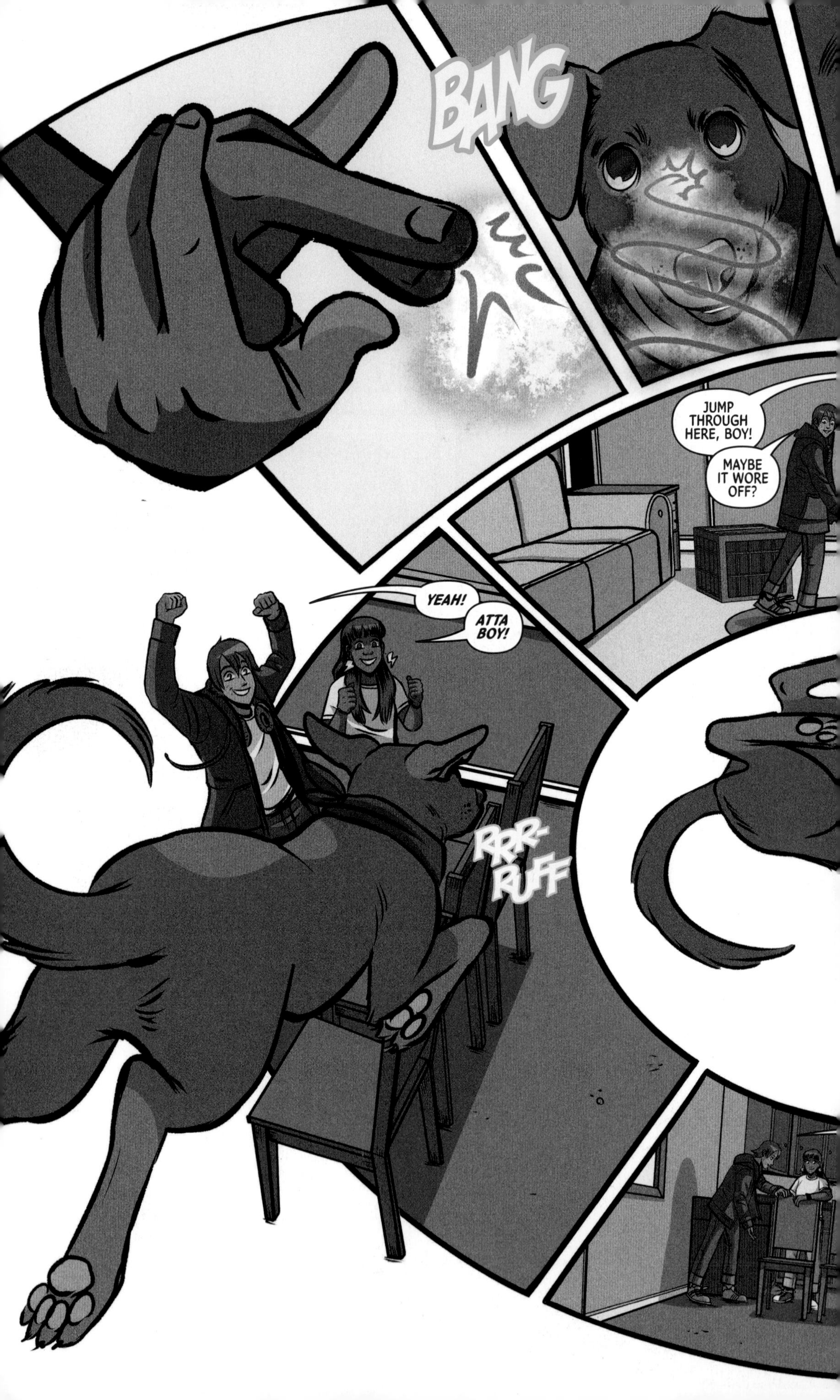
BANG
JUMP THROUGH HERE, BOY!
MAYBE IT WORE OFF?
YEAH!
ATTA BOY!
RRR-RUFF

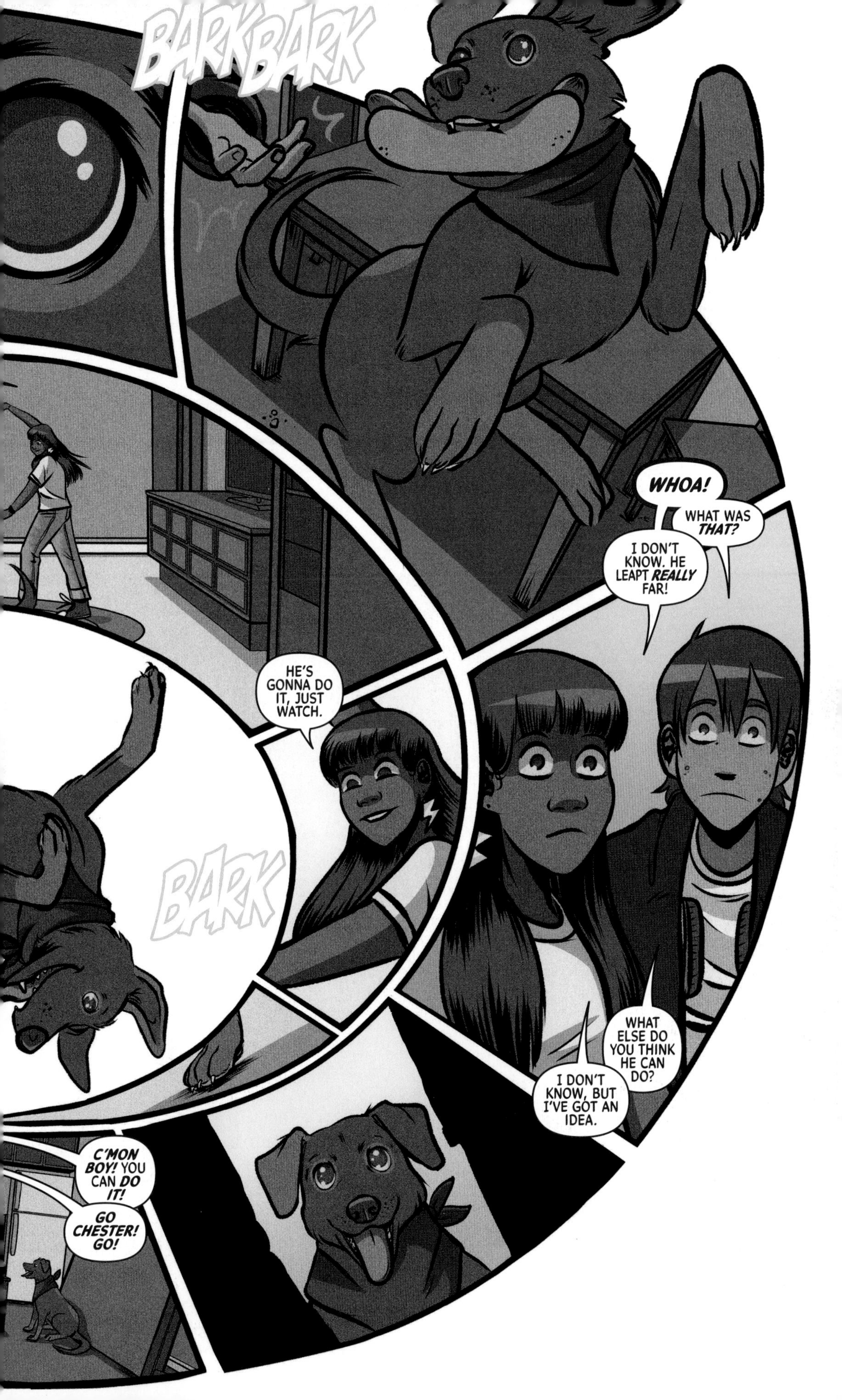
BARK BARK
WHOA!
WHAT WAS THAT?
I DON'T KNOW. HE LEAPT REALLY FAR!
HE'S GONNA DO IT, JUST WATCH.
BARK
WHAT ELSE DO YOU THINK HE CAN DO?
I DON'T KNOW, BUT I'VE GOT AN IDEA.
C'MON BOY! YOU CAN DO IT!
GO CHESTER! GO!

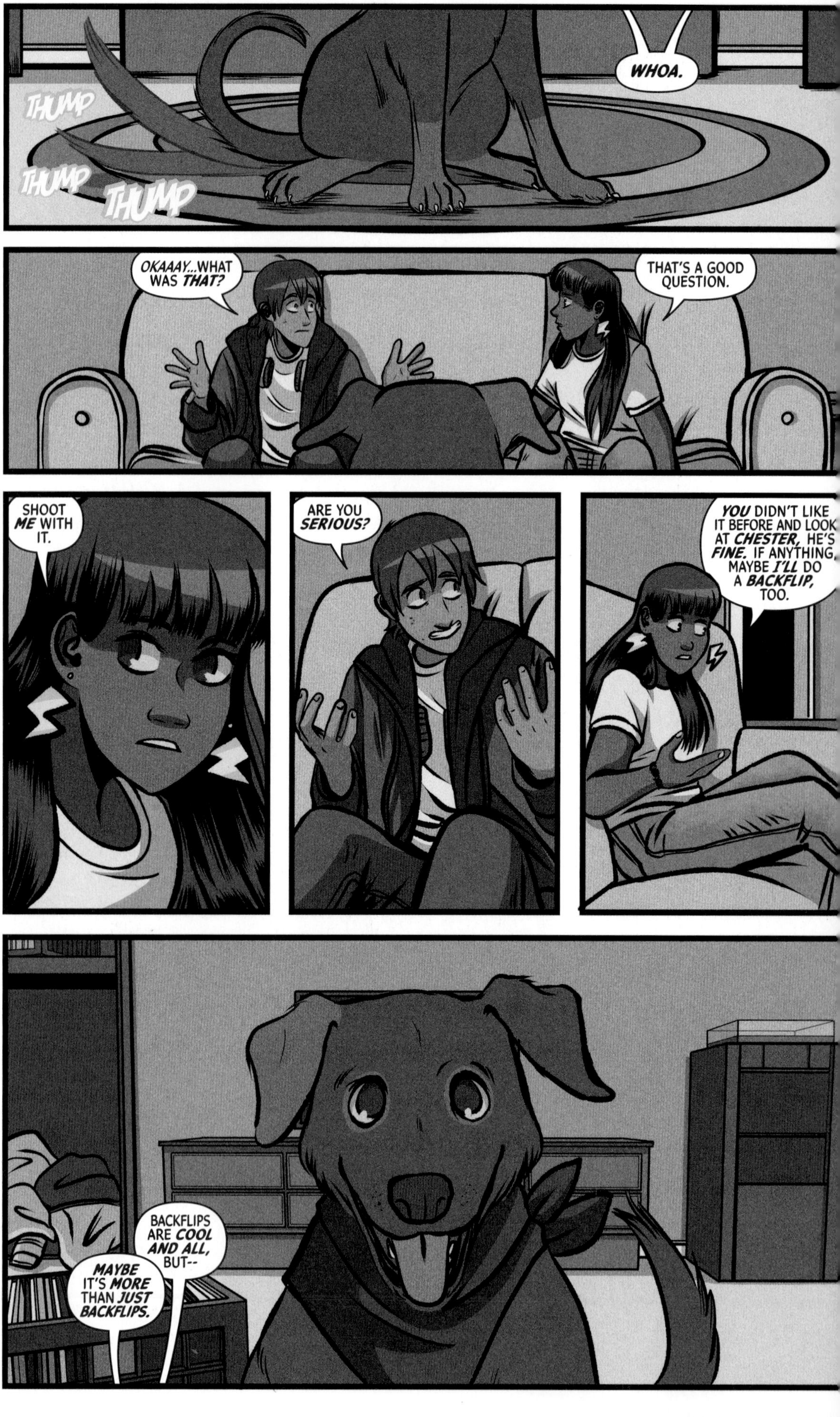
THUMP
THUMP
THUMP
WHOA.
OKAAAY...WHAT WAS THAT?
THAT'S A GOOD QUESTION.
SHOOT ME WITH IT.
ARE YOU SERIOUS?
YOU DIDN'T LIKE IT BEFORE AND LOOK AT CHESTER, HE'S FINE. IF ANYTHING, MAYBE I'LL DO A BACKFLIP, TOO.
BACKFLIPS ARE COOL AND ALL, BUT--
MAYBE IT'S MORE THAN JUST BACKFLIPS.

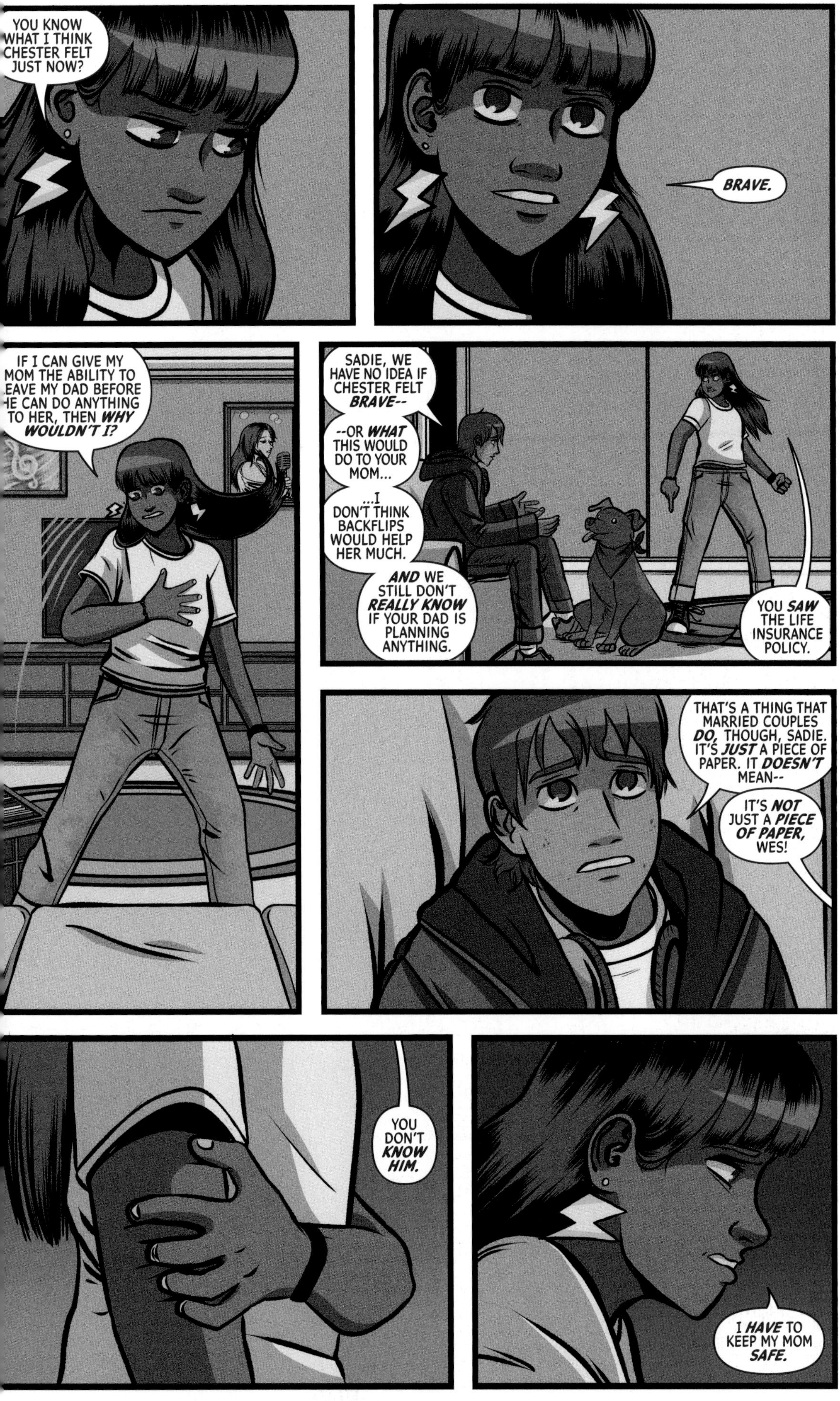
YOU KNOW WHAT I THINK CHESTER FELT JUST NOW?
BRAVE.
IF I CAN GIVE MY MOM THE ABILITY TO LEAVE MY DAD BEFORE HE CAN DO ANYTHING TO HER, THEN WHY WOULDN'T I?
SADIE, WE HAVE NO IDEA IF CHESTER FELT BRAVE--
--OR WHAT THIS WOULD DO TO YOUR MOM...
...I DON'T THINK BACKFLIPS WOULD HELP HER MUCH.
AND WE STILL DON'T REALLY KNOW IF YOUR DAD IS PLANNING ANYTHING.
YOU SAW THE LIFE INSURANCE POLICY.
THAT'S A THING THAT MARRIED COUPLES DO, THOUGH, SADIE. IT'S JUST A PIECE OF PAPER. IT DOESN'T MEAN--
IT'S NOT JUST A PIECE OF PAPER, WES!
YOU DON'T KNOW HIM.
I HAVE TO KEEP MY MOM SAFE.

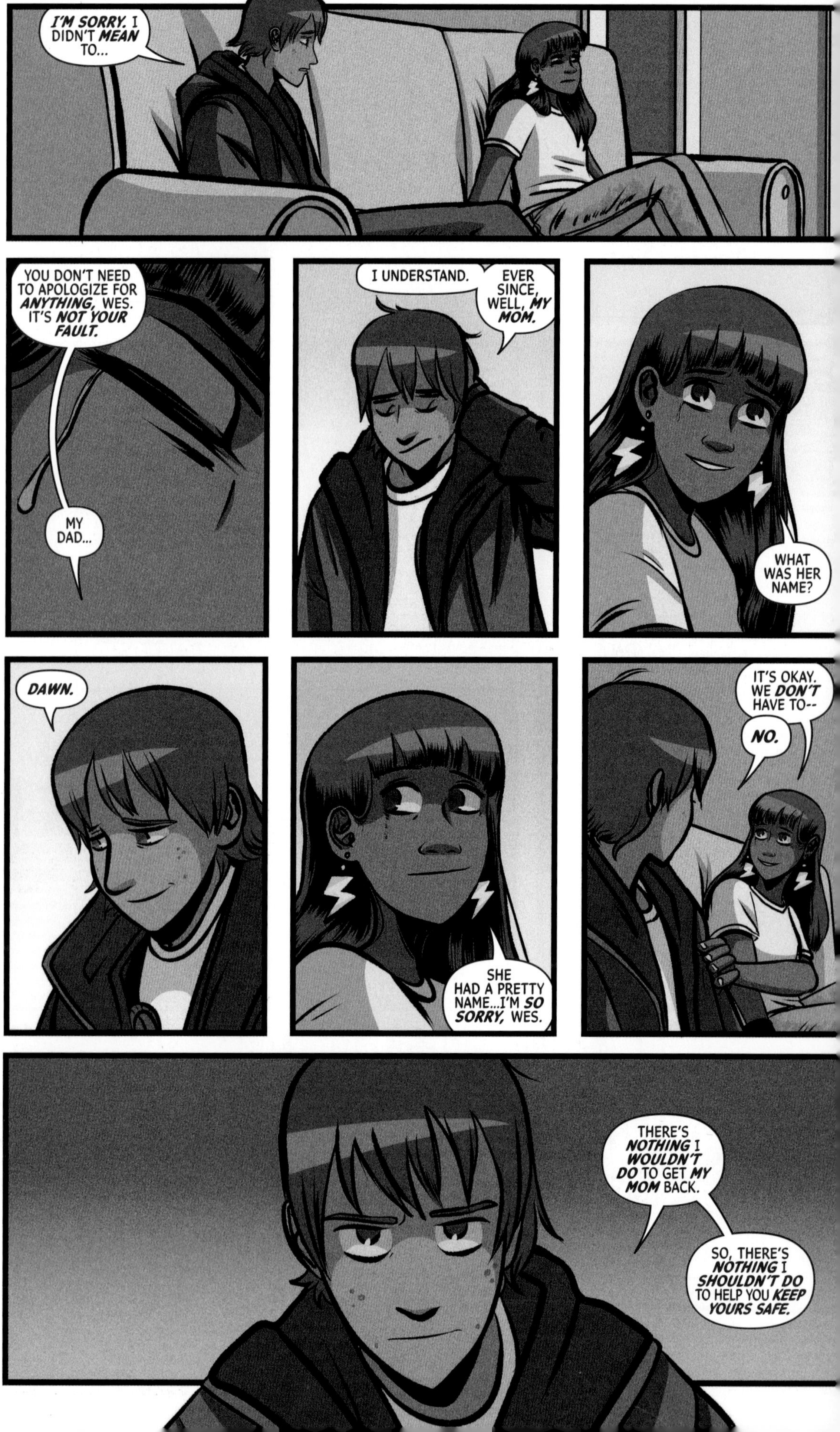

I'M SORRY. I DIDN'T *MEAN* TO...
YOU DON'T NEED TO APOLOGIZE FOR *ANYTHING,* WES. IT'S *NOT YOUR FAULT.*
MY DAD...
I UNDERSTAND.
EVER SINCE, WELL, *MY MOM.*
WHAT WAS HER NAME?
DAWN.
SHE HAD A PRETTY NAME...I'M *SO SORRY,* WES.
IT'S OKAY. WE *DON'T* HAVE TO--
NO.
THERE'S *NOTHING* I *WOULDN'T DO* TO GET *MY MOM* BACK.
SO, THERE'S *NOTHING* I *SHOULDN'T DO* TO HELP YOU *KEEP YOURS SAFE.*

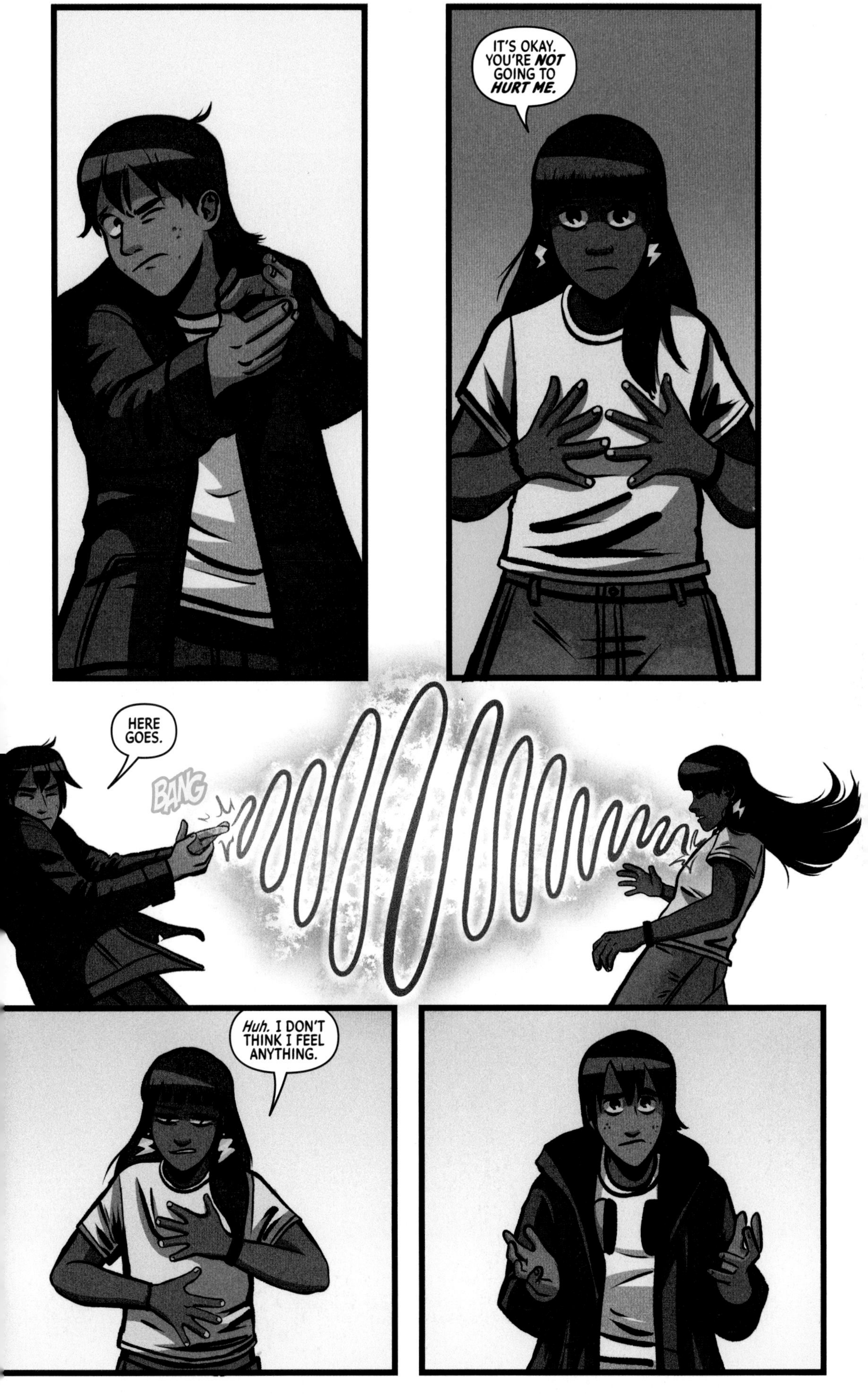
IT'S OKAY. YOU'RE *NOT* GOING TO *HURT ME.*
HERE GOES.
BANG
Huh. I DON'T THINK I FEEL ANYTHING.

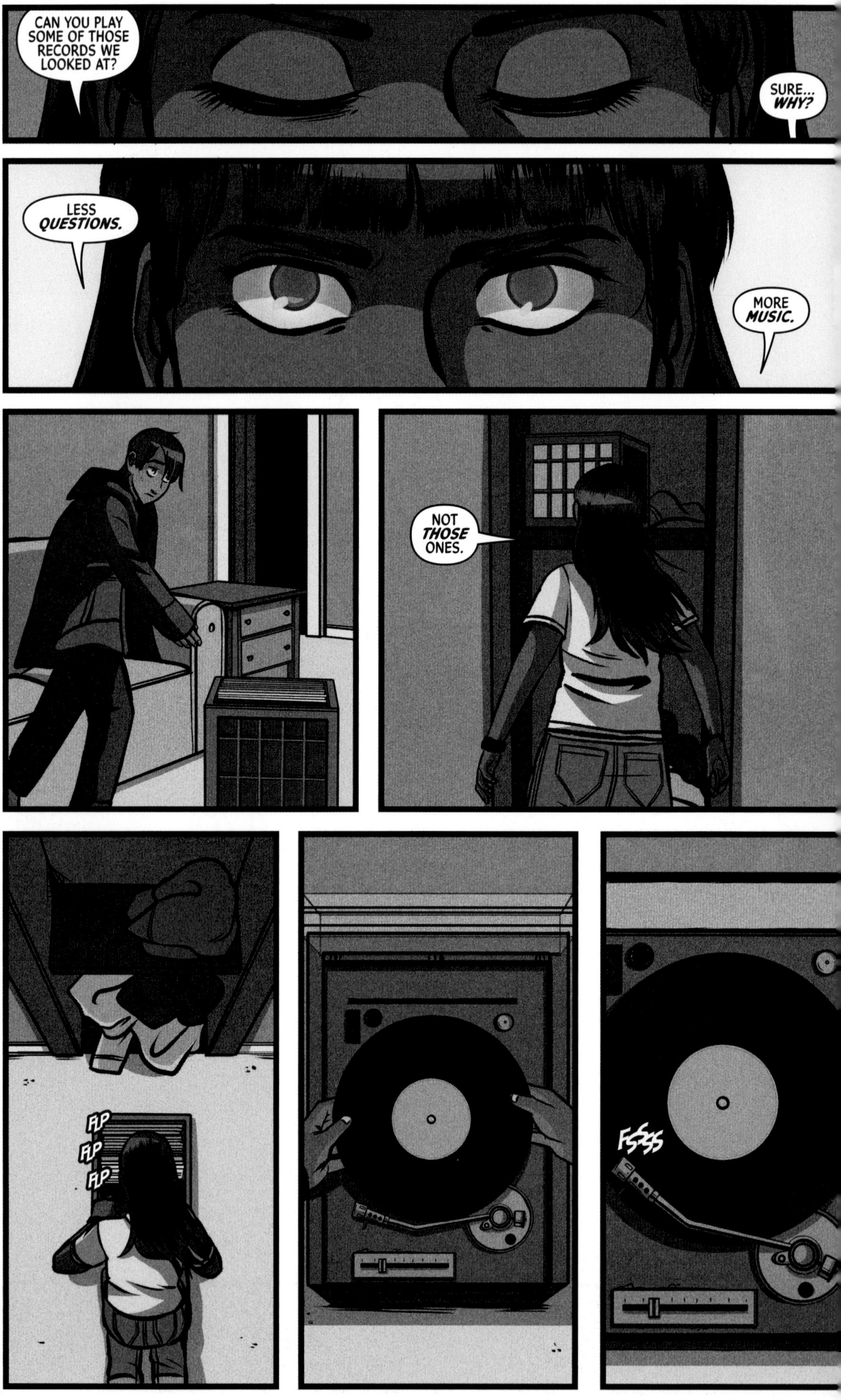
CAN YOU PLAY SOME OF THOSE RECORDS WE LOOKED AT?
SURE... WHY?
LESS QUESTIONS.
MORE MUSIC.
NOT THOSE ONES.
FLIP
FLIP
FLIP
FSSSS

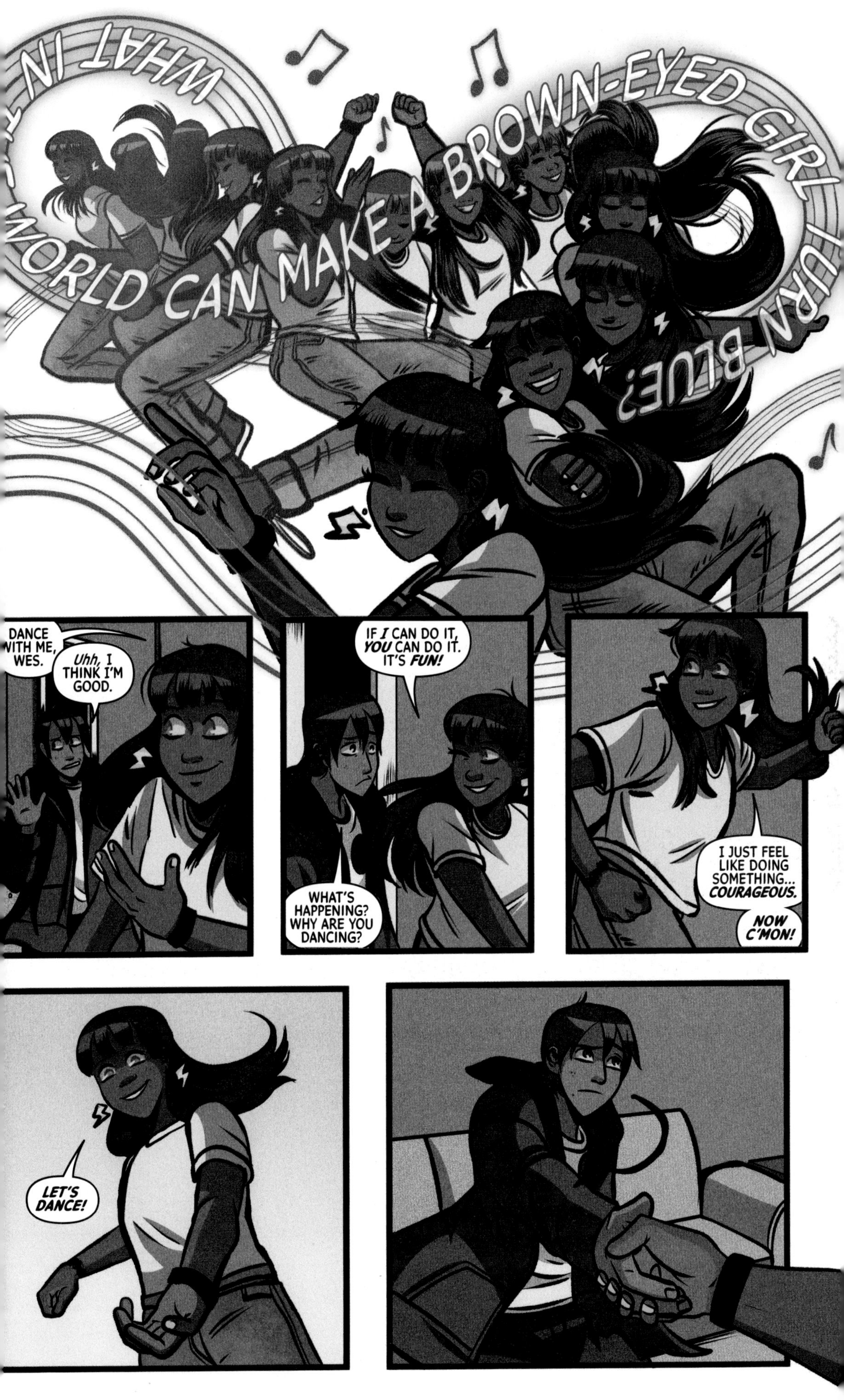
WHAT IN
WORLD CAN MAKE A BROWN-EYED GIRL TURN BLUE?
DANCE WITH ME, WES.
Uhh, I THINK I'M GOOD.
IF *I* CAN DO IT, ***YOU*** CAN DO IT. IT'S ***FUN!***
WHAT'S HAPPENING? WHY ARE YOU DANCING?
I JUST FEEL LIKE DOING SOMETHING... ***COURAGEOUS.***
NOW C'MON!
LET'S DANCE!

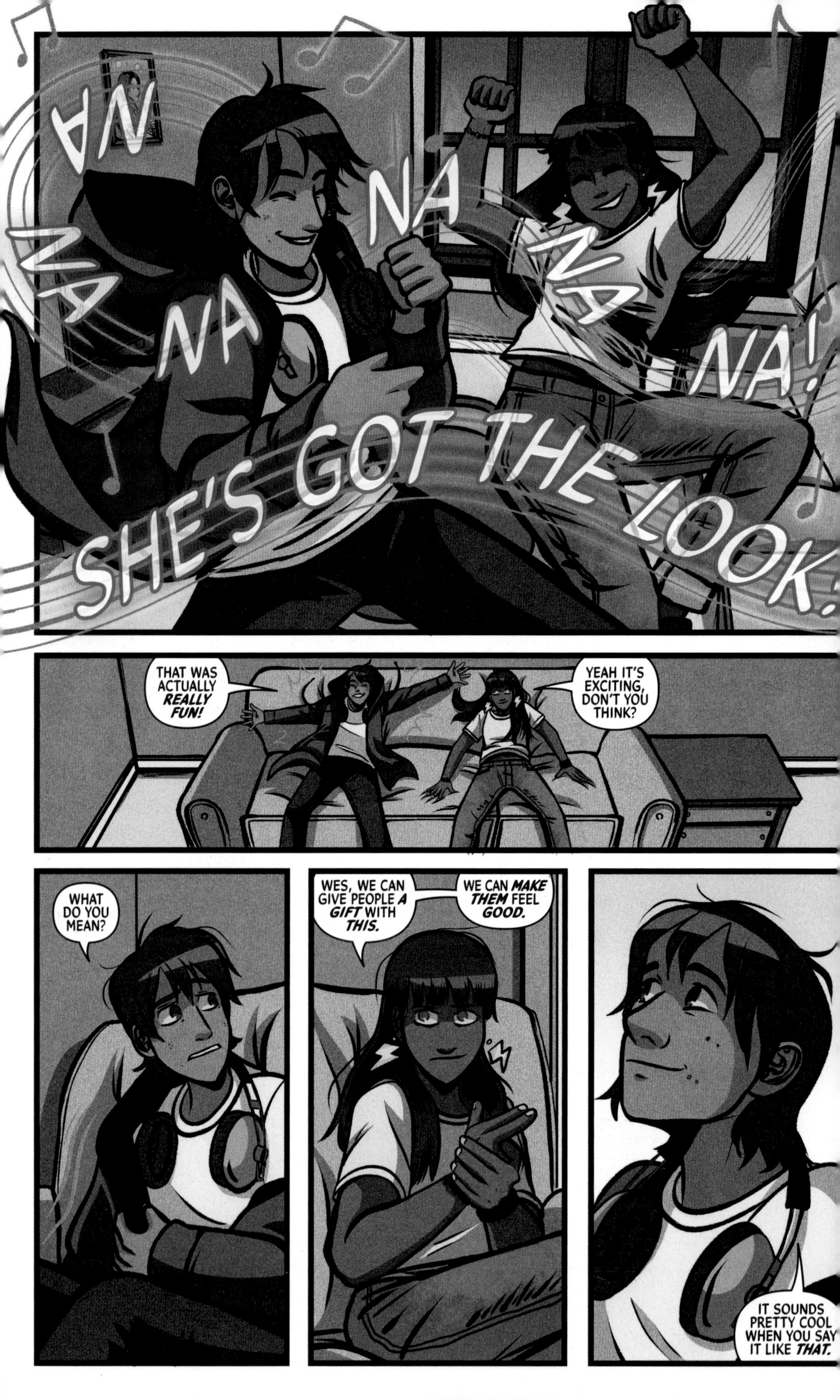

NA NA NA NA NA NA!
SHE'S GOT THE LOOK!
THAT WAS ACTUALLY REALLY FUN!
YEAH IT'S EXCITING, DON'T YOU THINK?
WHAT DO YOU MEAN?
WES, WE CAN GIVE PEOPLE A GIFT WITH THIS.
WE CAN MAKE THEM FEEL GOOD.
IT SOUNDS PRETTY COOL WHEN YOU SAY IT LIKE THAT.

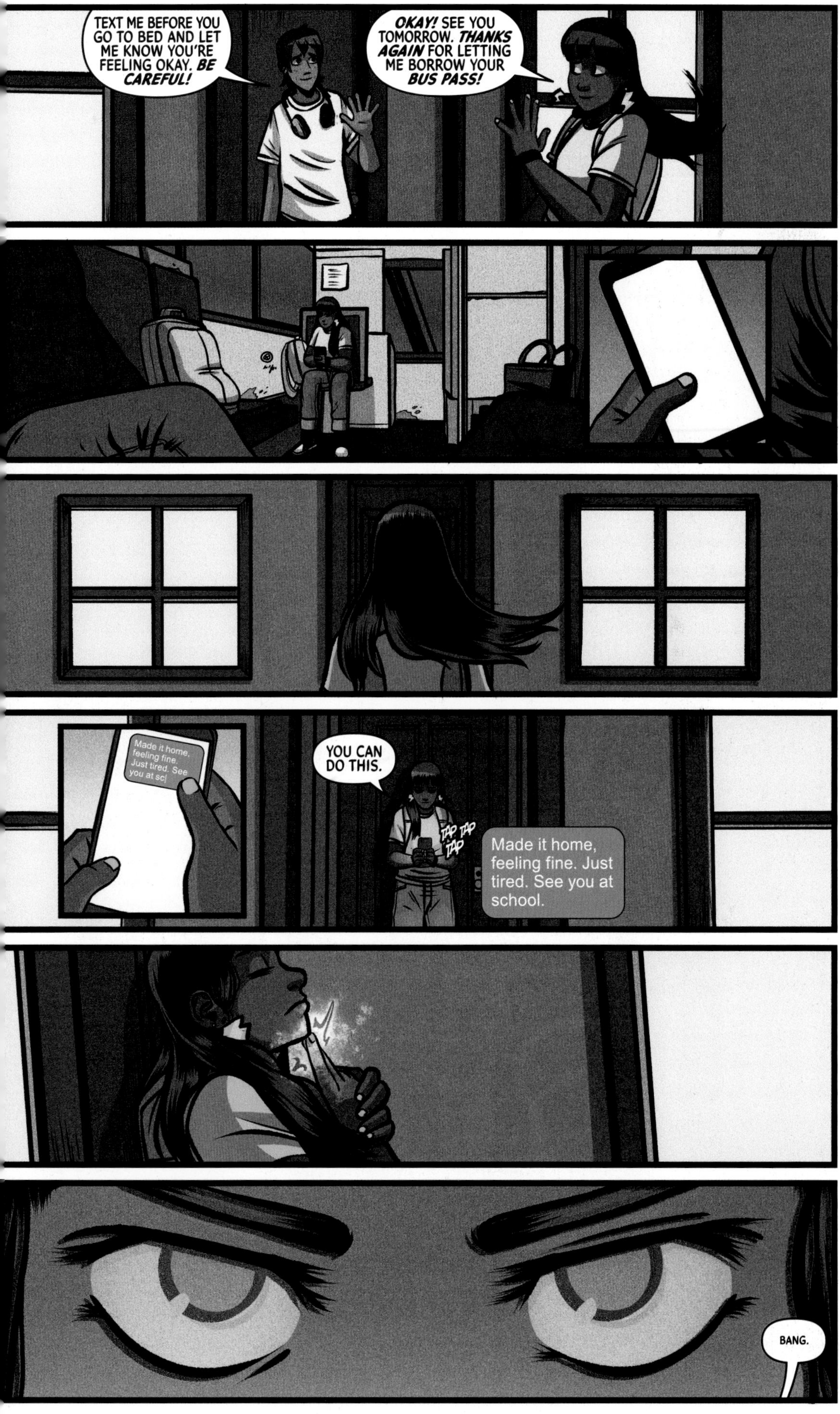
TEXT ME BEFORE YOU GO TO BED AND LET ME KNOW YOU'RE FEELING OKAY. BE CAREFUL!
OKAY! SEE YOU TOMORROW. THANKS AGAIN FOR LETTING ME BORROW YOUR BUS PASS!
Made it home, feeling fine. Just tired. See you at sc
YOU CAN DO THIS.
TAP TAP TAP
Made it home, feeling fine. Just tired. See you at school.
BANG.

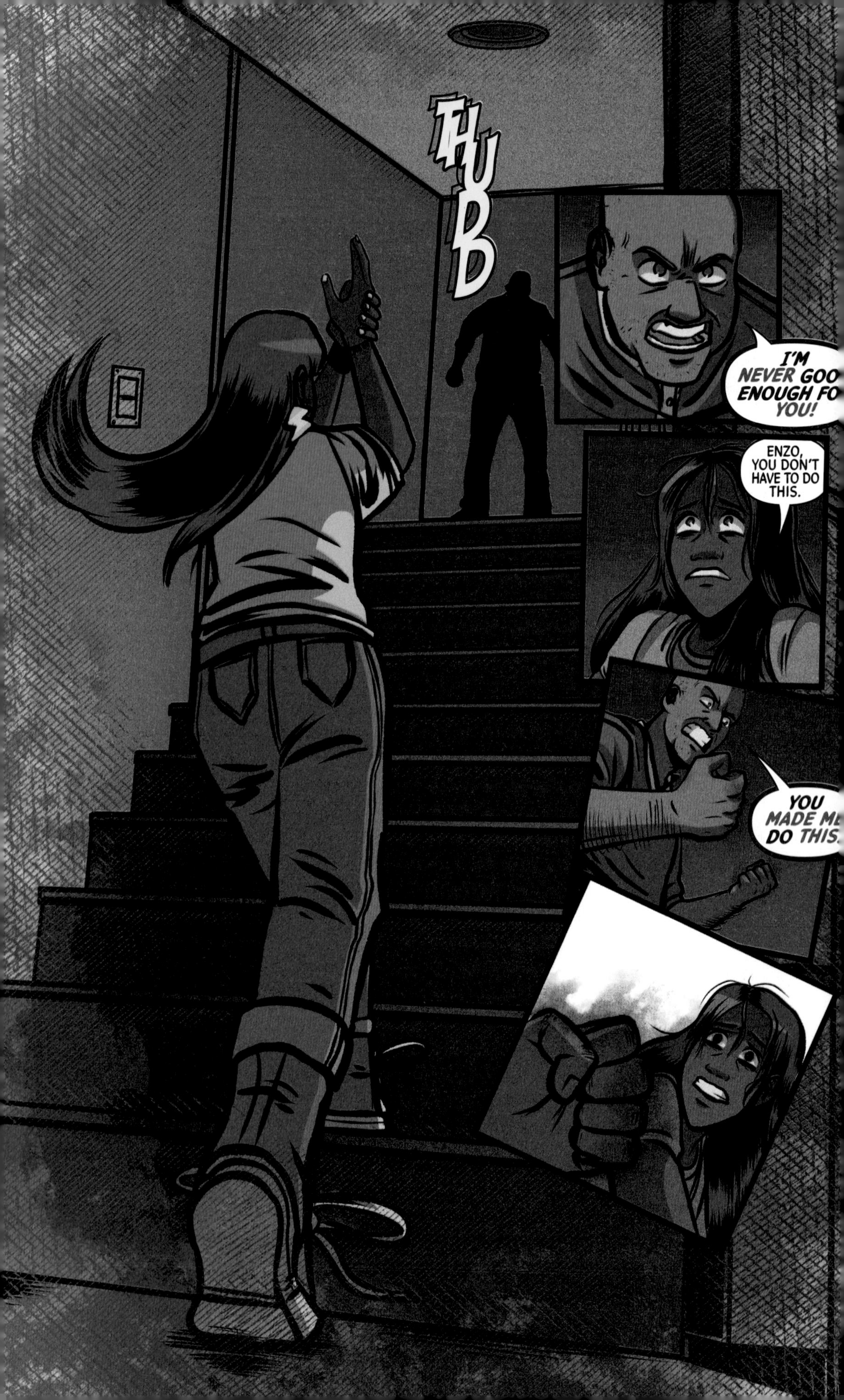
THUD
I'M NEVER GOO ENOUGH FO YOU!
ENZO, YOU DON'T HAVE TO DO THIS.
YOU MADE ME DO THIS.

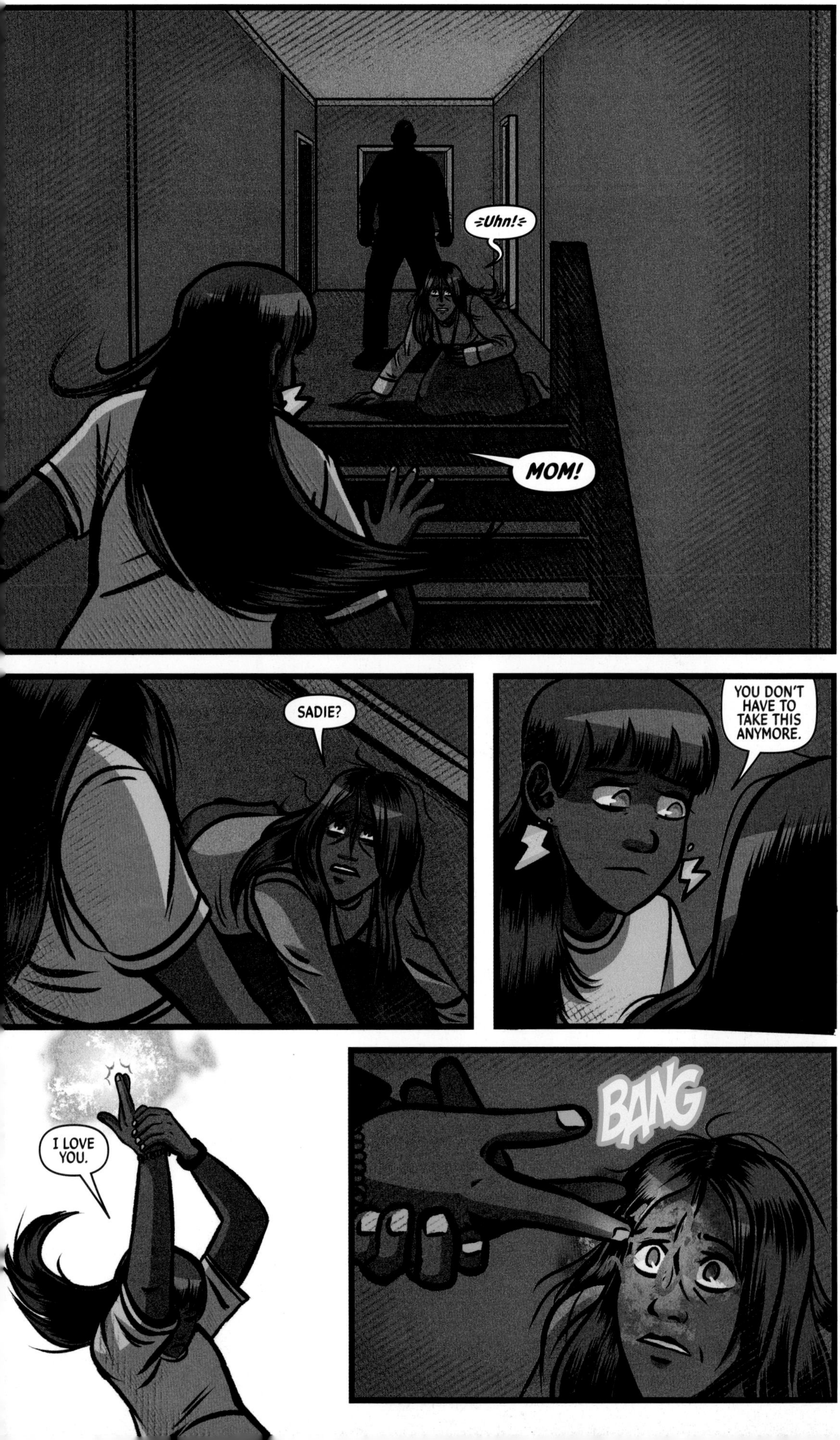
Uhn!
MOM!
SADIE?
YOU DON'T HAVE TO TAKE THIS ANYMORE.
I LOVE YOU.
BANG

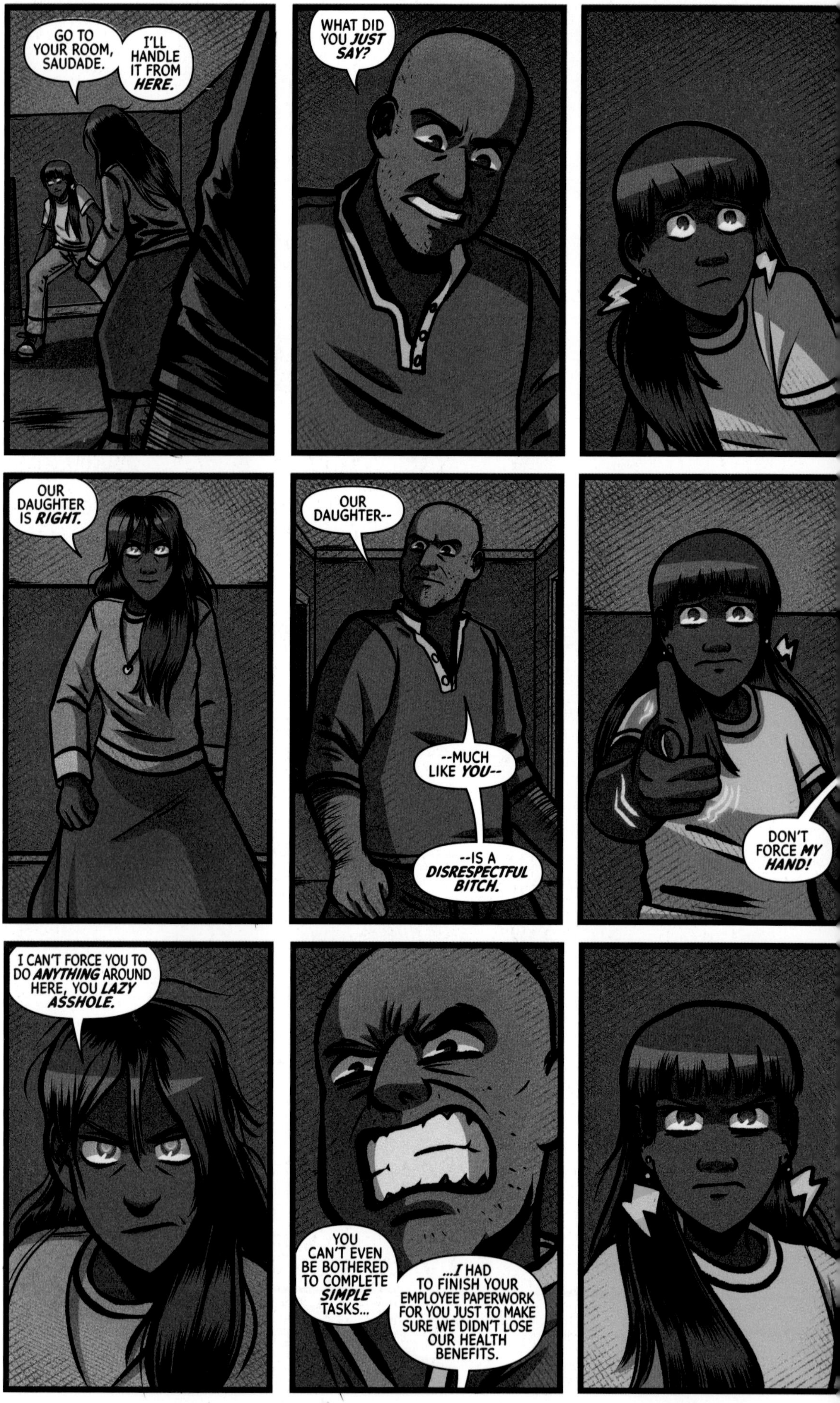
GO TO YOUR ROOM, SAUDADE.
I'LL HANDLE IT FROM *HERE.*
WHAT DID YOU *JUST SAY?*
OUR DAUGHTER IS *RIGHT.*
OUR DAUGHTER--
--MUCH LIKE *YOU*--
--IS A *DISRESPECTFUL BITCH.*
DON'T FORCE *MY HAND!*
I CAN'T FORCE YOU TO DO *ANYTHING* AROUND HERE, YOU *LAZY ASSHOLE.*
YOU CAN'T EVEN BE BOTHERED TO COMPLETE *SIMPLE* TASKS...
...*I* HAD TO FINISH YOUR EMPLOYEE PAPERWORK FOR YOU JUST TO MAKE SURE WE DIDN'T LOSE OUR HEALTH BENEFITS.

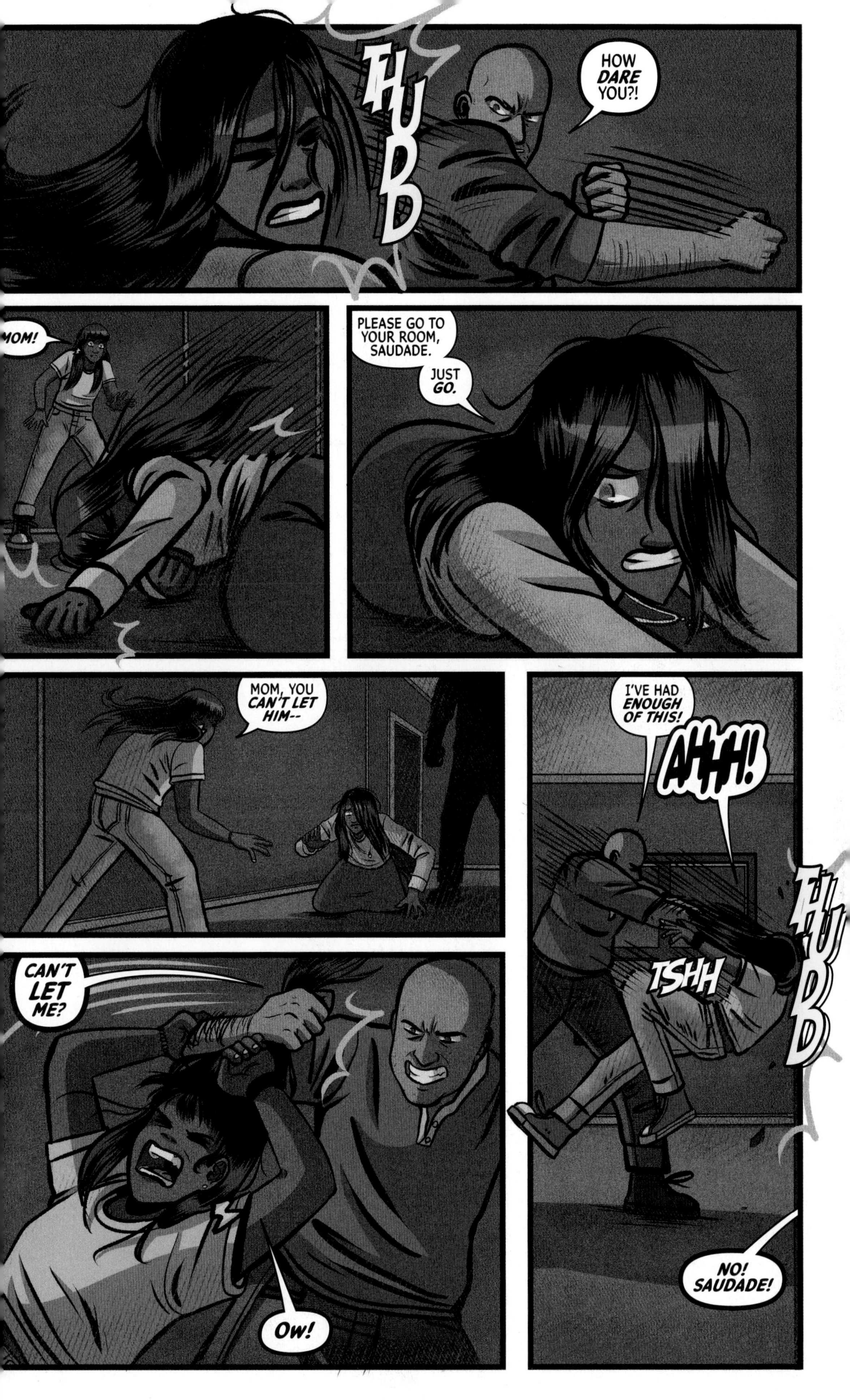
THUD
HOW DARE YOU?!
MOM!
PLEASE GO TO YOUR ROOM, SAUDADE.
JUST GO.
MOM, YOU CAN'T LET HIM--
CAN'T LET ME?
Ow!
I'VE HAD ENOUGH OF THIS!
AHHH!
TSHH
THUD
NO! SAUDADE!

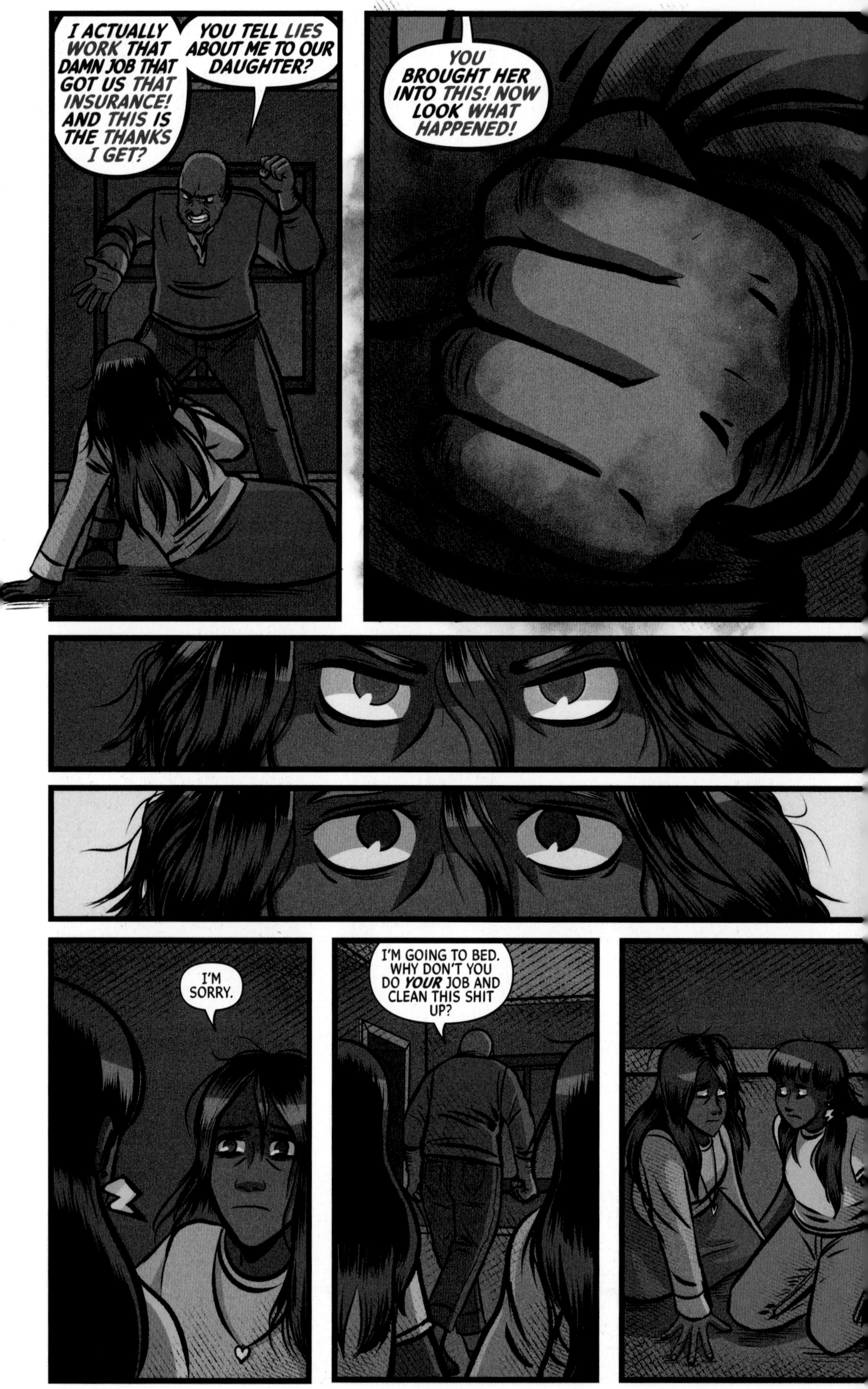
I ACTUALLY WORK THAT DAMN JOB THAT GOT US THAT INSURANCE! AND THIS IS THE THANKS I GET?
YOU TELL LIES ABOUT ME TO OUR DAUGHTER?
YOU BROUGHT HER INTO THIS! NOW LOOK WHAT HAPPENED!
I'M SORRY.
I'M GOING TO BED. WHY DON'T YOU DO YOUR JOB AND CLEAN THIS SHIT UP?

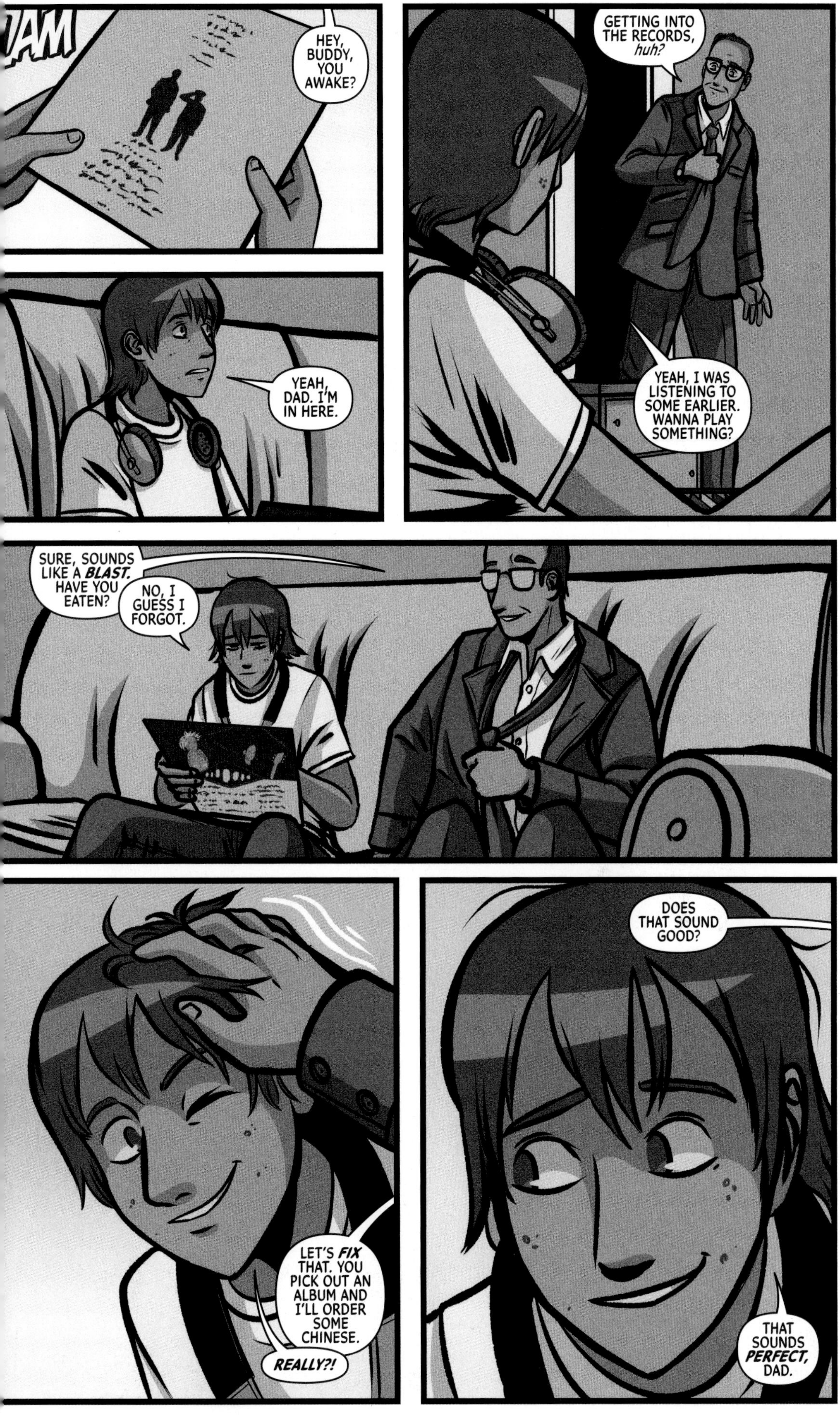

AM
HEY, BUDDY, YOU AWAKE?
GETTING INTO THE RECORDS, *huh?*
YEAH, DAD. I'M IN HERE.
YEAH, I WAS LISTENING TO SOME EARLIER. WANNA PLAY SOMETHING?
SURE, SOUNDS LIKE A ***BLAST.*** HAVE YOU EATEN?
NO, I GUESS I FORGOT.
DOES THAT SOUND GOOD?
LET'S ***FIX*** THAT. YOU PICK OUT AN ALBUM AND I'LL ORDER SOME CHINESE.
REALLY?!
THAT SOUNDS ***PERFECT,*** DAD.

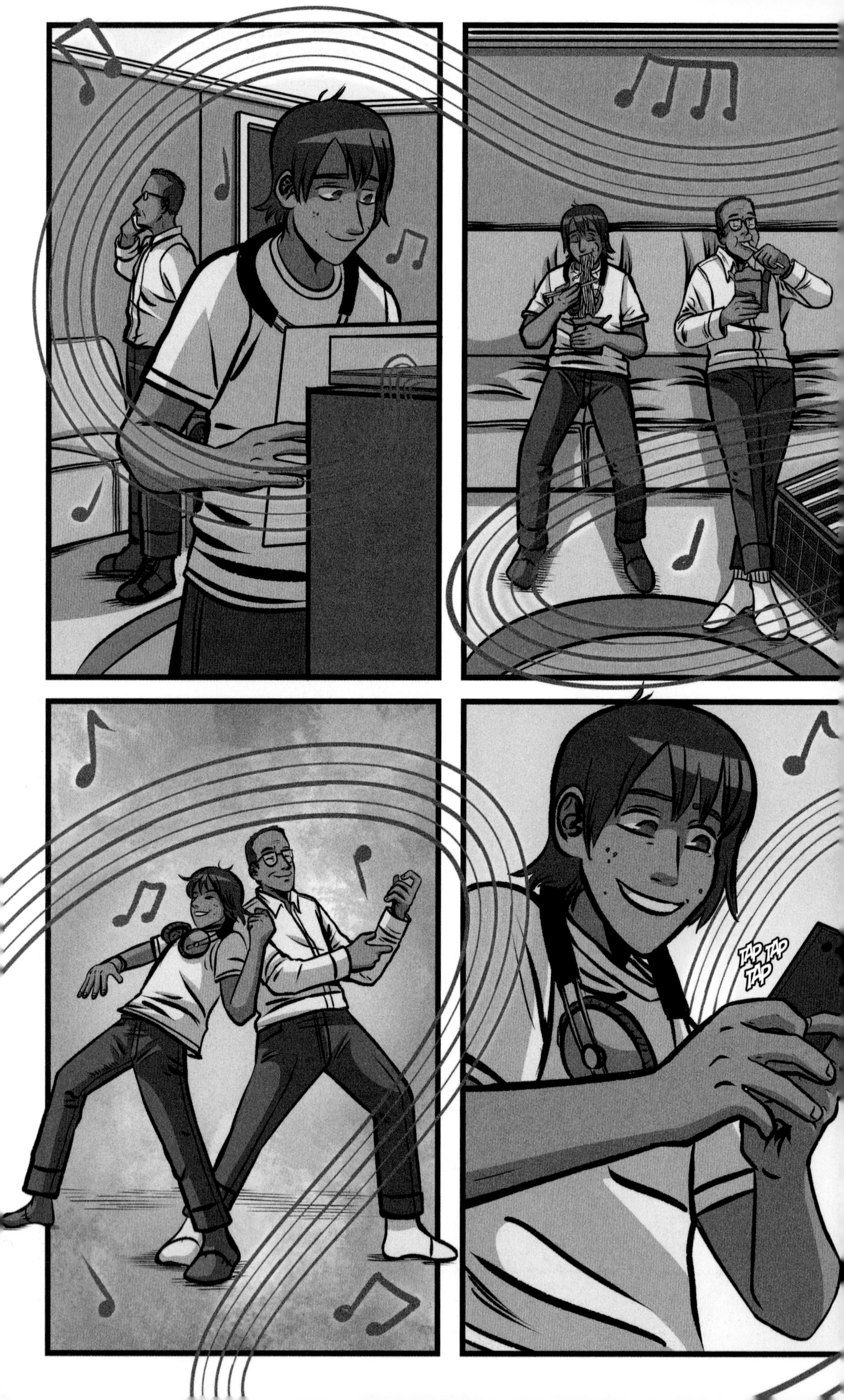
TAP TAP TAP

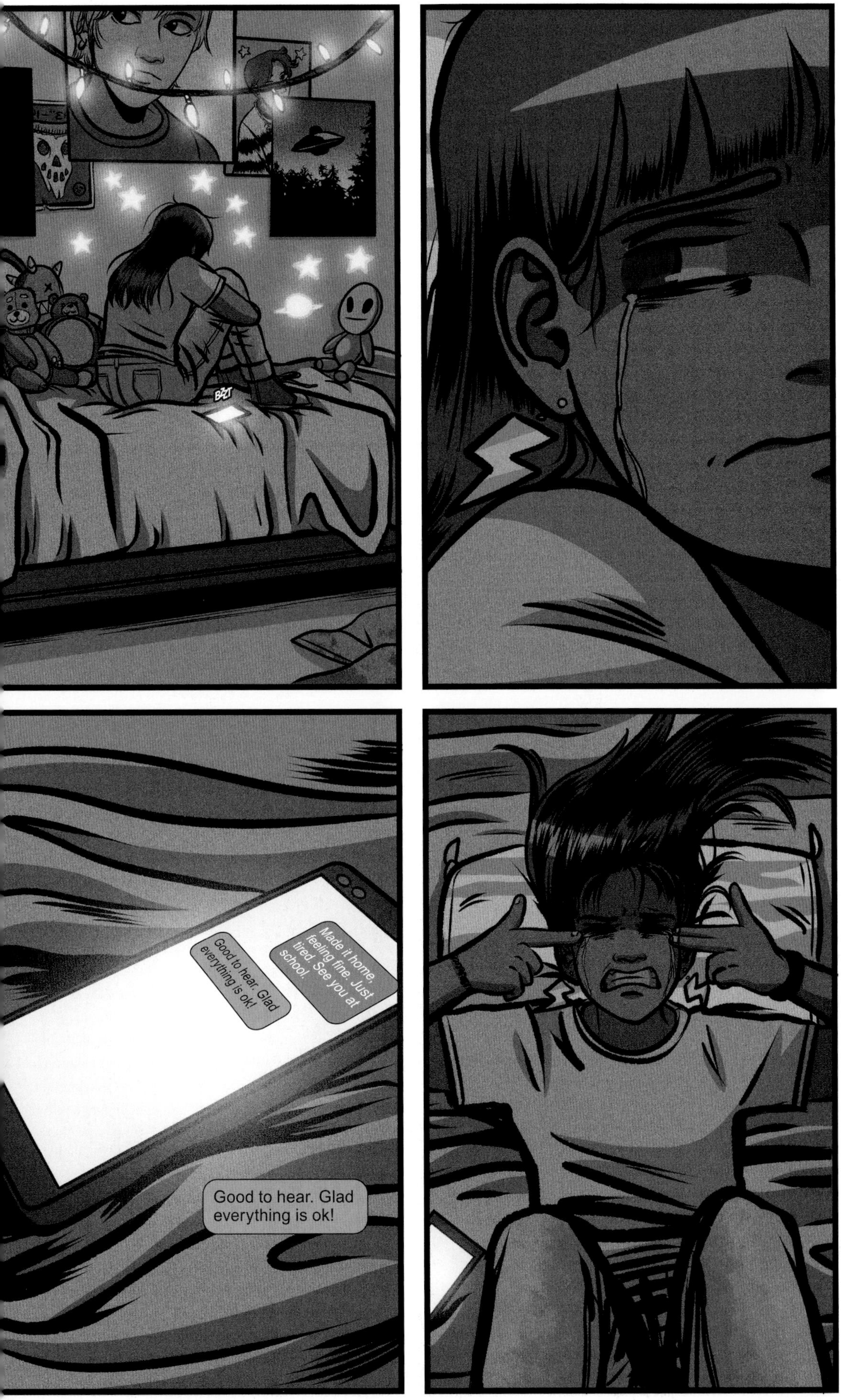
BZZT
Made it home, feeling fine. Just tired. See you at school.
Good to hear. Glad everything is ok!
Good to hear. Glad everything is ok!

FOUR

JUMPING THE GUN

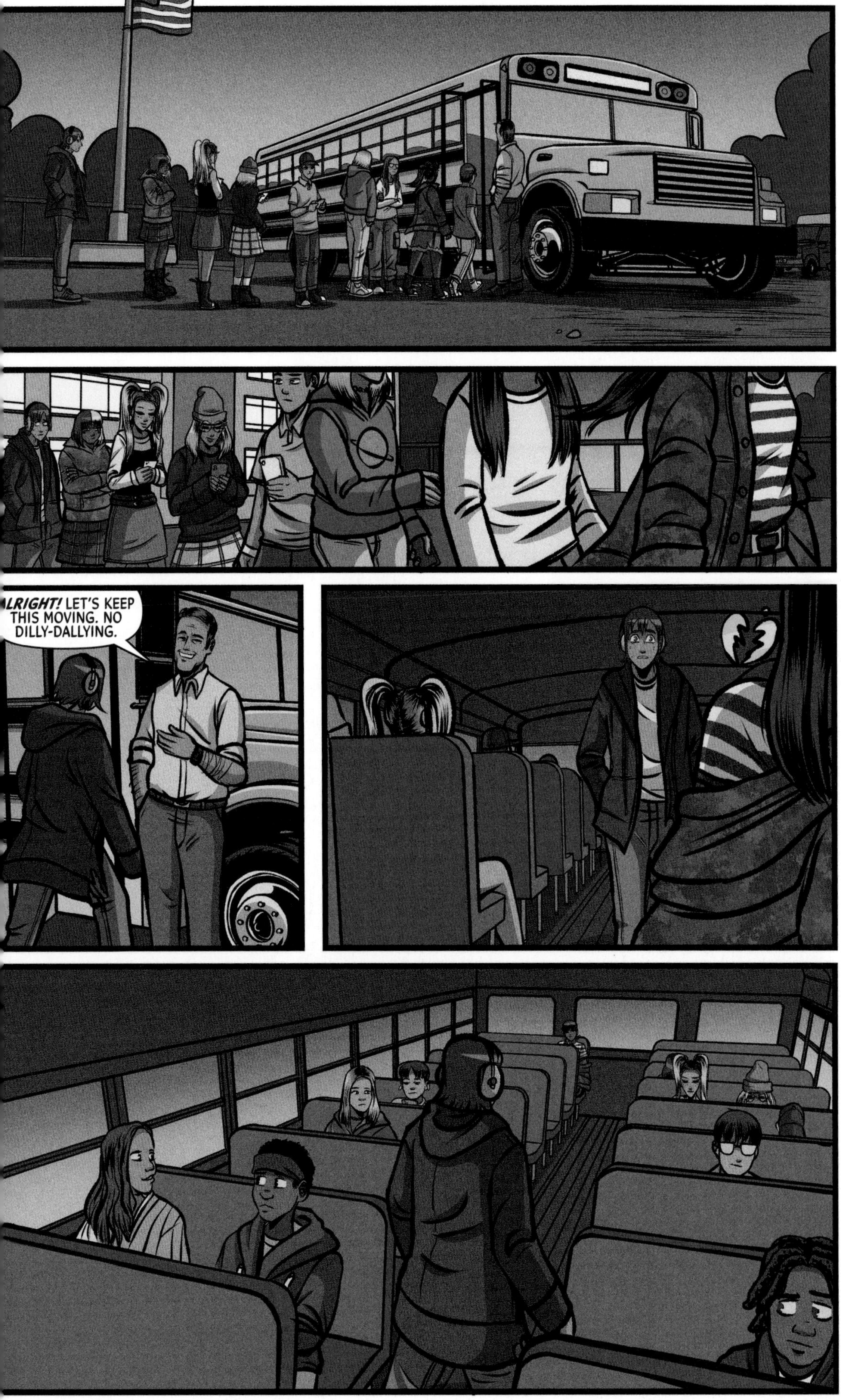
LRIGHT! LET'S KEEP THIS MOVING. NO DILLY-DALLYING.

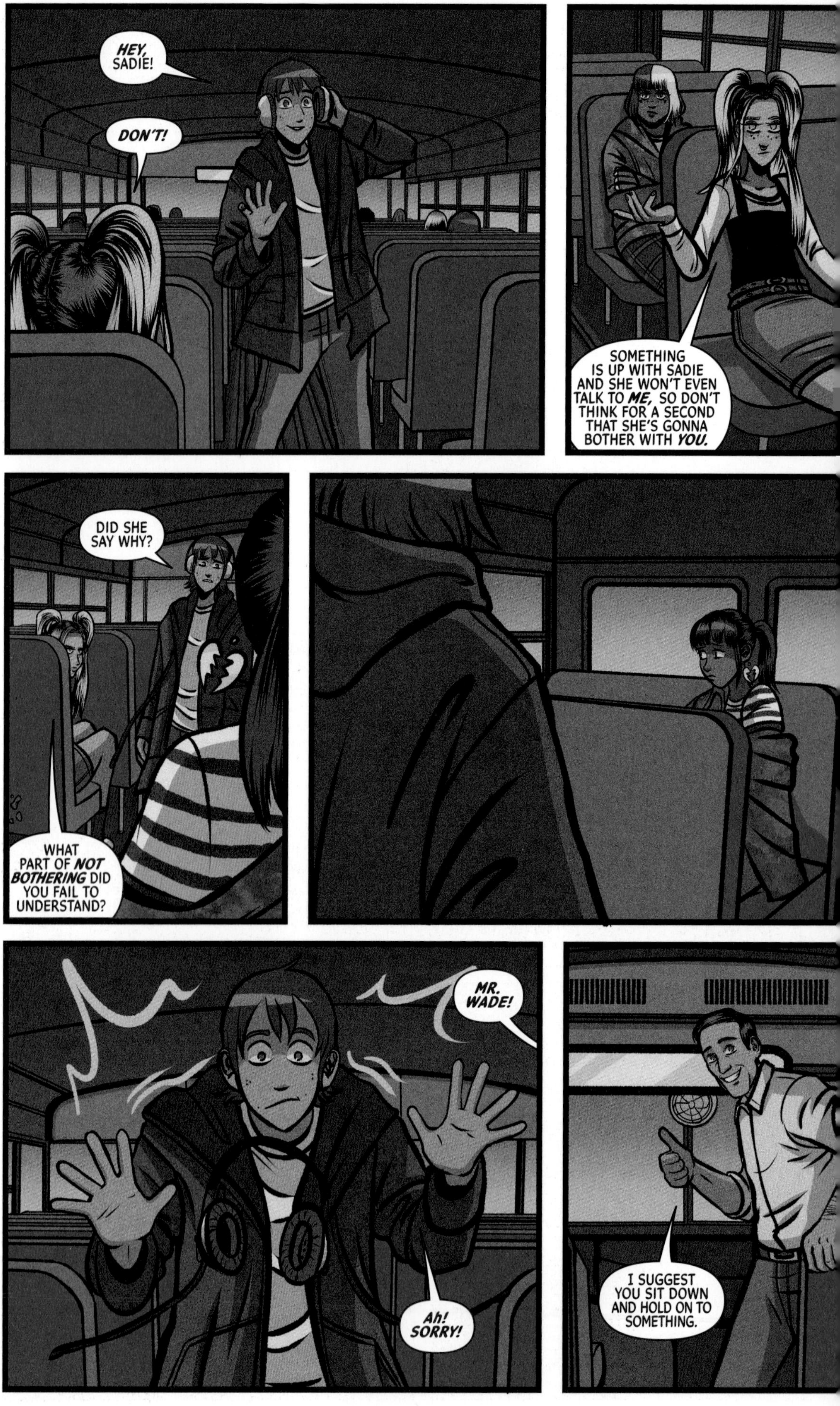
HEY, SADIE!
DON'T!
SOMETHING IS UP WITH SADIE AND SHE WON'T EVEN TALK TO ME, SO DON'T THINK FOR A SECOND THAT SHE'S GONNA BOTHER WITH YOU.
DID SHE SAY WHY?
WHAT PART OF NOT BOTHERING DID YOU FAIL TO UNDERSTAND?
MR. WADE!
Ah! SORRY!
I SUGGEST YOU SIT DOWN AND HOLD ON TO SOMETHING.

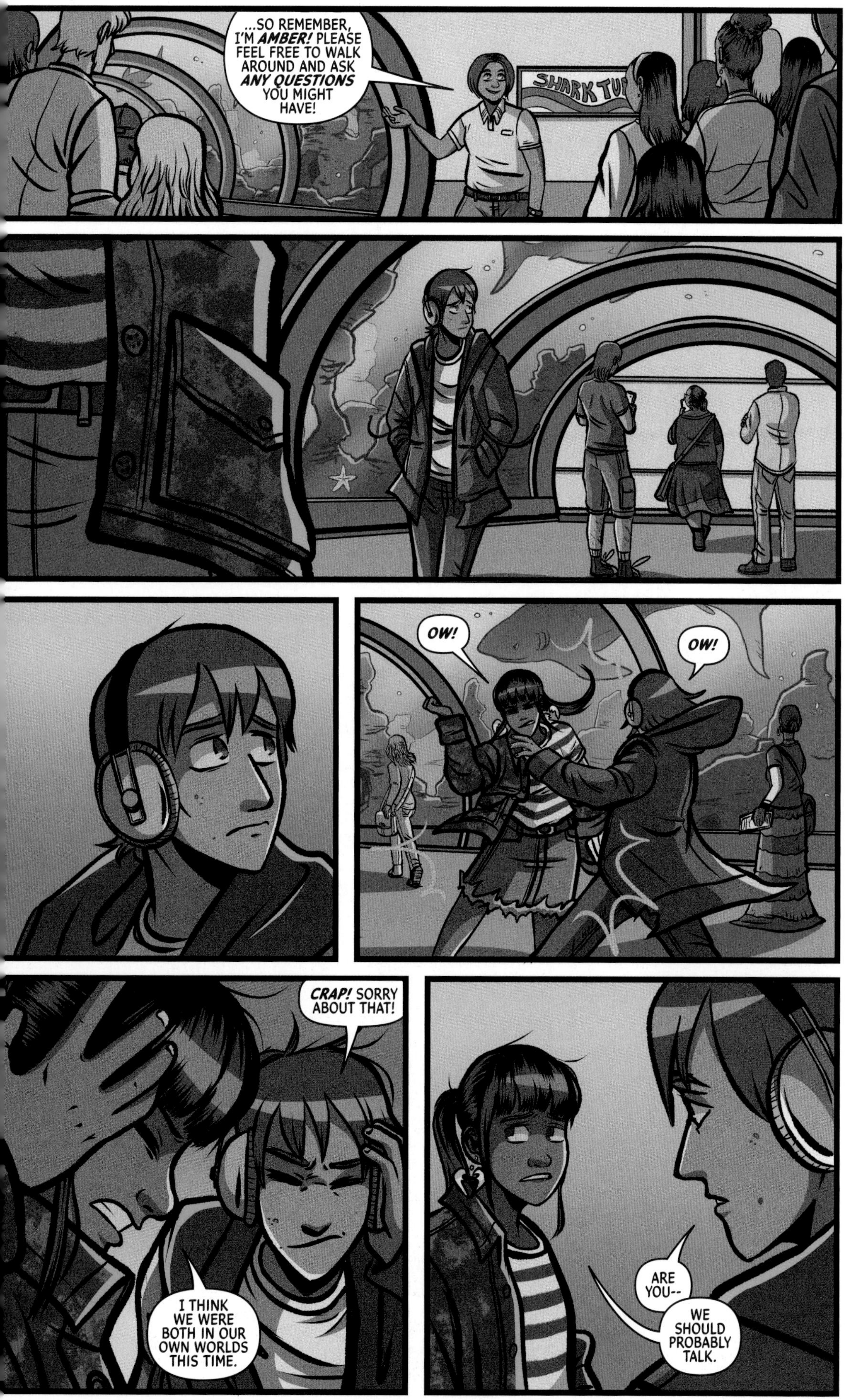
...SO REMEMBER, I'M AMBER! PLEASE FEEL FREE TO WALK AROUND AND ASK ANY QUESTIONS YOU MIGHT HAVE!
SHARK TU
OW!
OW!
CRAP! SORRY ABOUT THAT!
I THINK WE WERE BOTH IN OUR OWN WORLDS THIS TIME.
ARE YOU--
WE SHOULD PROBABLY TALK.

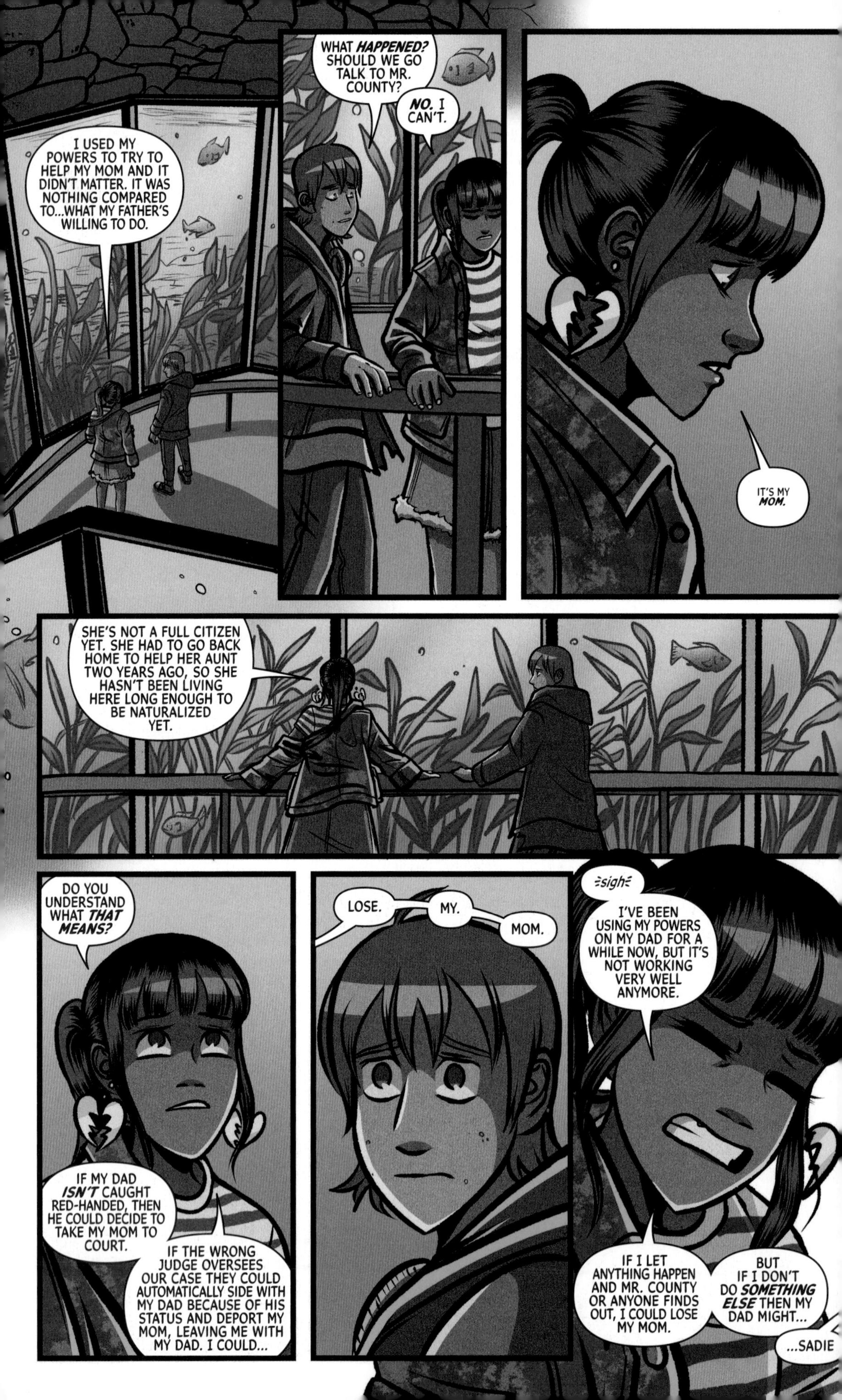

I USED MY POWERS TO TRY TO HELP MY MOM AND IT DIDN'T MATTER. IT WAS NOTHING COMPARED TO...WHAT MY FATHER'S WILLING TO DO.
WHAT *HAPPENED?* SHOULD WE GO TALK TO MR. COUNTY?
NO. I CAN'T.
IT'S MY *MOM.*
SHE'S NOT A FULL CITIZEN YET. SHE HAD TO GO BACK HOME TO HELP HER AUNT TWO YEARS AGO, SO SHE HASN'T BEEN LIVING HERE LONG ENOUGH TO BE NATURALIZED YET.
DO YOU UNDERSTAND WHAT *THAT MEANS?*
IF MY DAD *ISN'T* CAUGHT RED-HANDED, THEN HE COULD DECIDE TO TAKE MY MOM TO COURT.
IF THE WRONG JUDGE OVERSEES OUR CASE THEY COULD AUTOMATICALLY SIDE WITH MY DAD BECAUSE OF HIS STATUS AND DEPORT MY MOM, LEAVING ME WITH MY DAD. I COULD...
LOSE.
MY.
MOM.
sigh
I'VE BEEN USING MY POWERS ON MY DAD FOR A WHILE NOW, BUT IT'S NOT WORKING VERY WELL ANYMORE.
IF I LET ANYTHING HAPPEN AND MR. COUNTY OR ANYONE FINDS OUT, I COULD LOSE MY MOM.
BUT IF I DON'T DO *SOMETHING ELSE* THEN MY DAD MIGHT...
...SADIE

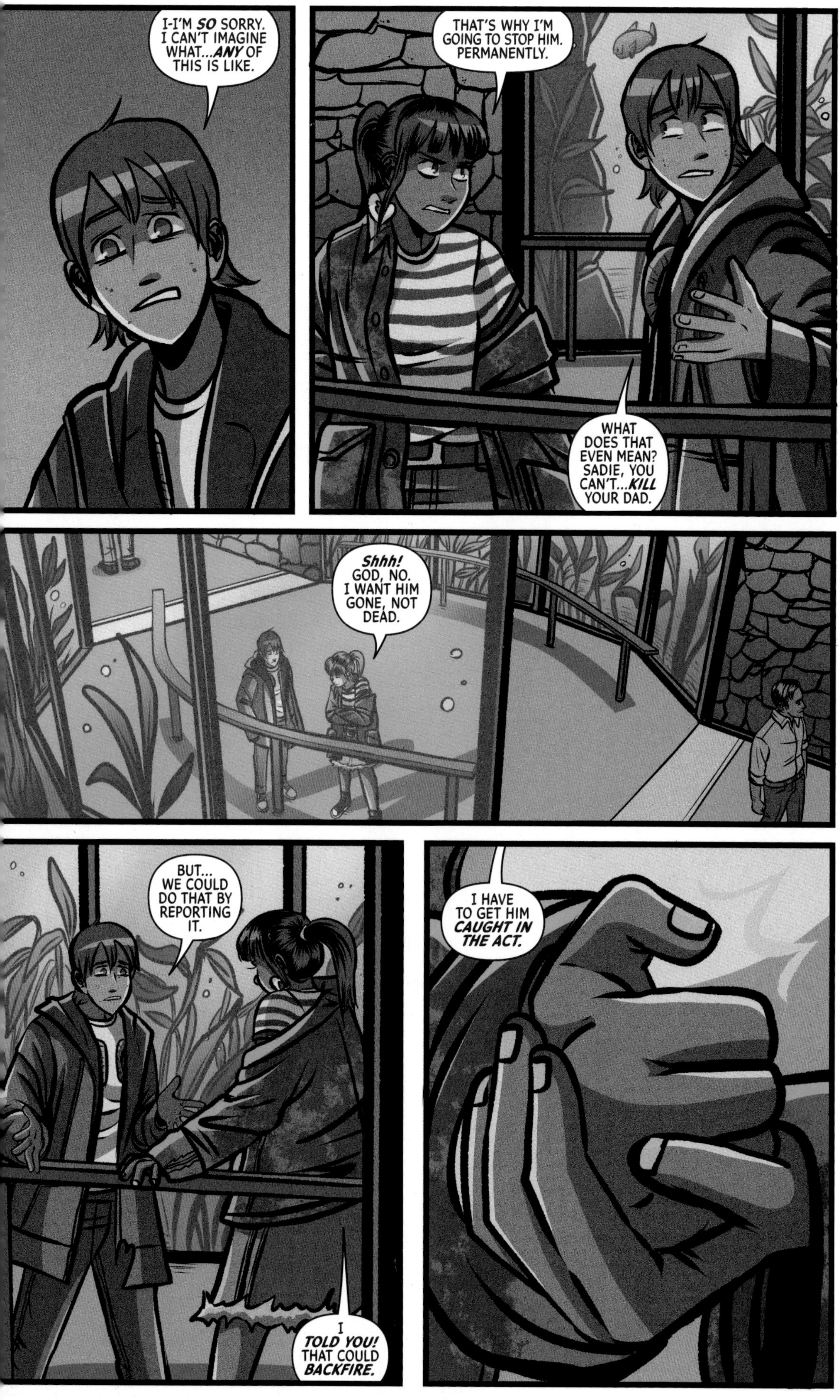
I-I'M SO SORRY. I CAN'T IMAGINE WHAT...ANY OF THIS IS LIKE.
THAT'S WHY I'M GOING TO STOP HIM. PERMANENTLY.
WHAT DOES THAT EVEN MEAN? SADIE, YOU CAN'T...KILL YOUR DAD.
Shhh! GOD, NO. I WANT HIM GONE, NOT DEAD.
BUT... WE COULD DO THAT BY REPORTING IT.
I TOLD YOU! THAT COULD BACKFIRE.
I HAVE TO GET HIM CAUGHT IN THE ACT.

HOW ARE YOU PLANNING TO DO THAT?

MY DAD'S BEEN WORKING NIGHT SHIFTS. WHEN HE LEAVES IN THE EVENING, I'LL BE WAITING IN THE BACK OF THE CAR.

WHEN HE GETS TO WORK, I'M GOING TO USE THE ANGER GUN ON HIM SO HE'LL MAKE A SCENE AND GET FIRED. I NEED YOU TO BE WAITING THERE TO BACK ME UP IF SOMETHING GOES WRONG.

SADIE, WE CAN'T DO THAT. THERE'S NO WAY THAT'S SAFE. EVEN IF THERE'S TWO OF US, THERE'S *WAY TOO MANY* VARIABLES.

WES, I WOULDN'T TELL YOU ANY OF THIS IF I DIDN'T TRUST YOU. I NEED YOUR HELP AND *THIS* IS THE ONLY WAY I CAN SAVE MY MOM. YOU *PROMISED* ME YOU'D *HELP ME*.

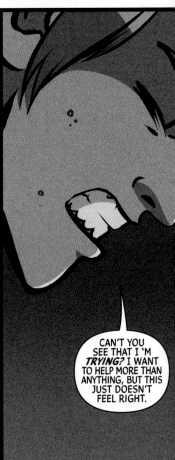

CAN'T YOU SEE THAT I'M *TRYING?* I WANT TO HELP MORE THAN ANYTHING, BUT THIS JUST DOESN'T FEEL RIGHT.

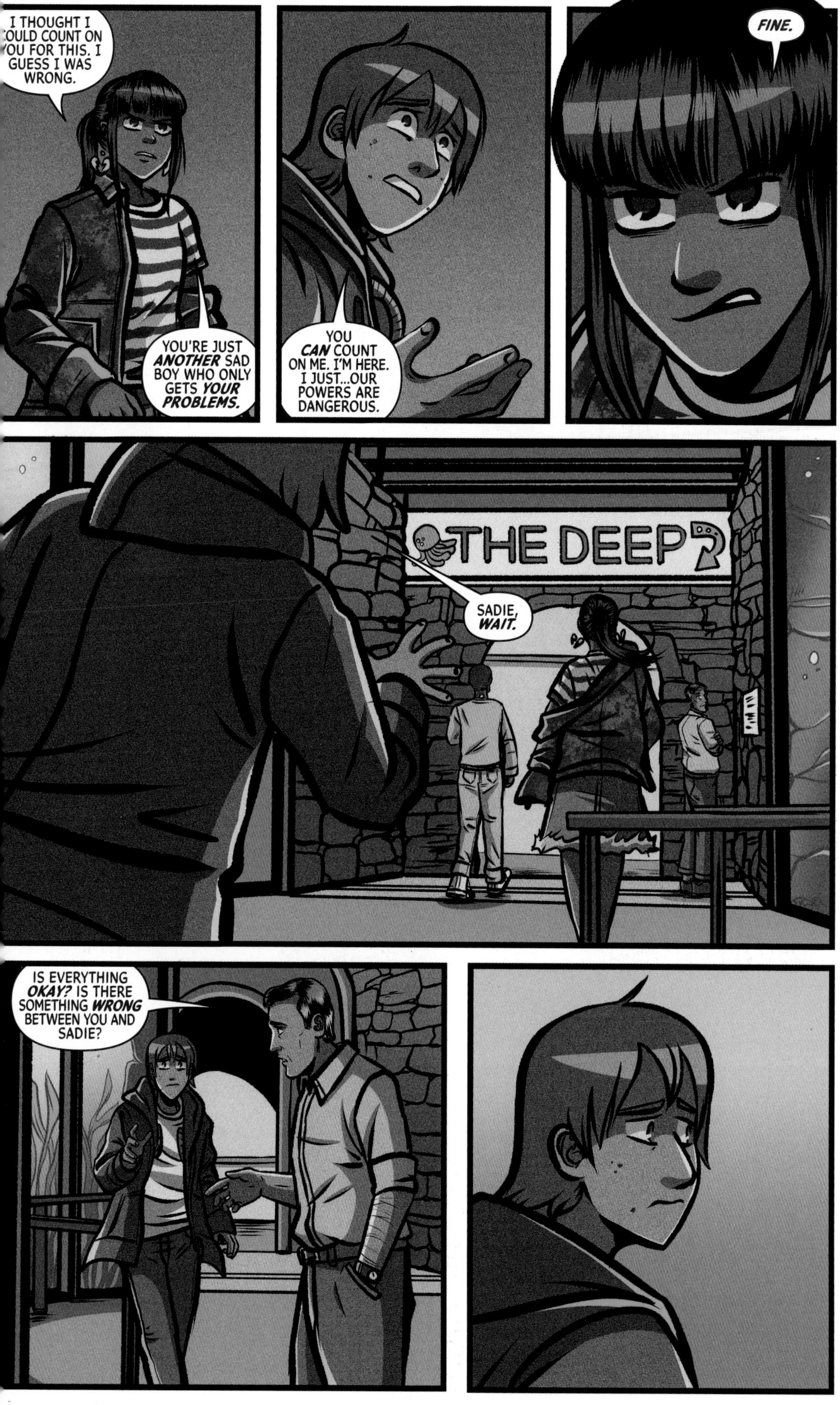
I THOUGHT I COULD COUNT ON YOU FOR THIS. I GUESS I WAS WRONG.
YOU'RE JUST ANOTHER SAD BOY WHO ONLY GETS YOUR PROBLEMS.
YOU CAN COUNT ON ME. I'M HERE. I JUST...OUR POWERS ARE DANGEROUS.
FINE.
THE DEEP
SADIE, WAIT.
IS EVERYTHING OKAY? IS THERE SOMETHING WRONG BETWEEN YOU AND SADIE?

Please don't tell anyone. I shouldn't have told you.
I've always taken care of things myself.
Nothing's changed.
Sadie, we should talk about this more.
Don't worry about it.
Let me know if I can help you in any other way. We should try to figure something out together.
Just don't say anything.
sigh
MY COD, WAS THAT AQUARIUM FUN! JUST DON'T FORGET KIDS, ANY FIN IS POSSIBLE IF YOU DON'T TROUT YOURSELF!
GROAN
GROAN
GROAN

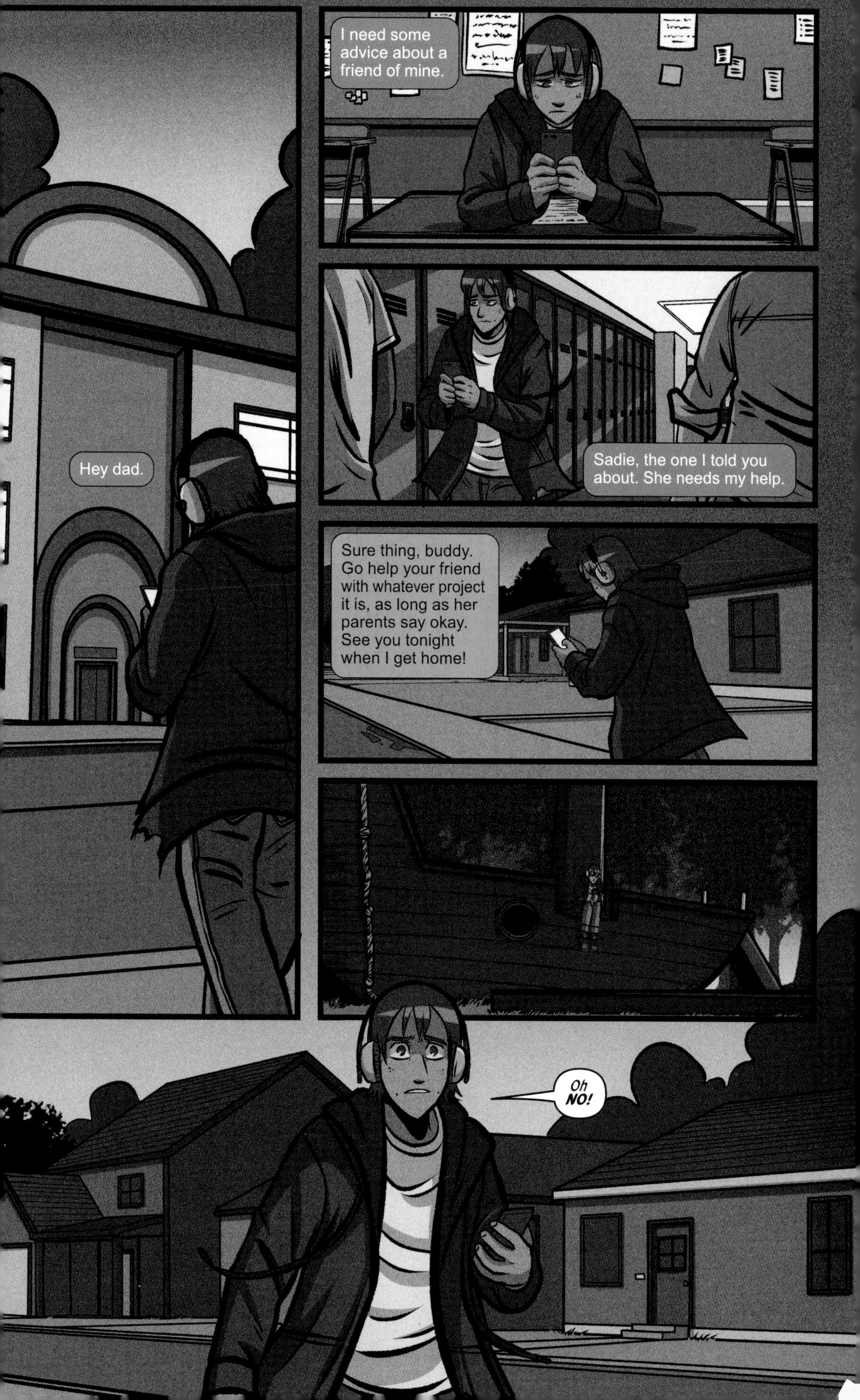

Hey dad.
I need some advice about a friend of mine.
Sadie, the one I told you about. She needs my help.
Sure thing, buddy. Go help your friend with whatever project it is, as long as her parents say okay. See you tonight when I get home!
Oh NO!

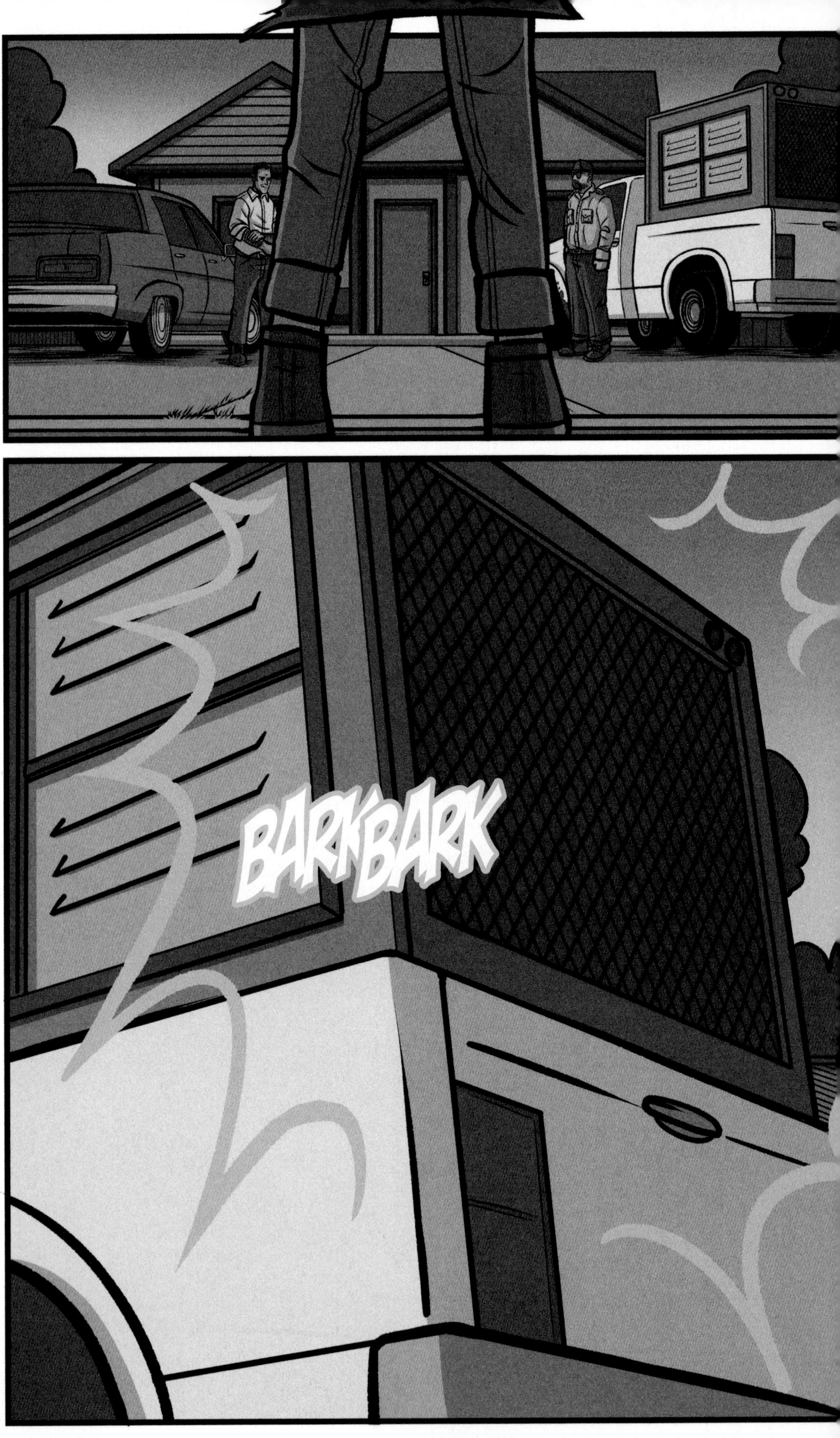
BARKBARK

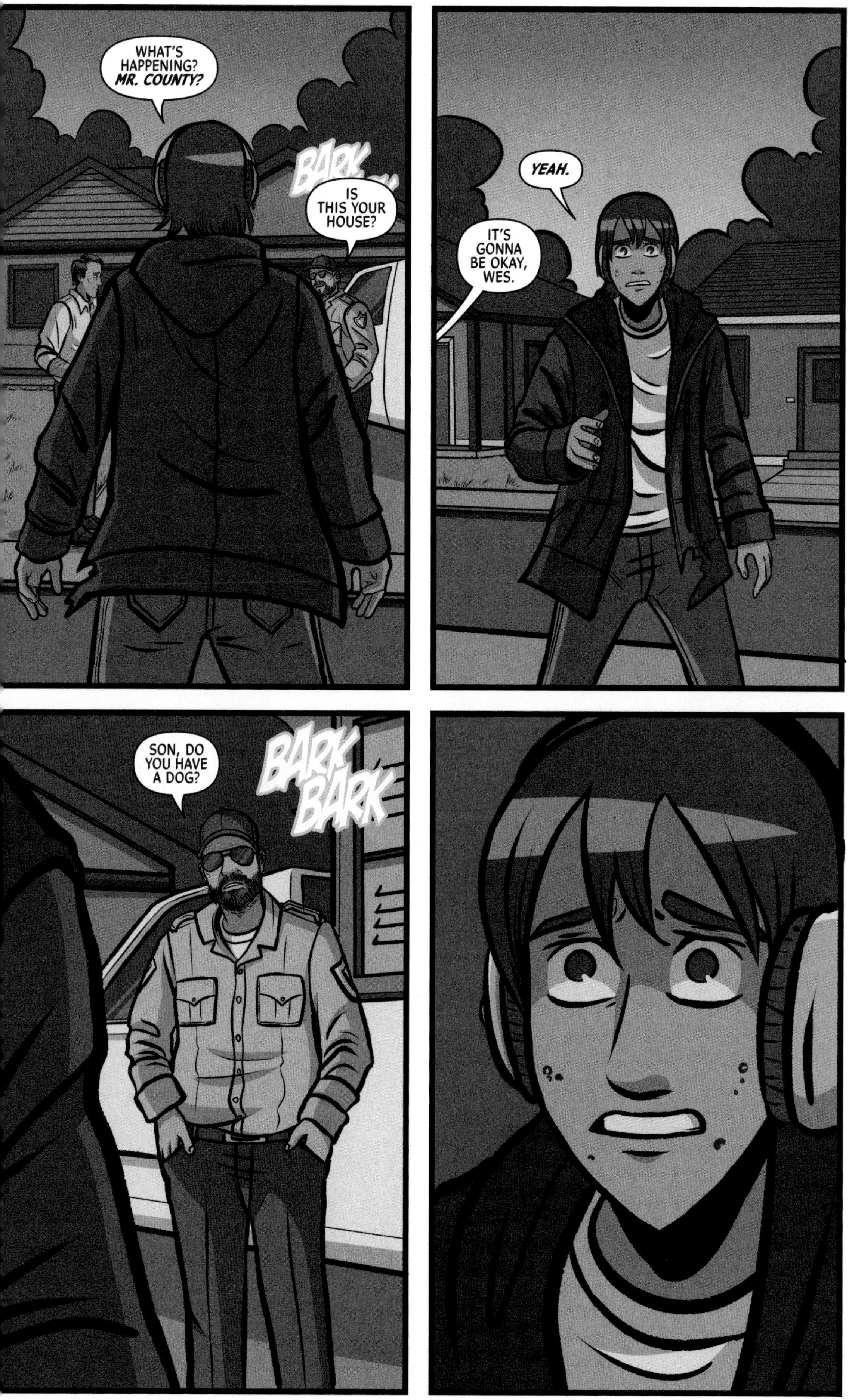
WHAT'S HAPPENING? MR. COUNTY?
BARK
IS THIS YOUR HOUSE?
YEAH.
IT'S GONNA BE OKAY, WES.
SON, DO YOU HAVE A DOG?
BARK BARK

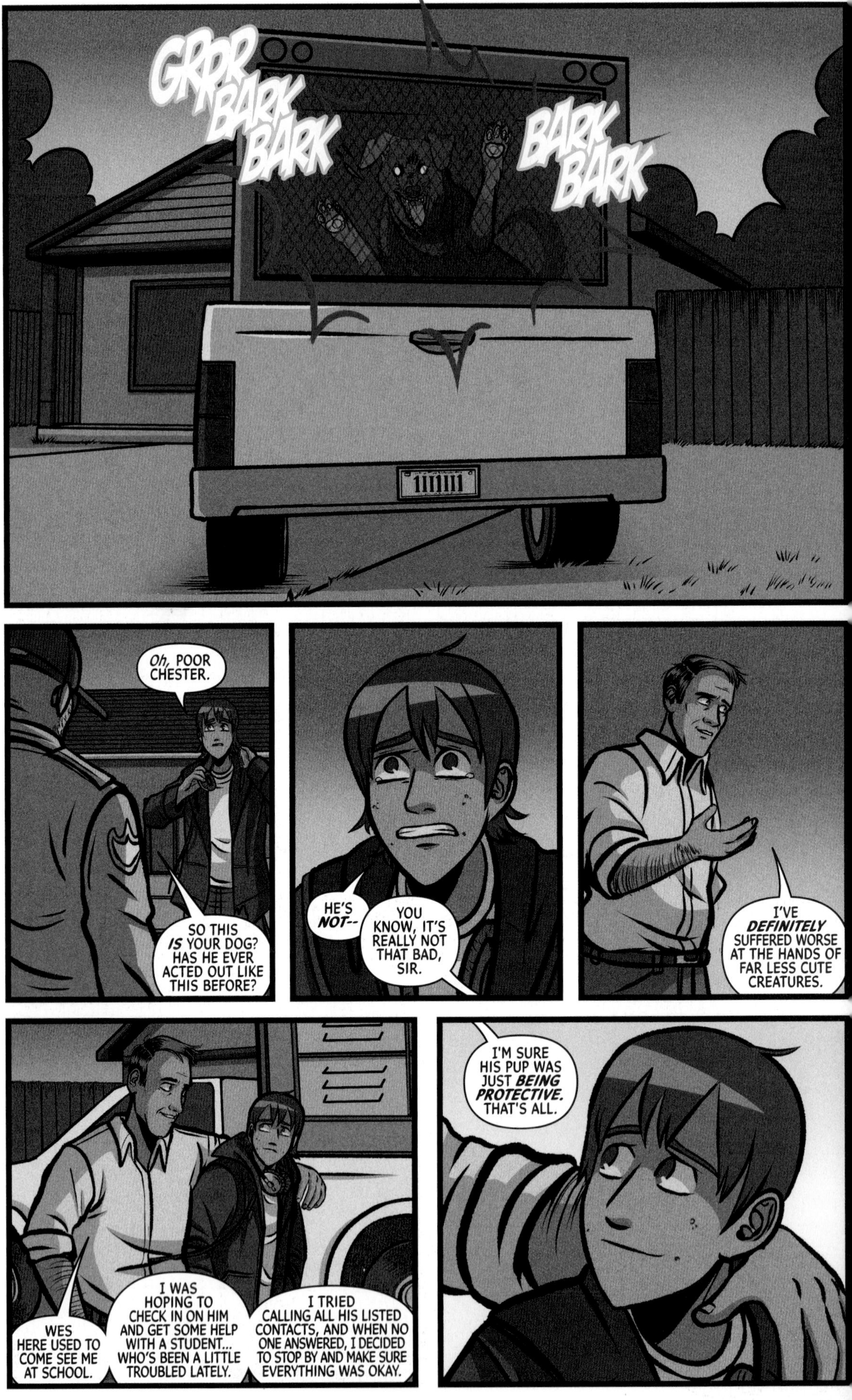
GRRR BARK BARK
BARK BARK
Oh, POOR CHESTER.
SO THIS IS YOUR DOG? HAS HE EVER ACTED OUT LIKE THIS BEFORE?
HE'S NOT--
YOU KNOW, IT'S REALLY NOT THAT BAD, SIR.
I'VE DEFINITELY SUFFERED WORSE AT THE HANDS OF FAR LESS CUTE CREATURES.
WES HERE USED TO COME SEE ME AT SCHOOL.
I WAS HOPING TO CHECK IN ON HIM AND GET SOME HELP WITH A STUDENT... WHO'S BEEN A LITTLE TROUBLED LATELY.
I TRIED CALLING ALL HIS LISTED CONTACTS, AND WHEN NO ONE ANSWERED, I DECIDED TO STOP BY AND MAKE SURE EVERYTHING WAS OKAY.
I'M SURE HIS PUP WAS JUST BEING PROTECTIVE. THAT'S ALL.

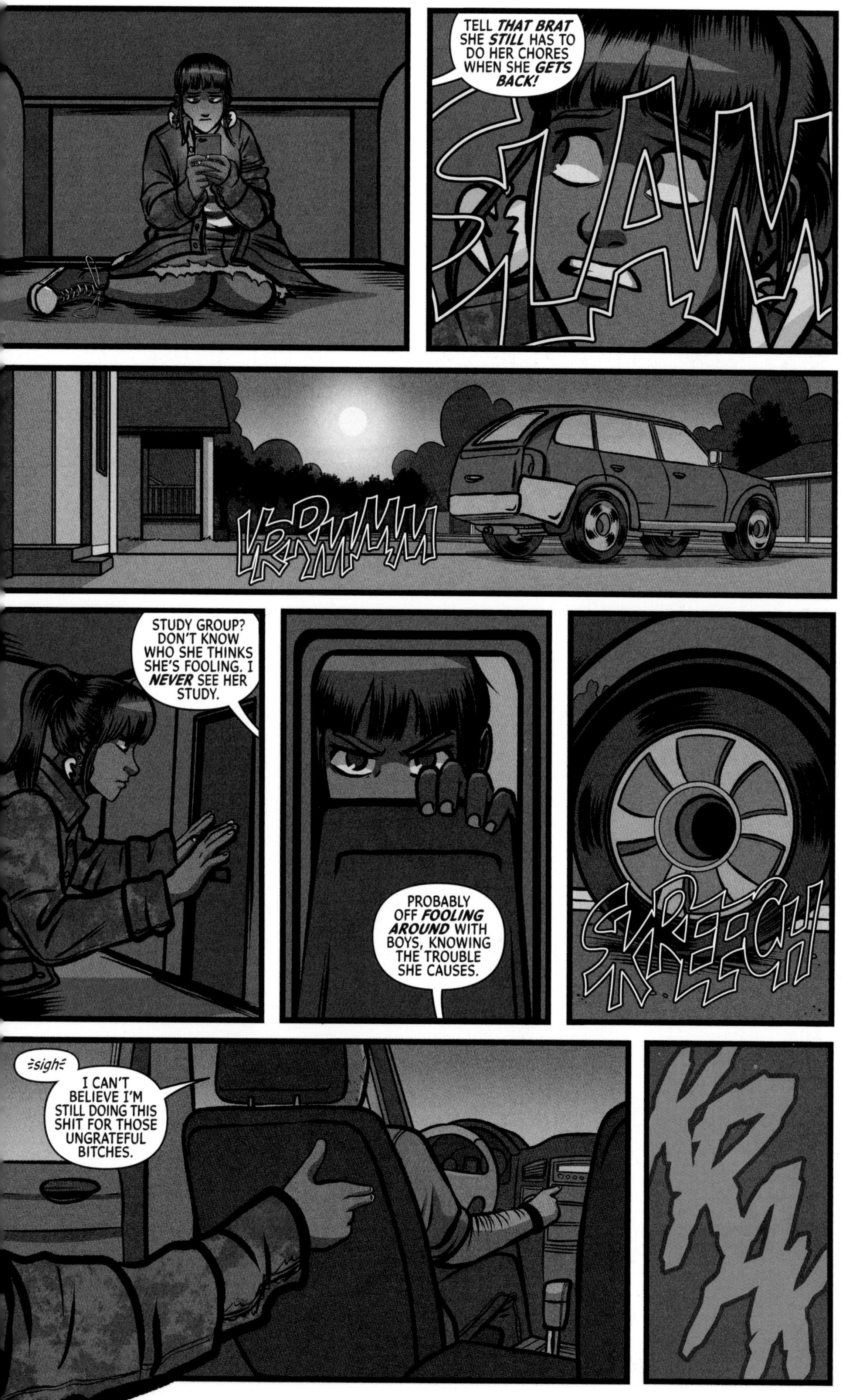
TELL THAT BRAT SHE STILL HAS TO DO HER CHORES WHEN SHE GETS BACK!
SLAM
VRRMMMM
STUDY GROUP? DON'T KNOW WHO SHE THINKS SHE'S FOOLING. I NEVER SEE HER STUDY.
PROBABLY OFF FOOLING AROUND WITH BOYS, KNOWING THE TROUBLE SHE CAUSES.
SKREECH
=sigh=
I CAN'T BELIEVE I'M STILL DOING THIS SHIT FOR THOSE UNGRATEFUL BITCHES.
KRA

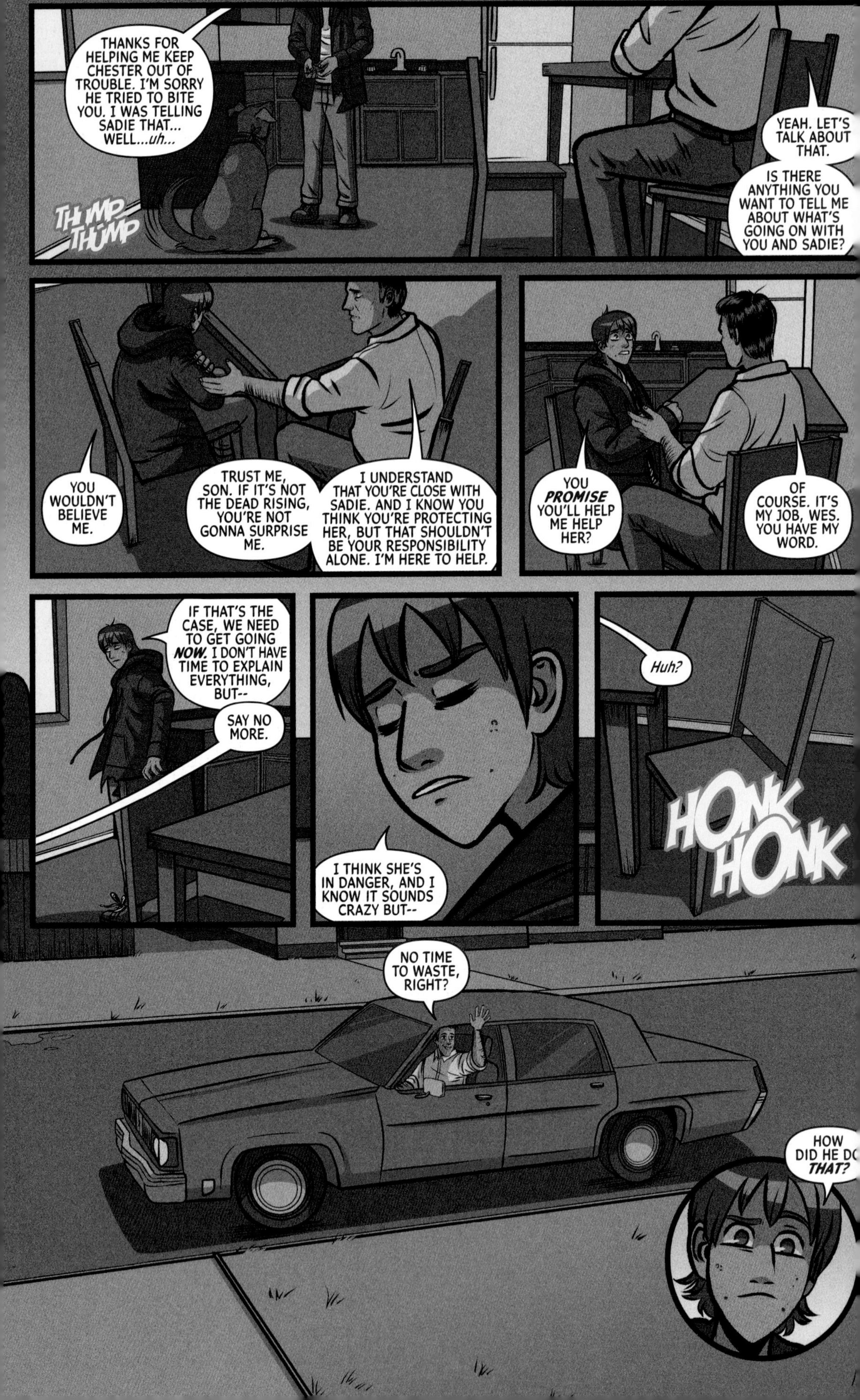
THANKS FOR HELPING ME KEEP CHESTER OUT OF TROUBLE. I'M SORRY HE TRIED TO BITE YOU. I WAS TELLING SADIE THAT... WELL...*uh...*
THUMP THUMP
YEAH. LET'S TALK ABOUT THAT.
IS THERE ANYTHING YOU WANT TO TELL ME ABOUT WHAT'S GOING ON WITH YOU AND SADIE?
YOU WOULDN'T BELIEVE ME.
TRUST ME, SON. IF IT'S NOT THE DEAD RISING, YOU'RE NOT GONNA SURPRISE ME.
I UNDERSTAND THAT YOU'RE CLOSE WITH SADIE. AND I KNOW YOU THINK YOU'RE PROTECTING HER, BUT THAT SHOULDN'T BE YOUR RESPONSIBILITY ALONE. I'M HERE TO HELP.
YOU ***PROMISE*** YOU'LL HELP ME HELP HER?
OF COURSE. IT'S MY JOB, WES. YOU HAVE MY WORD.
IF THAT'S THE CASE, WE NEED TO GET GOING ***NOW.*** I DON'T HAVE TIME TO EXPLAIN EVERYTHING, BUT--
SAY NO MORE.
I THINK SHE'S IN DANGER, AND I KNOW IT SOUNDS CRAZY BUT--
Huh?
HONK HONK
NO TIME TO WASTE, RIGHT?
HOW DID HE DO ***THAT?***

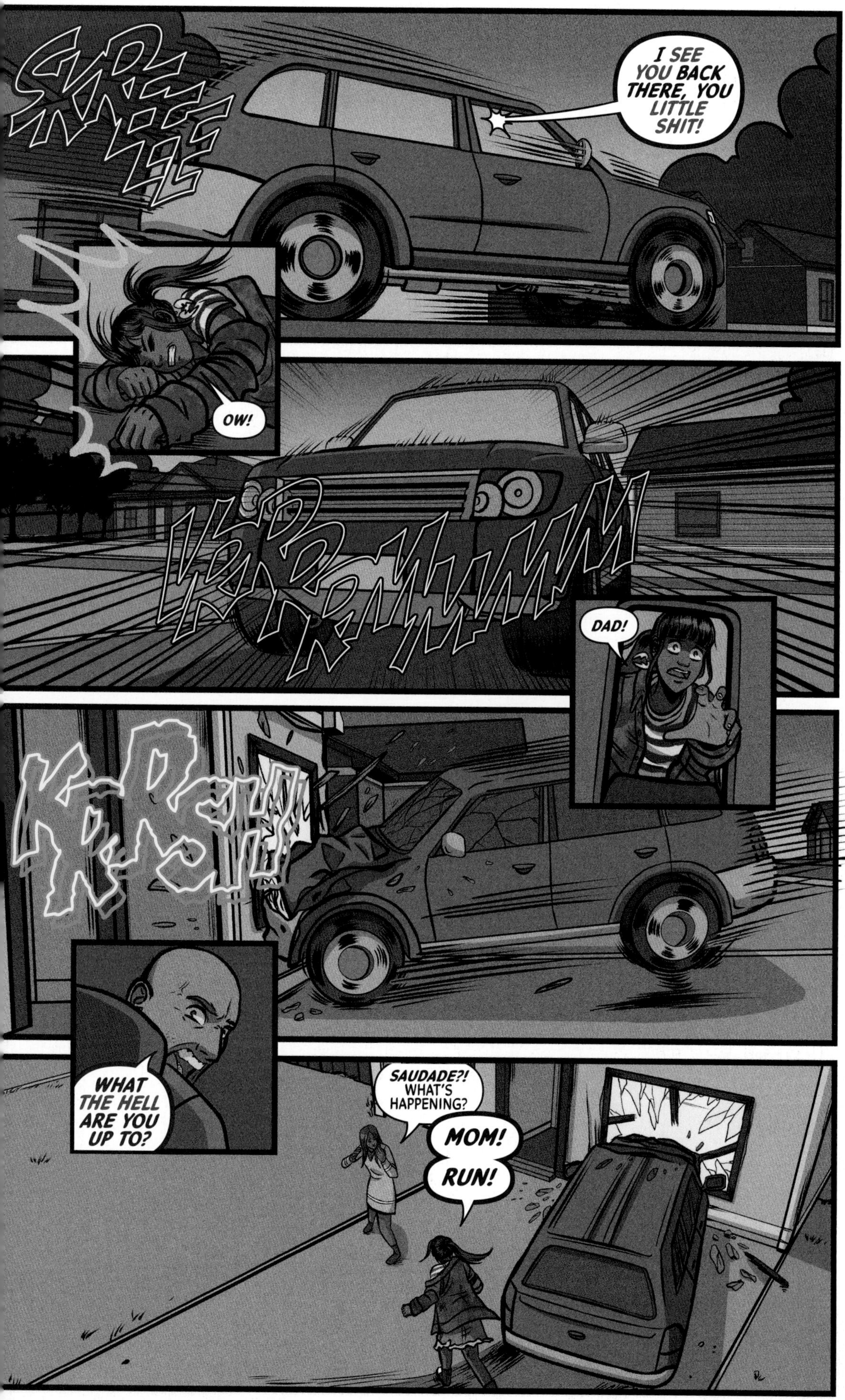
SKREEEEE
I SEE YOU BACK THERE, YOU LITTLE SHIT!
OW!
VRRRRMMMMM
DAD!
KRRSH!
WHAT THE HELL ARE YOU UP TO?
SAUDADE?! WHAT'S HAPPENING?
MOM!
RUN!

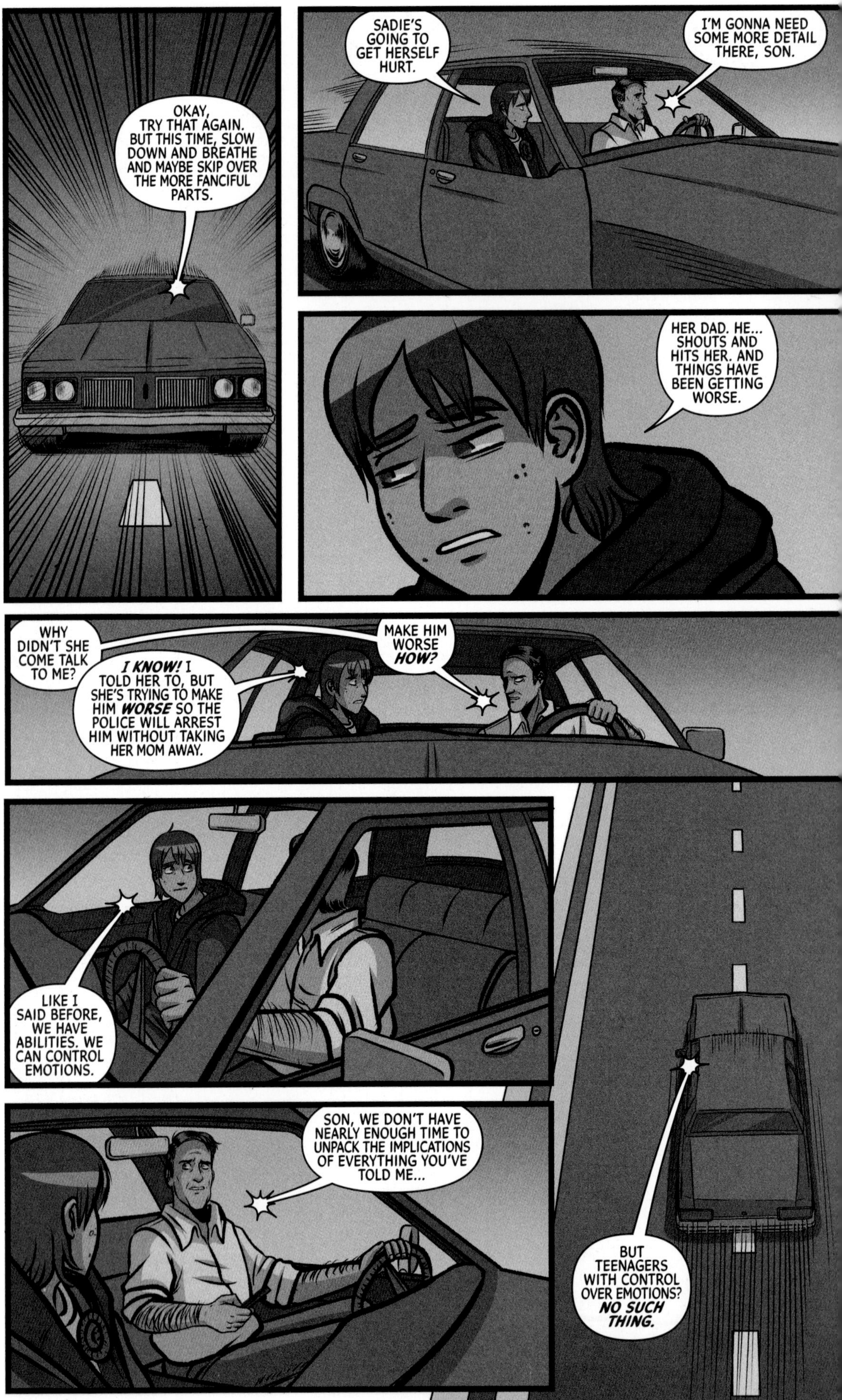
OKAY, TRY THAT AGAIN. BUT THIS TIME, SLOW DOWN AND BREATHE AND MAYBE SKIP OVER THE MORE FANCIFUL PARTS.
SADIE'S GOING TO GET HERSELF HURT.
I'M GONNA NEED SOME MORE DETAIL THERE, SON.
HER DAD. HE... SHOUTS AND HITS HER. AND THINGS HAVE BEEN GETTING WORSE.
WHY DIDN'T SHE COME TALK TO ME?
I KNOW! I TOLD HER TO, BUT SHE'S TRYING TO MAKE HIM WORSE SO THE POLICE WILL ARREST HIM WITHOUT TAKING HER MOM AWAY.
MAKE HIM WORSE HOW?
LIKE I SAID BEFORE, WE HAVE ABILITIES. WE CAN CONTROL EMOTIONS.
SON, WE DON'T HAVE NEARLY ENOUGH TIME TO UNPACK THE IMPLICATIONS OF EVERYTHING YOU'VE TOLD ME...
BUT TEENAGERS WITH CONTROL OVER EMOTIONS? NO SUCH THING.

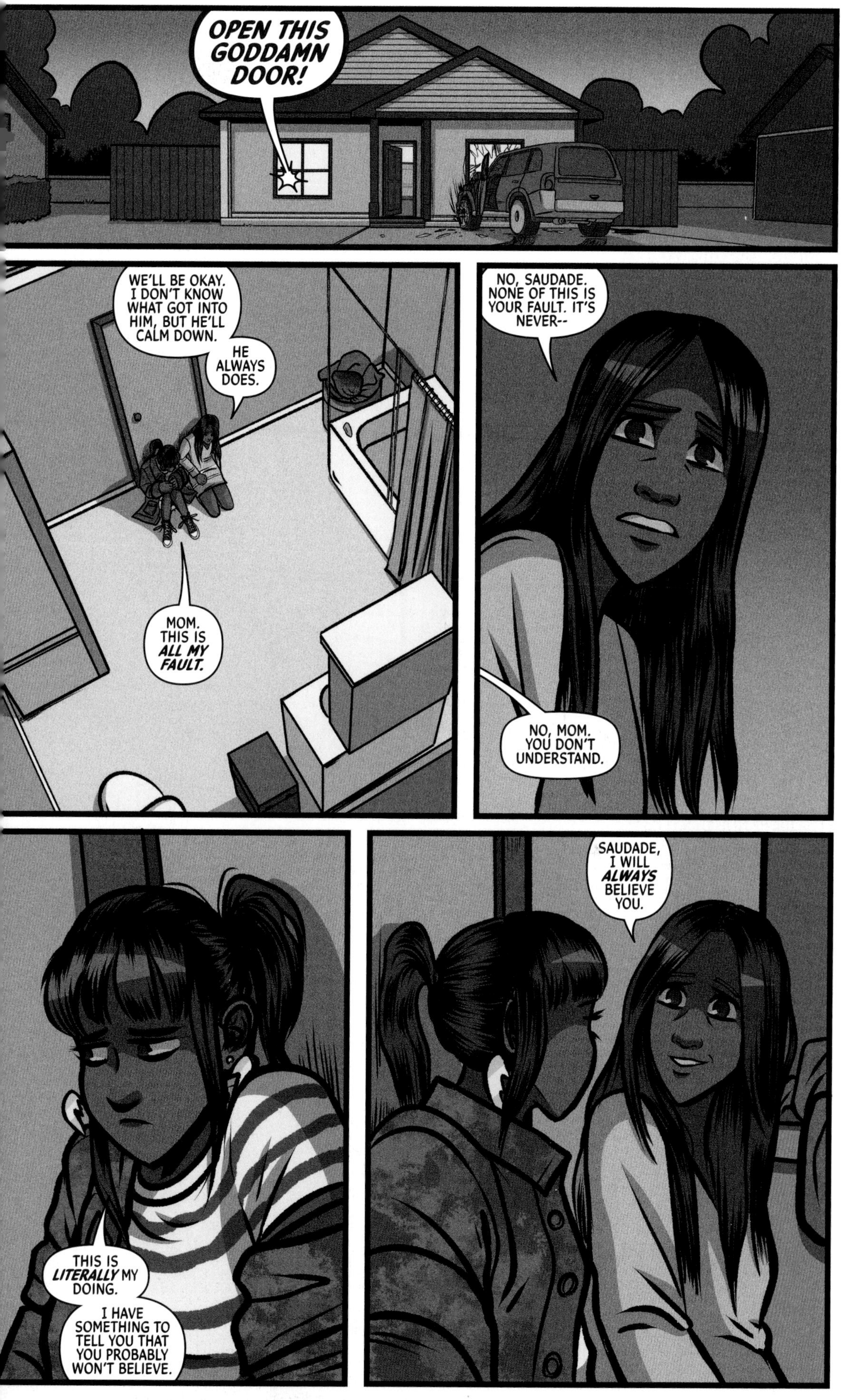
OPEN THIS GODDAMN DOOR!
WE'LL BE OKAY. I DON'T KNOW WHAT GOT INTO HIM, BUT HE'LL CALM DOWN.
HE ALWAYS DOES.
MOM. THIS IS ALL MY FAULT.
NO, SAUDADE. NONE OF THIS IS YOUR FAULT. IT'S NEVER--
NO, MOM. YOU DON'T UNDERSTAND.
THIS IS LITERALLY MY DOING.
I HAVE SOMETHING TO TELL YOU THAT YOU PROBABLY WON'T BELIEVE.
SAUDADE, I WILL ALWAYS BELIEVE YOU.

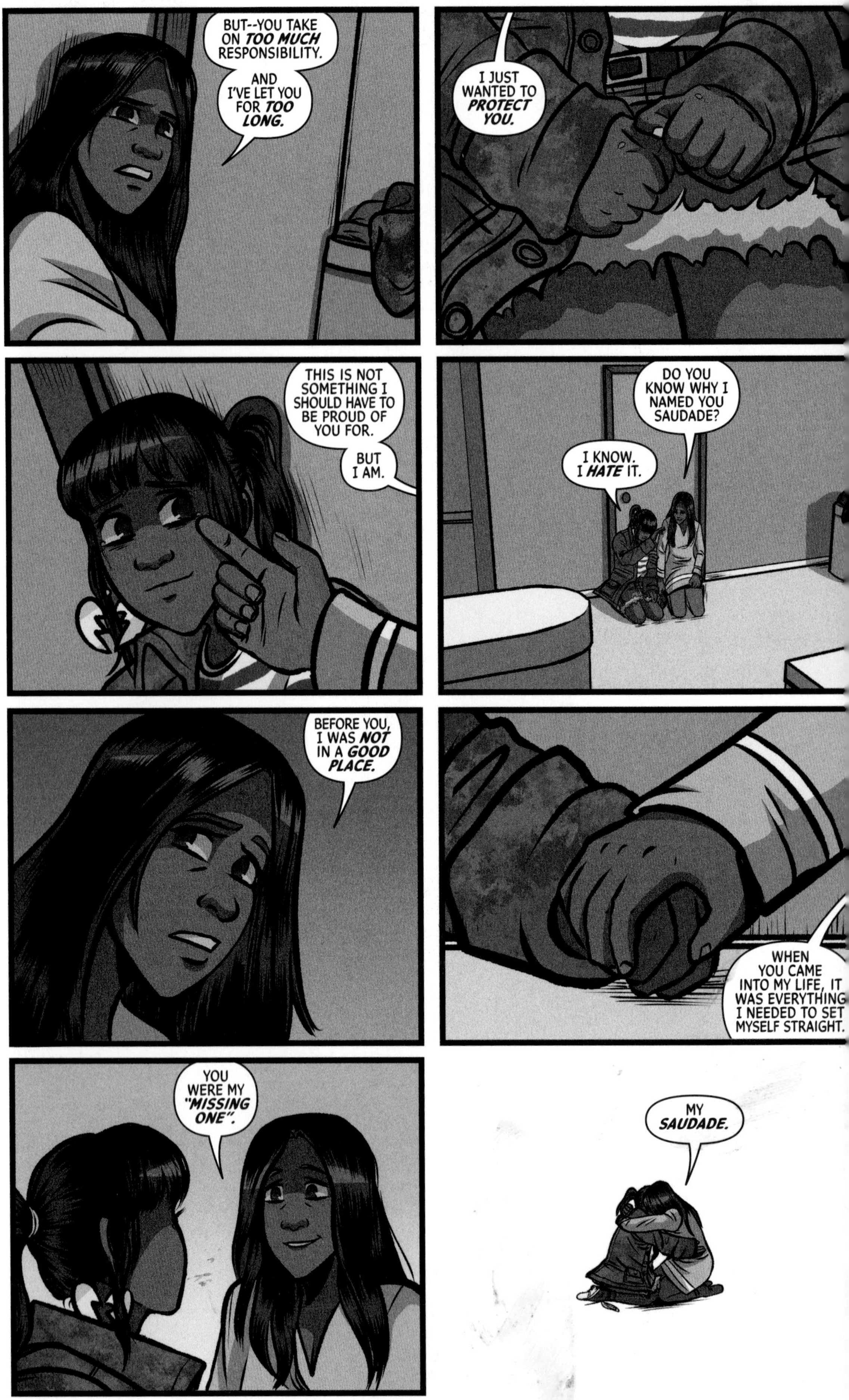
BUT--YOU TAKE ON *TOO MUCH* RESPONSIBILITY.
AND I'VE LET YOU FOR *TOO LONG.*
I JUST WANTED TO *PROTECT YOU.*
THIS IS NOT SOMETHING I SHOULD HAVE TO BE PROUD OF YOU FOR.
BUT I AM.
DO YOU KNOW WHY I NAMED YOU SAUDADE?
I KNOW. I *HATE* IT.
BEFORE YOU, I WAS *NOT* IN A *GOOD PLACE.*
WHEN YOU CAME INTO MY LIFE, IT WAS EVERYTHING I NEEDED TO SET MYSELF STRAIGHT.
YOU WERE MY *"MISSING ONE".*
MY *SAUDADE.*

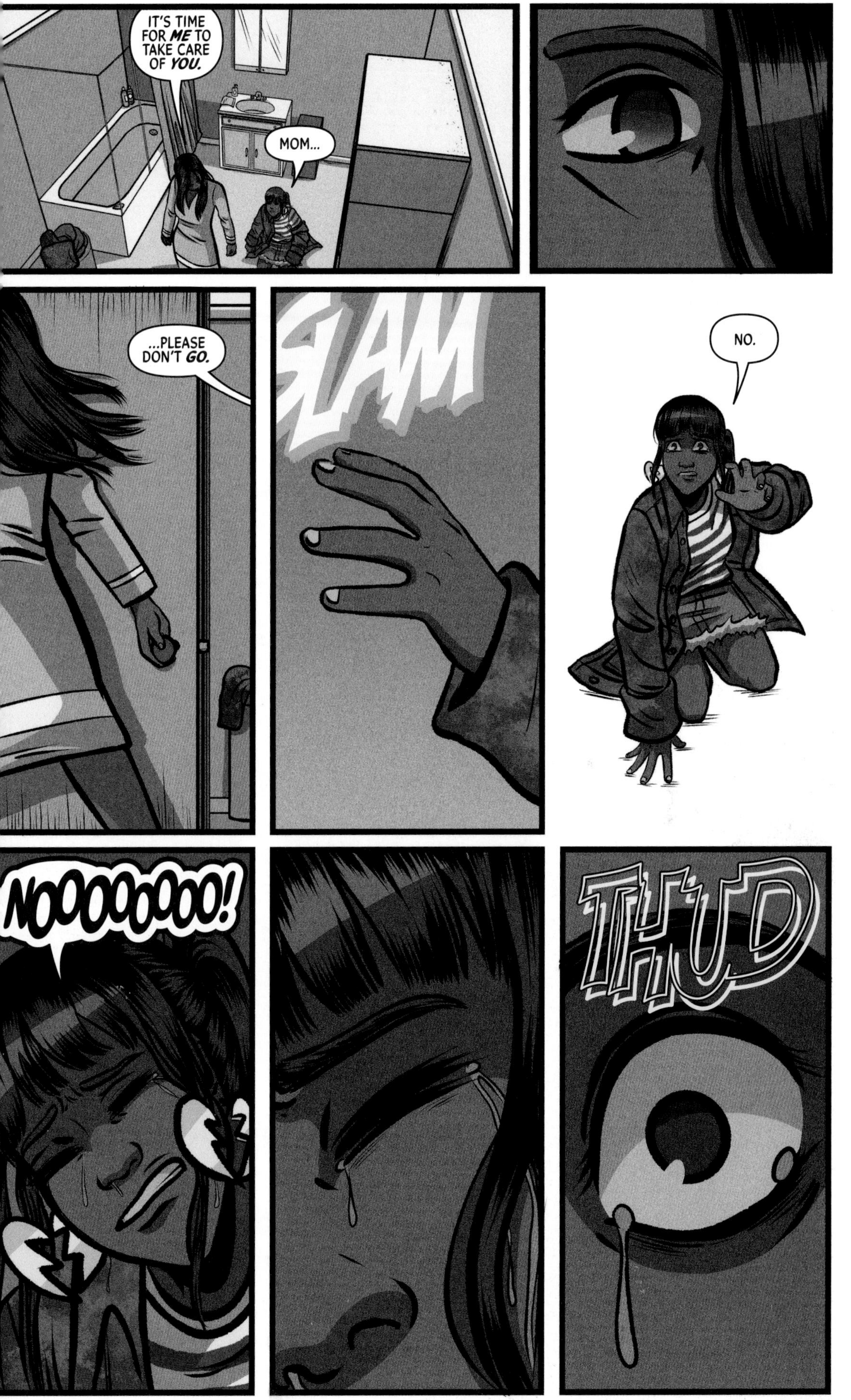
IT'S TIME FOR *ME* TO TAKE CARE OF *YOU.*
MOM...
...PLEASE DON'T *GO.*
SLAM
NO.
NOOOOOOOO!
THUD

SAUDADE. STAY BACK.

MAMA!

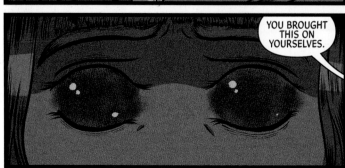

YOU BROUGHT THIS ON YOURSELVES.

I'VE HAD ENOUGH OF YOU BOTH.

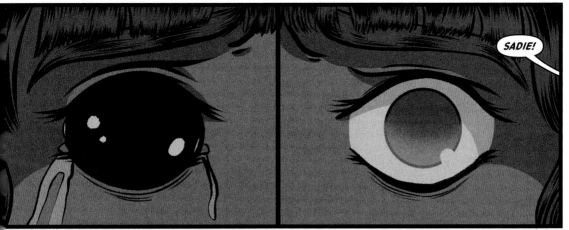
SADIE!

SORRY I'M LATE.

SAUDADE!

NO!

YOU DON'T *EVER* CALL ME *THAT*! I'M *HER* SAUDADE, NOT YOURS. *YOU COWARD.*

GET OUT OF MY HOUSE, YOU *WORTHLESS SHIT!*

DO YOU HEAR ME? **YOU'RE A COWARD!**

AND YOUR DAYS OF HURTING US *ARE OVER.*

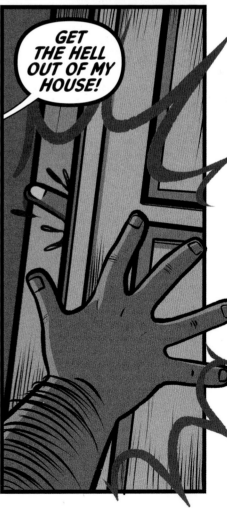
GET THE HELL OUT OF MY HOUSE!

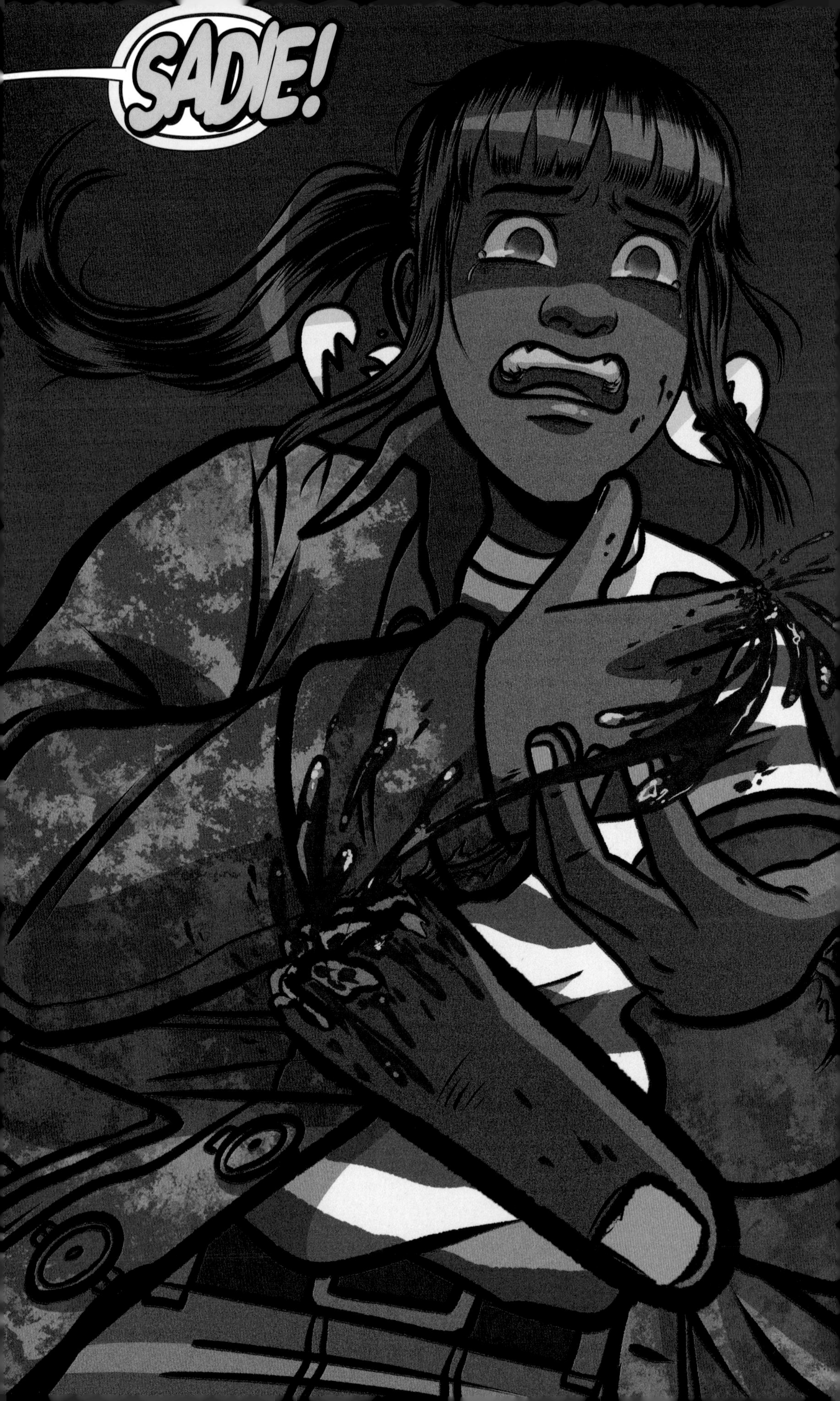
SADIE!

A PARTING SHOT

FIVE

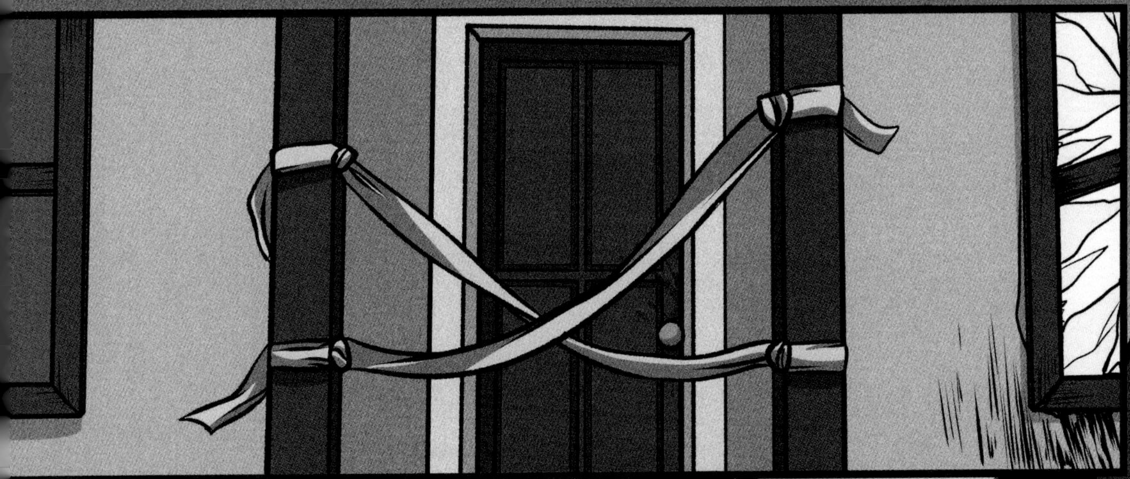

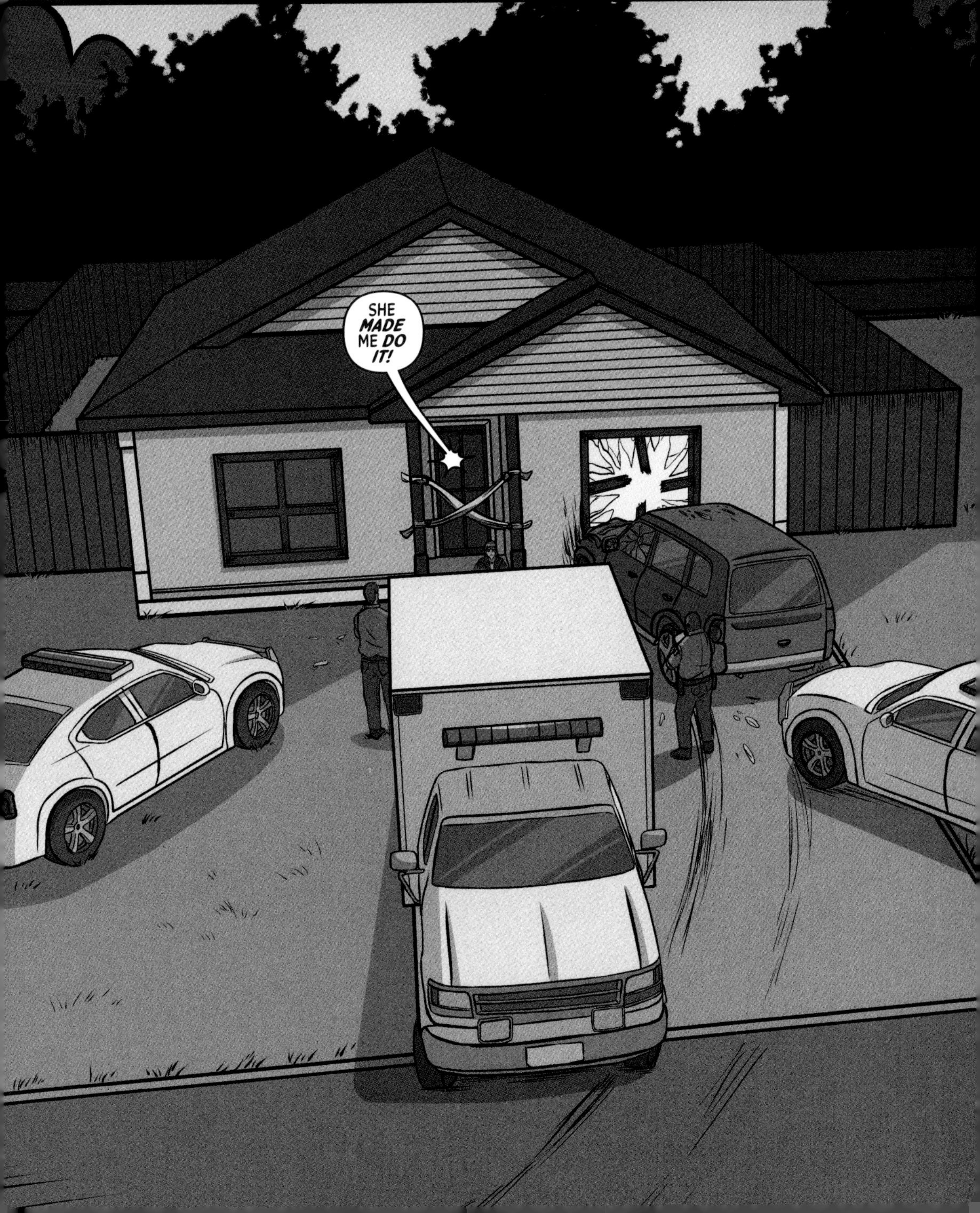
SHE *MADE* ME *DO IT!*

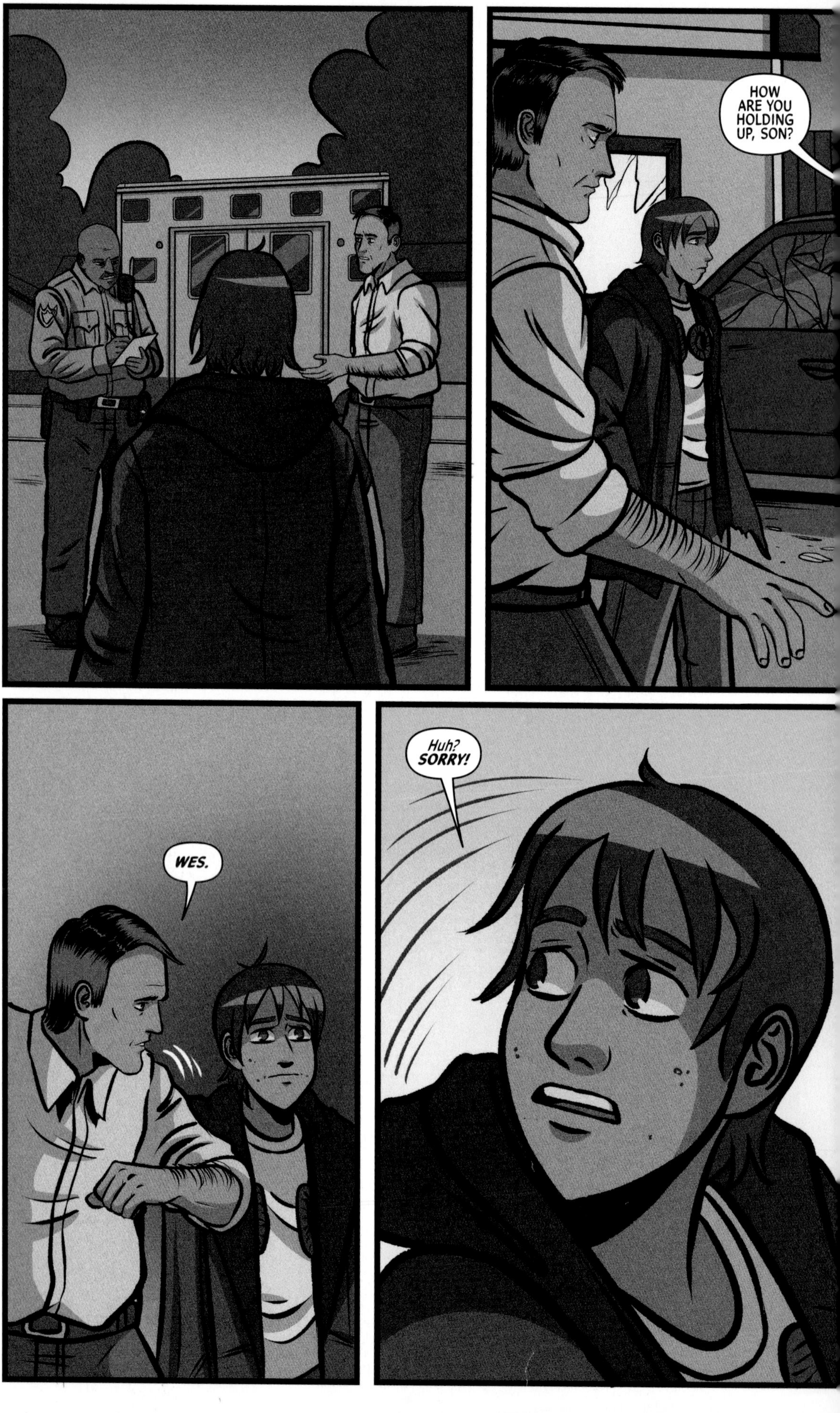
HOW ARE YOU HOLDING UP, SON?
WES.
Huh? SORRY!

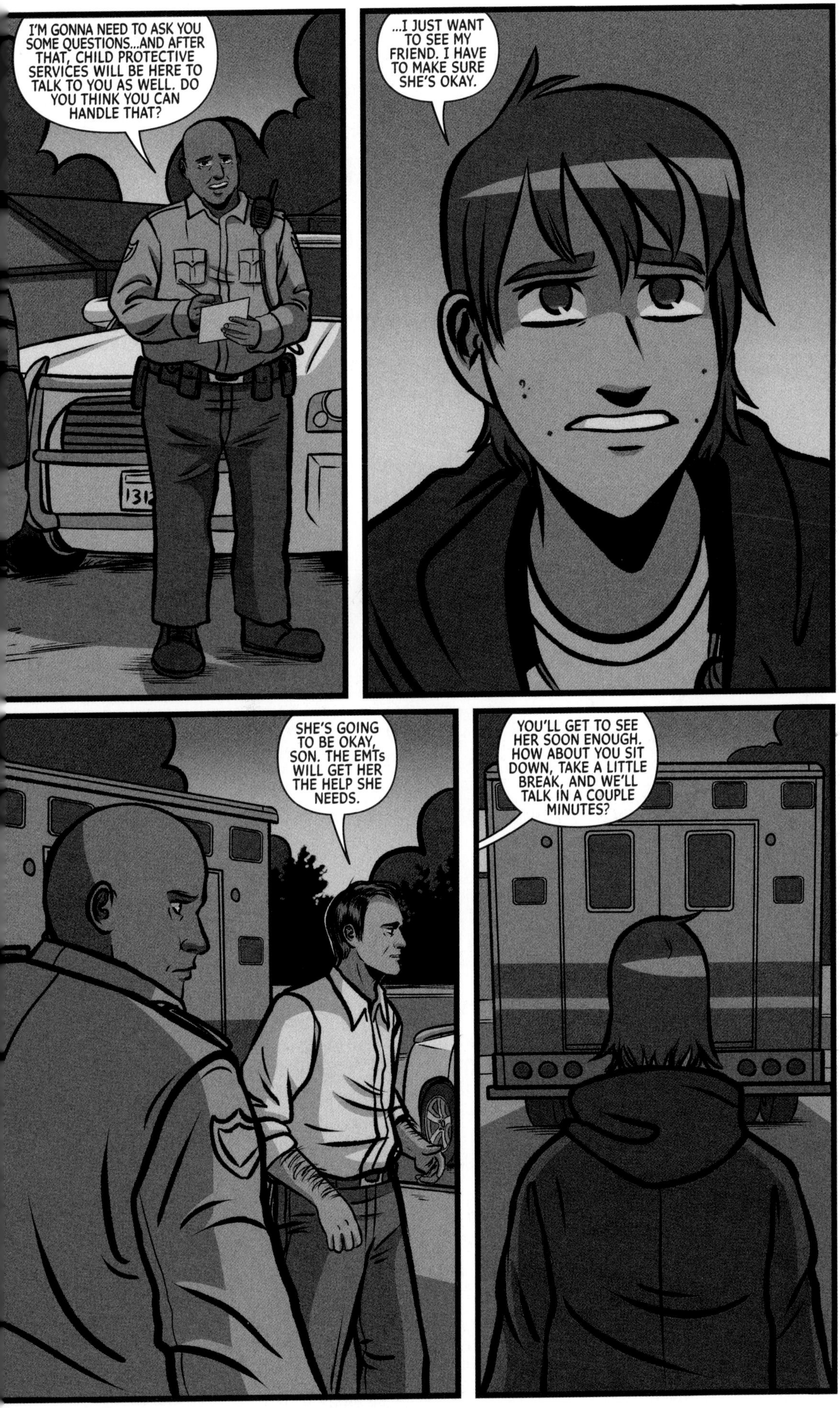
I'M GONNA NEED TO ASK YOU SOME QUESTIONS...AND AFTER THAT, CHILD PROTECTIVE SERVICES WILL BE HERE TO TALK TO YOU AS WELL. DO YOU THINK YOU CAN HANDLE THAT?
...I JUST WANT TO SEE MY FRIEND. I HAVE TO MAKE SURE SHE'S OKAY.
SHE'S GOING TO BE OKAY, SON. THE EMTs WILL GET HER THE HELP SHE NEEDS.
YOU'LL GET TO SEE HER SOON ENOUGH. HOW ABOUT YOU SIT DOWN, TAKE A LITTLE BREAK, AND WE'LL TALK IN A COUPLE MINUTES?

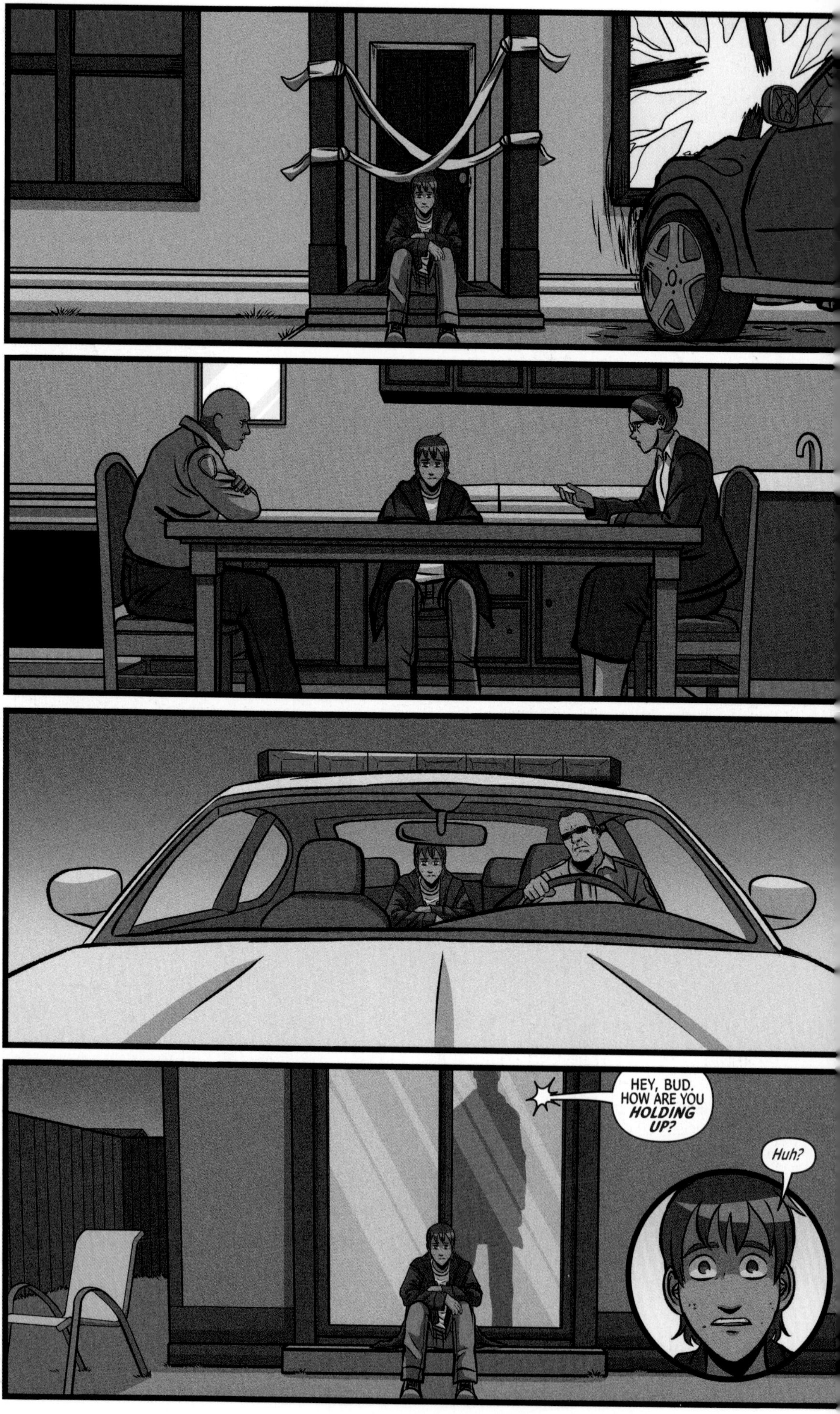
HEY, BUD. HOW ARE YOU HOLDING UP?
Huh?

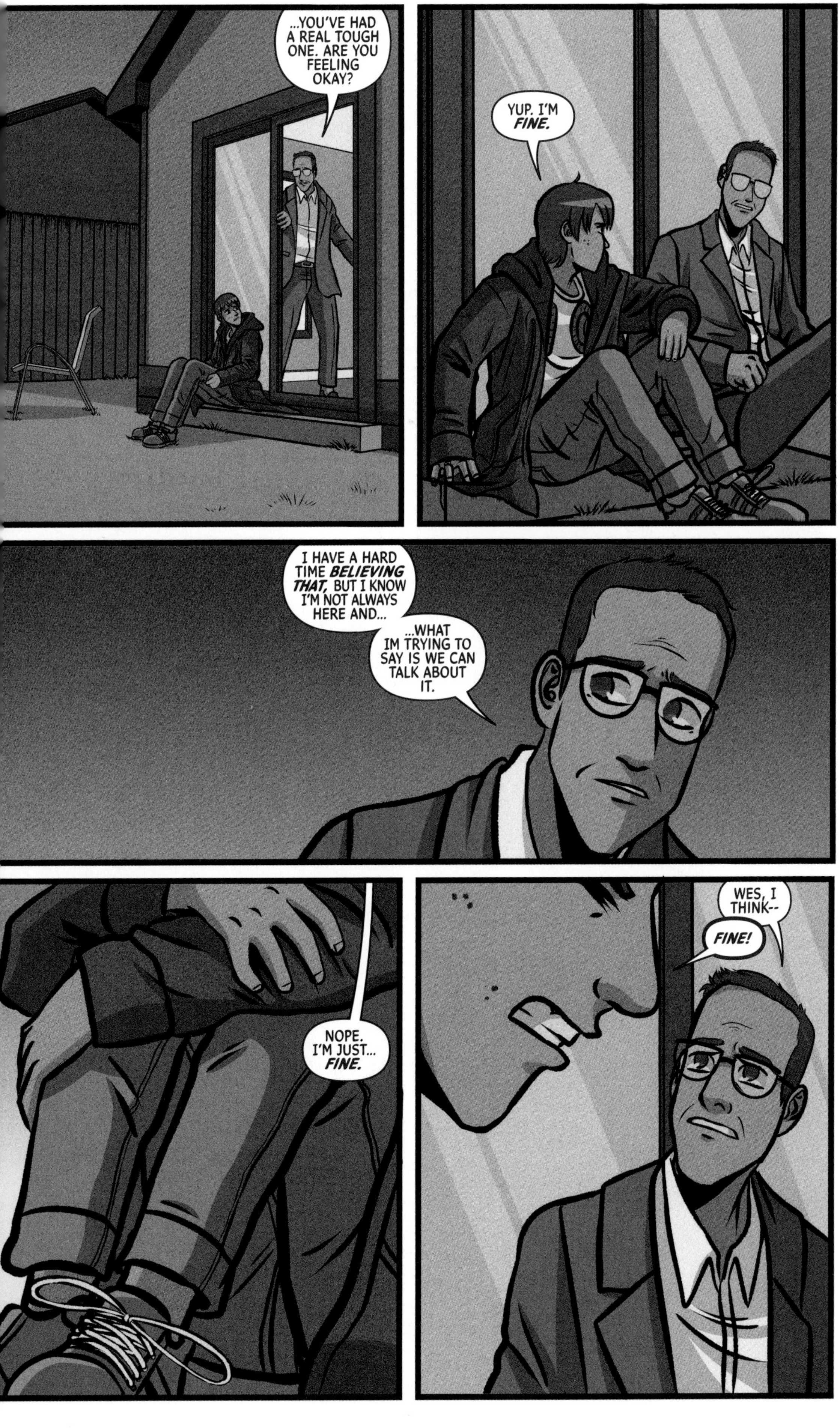
...YOU'VE HAD A REAL TOUGH ONE. ARE YOU FEELING OKAY?
YUP. I'M *FINE.*
I HAVE A HARD TIME *BELIEVING THAT,* BUT I KNOW I'M NOT ALWAYS HERE AND...
...WHAT IM TRYING TO SAY IS WE CAN TALK ABOUT IT.
NOPE. I'M JUST... *FINE.*
WES, I THINK--
FINE!

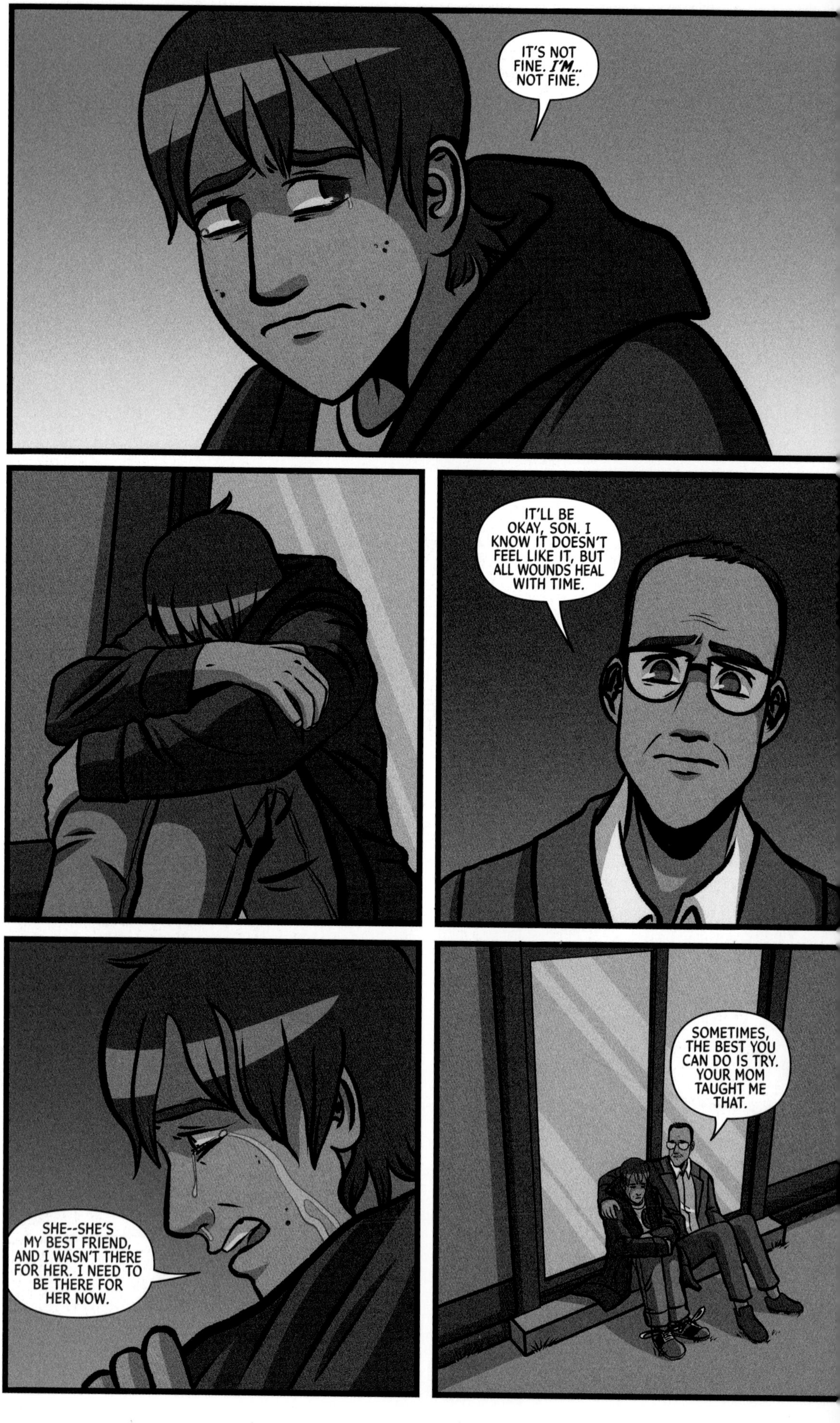
IT'S NOT FINE. *I'M...* NOT FINE.
IT'LL BE OKAY, SON. I KNOW IT DOESN'T FEEL LIKE IT, BUT ALL WOUNDS HEAL WITH TIME.
SHE--SHE'S MY BEST FRIEND, AND I WASN'T THERE FOR HER. I NEED TO BE THERE FOR HER NOW.
SOMETIMES, THE BEST YOU CAN DO IS TRY. YOUR MOM TAUGHT ME THAT.

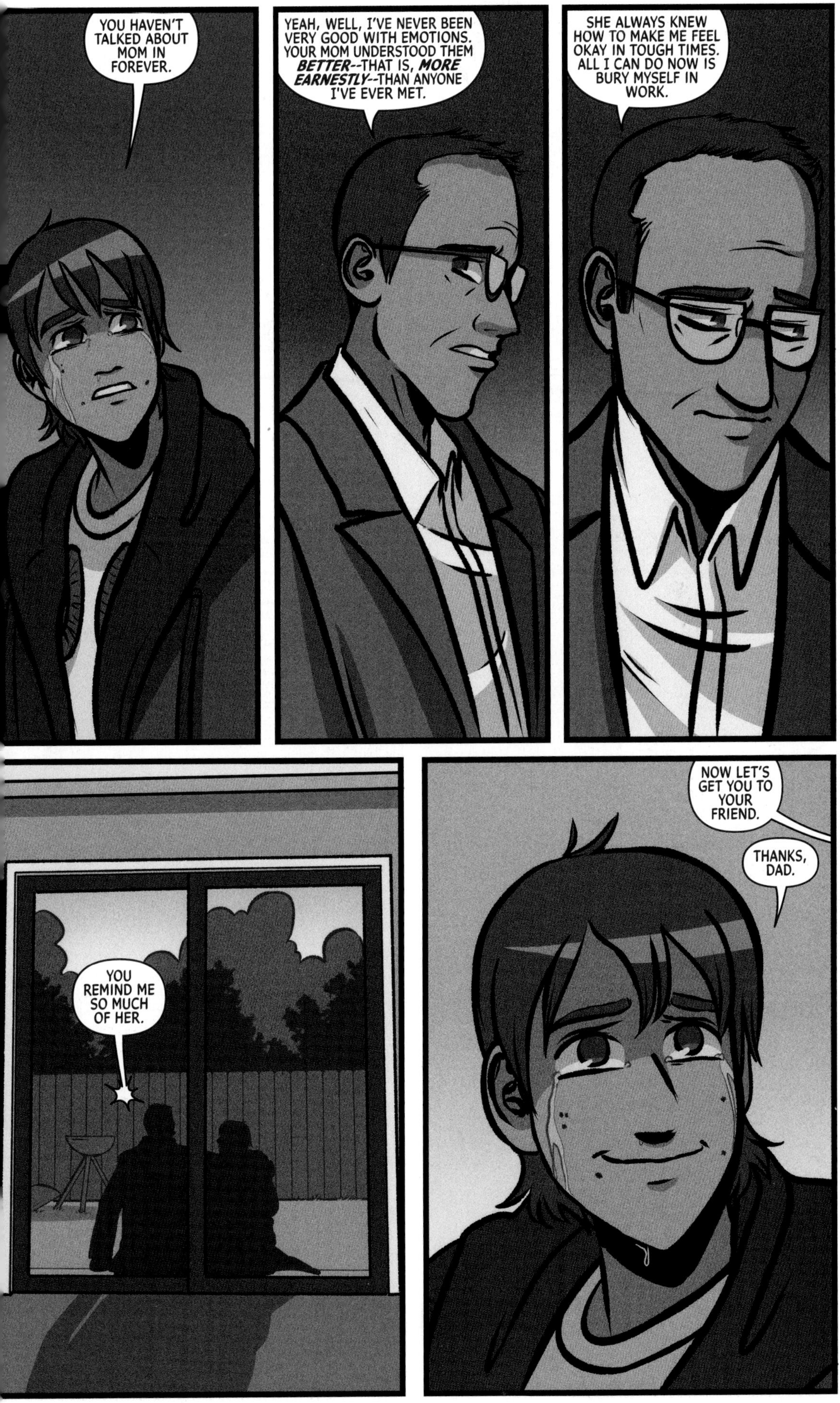
YOU HAVEN'T TALKED ABOUT MOM IN FOREVER.
YEAH, WELL, I'VE NEVER BEEN VERY GOOD WITH EMOTIONS. YOUR MOM UNDERSTOOD THEM BETTER--THAT IS, MORE EARNESTLY--THAN ANYONE I'VE EVER MET.
SHE ALWAYS KNEW HOW TO MAKE ME FEEL OKAY IN TOUGH TIMES. ALL I CAN DO NOW IS BURY MYSELF IN WORK.
YOU REMIND ME SO MUCH OF HER.
NOW LET'S GET YOU TO YOUR FRIEND.
THANKS, DAD.

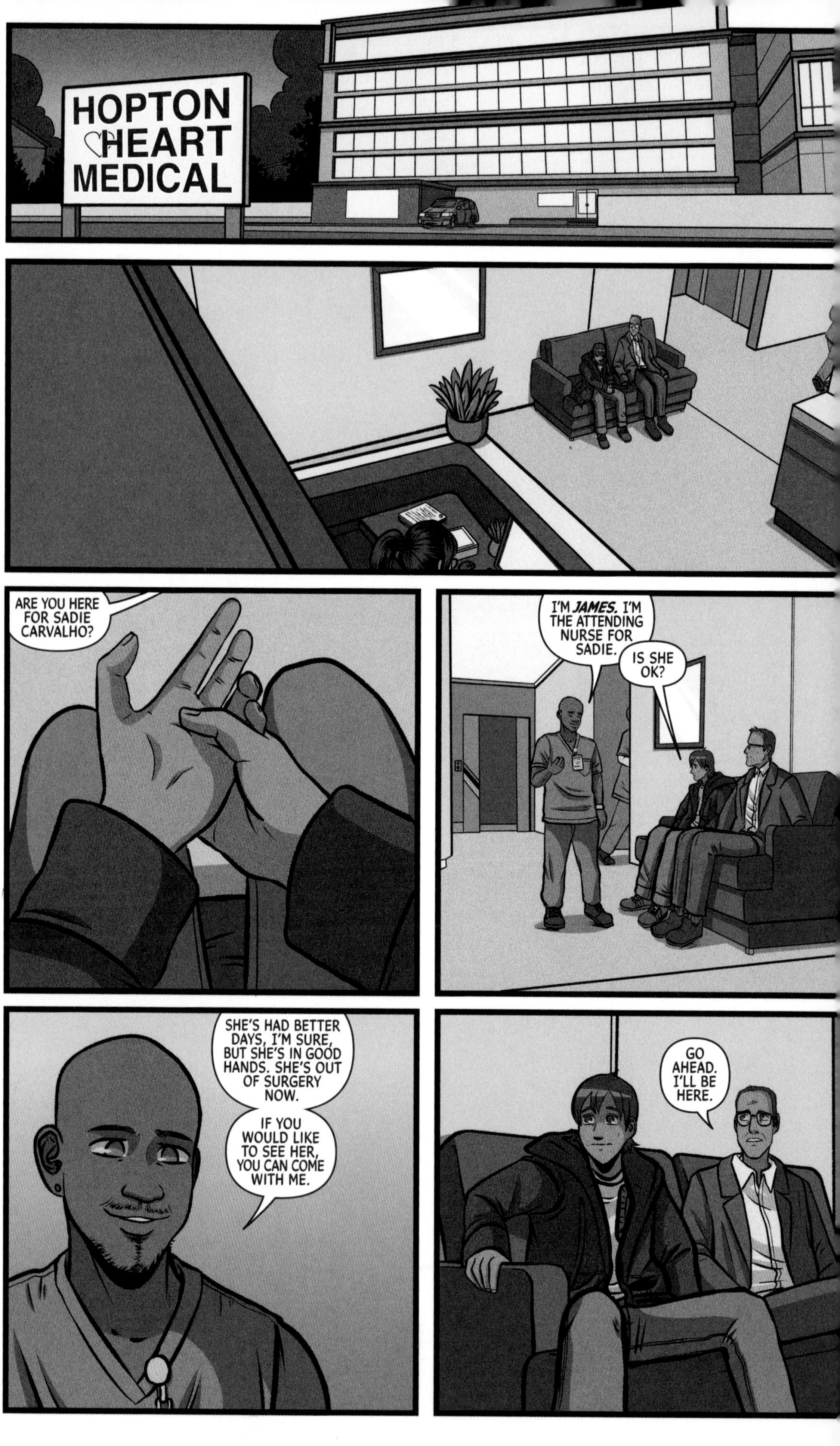

HOPTON HEART MEDICAL
ARE YOU HERE FOR SADIE CARVALHO?
I'M *JAMES.* I'M THE ATTENDING NURSE FOR SADIE.
IS SHE OK?
SHE'S HAD BETTER DAYS, I'M SURE, BUT SHE'S IN GOOD HANDS. SHE'S OUT OF SURGERY NOW.
IF YOU WOULD LIKE TO SEE HER, YOU CAN COME WITH ME.
GO AHEAD. I'LL BE HERE.

NÓ
NÓK

HEY, SADIE. YOUR FRIEND IS HERE TO SEE YOU.

I'LL LEAVE YOU TO IT. JUST RING IF YOU NEED ME, SADIE.

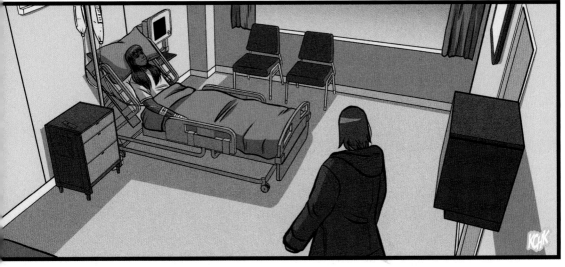

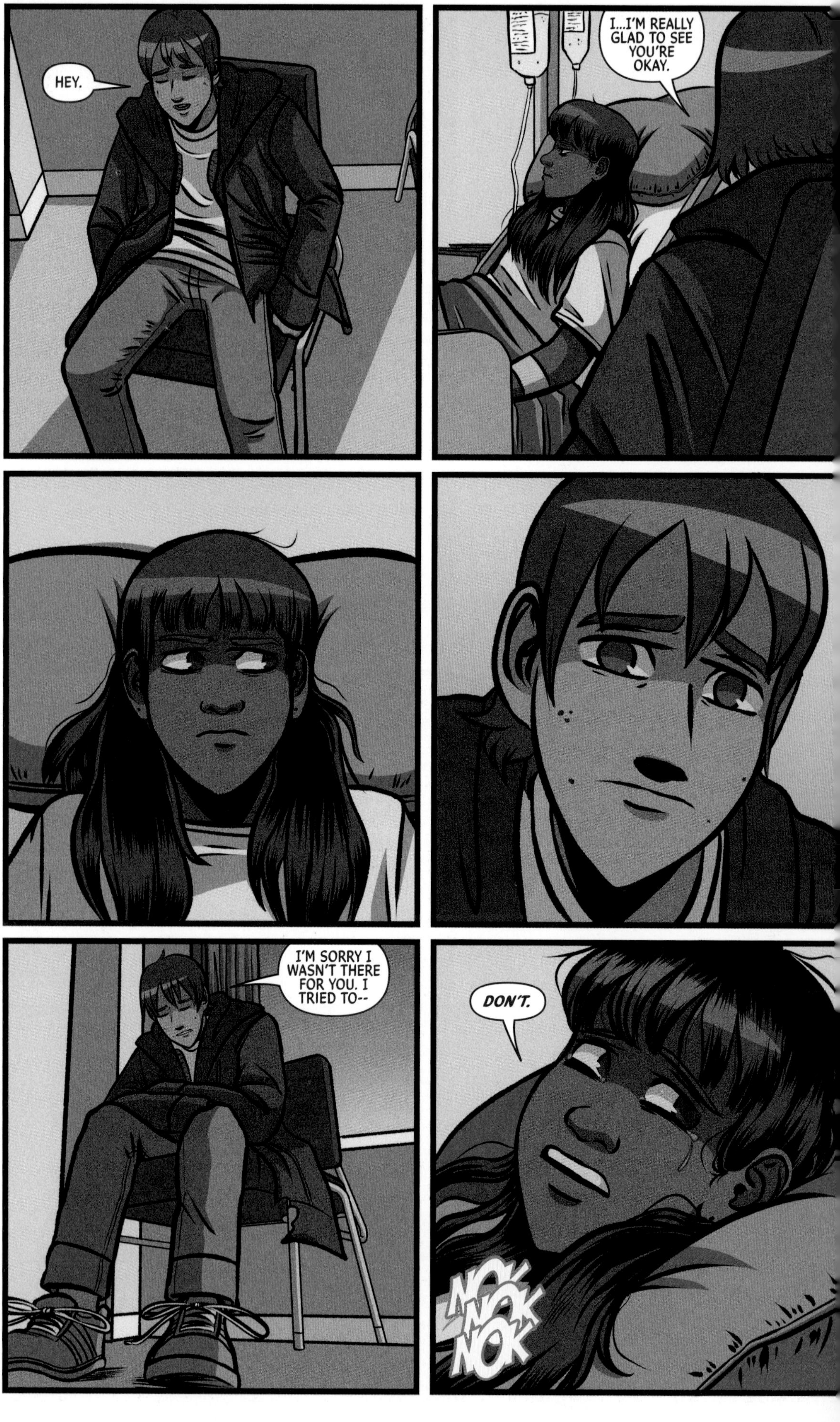
HEY.
I...I'M REALLY GLAD TO SEE YOU'RE OKAY.
I'M SORRY I WASN'T THERE FOR YOU. I TRIED TO--
DON'T.
NOK NOK NOK

HELLO, SORRY TO INTRUDE.

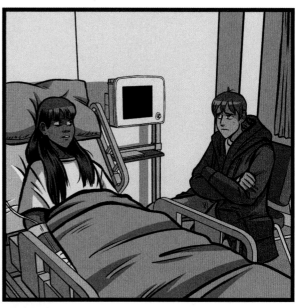

SADIE, ARE YOU COMFORTABLE DISCUSSING YOUR MEDICAL PROCEDURE IN FRONT OF YOUR FRIEND HERE?

YEAH, IT'S FINE.

WELL, I'M HAPPY TO SAY THAT I COME BEARING GOOD NEWS.

THE REATTACHMENT WAS VERY SUCCESSFUL.

WE WERE ABLE TO REPAIR YOUR EXTENSOR AND FLEXOR TENDONS, AND THE BODY IS PRETTY DARN GOOD AT HEALING AROUND DAMAGED SAGITTAL BANDS-- THE LITTLE GUYS THAT HELP KEEP YOUR FINGER STABLE. WHICH MEANS...

...WHILE IT MAY TAKE A WHILE, WITH HARD WORK AND PHYSICAL THERAPY YOU SHOULD BE ABLE TO REGAIN MOST--

--IF NOT ALL--

--OF YOUR RANGE OF MOTION AND STRENGTH.

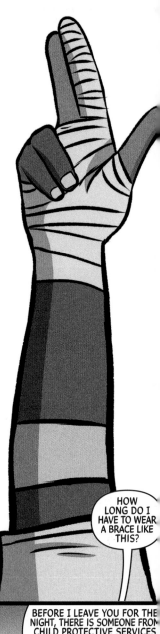

HOW LONG DO I HAVE TO WEAR A BRACE LIKE THIS?

IT ALL DEPENDS ON HOW IT HEALS. WE'RE GONNA HAVE TO FEEL IT OUT AS WE GO, BUT IT'S VERY IMPORTANT TO LEAVE THE BRACE ON UNTIL YOUR *PT* SAYS IT'S READY TO COME OFF.

BEFORE I LEAVE YOU FOR THE NIGHT, THERE IS SOMEONE FROM CHILD PROTECTIVE SERVICES HERE TO TALK TO YOU...AND YOUR FRIEND IS GONNA HAVE TO STEP OUTSIDE WHILE THEY ASK YOU SOME QUESTIONS.

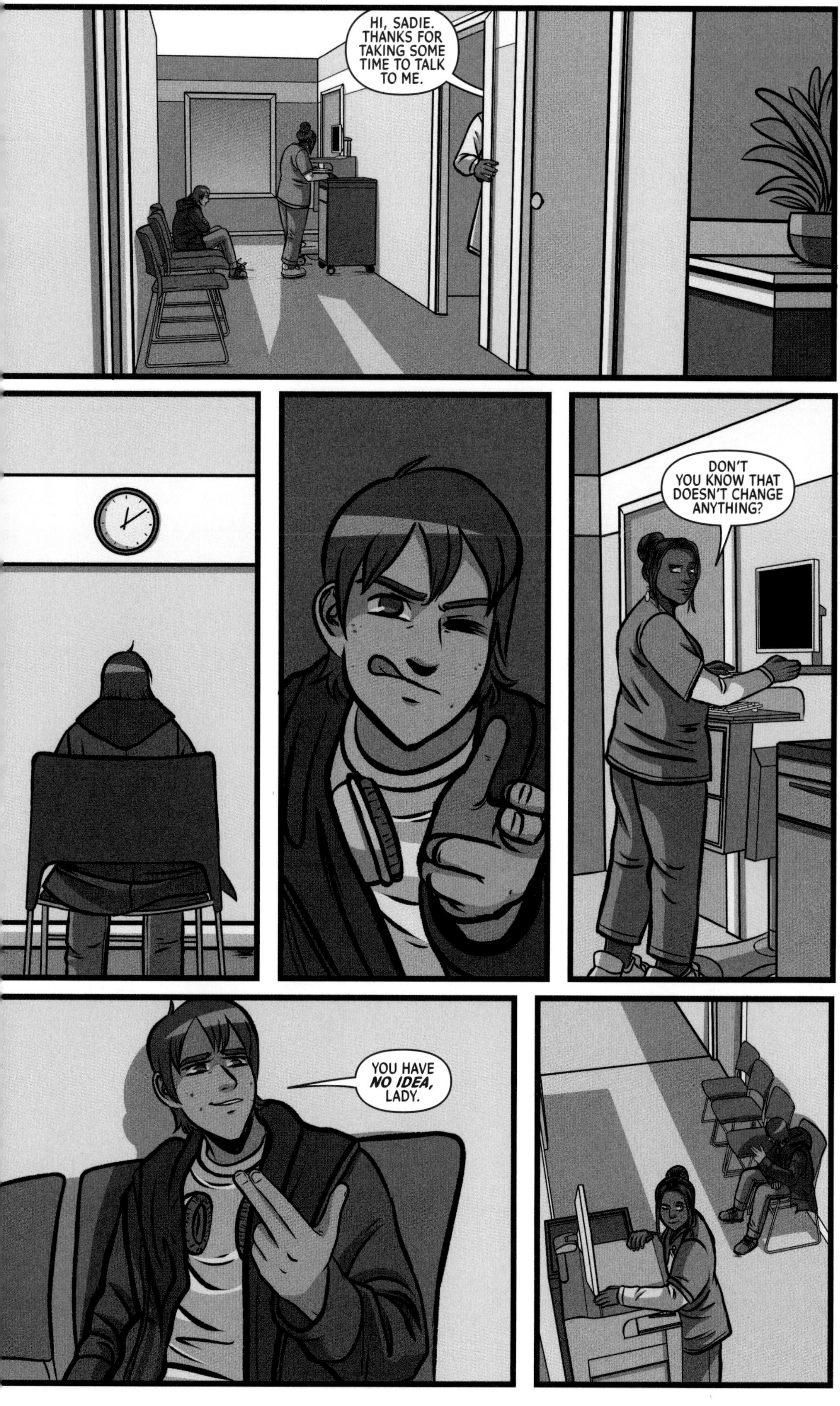
HI, SADIE. THANKS FOR TAKING SOME TIME TO TALK TO ME.
DON'T YOU KNOW THAT DOESN'T CHANGE ANYTHING?
YOU HAVE *NO IDEA,* LADY.

THANKS FOR LETTING US BORROW HER.

SHE'S ALL YOURS NOW.

HEY. HOW'D IT GO?

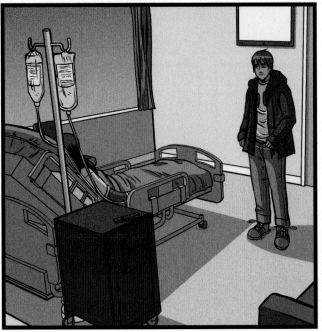

SADIE, I'M SO SORRY. I SHOULD'VE BEEN A BETTER FRIEND.

NO.

THIS WASN'T *YOUR* FAULT. IT'S MINE. I DID THIS.

I SHOULD'VE LISTENED. I WAS STUPID.

THIS ISN'T YOUR FAULT. YOUR DAD...

...SOMETHING HAD TO BE--

NO, I MESSED UP. I *KNEW* HE'D GET MAD IF I *PROVOKED* HIM. I KNEW I WASN'T GOING TO CHANGE HIM, BUT *I DIDN'T CARE.*

I EVEN *LOOKED FOR REASONS* TO DO IT. THE WHOLE THING WITH THE *LIFE INSURANCE* WAS *SO STUPID!*

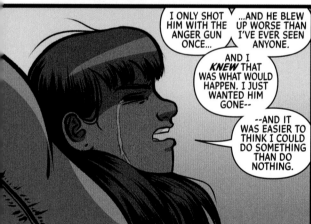

I ONLY SHOT HIM WITH THE ANGER GUN ONCE...

...AND HE BLEW UP WORSE THAN I'VE EVER SEEN ANYONE.

AND I *KNEW* THAT WAS WHAT WOULD HAPPEN. I JUST WANTED HIM GONE--

--AND IT WAS EASIER TO THINK I COULD DO SOMETHING THAN DO NOTHING.

I JUST WISH I WAS ABLE TO CONTROL MYSELF.

BUT... YOU *WEREN'T WRONG.* HE WAS A *DANGER* TO YOU *AND* YOUR MOM.

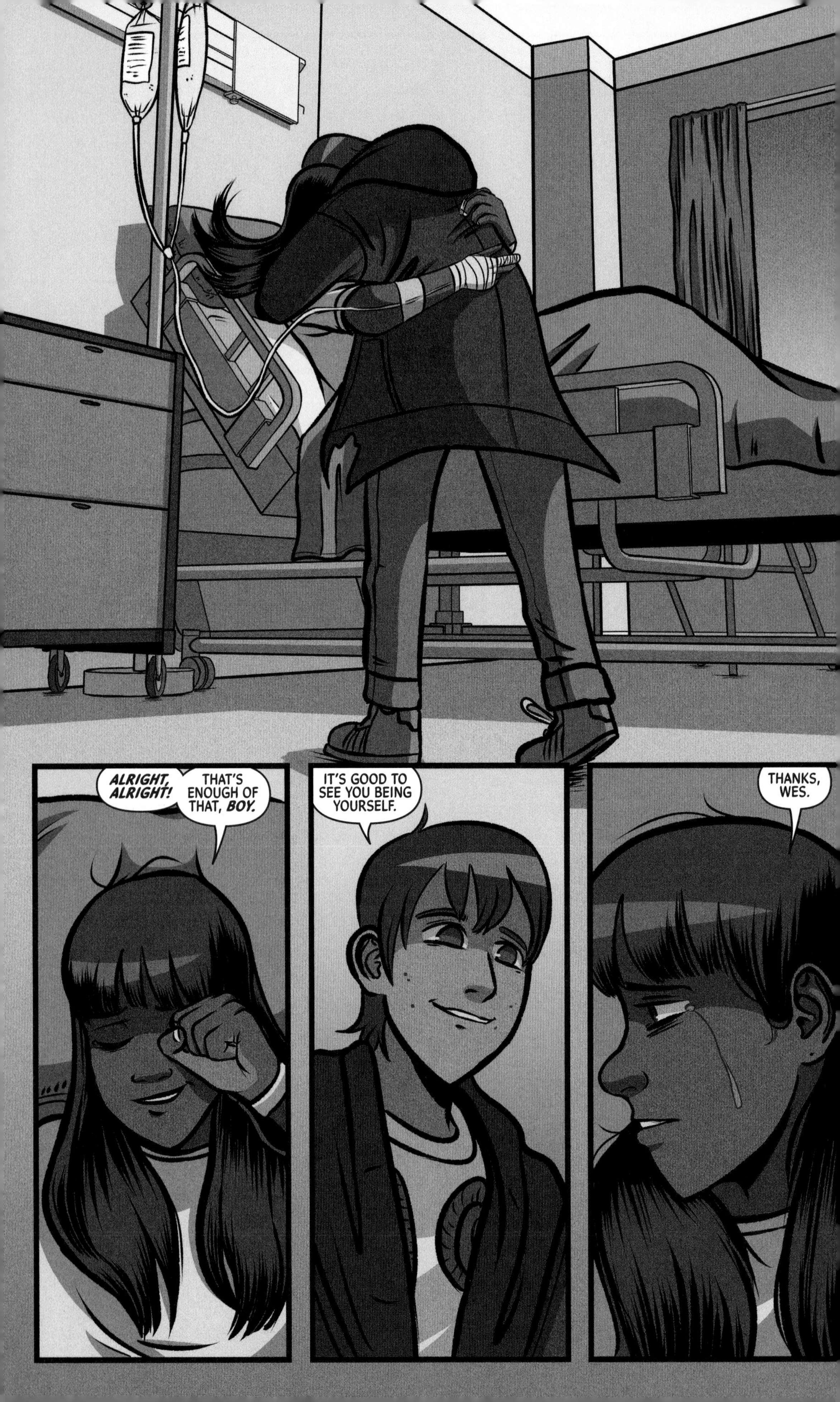
ALRIGHT, ALRIGHT!
THAT'S ENOUGH OF THAT, *BOY.*
IT'S GOOD TO SEE YOU BEING YOURSELF.
THANKS, WES.

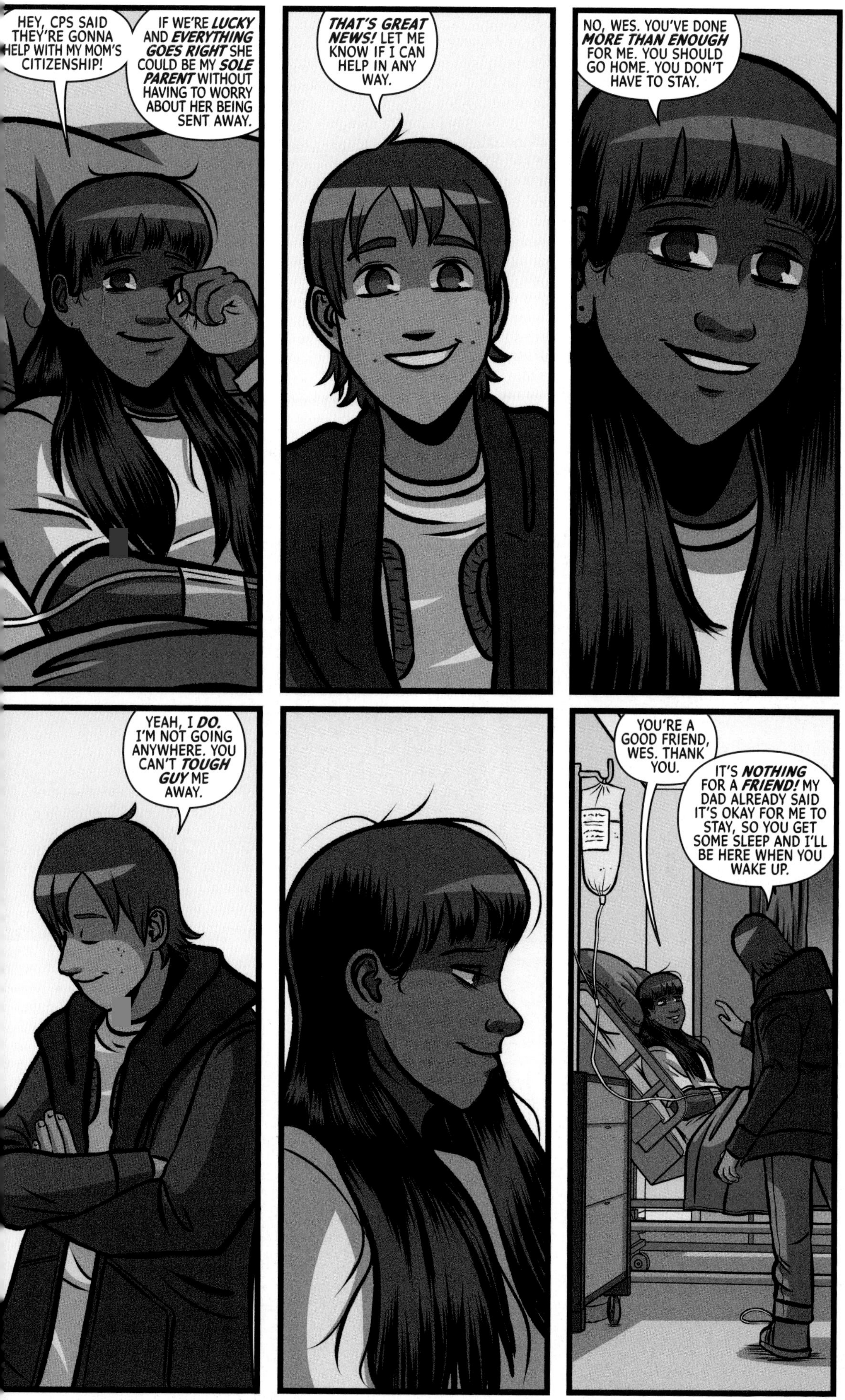

HEY, CPS SAID THEY'RE GONNA HELP WITH MY MOM'S CITIZENSHIP!
IF WE'RE LUCKY AND EVERYTHING GOES RIGHT SHE COULD BE MY SOLE PARENT WITHOUT HAVING TO WORRY ABOUT HER BEING SENT AWAY.
THAT'S GREAT NEWS! LET ME KNOW IF I CAN HELP IN ANY WAY.
NO, WES. YOU'VE DONE MORE THAN ENOUGH FOR ME. YOU SHOULD GO HOME. YOU DON'T HAVE TO STAY.
YEAH, I DO. I'M NOT GOING ANYWHERE. YOU CAN'T TOUGH GUY ME AWAY.
YOU'RE A GOOD FRIEND, WES. THANK YOU.
IT'S NOTHING FOR A FRIEND! MY DAD ALREADY SAID IT'S OKAY FOR ME TO STAY, SO YOU GET SOME SLEEP AND I'LL BE HERE WHEN YOU WAKE UP.

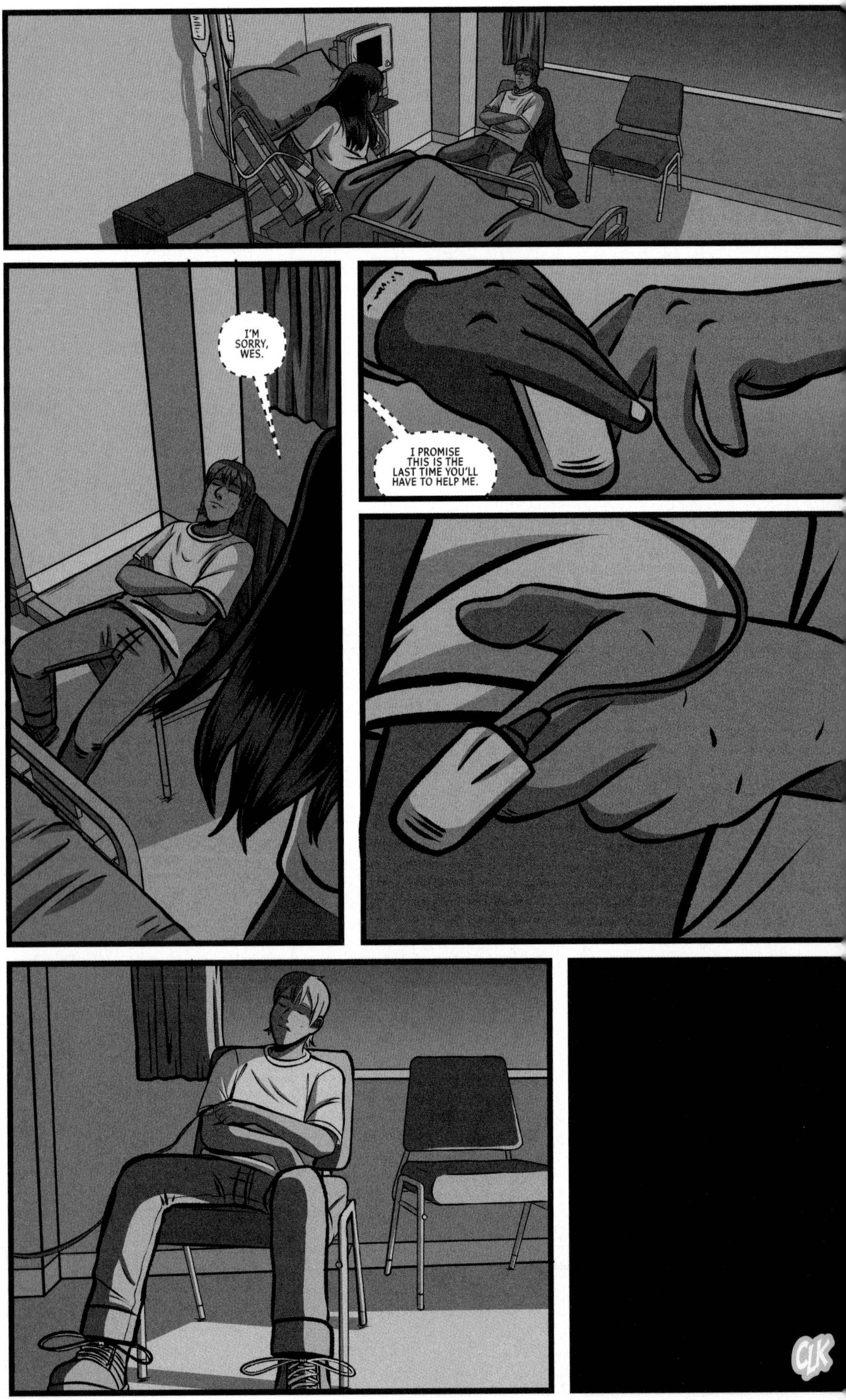
I'M SORRY, WES.
I PROMISE THIS IS THE LAST TIME YOU'LL HAVE TO HELP ME.
CLK

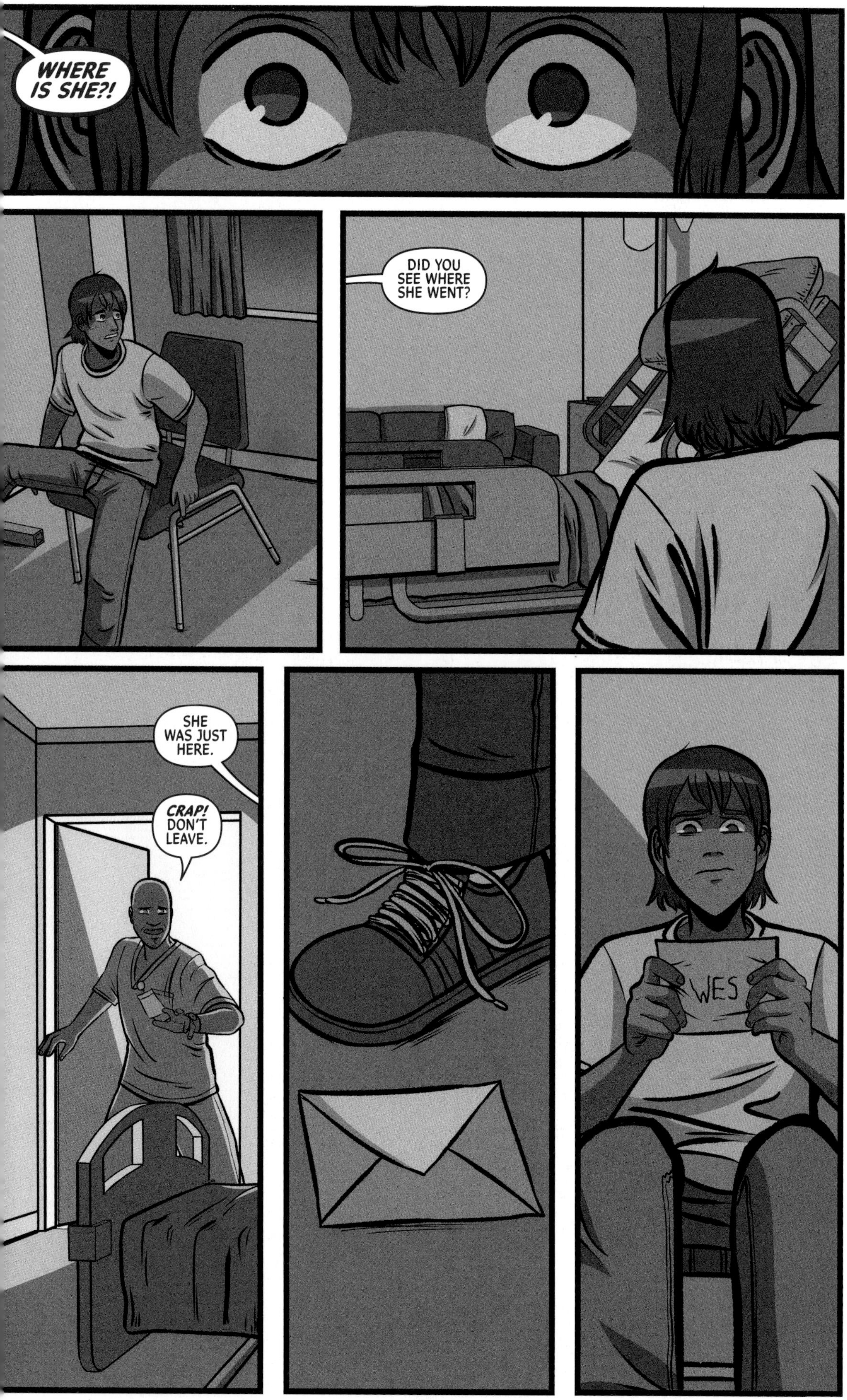
WHERE IS SHE?!
DID YOU SEE WHERE SHE WENT?
SHE WAS JUST HERE.
CRAP! DON'T LEAVE.
WES

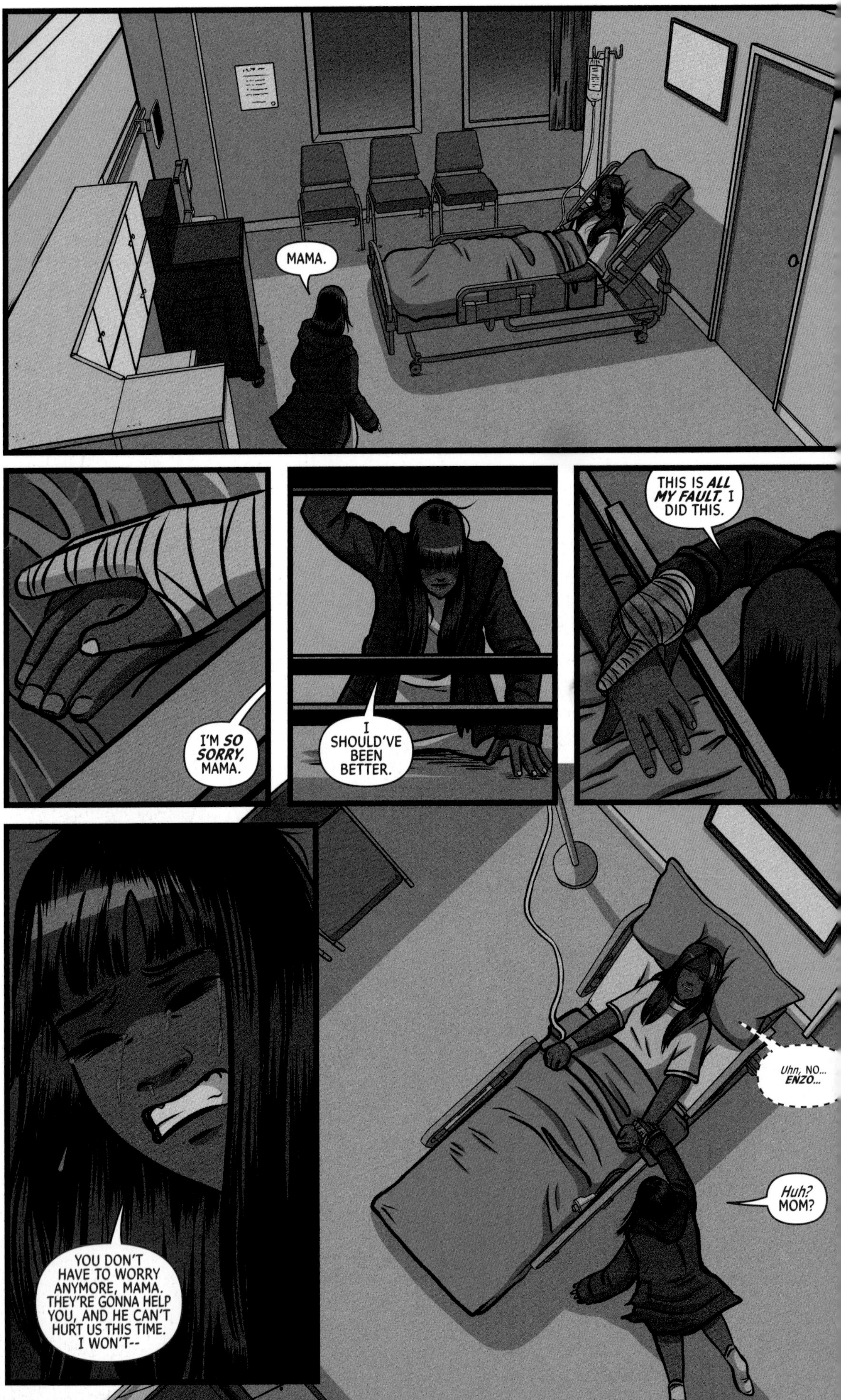
MAMA.
I'M SO SORRY, MAMA.
I SHOULD'VE BEEN BETTER.
THIS IS ALL MY FAULT. I DID THIS.
YOU DON'T HAVE TO WORRY ANYMORE, MAMA. THEY'RE GONNA HELP YOU, AND HE CAN'T HURT US THIS TIME. I WON'T--
Uhn, NO... ENZO...
Huh? MOM?

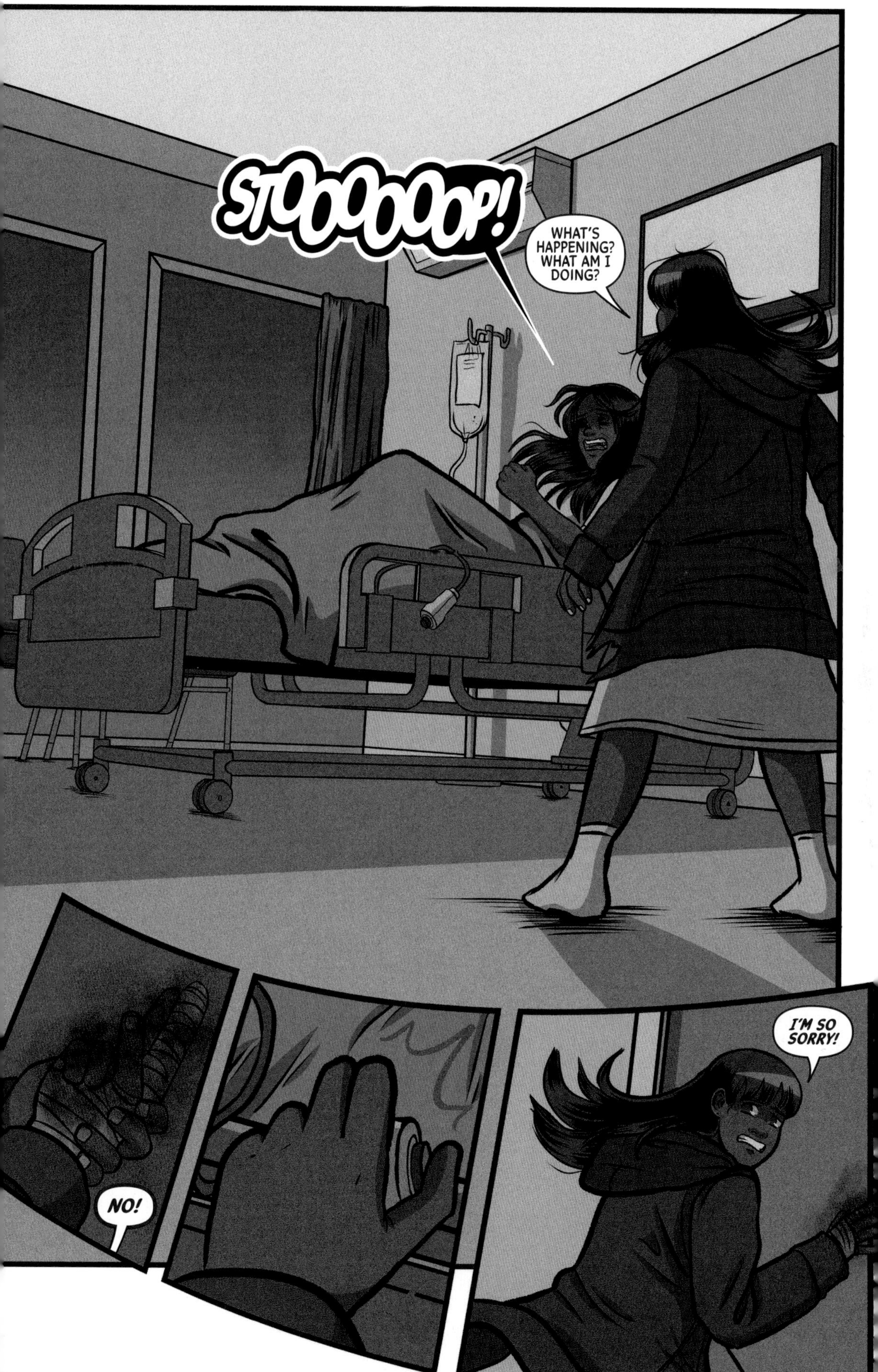
STOOOOOOP!
WHAT'S HAPPENING? WHAT AM I DOING?
NO!
I'M SO SORRY!

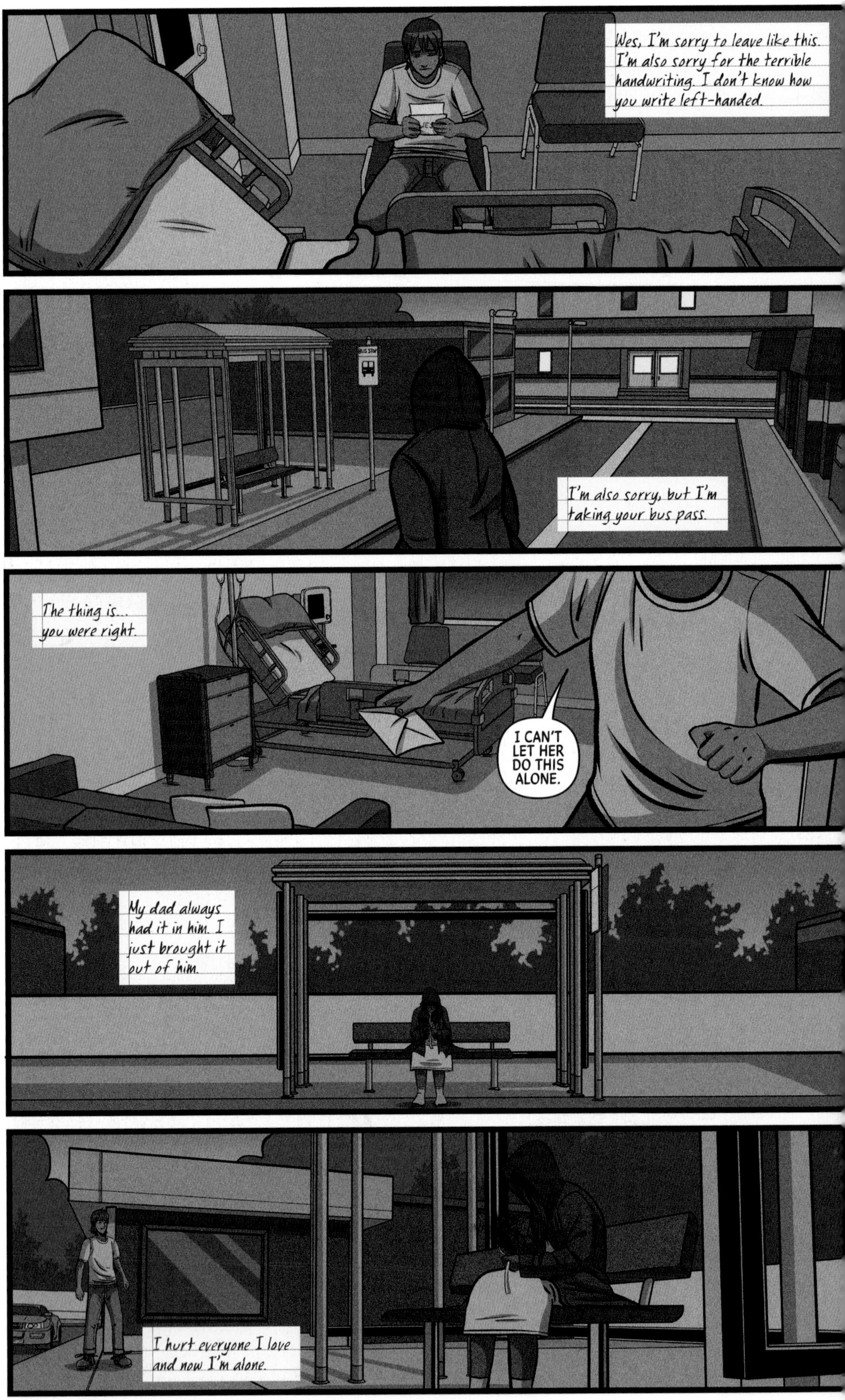
Wes, I'm sorry to leave like this. I'm also sorry for the terrible handwriting. I don't know how you write left-handed.
BUS STOP
I'm also sorry, but I'm taking your bus pass.
The thing is... you were right.
I CAN'T LET HER DO THIS ALONE.
My dad always had it in him. I just brought it out of him.
I hurt everyone I love and now I'm alone.

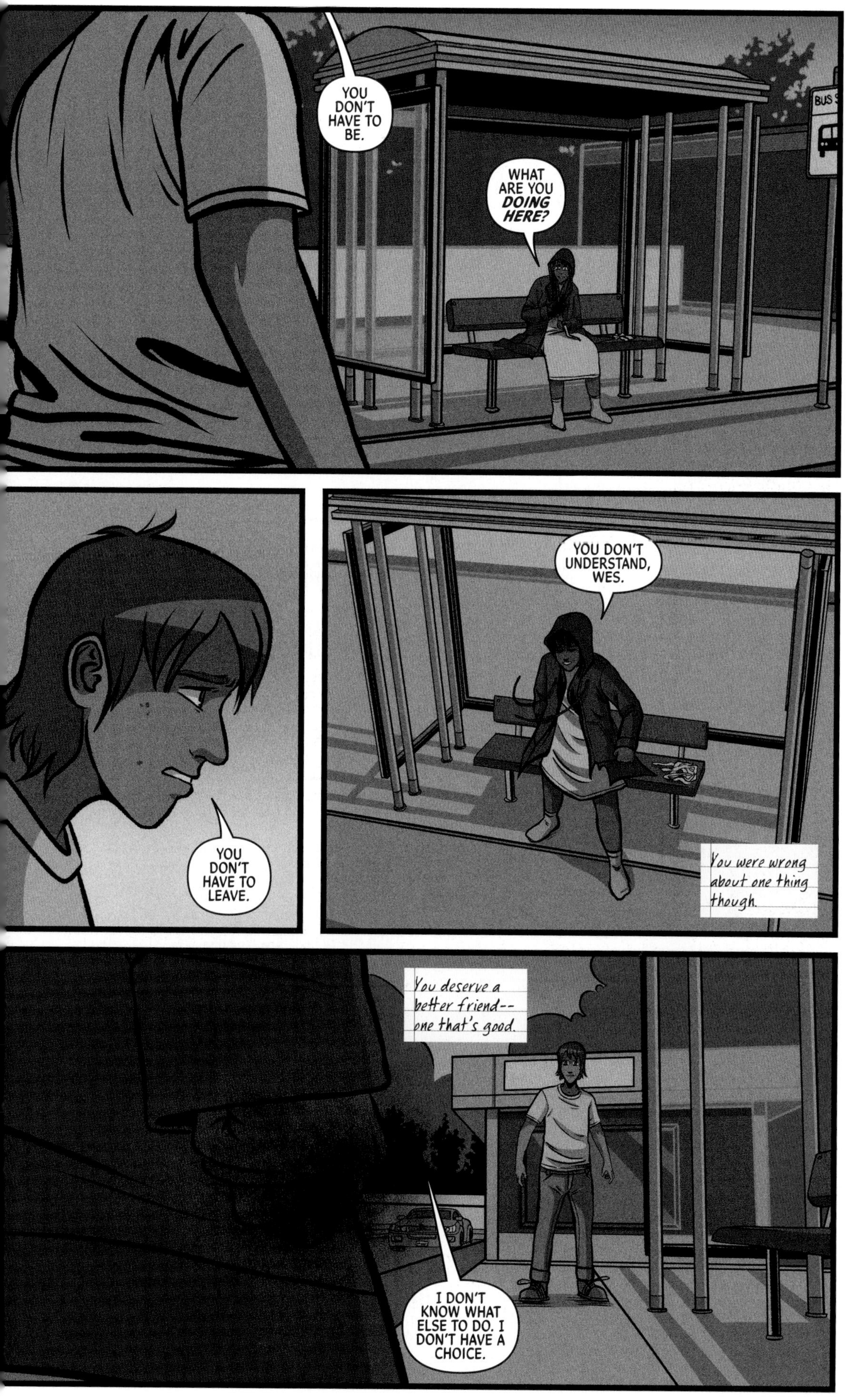

YOU DON'T HAVE TO BE.
WHAT ARE YOU DOING HERE?
BUS
YOU DON'T HAVE TO LEAVE.
YOU DON'T UNDERSTAND, WES.
You were wrong about one thing though.
You deserve a better friend-- one that's good.
I DON'T KNOW WHAT ELSE TO DO. I DON'T HAVE A CHOICE.

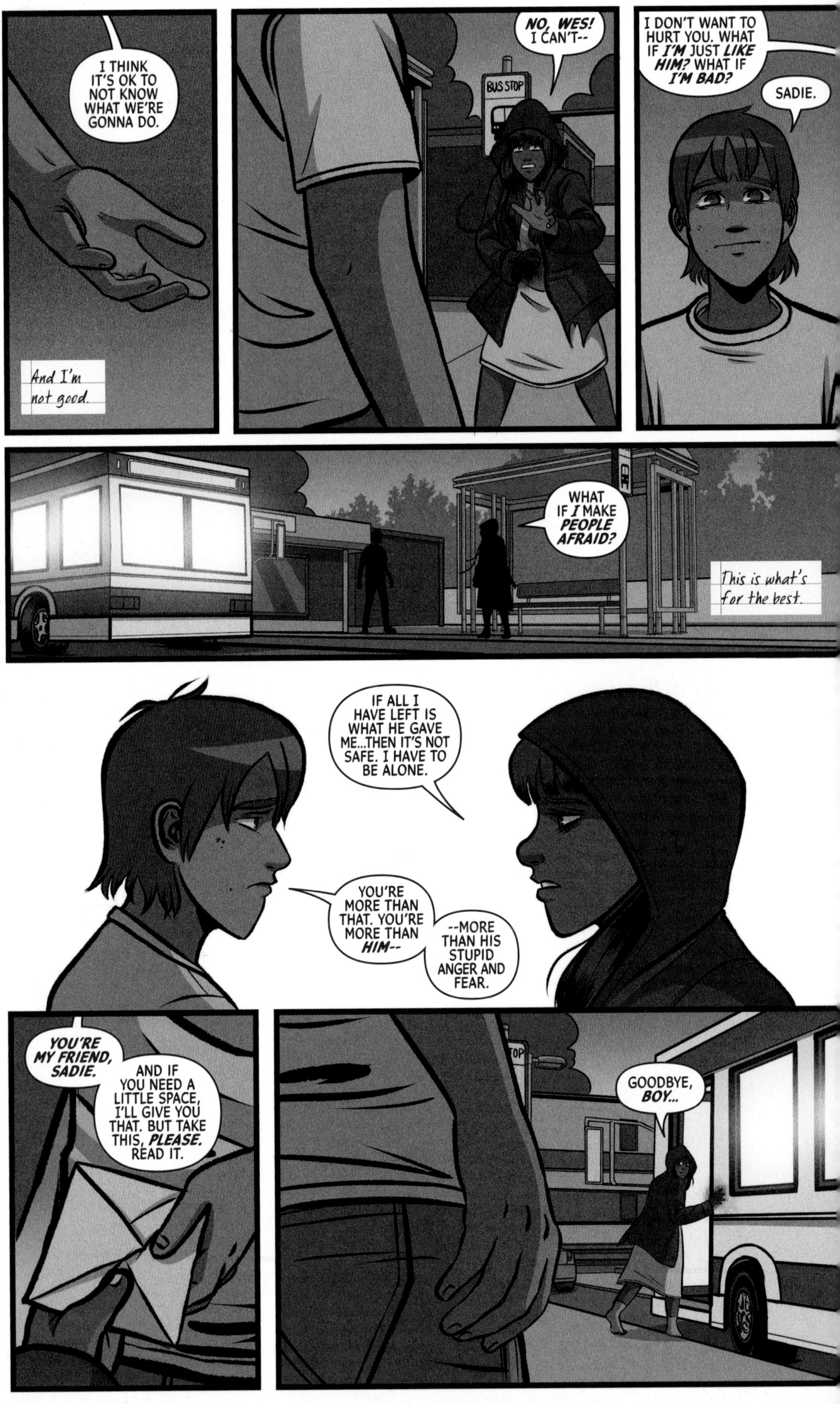
I THINK IT'S OK TO NOT KNOW WHAT WE'RE GONNA DO.
And I'm not good.
NO, WES! I CAN'T--
I DON'T WANT TO HURT YOU. WHAT IF I'M JUST LIKE HIM? WHAT IF I'M BAD?
SADIE.
BUS STOP
WHAT IF I MAKE PEOPLE AFRAID?
This is what's for the best.
IF ALL I HAVE LEFT IS WHAT HE GAVE ME...THEN IT'S NOT SAFE. I HAVE TO BE ALONE.
YOU'RE MORE THAN THAT. YOU'RE MORE THAN HIM--
--MORE THAN HIS STUPID ANGER AND FEAR.
YOU'RE MY FRIEND, SADIE.
AND IF YOU NEED A LITTLE SPACE, I'LL GIVE YOU THAT. BUT TAKE THIS, PLEASE. READ IT.
GOODBYE, BOY...

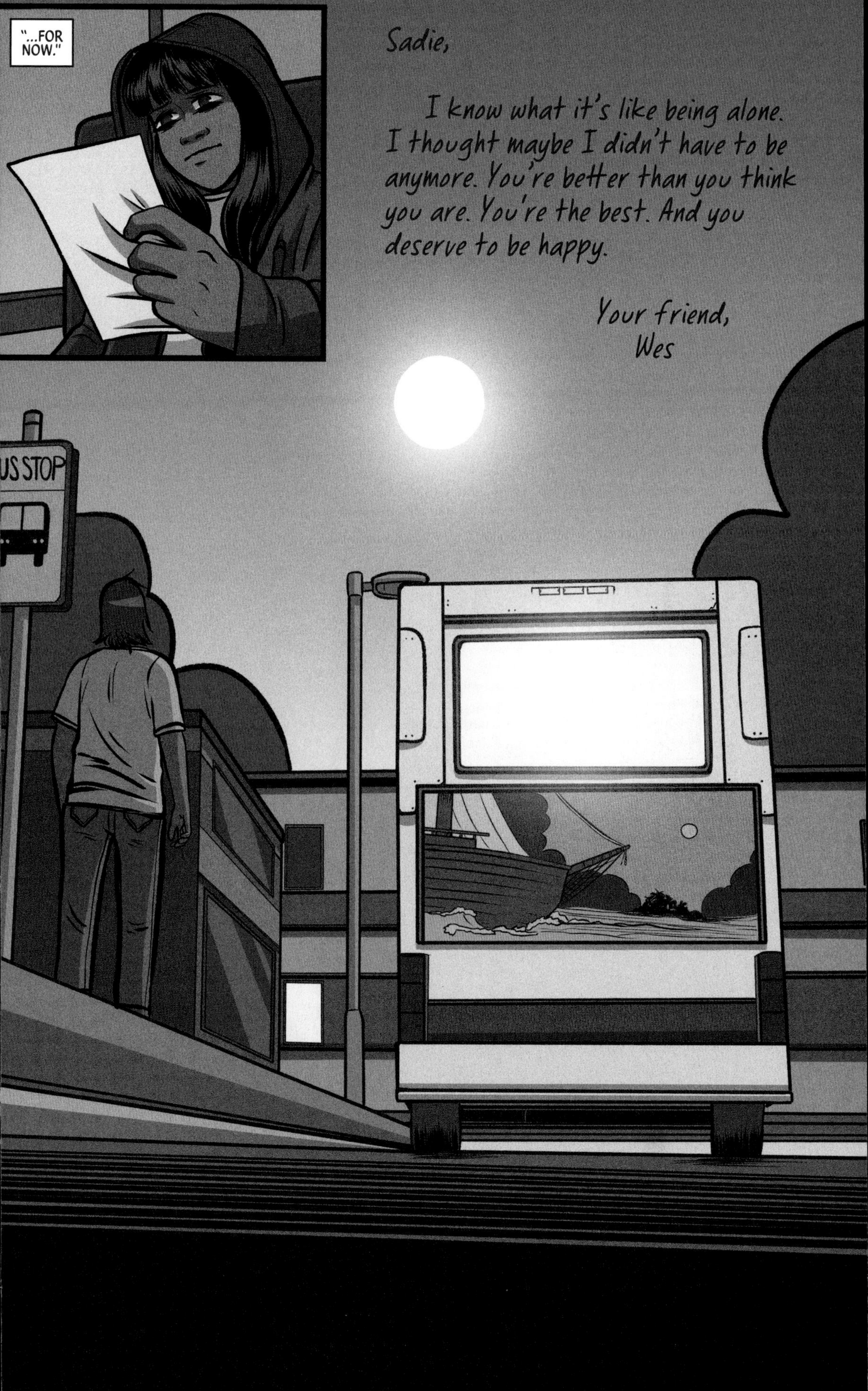
"...FOR NOW."
Sadie,
I know what it's like being alone. I thought maybe I didn't have to be anymore. You're better than you think you are. You're the best. And you deserve to be happy.
Your friend,
Wes
US STOP

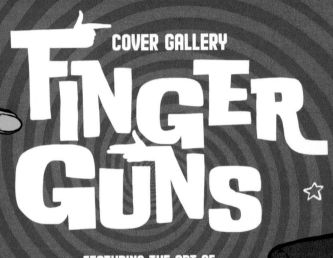

COVER GALLERY

FINGER GUNS

FEATURING THE ART OF

VAL HALVORSON

&

JEN HICKMAN

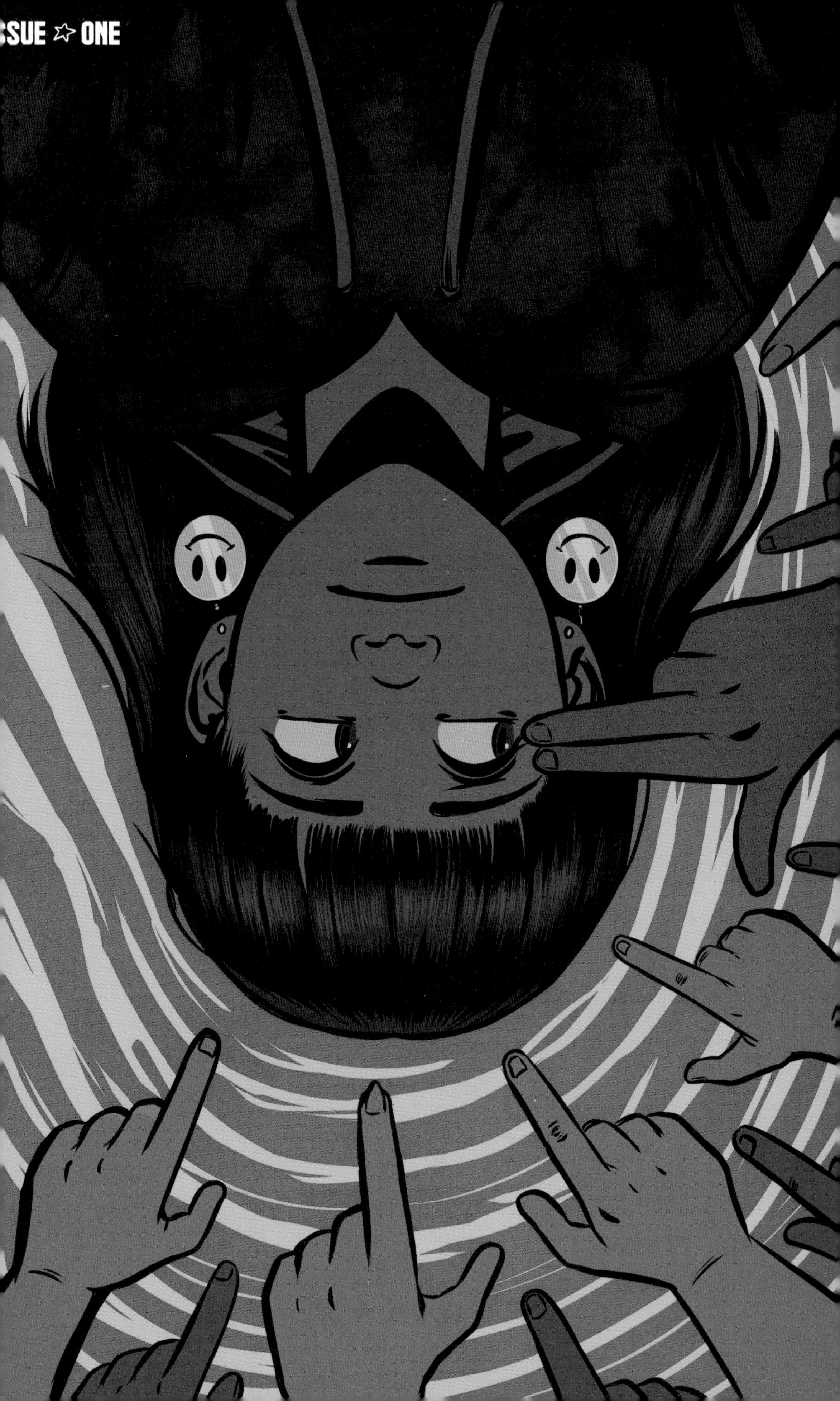
SSUE ☆ ONE

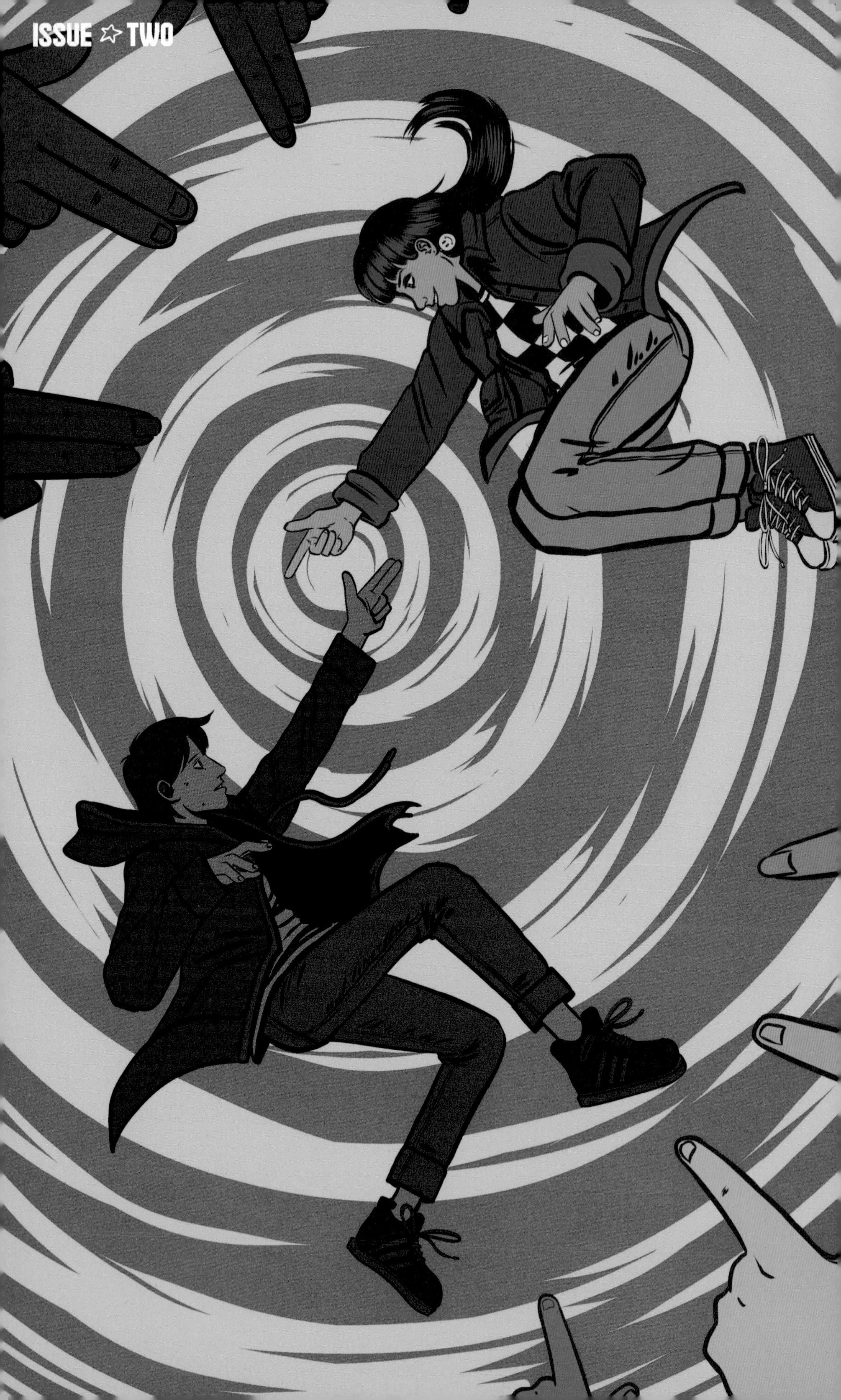
ISSUE ☆ TWO

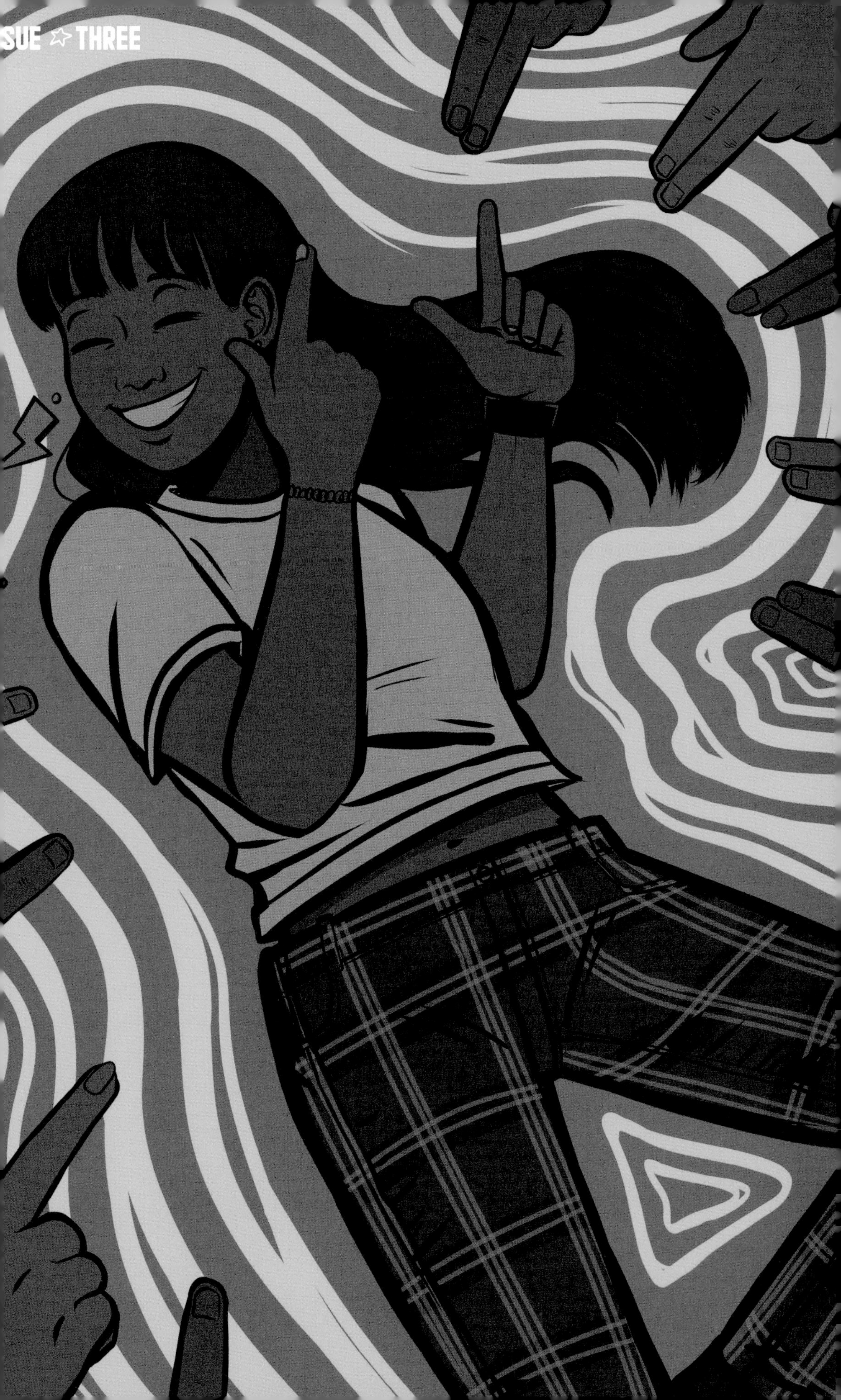

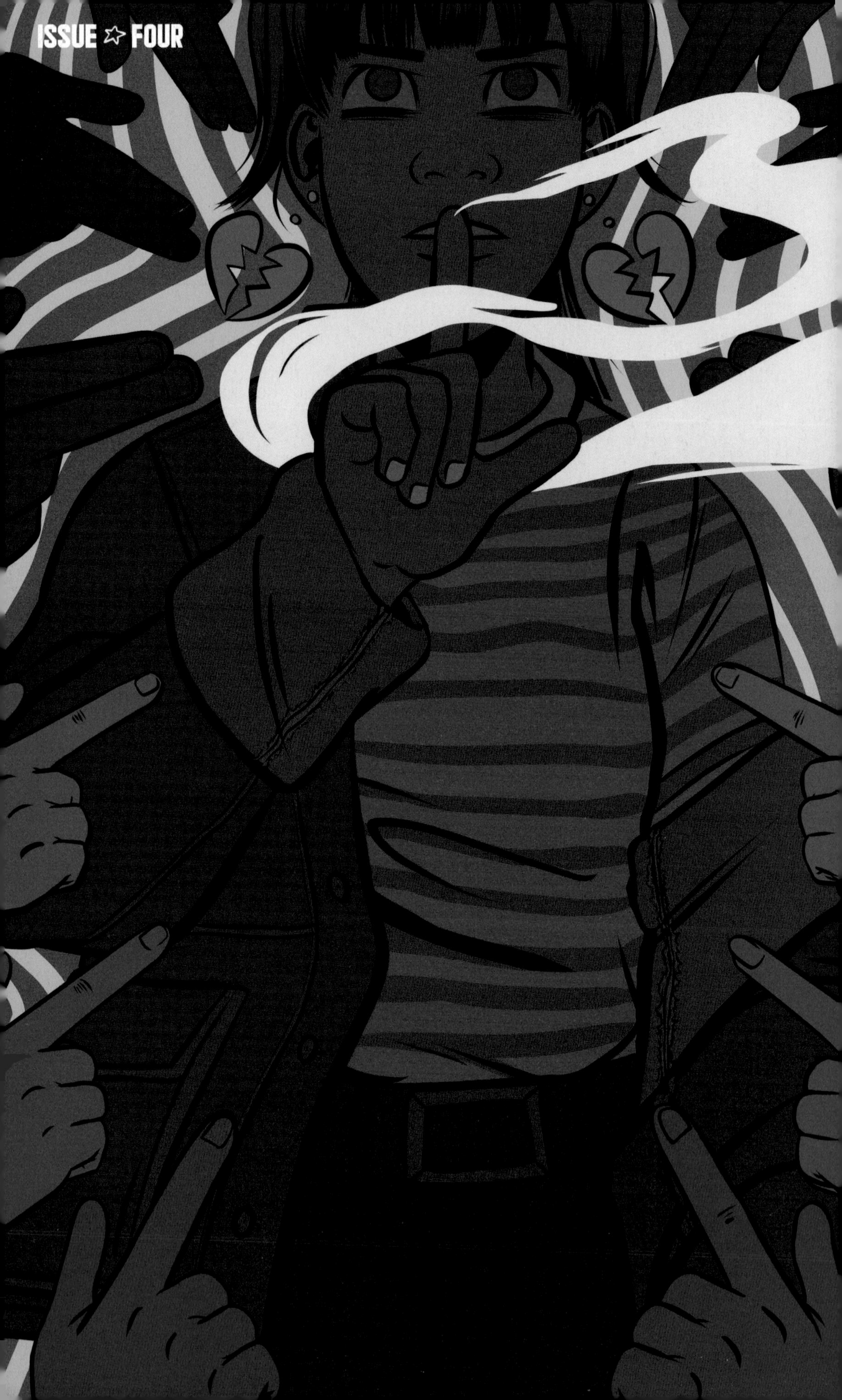
ISSUE ☆ FOUR

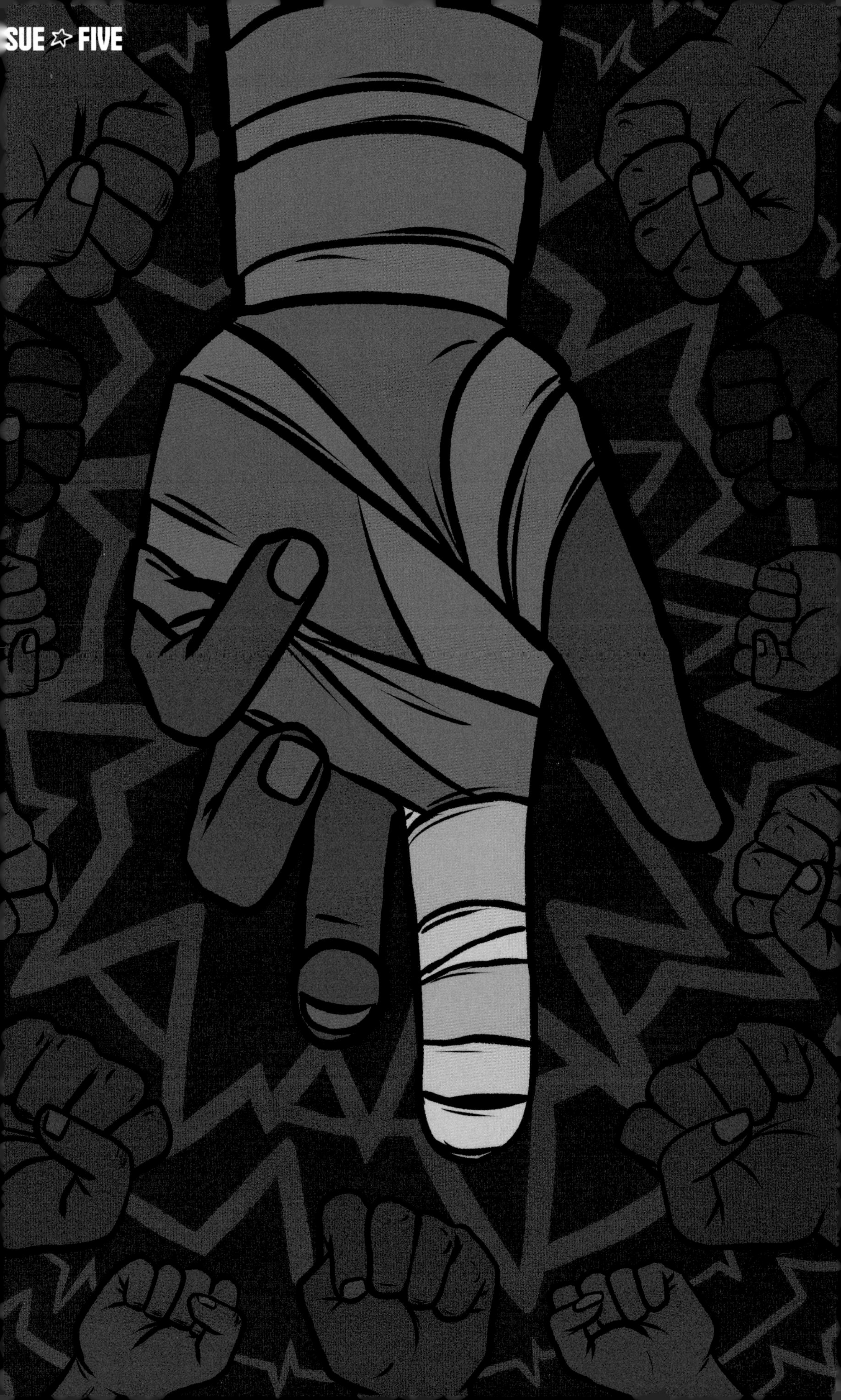
SUE ☆ FIVE

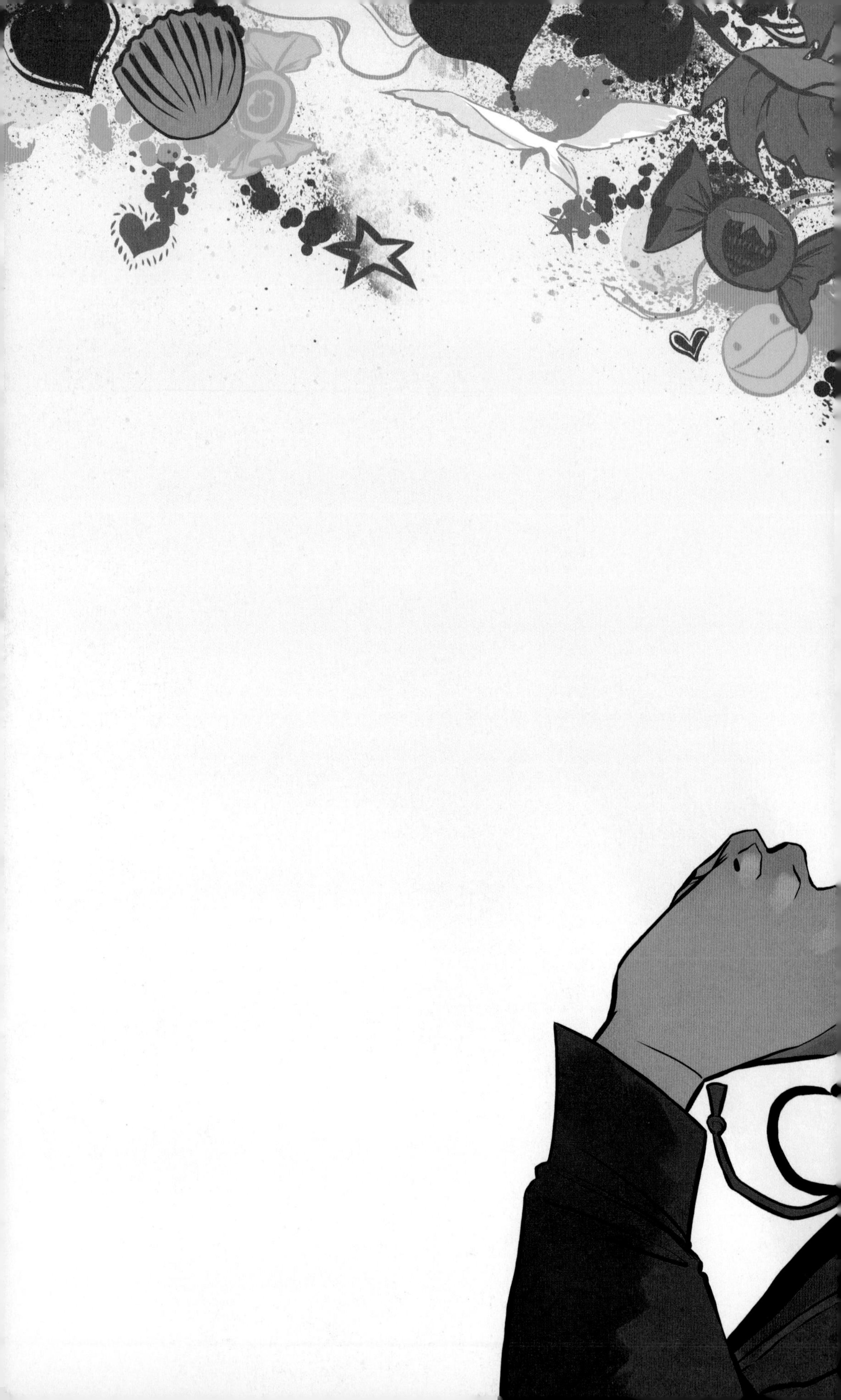

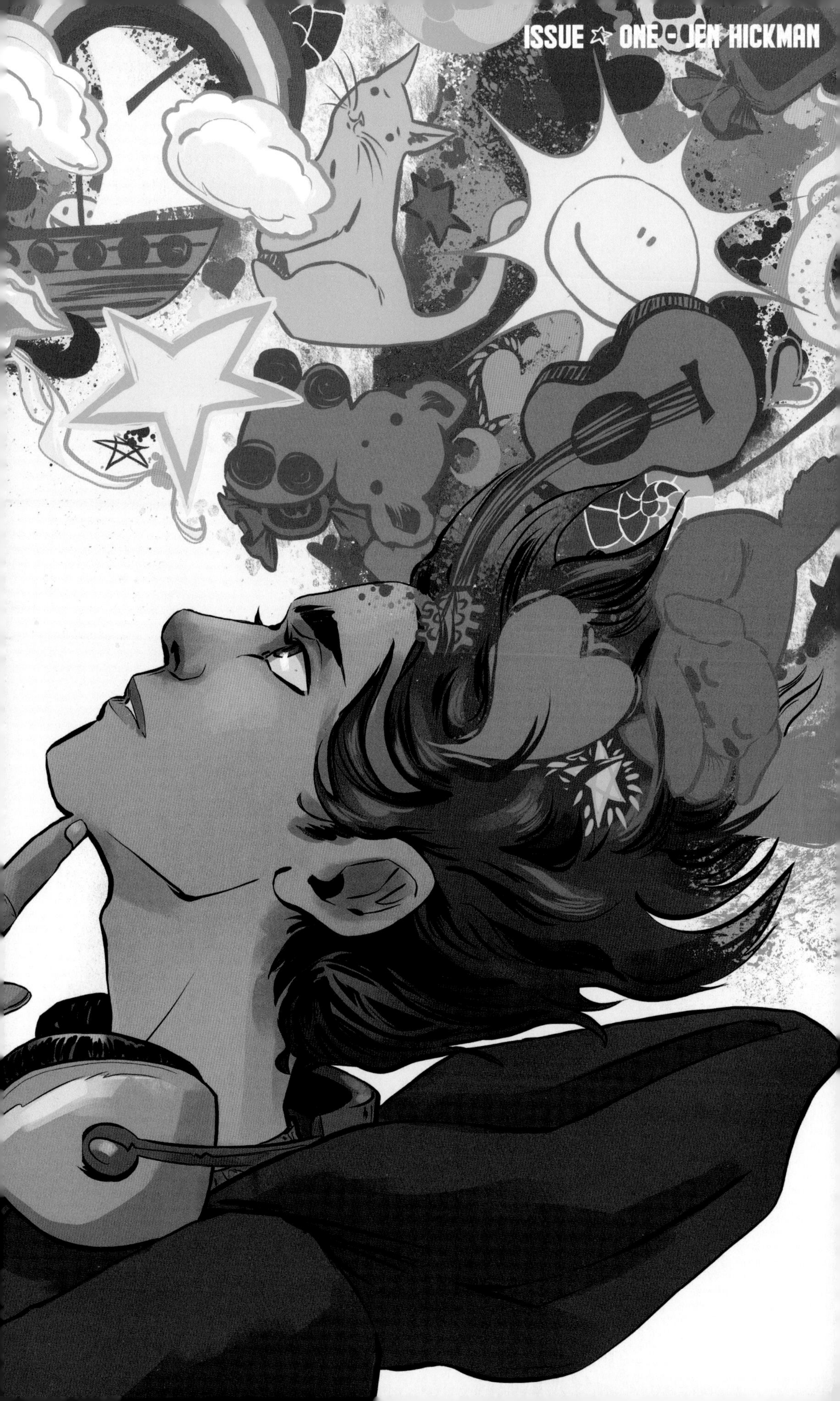

A NOTE FROM WRITER JUSTIN RICHARDS

DEAR READER,

IF YOU OR SOMEONE YOU KNOW IS A VICTIM OF DOMESTIC ABUSE, PLEASE SEEK HELP BY VISITING:

—

THEHOTLINE.ORG

OR CALLING:

NATIONAL DOMESTIC VIOLENCE HOTLINE

1-800-799-7233